I0637495

HUNTING THE DEAD

A Novel by

Blair James Lindsay

Preface

Beginning in 2007 and sharply accelerating in 2010, an organization known as WikiLeaks began releasing a large number of classified documents—mostly pertaining to the post-9/11 wars in Afghanistan and Iraq—and eventually a large number of US State Department diplomatic cables.

The authenticity of each document could not be verified in every case. However, in late 2010, a number of intelligence analysts noted a sudden surge in cyber-attacks against servers of both public and private computers hosting or downloading the leaked files. Initially these attacks were broad and obviously targeted at erasing any portion of the stolen documents that could be accessed. However, in March 2011, these independent think tanks concluded that this broad attack was becoming far more sharply focused.

Detailed analysis of early 2011 cyber traffic revealed that the files targeted for priority destruction included:

- Historical written and photographic documentation pertaining to Confederate Army activities in the southwest during 1862
- FBI memos and action reports from the 1960s and 1970s concerning attempts by the agency to capture a fugitive known as "Solenne Doe"
- Files from the 1970s to the 1990s from the US Defense Advanced Research Projects Agency (DARPA)

- Viral epidemiological research from the 1970s to the 1990s by the US Centre for Disease Control (CDC)

Related files were designated for top-priority erasure through any means necessary by the National Security Agency (NSA) as well as by several other cyberwarfare organizations in a variety of NATO-allied countries. Collectively, this set of files was referred to as documentation of the *Arizona Incident*.

This concentrated effort by Western cyberwarfare organizations was remarkably effective. Networks worldwide experienced catastrophic and unrecoverable data loss when any of their files contained even the vaguest references to matching key words in *Arizona Incident* files.

Paradoxically, given the obvious desire by the US and NATO to eradicate these files, the notoriety this search generated virtually guaranteed that at least some of the information would survive—diligently hidden, duplicated, and passed on by a variety of covert means. Fragments of these files have been reassembled and repaired by a number of professionals around the world whose goal was to make the truth known despite the massive forces attempting to hide it.

This book is based on facts documented in numerous government reports regarding the *Arizona Incident*.

# Chapter One

The undead did not dream and had no memory. Solenne envied them for that.

Her dreams were always the same. A slaughtered village, a dying mother, a plague raging westward like a prairie fire… because she had failed to stop it. Why did her mind bring the past back like this, again and again?

*A chance to learn from my mistakes.*

Solenne had forgotten the name of the town. It was nothing more than a small collection of grimy, worn structures thrown together as if by the haphazard hand of a child at play. Constructed in the aftermath of a gold strike nearby, the buildings now seemed to be sinking into the desert floor as though the earth were reclaiming them now that most of the populace had departed—perhaps in compensation for all the gold that had been taken from the surrounding hills.

Three horses were tied to the rack outside the saloon, and Solenne's cursory glance at the animals as she walked by revealed fresh blood on the saddle of one of them, along with deep gouges on its flank. She spread her hand over the gashes, raw and still oozing blood. They had been made by a human hand—or, more accurately, by the hand of something that had once been human.

The flesh of lower animals held no interest for the risen dead, so it seemed likely that the reaper had raked the flesh out of the man's mount while attempting to batten on to its intended victim.

The riders had executed their attacker. Solenne had found the body about five miles outside of town, riddled with enough bullets to have killed any living man four times over—and one lucky shot to the head that had finally dispatched the monster.

Solenne had often found herself in these circumstances before, chasing a still-living man who was doomed but did not know it, contaminated with a disease that would fester and grow and eventually rise in him, bright and burning, as inevitably as a new day's dawn.

Flipping her coat back and thumbing the keepers off her guns, Solenne pushed open the saloon doors and stepped inside, her gaze moving through the room like a wave washing up on shore, missing nothing.

It was just before noon and the place was virtually empty, though the stink of sweat and cigars in the room spoke of how it would later fill with men set on winning enough at cards that they might afford to drink through the night. The floor was a pastiche of stains from tobacco, horseshit, spilled whiskey, and—no doubt—blood.

A squat bartender with a tattered red beard and two dust-covered men in riding gear glanced up from the bar and looked her over, frowning. A group of four men playing poker in the corner flicked their gaze up at her only long enough to assure themselves the newcomer was intent on neither robbing nor arresting them before turning back to their cards.

Solenne saw that everyone wore a gun. There was nothing unusual about that, of course, but it would likely be bothersome, given why she had come. She saw nothing else she had not seen in dozens of small town saloons—save perhaps for the absence of the worn-out, dolled-up whore in a tattered dress who was typically on offer in such places.

After a moment, she saw the card players look at her again. Their eyes held a look she had seen before. She knew from experience, however, that what they saw was, for them, something quite out of the ordinary.

They saw a tall, lean, athletic woman of Mexican descent. A woman who, while not unattractive, had obviously led a rough life. Proof of this was plain in the raised white scars that twisted below her shirt collar and in her slightly crooked nose, evidently broken at some point in the past. Those with good vision might have noticed her blue eyes and wondered about her parentage.

None of these things truly set Solenne apart though. Women in the southwest were often treated roughly by the environment and by the men.

Solenne stood out because she was dressed like a gunslinger, her dusty black coat pulled back to reveal two .44 calibre Remington revolvers riding low on her hip, hitched to gun belts slung with speed load cylinders. Only the more perceptive might pick up on the other things that distinguished her—the easy confidence in her stance and the fearless way her eyes flitted across the men, as if she were examining a herd of dull-eyed cattle.

Outside of some pathetic Wild West show these men might have once seen, no woman they had ever laid eyes on dressed like this apparition. So the sensation of being stared at by every man in the room elicited no particular surprise in Solenne.

The beefy bartender was first to speak. "Help you . . . ma'am?"

Solenne had an odd linguistic history. She had grown up speaking what her elders called *Ch'olti*, then later learned what the whites called *Mexican* but she knew as *Spanish*. Finally, she had learned English. She was acquainted with proper English from the odd book she had managed to obtain and from the patience of one or two teachers, but her travels tended to throw her frequently among the rougher characters who inhabited these lands, and so she knew her speech patterns ran the gamut from strictly formal to cowpoke slang.

"Seems likely you can. I'm looking for the man who rode in on that bloodied horse outside."

The bartender glanced at the two men across from him, who narrowed their eyes and glanced at each other. The taller of the two tipped his shot glass up and swallowed before chuckling and elbowing his partner in the ribs.

"I reckon Tom'd be proud to hear a woman chased his ass all the way out here."

The man grinned at her, a smile devoid of a significant number of teeth and little better for the crooked yellow ones remaining.

"Tom's sick upstairs, missy, but he'd expect Manny and me to buy you a drink in the meantime."

Solenne did not return the smile. "His being *sick* is why I'm here."

Neither of the two men at the bar looked especially pleased about this, but she had not expected they would and continued. "He got bit, am I right? By some kind of . . . crazy man? Maybe a man who looked like he'd gone and caught rabies?"

The shorter of the two men tipped his hat back. "Not sure what you're after, little honey. That man *was* crazy, and we did what we had to do. If he was some friend or kin of yours—"

There was no amiability in the taller man's elbow this time. He shot it hard into his companion's ribs. "Don't fucking talk about that, Manny."

"And don't you fucking hit me, Matt." Manny looked wounded, but Matt's glower seemed to dissuade him from further comment.

Solenne held up a hand. "Not worried about the dead man. He wasn't any kin or friend of mine. Not revenge I'm after."

She stepped toward the centre of the room, removing her hat and shaking out her shoulder-length raven hair. She slapped the desert dust off the hat while her eyes swept up the stairway to the second floor, always keeping the card players in her peripheral vision. Most of them had turned to watch the conversation between her and the two cowboys, but now she saw that one of the men at the table was peering from her to a ragged piece of paper he had plucked from his shirt pocket.

"I know for a fact the man who attacked you *was* crazy. I expect you had no choice but to kill him."

Manny nodded even as Matt shook his head. "Missy, we *ain't* gonna talk to you about this."

"Don't want no talk about killing in my place," the bartender chimed in.

Matt turned to him with a dead look on his face. "And that's why we *ain't gonna*. Now, stay outta this, asshole. Do what you do best and fill us up again." He punctuated his order by slamming his shot glass down on the bar.

The bartender shrugged, his eyes hooded and his face

expressionless as he pulled a half-full bottle of murky amber liquid from under the bar and spilled some into Matt's glass. Most of the bar's customers were relatively friendly folk, but the bartender was used to being sworn at, and every so often some hard ass—or at least some cowpoke who fancied himself a hard ass—came through town looking for trouble. It rarely amounted to anything, but when it did, the double-barrelled shotgun under the bar always proved useful for defusing the situation—or for ending the problem with a severe finality.

Having beaten enough dust from her hat to satisfy herself that only an hour more of pounding would ever bring it somewhere near clean, Solenne put it back on. She noticed the man at the poker table continued to squint from the crumpled piece of paper in his hand to her and back again with what seemed like building excitement. Trouble was coming like a storm on the horizon, but she could not leave now without allowing something far worse to happen.

"The crazy man—he bit Tom, I expect?"

The look on Manny's face told her that's exactly what had happened. "Fellas," she continued, "this'll sound a bit strange, but I need to see Tom. That bite? It's gonna make him real sick."

Solenne followed Manny's gaze as it drifted to the rooms above. Tom, of course, was already extremely sick—with what Solenne's people had called "growing the curse" within him.

"You a doctor?" Manny ventured.

"Not exactly."

Matt walked over to Solenne until his face was scarcely a foot from hers. He towered over her, putting what an outsider might have wrongly construed as a friendly hand on her shoulder. The gunmetal stare she turned on him reminded him of something, but not until it was too late would he connect it with the time he'd looked up from filling his canteen at a pond and spotted a mountain lion watching him. Nearly three hundred pounds, he'd guessed afterward. This was the same passionless stare by a creature that knew it could kill you and was merely deciding if the deed was worth the effort.

But he had remembered that *later. Then*, he had squeezed her shoulder. Hard.

"Missy, I'm sure Tom'd be pleased to see you. Tell you what—why don't you have a drink with us, and maybe in a while we'll take you up to him. You can lie down with him and nurse him back to health." As he laughed at his own joke, he took his hand from her shoulder and caressed her cheek. "Heck, I think I may be a little sick as well. We could go upstairs and you could nurse me too—"

*That's enough of that.* Solenne became a whirlwind.

Shoulder. Hand. Twist and kick. Matt found himself suddenly pinned on his stomach, Solenne's boot heel grinding down on the back of his neck as if he were a bug. She held one of his wrists coiled up at a near impossible angle in her right hand while her left hand had suddenly grown a pistol. And she was pointing it directly at Manny, watching him with the same predatory expression that Matt would, hours later, associate with a wildcat.

Beneath her, Matt wiggled and strained, cursing as he searched for a position that did not send lightning strikes of agony into his shoulder. He could feel ligaments and tendons popping throughout his tortured arm and knew instinctively that only a few more ounces of pressure would tear his shoulder to pieces.

"Not going to be any kind of nursing." Solenne's eyes danced around the room. "Got to go check out your friend. That's all. If he's sick with what I think he's got, he—"

The card player who'd been looking at the piece of paper stood abruptly, as if his chair had suddenly caught fire, and Solenne's eyes locked on him. He was a rough-looking Mexican who looked vaguely familiar to her—and she knew what he would say almost before he said it.

"Santa Muerte!"

The other men around the table looked puzzled and tensed, their hands edging toward their sidearms.

Solenne sighed. So few people, and yet coming in here in daylight might have been a mistake. She could have been stealthier and waited until dark. Trouble was, by then, the sick man would likely have been dead. Dead and risen again—and spreading the curse into others.

No, *this* had not been the mistake.

"La Bruja!"

The Mexican was holding out the tatty piece of yellowed paper to his companions with the air of a man who had won a prize in a game. Even from across the room, Solenne recognized the wanted poster. She'd seen it plastered up among others outside general stores or on post office walls in various towns through which she'd passed.

*Such a poor likeness. Hardly recognizable . . . Definitely not my good side.*

But the damning thing was that male outlaws were a dime a dozen and dark-skinned female gunslingers were rare things indeed.

"The Mexican Witch!" the man continued. "She's wanted in California, see?" He turned back to Solenne, his eyes tiny and calculating. "Six-hundred-dollar reward."

She saw interest flicker to life like lit candles in the eyes around the table. Chairs edged back, grinding across the pitted wood floor.

Below her, Matt yelled, "Manny! Shoot this fucking bitch!"

And that—again—was enough of that.

Solenne twisted slightly and Matt's upper arm snapped just below the shoulder, the gunshot crack of bone echoing through the room. By the time he began to shriek with the pain, Solenne's right hand had let his slip and had likewise grown a gun to match the one in her left. She pointed this one more or less at the group of men coming to their feet around the table. She stepped back from Matt, who made no effort to rise from the floor and simply cradled his fractured limb in shock.

Solenne noticed Manny looking at Matt's broken arm and knew he was wondering if this was by chance or intent as she watched his hand drift toward his pistol. She shook her head and mouthed *No*—an order that he obeyed.

"Come on, amigos. Six hundred!" the Mexican said. "We can take her—"

Solenne shot him in the groin without even looking away from Manny, and he collapsed, clutching at the blood suddenly spurting from between his legs.

"Took me a moment, but I believe I know your face too, *hijo de puta*." Solenne spat. "Expect you're the only one who reads wanted posters, asshole? Raped and killed two sisters down in Sonoyta, as I recall."

One of the Mexican's companions was bending over him and attempting to help staunch the flow of blood. The man beside them simply stared in shock. But the fourth man paid not a lick of attention to the wounded companion he'd amiably been playing cards with moments ago. He stared at Solenne, licking his lips like a starving dog that had come across an unexpected meal. She knew he was busy convincing himself how good his chances were of ending the day six hundred dollars richer despite the fact that his gun was still in its holster.

A door slammed open upstairs and Solenne's flinty eyes flashed toward the noise.

What must have been—not more than an hour or two before—Matt and Manny's friend Tom staggered onto the balcony that looked down over the bar. He groped at the air and slammed into the railing as if blind.

*Everything so slow in the dreamtime. But the mistakes were plain enough . . .*

For some reason the thing looked directly at her from the upper floor. The newly risen dead sometimes retained a semblance of humanity, but the Tom creature's grey-yellow face was already sporting a long, black, bloodless gash on its left side that tore up into an enucleated eyeball dribbling thin greenish gore down its cheek.

She heard the sharp crack of the bolt action on the bartender's shotgun as he aimed at her and readied to shoot. The dead thing on the landing had distracted her, but her eyes were everywhere now. Reality shimmered in slow motion before her.

The bartender was trembling, but with the shotgun pointed enough in her general direction so that it would kill her even if his aim was off. Manny was plainly frightened of her—but whether too scared to draw his gun or too scared *not to* was yet to be determined. Matt was trying to get to his feet, searching with his good left hand for the gun holstered at his right side. The Mexican and his friend were out of the game, but the two others by the card table were looking at her with hard eyes. One of them had a pistol in his right hand now. She wondered when that had happened.

*Mistakes.*

The creature saved her from her mistakes this time. She looked it in the eye and it moaned in hunger. It floundered toward her with a yawning moan and pitched over the railing, thrashing in the air like a drowning man as it plummeted directly onto the bartender.

Manny took his chance and drew his gun. Solenne shot him in the shoulder, and he slammed backward against the bar and collapsed. Later she would be glad she hadn't killed him, but it wasn't by intention; she had been trying for the centre mass of his chest.

A second shot rang out almost simultaneously, and Solenne whirled to see the other man by the table go down beside the Mexican and his friend, clutching a bloody, mutilated hand as his smoking gun dropped with him to the floor.

The bullet had exploded in the chamber. A man who hadn't cared for his gun properly.

*Lucky, lucky, despite the mistakes . . .*

The last man standing by the table—the man who had been busy convincing himself he could be six hundred dollars richer—looked her in the eye and knew, almost at the moment Solenne did, that she couldn't chance he would try. She shot him dead centre in the chest, and he pitched backward onto the floor and lay gasping and trembling as death crawled up into him.

Between spitting and cursing, Matt had almost managed to get his gun out. Solenne took a quick step forward and kicked him in the head with what she would later remember in shame as a savage joy, and he fell back, limp and unmoving.

Manny had dropped his gun and seemed to have no interest in retrieving it. He had ripped part of his shirt off and was trying to staunch the steady dark flow of blood from his shoulder.

Solenne could hear shouts from people outside now.

*Time slipping away . . .*

Moans and cries came from all over the room, but she focused on the wet, slippery sound of teeth tearing apart flesh coming from behind the bar.

She stepped sideways, still covering the men near the table with one pistol while she pointed the other toward the creature.

The reaper had ripped the bartender's throat out and was chewing into his neck with a furious intensity as the last contractions of the man's dying heart pumped blood up in a fountain around the monster's face. Solenne shot the thing in the head and it collapsed on top of the bartender. She moved in closer and shot the barkeep through the head as well. Life had shaped Solenne into a ruthless creature almost from the very moment of her birth.

There was more shouting just outside, and she moved quickly toward the back door, away from the mayhem left in her wake, and slipped outside. She had left her own horse tied behind the saloon and was on it and away seconds later.

*Mistakes . . .*

*Going into the bar so brazenly. Concerned about saving lives or overconfident?*

*Forgetting the bartender . . .*

*Finally and worst—assuming the undead thing had injured* itself. *The gouge on its face, the punctured eyeball . . .*

The hungry dead tore themselves up constantly in their incessant pursuit of human flesh, so it had been a natural assumption.

*A stupid assumption.*

Solenne fled the town, and it was days before she learned the man upstairs had *not* been alone. When she had walked into the saloon she had noted the absence of a prostitute—something typically found in such places—but she had not asked herself *why* that might be so.

There *had* been a prostitute in the bar, but Tom's friends had hired the woman to lie with him, and the dead man had woken and fed on her, perhaps even before Solenne arrived.

The newly born monster's first victim had fought with it and scratched its eye out. And died. Died and then risen—and made more of them.

*Mistakes. . . .*

\*\*\*

Solenne woke and rolled over, squinting at the rising sun.

Her horse was looking down at her indifferently as it chewed morsels of some grassy plant it had found nearby with the slow, steady focus of an untroubled mind.

The horse was well muscled and healthy but lean, much like its rider. In its life with her, the animal had never enjoyed any long moments of leisure to feed and grow fat. Perhaps it hoped she would simply go back to sleep so it could continue grazing on the grass by the river.

Solenne had slept only a few hours and still ached for more rest, but the risen dead never rested, and there was one of them not far ahead of her.

She got to her feet and stretched, then took her canteen and splashed some water in her eyes, blinking rapidly to wash the grit out of them. Her joints felt similarly dry and stiff, like gears in an aging machine, caked with the same desert dust.

She thought the horse looked disappointed.

## Chapter Two

Brennan was quite certain he had spotted the three riders on the ridge ahead before they had seen him, and he immediately pulled on the reins of his mount to shift his direction so as to pass a good distance north of the other horsemen.

He frowned when he saw the three men subsequently alter their own course so that it would intercept his.

Brennan's instinct was that this was no friendly gesture, that a problem was coming to a boil. But there was no point in trying to flee unless he wanted to kill his horse, who was near exhaustion after running hard earlier in the day from a group of hostile Apaches. And there was certainly no place to hide in the open desert.

He considered who these men might be. Out here, there were few possibilities, and none of them comforting to a lone man interested in seeing the next sunrise.

Theoretically it was possible he might encounter Confederate or Union troops, though meeting either was more than a little unlikely. Arizona was disputed territory, but neither side considered it strategically important.

Encountering soldiers from either side might prove awkward, though. They might hang him as a deserter or as a sympathizer to the opposite side without any evidence, but simply for the good of general troop discipline. Or they might "draft" him into their army. This second prospect was, in Brennan's mind, only slightly more attractive than the first. He'd heard that whole battalions of Confederate troops had starved nearly to death on the march, collapsing with shoes worn off their feet and flesh melted from their bones like tallow from a burnt-out candle.

The one thing any soldiers who found him would *not* do was let him keep what was in his saddlebags.

But after a moment Brennan knew these were not soldiers. Either side would probably have appeared as a larger force or a single scout, not a group of three, but this realization was no relief. Soldiers were only one possible level of bad out here in the spaces between civilizations.

There were a number of possible reasons men riding through the desolate, soul-baking desert might want to meet a stranger. They might be lost, or short on water, or some other such essential and be looking to trade . . . maybe buy some tobacco off a fellow traveller. It was equally possible that after days of riding, they might just be looking for news of how the war was going or simply some knowledge about what lay ahead on the trail.

While these were all possibilities, Brennan was of a mind that the men riding toward him were after none of these things. A decade and a half of wandering through the American southwest had taught him to tell the cowhands and travellers from the thieves and cutthroats. Often it was obvious, but sometimes it was the little things—how far apart the men rode from each other, how they wore their guns, and even subtle cues in body language.

Even from a half mile away, Brennan could see obvious tension in the approaching group. The men kept glancing at each other, whispering in low voices as they came closer. The final tell was that each moved a hand off his reins and rested it near his gun. Three *friendly* strangers should not have appeared nervous approaching a lone rider. That they did spoke of a readiness to inflict pain.

He thought again about turning and running, but his horse would never last through another hard gallop without a night's rest, water, and food. Besides, there was nothing good behind him. The Apache scouting party had chased him hell-bent for leather for a good hour before he'd lost them in the twists of a dry arroyo. They would be keen to find him again, and where there was one such party, there were likely others. Moving away from them was his only choice.

As the riders drew close, Brennan saw that one of their horses was about to go lame. It was just barely visible—a small tic as it lifted its left front foot—but it was enough to tell him something was wrong with that leg or perhaps a stone was caught in its shoe. A lame horse out here would be no small problem—unless of course Brennan's became available to them.

The men seemed in far worse shape than the horse, though. Their clothing was torn, and they were covered with all manner of bruises and scratches. The one riding on the left looked as if he'd taken the worst of it. He was deathly pale, with what looked like claw marks on his neck and arms and a bloody makeshift bandage on his hand. Brennan fancied he could smell the stink of gangrene coming from the man and was not overly surprised, given his appearance. Pale and shivering even in the hard desert sun, he had the same desperate, darting eyes Brennan had once seen in a victim of consumption in a California sanitarium.

Brennan reined in his horse as the approaching men did likewise, and he nodded toward them.

"Howdy."

"Well, howdy to you too, mister."

The man in the centre addressed Brennan, apparently the leader. He exuded the combination of arrogance and uncomplicated intellect that in Brennan's experience often seemed to go hand in hand among third-rate desperados. His nose was swollen and red and had apparently been mashed crooked in whatever recent skirmish they had all obviously endured. He immediately thought of the man as *Squished-Nose* and watched with flat, incurious eyes as Squished-Nose assessed him in turn.

Squished-Nose saw a tall man with dirty-blond hair who might have been anywhere between thirty and forty. He was tanned and tempered like a blade by many hours under the Arizona sun. His clothes were dusty, but they were of better quality and in better repair than those of the three men staring at him.

Perhaps a thoughtful man would have been rendered more cautious by the sight of the two pistols slung around Brennan's waist, as well as the fine rifle strapped down beside his saddle. Unlike Brennan's clothing, his guns were pristine and gleamed in the sun. For good reason, though, Squished-Nose had never been called *thoughtful*. He saw only things worth taking and knew that three against one meant they *would* be taking anything they wanted from this man. Of all the things he saw, most interesting to Squished-Nose was the bulging and rather heavy-looking set of saddlebags on the back of Brennan's horse. After last night's lunacy— the killing of the madman who'd attacked them and then having to abandon Earl—Squished-Nose felt almost giddy to be getting back into the gang's comfortable routine of theft and mayhem.

Squished-Nose stretched his lips into what Brennan thought might have been a parody of a smile, exposing yellow-brown buckteeth. "Don't meet many folks out here."

Brennan fixed an amiable smile upon his own face. He could almost feel his guns in his hands. "That's a fact."

Squished-Nose frowned just a little. He was accustomed to people in such circumstances betraying nervousness, if not outright fear. In similar past encounters, most men had tried to be friendly—of course they would, outnumbered by armed men—but their tension and anxiety had always shone through. This man did not appear the least bit worried, and after the events of the previous night, this was even more irritating than it otherwise might have been.

Squished-Nose spat and said, "Where you coming from, mister?"

After a beat, Brennan nodded over his shoulder. "Back there a ways."

The reply provoked a particularly confused looked on the face of the man Brennan had mentally tagged as *Torn-Ear*—given that it looked like someone had tried to rip off his ear and only barely missed in succeeding, dried blood covering the left side of his head. The third was *Bandage-Hand* in his mind, although *Yellow-Skin* or *Dying-Man* would have been equally appropriate.

"Well, where you headed?" Torn-Ear said.

Brennan nodded toward the west this time. "Over there a ways."

The three men facing Brennan realized after a moment that they were waiting in vain for him to elaborate, and any residual good humour they held at the prospect of stealing the stranger's possessions seemed to drain out of them.

Eventually Squished-Nose, frowning, pointed behind Brennan. "D'you know you got an arrow sticking out of your saddlebags?"

Despite himself, Brennan could not help glancing behind him.

There was indeed an Apache arrow lodged in his left saddlebag, a souvenir of his run from them earlier. A pained look passed over his face as he turned back and lied. "It'd come to my attention."

Squished-Nose opened his mouth to reply but Bandage-Hand cut in, looking to his partners. "Fellas, I'm not feeling real good . . . Can we just find some water, or maybe this fella knows where the nearest town is?" He glanced at Brennan.

"Shut up, Jake," Squished-Nose said. "We'll make camp in a piece, and you'll just have to hold out till then." Turning to Brennan, he continued, "You're not too friendly, are you? Don't have much to say."

Brennan leaned back slightly. A practised eye may have noticed that this position made for an easier draw on his pistols. He smiled. "You one of those newspaper fellas? Want to write a story on me?"

While Squished-Nose absorbed this, Brennan continued. "Look, fellas, I've got a bit of a ride ahead, so I'm gonna press on. As maybe you'd guessed, there's a few Apaches an hour or two east of here. You may want to avoid going in that general direction."

Brennan lifted the reins and directed his horse to move around the men, but Squished-Nose was quick to manoeuvre his own horse into Brennan's path. "Just a minute, mister. It occurs to me that your horse"— he waved at Brennan's saddlebags—"looks a might overburdened."

Brennan smiled again, but there was no warmth in it. "I'm lighter than I look."

17

Torn-Ear piped up again, pointing at the ground behind Brennan. "Looks like you're leaking out some of your load too, mister."

Betrayed by a protective instinct regarding the contents of his saddlebags, Brennan glanced back again. Several gold coins littered the ground by his horse's left rear leg, and as he watched, another fell from the hole torn by the arrow in his saddlebag.

Brennan dropped the reins and flexed his fingers.

"Get down off the horse slowly, mister." Squished-Nose and Torn-Ear had their guns out now, pointed more or less at Brennan's chest. Bandage-Hand was slower to follow his friends' lead but eventually got his own gun out too.

Brennan sighed and dismounted in what he hoped was a manner leisurely enough to be irritating, holding his hands up at shoulder height.

"Fellas, I know this seems like a good idea to you, but those Apaches may not be quite as far back as I'd—"

"Shut up!" Squished-Nose tried to strike an angry tone, but self-satisfaction intruded. Finding saddlebags full of gold coins almost made the mess of the previous night worth it to him. He thought it was a terrible shame that poor Earl would never share in their good fortune, but that was how things worked out sometimes.

"Now that I think about it, mister, you look a little overburdened yourself. Why don't you—slowly now—just unbuckle those gun belts of yours and let 'em drop."

Brennan nodded as if he had expected the demand and loosed his guns to fall on the ground.

"Mighty good, mister." Squished-Nose grinned. "Now let's take care of that poor horse of yours." He gestured with his gun, indicating Bandage-Hand. "Hand those saddlebags to Jake, there."

Brennan glanced at Jake/Bandage-Hand as he unbuckled his saddlebags. The man's skin was a sickly colour, and he seemed increasingly tremulous and less impressed than most men would have been at the prospect of being handed a bag of gold.

Brennan grunted as he hefted the saddlebags off his horse. They *were* heavy, and his mount actually had the poor grace to look a bit more cheerful for their absence. Trudging over to Jake/Bandage-Hand's mount, he noted there was indeed a distinct scent of decay coming from the man.

"That's it, mister. Go on and put 'em on Jake's horse."

"See that you're not worried much about overburdening *him*, I reckon," Brennan muttered, trying his best to sound angry, which he was, and defeated, which he was not. Not yet, at least.

In a few seconds, Squished-Nose would realize he had made an error in letting Brennan put a horse between himself and the only two healthy gunmen among the three.

Torn-Ear chimed in at—from Brennan's point of view—exactly

the right time.

"Well, now, don't that horse of his look better already? It's a shame we had to leave Earl behind. He'd've enjoyed this."

Squished-Nose shook his head and chuckled. "He shouldn't've been letting a bite slow him down." Torn-Ear laughed back after a few seconds. The sound of coins jingling as Brennan threw the saddlebags onto Jake's horse made him turn back. "Why thank you, mister. I know—"

He stopped as he noticed the arrow from the saddlebag was now in Brennan's hand. Before he could bring his gun up, Brennan stabbed the arrow into Jake's leg, leaning in and putting all his weight behind the thrust.

Sick as he was, Jake was jarred more by the violent impact than anything else—at first. He stared down at the arrow protruding from his leg, eyes bulging as his gun slithered out of his hand like an oiled snake, then watched Brennan snatch the falling weapon out of the air.

After a few seconds, pain signals worked their way through Jake's rapidly deteriorating nervous system to his brain, and he cried out in pain. His horse, perhaps having had enough of the scent of blood and the screaming of men in the last few hours, bolted.

"Shit! Jake—"

Torn-Ear had only enough time to bring his gun up before Brennan's first shot caught him in the chest and ploughed through his heart. He jerked, twisted off his horse, and fell face down into the sand.

Brennan watched Torn-Ear fall, then glanced at Jake, but by the time his weapon was turning toward Squished-Nose, the man already had his gun aimed squarely back at Brennan. Squished-Nose fired three shots in rapid succession, the first two whizzing by Brennan's left ear and the third going wildly high above his head.

Brennan had seen this many times before. Most "gunmen" killed by firing as quickly as possible and hoping at least a few of their shots told on their adversaries. Such a strategy worked better with force of numbers than one-on-one.

Taking a moment to draw a deliberate bead on the gunman, Brennan took a deep breath and shot twice. The second bullet flew squarely through Squished-Nose's left eye and tumbled out the back of his head in a sludgy red burst of brain matter and skull fragments. The shot man tumbled like a broken thing onto the ground, where he convulsed for a second before lying still.

Brennan turned his eyes on his remaining adversary.

Death was wrapping its eager arms around Jake like a passionate lover who would not be denied. His organs were failing and his brain was flickering like a dying fire as the infection tore through him. In the muddy water that his thoughts had become, he was dimly aware that his movements were increasingly slow and clumsy, but still, the moments

Brennan had spent dealing with his two friends had allowed him the requisite time to get his horse under control. He had turned his mount back toward the fight and had managed to pull his remaining pistol. Now he was unsteadily trying to bring it to bear on the man who'd killed his friends.

Brennan did a zigzag run toward Jake, took a shot, and heard nothing but the click of the hammer falling on an empty chamber. More pulls on the trigger produced the same empty sound. Brennan grimaced; after stealing the man's gun, he was paying the price for the owner's idiocy in leaving the weapon half-empty.

Jake had flinched when he saw Brennan take aim but now realized that Brennan's gun—well, *his* gun—was empty. The disease coiling within him made it challenging for him to control fine motor movements, but with some force of will, he brought his own weapon to bear on Brennan's chest.

"Don't fucking move! I swear, fucking move just once and I'll shoot your fucking heart out!"

Brennan halted his advance, wondering why the man wasn't doing just that. He watched as Jake looked down at the arrow embedded in his leg, black-red blood oozing out around the wound.

"You fucker!" Jake spat. "Fucked my leg up good, and killed my friends into the bargain."

Brennan let his eyes wander briefly to the two bodies lying still in the sand, nodding after a moment. "True enough." He licked his lips. "But surely you must admit there was a . . . mutuality of intent among us."

Jake's face twisted into a grimace. "What? Mutuality of what?"

"Well—"

"Shut up! Shut up!" Jake's gun hand trembled. "Mister, I'm fucking tired of people biting and stabbing and shooting at me. Now drop that fucking gun."

Brennan looked at the gun in his hand and took a step toward the other man, smiling. "It's empty." He took another step as he pulled the chamber open. "See?"

"Drop it!"

"Okay, okay." As Brennan threw the gun down, he took another stride forward.

"Don't! Not one more step, shitheel. I swear to God, I'd shoot you dead right now if I wasn't so sick. Now, you help me out and I'll let you keep half of your gold."

"Half, huh?" Brennan's smile widened. "Generous man."

Jake's jaw hardened and a thin line of black gore dribbled out of the left side of his mouth. "Who the fuck do you think you are, fucker? Ain't I the one with the gun?"

"All these questions. You sure you're not one of those newspaper fellas?"

"Fuck you! Now you go get that fucking horse—"

Jake shifted his gaze and his pistol to point at the horse he wanted Brennan to catch, and that was the moment.

When Jake looked back, he saw something in Brennan's hand, but with his ever-dimming vision, he found it difficult to see exactly what the object was. And even more difficult now because the man's arm was moving, throwing—

Brennan's knife impaled itself high up on Jake's gun arm.

Crying out in equal parts fright and frustration, Jake again dropped his gun and used his other hand to grope at the knife with ineffectual, spastic movements. More by chance than intent, he succeeded in pulling it out, and jets of oily black blood fountained from the wound.

Brennan had been running from the moment the knife left his hand, but the wounded man's horse—spooked once again and far beyond easy calming this time—reared up at Brennan's approach, nearly unseating his rider. Brennan jumped back from the reeling horse and fell on his backside. The horse bolted for the horizon, the screaming man still atop it.

Cursing, Brennan dived for his discarded pistol belt, fumbled his own gun out, and then rolled onto his back and fired at the rapidly retreating horse and rider.

No man who'd ever seen Brennan shoot would have been loath to describe him as a marksman, but Jake's horse was fleeing at top speed and the man upon it was pitching unpredictably back and forth with every gallop. In a few moments, the man and his mount dipped below a small rise and were effectively out of range.

"Hey!" Brennan was on his feet now and running, for he had no hope in the short term of catching any of the other loose horses, confused and terrified as they were.

"Stop! Not that way! Ah, shit . . ."

The wild horse—Brennan's gold still aboard—was heading straight back the way he'd come.

Toward the Apaches.

## Chapter Three

Even from a half mile away, Solenne could smell death in the camp by the river. But not true death. Not final death.

The horse could smell it too and tossed its head, tugging at the reins and whinnying. Solenne nudged it forward anyway, and her mount snorted as if in disgust.

She had been stalking the reaper for several days, losing the trail for a time when the clumsy thing stumbled into a river and was carried away downstream. A mile or so downriver, she had found traces on the riverbank where the creature had managed to drag itself out of the water. Vultures circled overhead nearby. No scavenger would touch reaper flesh. Even flies would not deign to lay eggs in the tissue of the infected. But Solenne had often seen vultures circling the carcasses of those recently killed. Once, she had even seen one approach and dip its beak to tear away a bit of contaminated flesh, then suddenly back away and fly off as if the meat were poisoned. She followed these vultures to the body of a rancher, who had been unlucky enough to be watering his cattle when the reaper had found him. She thought that the scent of the man had probably served as an impetus for the monster to exit the water.

Solenne had looked down at the rancher from atop the horse. In feeding on the man, the reaper had ripped into his abdomen and scattered remnants of bloody organs all around the body. Torn virtually apart, the rancher had looked dead as yesterday's news, but Solenne had shot him in the head anyway to make absolutely sure his first death was his last. She had felt bad about the rancher, who'd looked old enough to perhaps be a grandfather, and who, even in violent death, seemed to her to have a kind face—one that hadn't deserved a bullet through it.

It had been near dusk when she'd found him, and by the state of the corpse and the bloody footprints the reaper had left, she figured the thing was just a few hours ahead. The trail had been clear from then on, even across the bare desert shale. The creature had left behind traces of the rancher's blood as it scrabbled across the desert, dragged on its vector of hunger by who knew what vague scents or impulses.

Solenne had chosen to ride most of the night though only a sliver of a waxing moon shone down on her. Her fervent hope was that she could catch up with her quarry before it came across anyone else, but she decided to sleep a bare hour or two before dawn to be certain she wouldn't be exhausted when she did find the thing.

On the trail again that morning, she'd grimaced when she'd seen the reaper's tracks break west suddenly to align with the wispy white smoke of what looked to be a dying campfire on the horizon. The undead retained enough of their faculties to be attracted to sound and movement, as well as human structures and fire.

The wind was coming from the west, and Solenne caught a waft of death on it even before she came over the last rise and saw the camp. The walking dead gave off a stink that clawed into the brain and scraped at it— a poisonous scent that declared not just death but death that *hungered*.

Solenne paused at the top of the low hill to survey the encampment while she murmured to calm the horse, which, like most animals, seemed to innately fear the undead.

There were two bodies around the remains of the campfire, one propped up against a fallen pine tree and the other splayed out some distance away; she immediately decided the second one was the creature she had been pursuing. Even from a distance, it was easy for her to see that it had reached the same desiccated stage most of the walking dead reached after several days, with its body missing some parts and most of its clothes scraped or worn off. The body propped against the log was still moving.

Solenne stroked her horse's neck as she spurred it down the hill. From the state of the ground around the camp and the tracks leading away, she could see that at least four people had bunked down around the campfire before the creature had come upon them. It seemed three had left on horseback some time after the cursed one had come into their camp. She wondered how many of those leaving had been bitten or injured. Contaminated.

Solenne dismounted where she could keep an eye on the live man while she examined the corpse of the creature.

It was definitely, finally, dead. Those it had comes across here had blasted it to pieces, their bullets tearing out chunks of flesh all over the creature's body. Eventually—likely through luck rather than by purpose— they had shot it in the head and put it down for good.

Now she turned her scrutiny toward the man propped against the log. She could see immediately that while he was still alive, he would not be for long. Experienced eyes took in the crusted, bloody bandage on his arm and the twisting, ropey, bluish lines running from underneath it up into his neck. His skin was already developing the unhealthy yellowish-grey cast typical of those bitten. As she approached him she saw that he had the fever. He was drenched in sweat and gasping like a fish tossed ashore and dying in the sun, but his bloodshot eyes still showed awareness. He shook his head and blinked rapidly as she came near.

Apart from a bedroll, the three who had departed had apparently stripped the camp. Left their friend to die? But no, there were a few odds and ends like a canteen and a small pack, and now she could see the man's horse through the trees, tethered by the river's edge.

She halted a few feet away from the dying man, watching him

shake his head as if plagued by flies and finally look up at her when she cleared her throat.

*

Earl focused on the woman before him and tried to decide if she were real. The delirium that had descended upon him over the last few hours made this difficult, and those who knew Earl well would have said that—even at the best of times—his thought processes were slow and murky as stagnant water.

For most of his adult life, Earl had been a horse thief. Then circumstances had forced him to choose between joining the Confederate Army or becoming better acquainted with a noose than most men would wish to. In his months of service since, he had been involved in a number of desperate battles with undependable comrades and had been forced to subsist on dependably bad food. Several months ago, he and three other like-minded "draftees" had seen their chance, stolen some horses, and deserted.

Since then, James, their self-appointed leader, had led the gang on a series of more or less successful robberies. Various farms, stagecoaches, and banks had all had occasion to surrender money or liquor to them over the last few weeks. Each episode of banditry had been followed by three or four days of hard riding to cross the Rio Grande and then a few of weeks of drinking and whoring around just over the border in Mexico.

They had slipped back into the Arizona territory two days prior and had been sitting around the fire the previous night debating the merits and perils of targeting the same bank twice when they'd heard noises out in the darkness—low, guttural moans punctuated by occasional brutal snarls, along with the distinctive sound of something large dragging itself over the ground toward them.

Earl had not even considered the possibility that the sounds were human and suspected some wounded animal was approaching. As the growls grew louder, he and his companions all grabbed for their guns and peered out into the darkness, cursing at the ghastly stink of sulfuric decay that was suddenly in the air.

The horror that stumbled into the periphery of their firelight seconds later was a nightmare caricature of a man—a gashed and ragged grey-skinned thing with oily yellow orbs where its eyes should have been. Despite its many wounds, the thing did not bleed. A thin inky fluid leaked from its wounds instead.

As it neared the men around the fire, the monster's mouth yawned open, its frayed lips peeling back over sparse yellow teeth. Thin, greasy drool spilled out of the creature's maw as it snarled at them, and the raw animal sound of it sent a river of ice down Earl's back.

"Stay back—" Earl started to say, but his voice only served to draw the creature's focus.

As the thing leapt at him, Earl shot it, and though he was sure his bullet had flown true, it had no visible effect. The thing's hands closed on his arms, its fingers like knives digging into his flesh. It sought to draw him within range of its teeth, and he stumbled backward, the monster falling on top of him and bearing him to the ground like a clumsy suitor. Teeth scraped against his neck as he struggled to hold the creature back. Reflexively, he punched at it with his gun, slamming his pistol into its jaw. He was rewarded with a spray of teeth and oily black blood, but the creature never paused in its attack.

By then his cohorts had come to his aid, kicking and punching at the creature, and they had managed to get it off him and throw it to the side.

Then the shooting had begun.

Earl and his army buddies had been of a uniformly ruthless mind as far as thievery was concerned. They had been ever ready to gun down any man at the least provocation should it mean more silver in their pockets. But for the most part, they had killed by force of numbers and surprise. None of them had ever squared off in a gunfight one-on-one; in fact, they had gone out of their way to avoid what any fair-minded person would have called an even fight. Circumstances had never before demanded from them any true marksmanship, and so it had taken a dozen or more shots between them to bring down their attacker. In the time that he'd had on his hands since then to brood on it, Earl had reckoned that half the bullets they'd fired at the thing hadn't even hit home. Only when James had placed his gun directly against the monster's head and shot it through the skull had it finally gone down.

"Hey. What happened to you, cowpoke?"

The woman's voice cut like a knife into Earl's reverie, its low timbre a surprise in and of itself. In his deepening delirium over the last few hours, he had been visited by numerous terrifying hallucinations, mostly taking the form of moaning skull-faced phantasms reaching out to him with bloody hands. None of the phantasms had spoken, however, so— at least in context of the last few hours—this was a surprising development.

"Hey."

None of the illusions had kicked him in the leg, either.

"Tell me what happened."

His desperate mind dismissed her slightly askew nose and the scars running down her neck and saw only the lithe feminine figure that reminded him of a dancer he'd seen once, long ago, in San Francisco. Her eyes looked like chips of blue ice and her hat hung from its wind strings down her back despite the glare of the midday sun, as if the desert heat couldn't touch her. Most astoundingly, she wore tied-down gun belts left and right. Earl had never seen a woman wearing guns, though he'd heard of one or two female trick shooters.

The only women in Earl's adult life who had deigned to spare him even a single word had, for the most part, been beggars and prostitutes, and so despite Solenne's questions and even her kick, Earl was unsure this wasn't just another hallucination.

"Hey. Cowpoke. What. Happened?" This time she punctuated each word with a kick to his right leg.

"Are you real?"

The woman squinted at him and tilted her head for a moment as if she were giving the question serious consideration. She evidently decided against answering and instead pointed at the monster's corpse, lying a few yards away.

"It bit you before you killed it, yes?"

Earl nodded after a moment, wincing and cradling his bandaged arm a bit tighter against his body.

"No! Not bit, but scratched me up real good. Fucker came in after dark. Crazy motherfucker. No fuckin' gun or nothin'. Just came in and jumped on me like . . . like he was wanting to eat me for dinner and then—"

Earl coughed, his chest heaving, and Solenne saw that the spit flying out of his mouth held traces of brackish gore.

She looked toward the trail leaving the camp. "Any of your friends get bit?"

"Ain't no fuckin' friends of mine. Fuckers . . . I'm just a little"—*cough*—"sick. Got a touch of cold or somethin'. Those bastards took off without me this mornin'." Earl paused as if to force himself to focus through the fever, and he looked sideways at the woman standing over him. "Just who the fuck are you anyway, missy?"

*

In the heat of the noon sun, Solenne watched Earl shiver as if he had just been pulled from a mountain river and knew he was close to death. The curse progressed quickly in its victims, surging through them like a flash flood. Toward the end, the fever threw them into terrible, bone-shaking rigours that sometimes set their teeth to chattering so hard they bit through their own lips. If she was to gain information from him, it must be soon, before he could no longer speak.

"Your friends, they—"

"Hey, tell you what, missy." Earl gasped. "I need some water. Canteen's dry. How about you get me some, huh?"

Solenne looked at Earl like a butcher wondering if a cut of beef was past its prime, lips pursed and eyes narrowed. After a moment, she toed her foot under the empty canteen lying at his feet and flicked it up into her hand.

"Will do, cowpoke, but want some answers first. How many of

your friends got bitten?"

Earl shook—with anger or fever, Solenne could not tell.

"You listen to me, you fuckin' bitch! I want some fuckin' water, and—"

When he opened his mouth to yell, Solenne saw that his gums were receding and his teeth appeared longer—a latent sign of the curse scribbling over its victim's soul. She did not have much time.

Leaning back slightly, Solenne kicked the man in his right side—*hard* this time, and with no regret. She felt a rib snap beneath the toe of her boot, and he howled in pain, gulping several times before breaking into a barrage of ragged coughs and then spitting up greenish-black liquid that she knew had been blood only hours ago. When he was done, he looked up at her and bright, incandescent hate was writ plainly on his face.

"Listen up now, cowpoke—"

"Earl! My name is Earl, you bitch!"

Solenne spat. "*Earl*, then. Listen to me, *Earl* . . . I ain't no nice woman." To emphasize this, she lifted her foot as if to kick him again and watched him flinch like a beaten dog. "Now, how long since they left, and how many were injured? Answer that—"

"You fuckin'—"

Another kick and a shriek of pain. Solenne held up a finger when Earl looked like he was going to start swearing again.

"Answer me."

"You—"

"*Answer me now* . . . and I'll get you some water."

"*Okay* . . . Jesus. They left this mornin'. Maybe a couple hours afore noon. Jake . . . I guess Jake was bit too. Not bad though."

Earl coughed up more dark fluid, staining the ground around him with a halo of inky droplets, as if some dark angel had laid claim to him.

"Fucker near tore my arm off. Jake just got bit on his hand. He was feelin' sick this morning' too, but not as bad as me. I couldn't even get on my fuckin' horse, so they left me behind. Fuckers."

Earl looked murderously up at Solenne again through eyes turning pus-yellow. She could see he was very close to turning now. The bluish discolouration on his arm had clawed its way from his neck up over his face even in the few minutes she had been talking with him.

"Now get me some *water*." A stream of black goo leaked unnoticed out of the corner of his mouth as he shouted at her.

Solenne considered the man through lidded eyes. She needed to be after his friends before they wandered into some town with the curse cooking to a boil in them. But she had promised this man water. Honour had been important to her people, and honour might be all she had left of them inside her.

She walked to the river's edge and knelt, replenishing Earl's canteen, as well as her own. When she came back up the riverbank, she saw with no particular dismay or surprise that Earl had managed to produce a pistol, though she wondered idly where it had come from since the man wore no gun belt. His friends must have left it for him, and he had kept it hidden until now.

He pointed the gun roughly at her abdomen, and Solenne had a moment of concern when a tremor ran through him as he cocked the hammer.

"Get over here, you bitch!" Earl smiled. He was missing several teeth, but the smile would have been spoiled all the same, Solenne thought, by the dark gore that continued to leak like tree sap from between his lips.

"You—" Earl shook again, almost a convulsion this time. "Come here."

Solenne moved toward the cursed man with unhurried steps. She tossed his canteen so it landed beside him. The man flinched again, gun hand shaking, and she took an involuntary breath. He grabbed the canteen with his left hand, keeping the gun on her with his right, and grinned at her out of a face become a death's-head rictus.

"You're a fine-lookin' girl." Earl coughed again. "And I'm a mite cold. Reckon I'll feel a whole lot better with a nice warm gal like yourself sittin' next to me, warmin' me up, like." He gestured beside him. "You come sit beside me for a bit."

Solenne looked at Earl with flat, stony eyes. "Earl, I'll tell you the truth. In about five minutes, you're going to turn into the same kind of monster that hurt you. The thing that attacked you has a disease, kind of like rabies; and it's in you now, killing you . . . All I can offer you—"

"Shut—"

There was a sharp crack as Earl's gun went off, the result of another tremor spasming through him, and Solenne flinched as the errant bullet whistled by her ear.

"Shut the fuck up, you bitch! You listen to me, now. You're gonna come sit by me and warm me up, you hear? Can't fuckin' believe I'm so fuckin' cold in this heat." He looked up at the sky and laughed, spraying out more black droplets before focusing again on Solenne. "You come sit beside me, sugar. Keep me company."

Solenne stepped toward him, her hands coming up toward her guns.

"Wait!"

Earl's head bobbed back and forth from one side to another, and Solenne suspected the man's sight was growing misty as his eyes clouded over with the yellow cataracts that characterized the gaze of the walking dead. Reapers found prey mostly by sound, scent, and perhaps heat, but their eyesight deteriorated quickly once the curse took hold of them.

"Slow down and take your time, missy . . . Maybe you'd better get comfortable. Take your guns off, for a start. Just reach easy like and unbuckle those babies. Do it now."

Solenne slid her hands slowly up to her waist and unbuckled both gun belts. They fell, one after another, at her feet.

"That's good." Earl said. "Now— Ahhh!" Earl rolled back and forth against the log as rigours ran up and down his spine. With obvious effort, he gained control of himself while Solenne watched, as still and patient as a statue.

"Now get your clothes off. Reckon I'll feel a lot better after an hour or two warmin' myself up with you."

Solenne could see the curse sleeting through the man like a mid-winter storm. His teeth seemed suddenly longer as his gums receded, and his colour was fading from pale to dark grey as the disease painted rapid strokes over him like some demon artist.

"Did you hear me, bitch? Get your clothes off!"

"I heard you."

She watched Earl closely as she shrugged off her vest and let it fall to the ground beside her guns. She went to unbutton her shirt and then smiled almost coquettishly at Earl, instead lifting her leg and reaching down to remove her right boot.

"That's it." Shivering though he was, Earl managed a grin. "Can't believe how fuckin' cold I feel."

He watched, tremor-wracked, as Solenne dropped the boot in the sand at her feet and then suddenly something flashed by his eyes—bright, metallic, and glinting in the sun.

The knife that Solenne kept sheathed in her boot was nine inches long, weighty, and well balanced. She kept it sharp as a razor and practised throwing it—alternating hands—nearly every night. Over the years she had developed a strike as deadly and quick as a viper.

The knife flew like an arrow and sliced through Earl's gun arm, slamming it back and impaling it against the log behind him. His fingers snapped apart and his pistol dropped to the ground beside him. He looked dumbly for a moment from Solenne to the knife, but it took time for his dying nervous system to communicate the full import of what had happened to his brain, so the cry of pain came several seconds later.

When it did come, his yell was a growl of unalloyed rage that ripped from the throat of something no longer human. His eyes were completely clouded over now, an unfocused buttery yellow colour, and his lips split as they drew back over prominent teeth. He snarled and lunged toward Solenne like a starving animal, held back only by the knife pinning his arm to the log.

"Hate to tell you this, Earl"—Solenne plucked a pistol out of one of her fallen gun belts—"but nothing this side of hell is going to warm you up again."

Earl snapped his teeth at her, dark spittle foaming out of his mouth.

Solenne had seen them slip over like this before. Occasionally, there was no death in between, just an abrupt conversion from human to monster. She stepped nearer and he wrenched forward, tearing his speared arm half-apart, his sensibility to pain fleeing along with his humanity.

Solenne raised her gun and shot him precisely between the eyes.

Earl's head snapped back as the bullet tore through his brain, and he collapsed into his final death like a discarded doll falling limp to the ground.

Solenne buckled her gun belts around her waist again, replaced her boot, and shrugged back into her vest. She looked up to see that her horse had wandered down to the river to join the dead man's mount in a drink.

Her knife was embedded deep into the log, and she had to step on what remained of Earl's torn arm and lean back to pull it out. She wiped the blade—greasy with dark blood—on his shirt and then replaced it in its sheath in her boot. Then she went down to the river, took the tackle off the man's horse, and turned the animal loose.

By the sun, she estimated she could perhaps catch up with the dead man's friends before dark if she hurried. The question was, did she *want* to catch them in daylight? History suggested such men would not respond with enthusiasm to suggestions that one of them was doomed to die and must be put down like a rabid dog.

Approaching them after dark might be equally hazardous. They would naturally be more watchful after what had happened to them the previous night—they might even set a guard—but then again, Solenne would not be battering in among them like a mindless monster; she would slide into camp like one of the wraith-like death-bringers from her people's mythos.

She whistled and her horse lifted its snout from the river with a reproachful look in its eyes, dismayed, as always, with the idea that she might want to ride some more when there was water and shade and greenery all around them. After a moment, it snorted and trotted over to her.

Tradition among Solenne's people dictated that she bury the corpse of a slain enemy, but Solenne didn't even consider it. The time it would take wasn't worth the chance that she might lose her quarry's trail.

Honour was for the living—always—before the dead.

She mounted the horse and rode out.

## Chapter Four

Blood trails flew back along the flanks of Colonel Simon Johnston's horse as he worked his spurs into the sides of the straining animal, relentlessly urging it to greater speed. The captains and lieutenants galloping alongside him knew they were all close to running their mounts to death, but the cautioning look that had darkened the colonel's face when one of them had suggested a slower pace kept them all silent now as they rocketed across the Arizona plain like thunder brought to earth.

Dust rose up behind them like a cometary tail, but Johnston worried little about the stamp their journey made upon the sky for anyone nearby to see. The chance of coming across some adversary they could not easily defeat out here was almost infinitesimal. Encountering Union troops this far south was beyond unlikely. Meeting hostile natives was certainly possible. But either danger—any danger—when weighed against the treasure he almost had within his grasp, was not worth slowing one iota to mitigate.

He had been dragging his increasingly ragged fifty-man troop around southern Arizona for nearly two months, and he had never been closer to his goal. His men and their mounts were near exhaustion, but he noted this only in terms of his requirements for a functional fighting force. He knew no man among them was without a profound fear of his colonel, which would always win out over fatigue, perhaps even to the point of death. He had taken great care over his time with them to cultivate such fear for this exact purpose. The troop had begun this journey sixty-four men strong, but matters of discipline and the ultimate value of the prize they pursued had necessitated sacrifices. Johnston needed his soldiers to be a sharp, reliable weapon, and so he had forged them into one, and he was no sorrier for the men lost along the way than a blacksmith sharpening a knife would lament the toll it might take on the leather strop.

Before the war, Johnston had been one of the wealthiest plantation owners in all of Virginia, an ancestral legacy handed down to him by his father, along with piracy, murder, and robbery. Johnston's father had passed on to his son a keen love of history and a particular interest in the explorers who'd ventured into Africa and the New World, braving unknown dangers in pursuit of knowledge. His father's support of his scholarly interests, though, had been accompanied by a deliberate cultivation of a merciless nature in his heir.

When his father had passed on, a victim of too much good southern whiskey, Johnston quickly became bored with plantation life and hired a manager so he could engage in more exciting pursuits. Longing to be known as the same kind of intrepid adventurer he had read of in school, he initiated journeys of exploration deep into the wild rainforests of South America to wander among long-abandoned dead cities, now reclaimed by the climbing vines and enfolding green of the ever-growing jungle. Even here, Johnston sought wealth as he had been conditioned to, and he found lost gold and gems left behind by civilizations destroyed by Spanish swords or smallpox a century earlier.

It was the last of these expeditions that he remembered most vividly. His group had penetrated much deeper into the primeval jungle than Johnston ever had before, following a long overgrown and barely recognizable path beside a river and far up into the mountains. Of the ten men who had set out with him, three died along the way of illness that made them bleed from every orifice, and another three simply disappeared into the night, dragged off after sundown by some beast they never identified, their screams echoing through the forest. Johnston and the others had spent the nights after that slung up in the trees whenever they could.

Eventually they found the temple they sought, and the stories they followed turned out to be true. The temple was filled with the gold they had been told would be there, along with the horrifying temple guardians they had thought to be mere invention calculated to frighten away potential thieves.

Johnston alone had survived the encounter.

On his return from South America, Johnston had found his beloved state under the growing influence of Northern tyrants who wanted to ruin his way of life, so he had joined the Virginia State Militia and risen quickly through the ranks to become a prized fighting mate of John Mosby, the "Grey Ghost" so despised by the North. By the time full blown war erupted, he had been promoted to the rank of colonel by Robert E. Lee himself.

Two months previously, Johnston had been readying his troop to depart Amarillo with orders to forge north and reinforce units fighting in Kansas. But the night before he was to leave, he chanced to read a hastily written entry in some nameless Confederate scout's log—a detailed account of cannibalism and madness among a small native tribe near the Arizona-Mexico border. The scout had seen humans eating other humans with his own eyes, and this had been no degeneration of men driven by starvation. By his account, written in a trembling hand, those he had encountered had acted like rabid dogs, seeking to kill any human who came within their reach with their bare hands and teeth.

The scout who had seen all this had been carrying documents from spies in California and had only by chance come across this village of demons while searching for a river to water his horse. He had fled as quickly as any sane man would upon viewing such horrors, so there were few other details, but in the moment of reading the account, Johnston's destiny was revealed to him in an epiphany. He saw immediately why he had been spared the horrible death that had befallen all his fellows in that savage jungle. There was a purpose to everything, and Johnston had divined his own in that hot, fetid jungle temple. The time had come to act.

Johnston ignored the orders that would have sent him and his men to Kansas and instead rode his troop hard toward the location the scout had described in his report. Two weeks later, he found the village—what was left of it. It was like riding into an uncovered graveyard. The whole tribe was wiped out, preserved in a ghastly tableau, and the cadavers—left where they had fallen—had shrivelled and desiccated for weeks in the summer sun. For some reason, there had been little or no predator activity, but it was apparent that many of the bodies had been partially eaten, quite obviously consumed by their fellow tribesmen.

But several had been killed by gunfire, and always by a bullet through the head.

Several trails led away from camp, shuffling marks in the sand obviously made by limping men. Johnston remembered the drunkard's gait of the creatures in the jungle and knew these tracks were left by men turned cannibal-demon. Alongside each trail were traces of someone following on horseback, and each had led to another corpse, twisted and baking in the desert sun, all shot in the head.

Johnston was not the only one pursuing these creatures.

In another nearby Apache village, there were more accounts of the dead risen as diseased cannibals. But there were also tales of a woman who hunted the infected down and destroyed them. The natives called her *la Bruja*—the Witch—and she was apparently well known to the indigenous people. She always appeared when the demons things did, and the local natives spoke of her reverently, even fearfully, as a spirit tasked with dragging the dead back to the underworld.

When the tribe's chief divined that Johnston was interested in finding her, he became angry and refused to speak anymore, and so Johnston ordered his men to burn the village and slaughter its inhabitants. He relented only when one of the natives proposed to scout for them and help them find what they sought if the village was spared.

Since then, Johnston and his troop had pursued the stories of madness and violence, racing from dead-end towns to deserted native villages to bloody trails that died out among the desert sands, and everywhere they found corpses of men, women, even children—heads torn asunder by bullets or smashed into pulp by some improvised club. All the bodies bore marks of having been fed upon or bitten. All had risen and then been killed by this witch.

Johnston guessed he would have had one of the creatures a month ago if not for this mythical woman whom their unwilling Apache recruit spoke of with such apprehension—a legend that would not bear belief in the cold light of day if he had not seen the animated corpses himself. Woman or no, supernatural or not, whatever force killing these creatures danced always just ahead of him, slaughtering the demons like an avenging angel and meddling with his God-given destiny. Each new annihilated corpse, spoiled beyond possibility of use, stoked his inner rage as if it were a blacksmith's fire.

But he was close now—closer than he'd ever been—and *one* of the diseased abominations was all he needed. One who was, not *alive*, of course, but still moving with whatever unholy power inhabited it.

Just one.

Johnston's glare turned from the trail ahead of them to Quinto, their pressed Apache scout, who was riding beside him. The man had been staring at him, perhaps also remembering the day the savage had sworn to aid Johnston lest his entire tribe be murdered.

After days of riding a ragged criss-cross trail near the last deserted village they had come across, Quinto had picked up clear signs of one of the creatures—stumbling prints, drops of dark ochre blood, and even the occasional ragged bit of torn flesh littering the ground.

One of *them*, still animate.

Now if he could only get to it before she did.

As it did more and more often now, the mere thought of her tore an oath from him. He scowled at Quinto. "How fresh are these tracks? How much further?"

It was late afternoon and, at this speed, the growing shadows must have made it difficult for the Apache to pick out the trail. Nevertheless, Quinto merely glanced at the ground ahead before gesturing at some vague signs only he could see. "From last night."

Johnston glowered anew. The heathen's words could mean anything. He could assume that the abominations moved no faster than a live man did, unless perhaps they were pursuing a victim. The thing might be hours away.

Or over the next ridge.

The troop came thundering over a small rise, and Johnston immediately saw the campsite by the river below and the two bodies lying near it. He reined in his horse so quickly that less well-trained cavalrymen might have run into him, but the entire group stopped within seconds of each other, stirring a brief haze of dust, and observed the scene below.

Naturally, none of Johnston's troops had ever themselves seen one of their colonel's abominations alive, but they had received explicit instruction from him on how the creatures were to be handled. In the early part of their journey, after arduous rides under the implacable Arizona sun, Johnston had often stood in front of the haggard, disbelieving faces crowded round him and told them about men that might *appear* dead—

even be dismembered or disembowelled—while still retaining a demonic spark of movement and hunger. He warned that they fed on the flesh of the living and that any human bitten would inevitably perish in pain and turn into one of the creatures themselves.

He had debated with himself about revealing what he considered a key piece of information—that one of these creatures could be killed only by annihilating its brain. This singular vulnerability had been only a conjecture after his battle in the jungle, but it had been confirmed for him after seeing the work of the Witch. He decided he could not have his men, in the panic they would surely experience upon seeing one of the things, killing what he so desperately needed, so instead he cautioned them on pain of death *not* to shoot for the head. Though he suspected that the corpses the Witch had left behind her had spoken plainly of the monsters' weakness to some of his men, he hoped they might simply interpret his caution as concern for capturing one of the cannibal-things alive.

Whatever the men might or might not have guessed about the nature of the corpses they found, they harboured no illusions or lack of clarity regarding their leader's philosophy of command and punishment. When the men saw Johnston—his mood over the last weeks increasingly befouled by every new withered corpse they had comes across—begin to shake with anger at what he saw down by the camp, every man in the troop tensed.

Quite obviously the Witch had been here . . . been and gone.

Neither of the bodies was moving, and Johnston knew the troop had made enough noise coming over the hill to make any of the abominations come crawling toward them if they had even one appendage left. Still, it was always worth being thorough.

"Captain Lewis."

"Sir?" Lewis was a tall, lean, dark-haired man, whom Johnston knew as unimaginative but quick, unquestioning, and efficient at fulfilling orders—an ideal subordinate.

"Take ten men and spread them out over this rise between the camp and the river. Quinto, Captain Barrett and I will go down and investigate."

Lewis nodded and turned to issue orders to the men, but Johnston turned with him and spoke ahead of him in a harsh yell that carried across the valley.

"Mark me, men." He pointed toward the camp. "Those two look to be dead, but it might just be that one of them is the thing I seek. If either of those things moves, you are to do exactly as we planned. You each have nets. If one of them comes at you, you cast your net and ride back a bit, if need be . . ."

The men had heard variations of this speech before and braced for the inevitable conclusion. Boredom was never long a fact of life in men serving under Simon Johnston.

"  . . . and if they get too close, you can shoot them in the legs. *The legs only!* Any man who shoots for the head, I will personally kill myself. Clear?"

A chorus of *yessirs* followed, and Lewis cut ten men out of the ranks and began ranging them along the top of the ridge.

Johnston nodded at Barrett, who plucked his rifle from its scabbard and ensured its readiness with the quiet efficiency of an expert gunman. While he appreciated Lewis's obedience and efficiency the way he might value a reliable pistol, Barrett was more like a knife—surgical and precise. Trouble was, Barrett was more of a thinker. Johnston could see it in his cold grey eyes. Thoughtful subordinates sometimes questioned orders, and Johnston could not abide that, but Barrett seemed to sense that as well, offering his judgment when asked, but *only* when asked; and he had always been respectful, hiding his true opinion—if he had one—about whatever orders he was issued.

Johnston had picked Barrett carefully for this mission, spiriting him away from another commander after hearing about his marksmanship. Despite Johnston's preference for unimaginative subordinates, Barrett was known as the best sniper in the whole Confederacy, and a man certain to hit one of the demons—not in the head, but with a disabling shot to the legs—was a profound asset.

As Johnston urged his horse down the hill, Quinto fell in to his left to examine the tracks that led down into the camp while Barrett placed himself between Johnston and the two corpses they were approaching. Barrett knew he was not exempt from Johnston's edict. If either of the two things on the ground moved, his bullets had best cripple rather than kill, or within seconds he would find himself lying dead on the ground beside them.

It quickly became obvious, though, that no bullets or nets would be required. The two corpses, lying just a few yards away from one another, had both received devastating, close-range head wounds.

One of the carcasses looked as if it had been dead for weeks, and Johnston supposed that it was the walking corpse he and his troop had been following for the last few days.

The other body, leaning up against a log in front of a still-smoldering campfire, looked freshly killed, perhaps dead for only a few hours, but Johnston took in the bandaged arm and discoloured skin and could see that the man had turned from human to flesh-eater before he had been executed.

Quinto had dropped from his horse and was skirting the campsite on foot, examining the ground closely.

Barrett walked his horse up to within a yard or two of the corpses and gave voice to what Johnston had been thinking. "Looks like they've been dead a while." He pointed. "Gunshot wounds look fresh, though." He held his hand over the remains of the campfire. "Still a bit of heat. Was stoked up this morning, I'd guess."

"Sounds likely, Captain."

Johnston turned to Quinto, who had apparently finished his inspection of the area and was waiting for Johnston's attention with the quiet patience that marked the man. Quinto's face was ever passive, unmarked by the rage he must have felt inside at being torn away from his family and home. While he had been cooperative enough to survive Johnston's erratic temper, he had never been overtly helpful. He would not speak unless spoken to, and he would volunteer no information unless asked for it.

"Quinto." Johnston spat. "What happened here?"

The Apache thought for a moment and then pointed toward the southeast. "Three men on horseback rode in here and made camp . . . last night. That one"—he nodded toward the corpse that looked weeks dead—"came in from the south. Later, someone else came on horseback, following it into camp. Maybe only this morning. Tracks are fresh."

He paused and scanned the ground, obviously playing the chaos of the many mixed trails, human and animal, through his mind. Quinto might not volunteer information, but in Johnston's experience he never ever lied, and he suspected that in Quinto's mind, his oath bound him from directly deceiving his captors.

"There was some kind of fight, as you may see." Quinto pointed to indicate the two corpses and flashed a tight grimace that might have passed for an ironic smile. "But these men did not die at the same time. I think this man, with the torn arm"—he gestured at what had once been Earl—"was alive till this morning and—"

Johnston waved his hand dismissively. "Never mind all that. Who left, and in which direction?"

Quinto raised a finger as if to admonish Johnston for rushing him, and every man who saw the gesture grimaced, knowing that anyone else who did such a thing would be dead seconds later.

"Three laden horses left in that direction." Quinto pointed roughly southeast, where several sets of hoof tracks were barely visible in the sand. "It was after they left that the other came into camp and killed him." He pointed again at Earl's body. "Then the killer followed the others."

Something on the ground caught Quinto's attention, and he bent and grabbed a handful of the loose soil, raising it to his nose and sniffing at it for a moment before letting it spill back out of his hand.

"One—maybe more—of the men who left earlier was wounded . . . bleeding."

"Bullshit . . . How the hell d'you know that?" Barrett said.

Quinto shrugged. "Can smell it." He held out his hand, his

forefinger and thumb barely an inch apart. "Just a little. Blood on the ground."

Barrett snorted.

"And who rode after them?" Johnston asked.

Quinto paused, looking at Johnston, eyes stony. "You know."

"Your witch again, was it?" Johnston was rewarded with a rising look of discomfort on the otherwise imperturbable face. He raised his voice. "Mr. Lewis."

From up on the rise the captain responded. "Yes, Colonel!"

"Oblige me, sir, and have two of your lieutenants help Mr. Carter dismount." He pointed into the crowd of riders on the ridge around the campsite precisely at a trooper, who immediately blanched and clutched at the horn of his saddle as if hanging onto it could somehow save him from the hell that was coming for him.

"No!" Carter said. "Colonel, no! I didn't do nothing—"

Lewis shouted, "Troopers. Help this man dismount. Now."

Carter had seen what had befallen the previous subjects of such punishment, and he looked from side to side with the frantic air of a deer cornered by a cougar, edging his horse backward as if seeking a way to escape. The two horsemen beside him looked equally frightened, but for a very different reason. They both knew if they let Carter elude them—even momentarily—or were overly slow in arresting him, they might easily find themselves sharing his punishment. Without hesitation, they grabbed the doomed man's reins and hauled his horse to a stop.

The men knew what was coming. Johnston's building frustration as they tracked back and forth fruitlessly through the desert had finally led him to try—as he termed it—"other measures" to realize his goal. The discovery of two corpses a week ago, whose bullet wounds had seemed recent, had prompted Johnston to attempt an experiment. In each case the troop had witnessed some luckless enlisted man—one who had committed some minor crime or infraction—singled out to "assist" with this experiment.

Under Lewis's direction, the two soldiers alongside Carter relieved him of his pistol and marched him down the rise. When Carter's knees gave way, the troopers hauled him roughly to his feet and half-carried him to stand before Johnston.

Barrett watched without expression and leaned over to the colonel, voice low. "You reckon to try this again, sir? Didn't work those other times."

"I do intend to try it again, Mr. Barrett," Johnston said, his voice flat. "As many times as I think it necessary to successfully fulfill my mission."

Johnston turned to the trembling man in front of him, and Carter looked back into his colonel's eyes as if searching for some undiscovered spark of compassion that might dwell within. Whatever he found caused him to begin crying, sputtering pleas for mercy between the sobs.

"Is it true, sir, that three nights ago you stole a pocket watch from one of your fellow soldiers?"

Carter blinked tears out of his eyes. "Sir! Colonel, sir. It wasn't like that. Smith'll tell you. He owed it to me from cards, and he wasn't gonna pay up. They'll tell you . . ." He looked up toward what had— moments ago—been his fellows, singling out one of them with his eyes. "Smithy! Tell him! Tell him, you bastard!"

Trooper Smith cast his eyes downward and hardened his jaw. All of them knew that nothing said or done now could save a man chosen by Johnston for punishment. Carter might as well have been a field mouse targeted by a hawk.

Johnston stepped closer to Carter and took him by his chin, directing the condemned man's gaze back up into the wintry eyes looking down on him.

"Sir, it matters not to me the circumstances of a theft, only that one has occurred." He stepped back and turned to the remainder of the troop, raising his voice to a shout. "This man was a Confederate soldier, one of your trusted comrades, who swore to fight with you, side by side, watching your back as you watched his . . . With his act of thievery, he has betrayed us all, as well the oath he took."

Johnston turned and strode toward what might be thought of as the most fresh of the two bodies. Earl's withering corpse lay slumped against the log, staring up at the sky with tar-coloured gore from Solenne's head shot staining his yellow-grey face. Johnston gestured impatiently with quick waves of his hand for the two troopers holding Carter to bring him along.

"And yet," he continued his speech, "this traitor amongst us may still serve our cause and, in some slight fashion at least, redeem himself." He stooped over Earl's body, staring into the clouded eyes as he plucked his riding gloves from his belt and pulled them on.

"No!" Carter screamed. "No, Colonel, please!"

Johnston wheeled and delivered a backhanded slap across Carter's face, splitting his lip and raining fresh flecks of blood amid the inky gore that surrounded Earl's body.

"You're a soldier," Johnston growled. "Face your fate like a man."

Carter began to gibber and beg, sputtering a mixture of tears, blood, and snot.

"Put him on his knees, gentlemen."

The troopers forced Carter to the ground. Having seen this sort of ritual before and wanting nothing more than to be done with what was inevitable, they dragged the man forward until he was lying halfway across Earl's corpse.

Johnston grasped Earl's head and wrenched the dead man's jaws wide open, producing sharp cracking sounds as ligaments and muscles in the cadaver's lower face ripped apart.

"His arm, please, gentlemen."

One of the troopers grabbed Carter's left arm and forced it down toward Earl's leathery face as Johnston pried the maw of the corpse fully open. A hopeless wail tore from Carter's lips, degenerating into pathetic mewls as the two troopers shoved Carter's forearm into the open mouth until the bare flesh grated against the few jagged yellow teeth Earl had remaining.

"Fear not, solider," Johnston said to Carter. "You may yet redeem yourself through this sacrifice." He slammed the corpse's mouth closed on Carter's flesh, pulling up hard with both hands to force the dead man's teeth deep into the muscle of Carter's arm.

Carter screamed again, not so much from the pain as from the knowledge of what the wound would eventually bring. The troopers holding him glanced bleakly at each other even while maintaining an iron grip on their victim..

Johnston methodically worked the corpse's jagged teeth back and forth into Carter's flesh until the man's skin was torn and streams of blood ran down his arm. He continued the grinding motion for a minute or so and then seemed satisfied. Pushing away from the dead man and rising to his feet, he gestured at the two troopers holding the captive man between them.

"Lash him over his horse, and *lash him tight*, mind? I want three troopers watching him at all times. One of them is to report to me each hour."

"Yes, sir," the troopers said simultaneously, dragging Carter—who was muttering curses under his breath—back to the horse he'd vacated only moments ago.

Barrett had watched the whole thing without a flicker of emotion. Again, his voice low, he asked, "Think it's likely to work this time, Colonel?"

Johnston smiled at Barrett. "Does no harm to try, Captain." He said this with the air of a man remarking that there was no harm in trying a new brand of tobacco. "He'll become one of the things I need or he'll die—either way he serves as an object lesson to the other men of the results of thievery in the ranks. Get the troops ready to move out, will you? They'll have ten minutes to fill their canteens and water their horses at the river. Then we ride."

Barrett nodded and moved toward the rise, passing the men lashing Carter—blood still running from his arm—over his horse. If this experiment progressed anything like the previous two Barrett had witnessed, Carter would sink quickly into a delirium and die in a feverish agony within half a day without any subsequent sign of the deadly resurrection the colonel hoped to achieve.

Johnston watched as Carter was lashed down. Satisfied that the troopers were carrying out their work with diligence, he turned to Quinto, who had watched the incident play out with a passive expression that had mirrored Barrett's.

Johnston stepped toward the scout, plucking his now-bloody riding gloves off and tucking them back in his belt. Quinto saw him glance around to assure himself his men were out of earshot.

"Mr. Quinto, I think it is time for us to talk. Truly talk." He wagged a finger at the man.

Quinto stared at him.

"You"—Johnston prodded him in the chest—"know a lot more about this than you have said. It is time, my boy"—he grinned—"to *tell me* what you know."

"I have told you everything I know about these creatures."

"Make me sure of that, Quinto. Make me sure, else I'll have you tied to four horses and torn apart." Johnston's smile never wavered. "Then I'll send a dozen of my men back to your village and have it burnt to ash."

The Apache took an involuntary step back, and Johnston took some small satisfaction in having finally spooked the man he thought of as a savage.

Quinto watched Johnston's hand wander toward his pistol. After weeks of watching this madman drive his troopers to the brink of exhaustion and starvation, torturing and killing those who offended him, Quinto would have welcomed death, but there was his tribe to think about. He spread his hands as if in surrender.

"'Everything I know' is not much. No one knows much about these things. Since I was a child, I have heard stories of demons—flesh-eaters. Parents tell children these stories to keep them from wandering. But when I was a young man, we heard from a village far south of us that the fables of our fathers had turned out to be true. They had met demon spirits who ate flesh and spread their appetites into those they killed, making new monsters."

Johnston waved at the two corpses. "These may have been the last of them. This was the only trail we picked up. It may be our final chance. So I want to know all about *her* now, Quinto. All about *her*. On your life . . . and the life of everyone you love."

Quinto nodded. "I believe you. But I should tell you that it is bad to speak too much of witches. Always dark spirits hear when men speak of such creatures—"

Johnston turned and shouted, "Lewis. Pick out a dozen men for a mission."

When Johnston turned back to Quinto, Lewis's acknowledgement echoing behind him, Quinto had paled appreciably.

"Please, Colonel, I will tell you. I promise . . . There are stories of this woman too, as you know, like the stories of the dead who walk, but the stories about the woman . . . they're not so old. I guess they started maybe ten, fifteen years ago. Some say she's from Mexico. In some of the tales, she comes from one of the old tribes from far southern lands—ones that died fighting the Spanish—and they say she knows the old magic they had."

"Have you ever seen her?" Johnston asked.

Quinto shook his head. "No. But if she is real, then it is as we have seen. Wherever the curse appears, she does too, giving the dead that walk back to the ground for good. She is said to be a skilled warrior, as well as a witch." He paused, thinking. "A few also claim that she *herself* is a spirit of some kind."

Johnston had been looking bored but he now stiffened, eyes boring in to Quinto's. "Why do they say that?"

"If she is real, we should not pursue her, Colonel. If she truly is a witch—"

"Pah. Bullshit."

"—she might curse us all to walk as dead things."

"Why do people think she's a witch? What's that got to do with any of these stories?"

"It has been said that she has made a spell binding Death himself. That the walking dead cannot harm her . . . Whatever disease they carry slides off her as if she is made of ice. She is immune to the curse."

Johnston smiled widely. And Quinto, who had witnessed horrors and cruelty without end in the Indian Wars and again in this most recent war between the whites, found himself thinking that Johnston's smile was one of the ugliest things he'd ever seen.

## Chapter Five

Solenne came upon the two dead men just after dusk.

Vultures and coyotes surrounded the bodies, darting in and ripping bits of flesh from the corpses and then dancing back, sharing their feast in an uneasy truce. The presence of the scavengers meant neither of the men had turned reaper before they died.

She rode around the bodies in growing circles, eyes roving over the tracks left behind by those who had left this encounter alive. There had obviously been a gunfight. Someone riding in from the east had met up with the three she had been trailing. She could plainly see the trail left by two burdened horses leading toward the southeast.

She was about to ride off when she caught sight of something glinting in the sand. She slid off the horse and crouched, plucking the object out of the dirt and holding it up to examine it in the dying sunlight.

A gold coin.

Solenne frowned. She recognized the coin. Elders in her village had possessed several just like them, handed down from generation to generation. They had been mementos of their early struggles against the invaders from the eastern sea, before the people were forced to flee the sickness and death the intruders brought with them. She knew the coin now as a Spanish escudo, and touching this one raised an odd mixture of emotion that was half nostalgia, half disquiet. She had come to associate such coins with death.

She tucked the escudo into a pocket in her vest and got back on her horse, scanning the sky to the west. With luck she could ride another hour or two before dusk forced her to decide whether to camp or ride through the night. She had sometimes ridden on through the darkness after one of the things, but the waxing moon would not offer much light and she might lose the trail if the horse injured itself in an unseen rabbit hole or some such thing.

Solenne would bet that the injured man or men would do as she would—ride until the darkness overtook them or until the illness brought them down. If infected, they would be dead before sunrise. Dead, risen, and wandering like blind men in the desert. If luck was with her, they would be easy enough to catch and kill before they hurt anyone else.

She headed east, following Brennan and the man he in turn pursued.

\*\*\*

Jake had allowed his horse to run many miles before he even began to try to rein in the animal.

During that time a mind-numbing fog had descended over him, and after all he had been through in the last day, it was not entirely unwelcome. While the pain from the bite had receded, it had been replaced by numbness as a dark, web-like discolouration climbed from the wound up his arm, twinned with a raging fever the likes of which he'd never felt before. His aching joints lanced signals of pain into his brain every time he moved, and sweat was rolling off him in a torrent even as dusk approached and the desert cooled. Through the haze that was thickening around his feverish mind, he had not given a single thought to where he was heading as long as it was away from the gunman behind him. Eventually he had begun to try to slow the animal, which had tired considerably. A few tugs on the reins brought the horse to a canter, and finally to a halt. The strength left Jake's arms and he let the horse have its head. Hungry, thirsty, and weary, it trotted toward a stream it noticed just ahead of them.

In the mist that was his mind, Jake did not noticed the group of Apaches who crested the rise just to his right and moved toward him.

As his horse drank, he blinked to try to clear away the fuzzy feeling in his head and then looked down at his dead arm. The ropey blue lines running up from the bite wound frightened him almost as much as the numbness in the limb. He slapped at his discoloured arm with his good hand, but the movement only brought fresh pain from his left leg, and he suddenly realized the gunman's arrow was still stuck in his thigh.

He tried to close his fists around the hilt of the arrow but found his left hand refused to obey him in any meaningful way, spasming in irregular, tetanic contractions when he tried to clench his hand. Cursing, he wrapped his right hand around the arrow's staff and heaved. Agony flared in his leg and a stream of loud curses tore out of him as he ripped the arrow from his thigh. There was an upwelling of dark, brackish blood, and his horse caught the scent—not just of the blood but also of the corruption growing within it—and it whinnied, lifting and tossing its head as if uncertain of the nature of the creature that now sat astride it.

The Apaches glanced wordlessly at each other when the man began cursing at the top of his lungs. They were all somewhat surprised to encounter a white man who seemed so witless and paid so little attention to his surroundings way out here in what any sane man should have considered hostile territory. He was obviously wounded, but only a fool would give vent to his pain by yelling and screaming, sounds sure to attract predators of all kinds.

The leader of the Apaches, Turak, unslung his bow, and his companions followed suit. Drawing an arrow from the quiver on his back, he prodded his horse slightly to the left and drew a bead on his target. He was surprised when he saw that the white man was holding an Apache arrow in his hands that he appeared to have just now pulled out of a wound on his leg, but this did not halt him from pulling his bowstring taut.

Jake continued to swear as he tossed the arrow aside and clutched at his torn leg, trying to staunch the flow of blood flooding from the ripped flesh.

At that moment Turak let his arrow fly, and it hurtled through the air to land—from Jake's point of view as if by magic—just a few inches lower down on his leg from the first wound.

Brennan had stabbed him with the arrow, but this was no mere stab wound. Turak's arrow sliced through the thick muscle of Jake's quadriceps and erupted out the other side, pinning the man's leg to his saddle fender. For a few seconds, Jake's mind simply refused to accept this supernatural reappearance of an arrow he'd just torn out of his leg, and then the pain lanced up into his brain and he screamed anew.

The Apaches had set their horses to a canter, and when Jake heard their war whoops, he tore his gaze from his new wound to look up at the approaching Apaches with dull, open-mouthed surprise. Hands shaking, he nevertheless grabbed for his rifle and had it halfway out of its scabbard before the next arrow sliced deep into the left side of his chest. The impact knocked him off his horse, and his crash to the ground drove the air out of his lungs. Eyes clouding, he watched as one of the Apaches snagged and secured the reins of his panicked horse while the others gathered around him.

The Apaches watched as the man on the ground shook with deep, racking coughs that grew more raggedly wet with each heave of his chest. He began spitting up foamy blood within a few breaths as the arteries torn open by the arrow's passage spewed blood into his lungs. He struggled to sit up for a moment before collapsing back onto the ground, eyes flitting back and forth among the hard faces of the men staring down at him.

Turak saw the man's gaze alight finally on the setting sun and wondered if he realized he was looking at his last sunset. The Apache knew only a few words of English, and in his experience few whites understood his language, but he gave voice to a question anyhow.

"I shot arrows at another white man not a day ago." Every Apache made his own weapons, and Turak had recognized his own handiwork easily in the arrow Jake had thrown aside. "One has found its way into your leg. How has this happened?"

Jake looked up at the men above him, choking as frothy blood filled his throat. A heavy glaze was darkening his vision, draining the sunlight from his eyes, but he managed to spit at the warrior closest to him and gurgle out a faint *fuck you*—one of the few phrases in English that Turak *did* clearly understand. Turak put his next arrow into Jake's heart, and the sunlight in his eyes faded away forever.

***

Solenne did not smell the campfire until she was nearly upon it. The man who had built the fire had taken some care to try to hide his

45

presence from passersby, taking shelter in what looked to be a dead-end canyon carved into one of the tall mesas scattered across the plain over which Solenne trailed her quarry.

Even with the quarter moon casting thin blue light, the trail she followed was barely visible now. When it had become too dark to ride, she'd waited for the moon and then dismounted and picked her way on foot, the horse trailing behind her. Slow going, but better than a lame horse.

Even in the twilight, though, she could see that one set of hoofprints carried on past the mesa while the other led up into the canyon. Both sets of tracks were about the same age, maybe a few hours old. This separation might have any number of possible explanations. A sick and dying man, desperate with the curse burning him up inside, might have decided to take shelter in the canyon until morning while his companion travelled on. Or any wary traveller might simply have decided that this was a safe and easily defensible place to overnight.

Early in her childhood, the tribe's Witch-woman had recognized in Solenne a nascent and rare ability to see elsewhere or elsewhen. Her people called such talents *spiritsense,* and the Witch-woman had nurtured this budding potential in Solenne like a carefully tended flower. Solenne closed her eyes now and reached out with the spiritsense. She could feel no animate dead thing close by, but that did not necessarily mean the curse was not growing its dark tendrils in whoever was up in that canyon; it simply meant that it had not yet bloomed.

Investigating the campfire was an imperative either way. She might hope the man—she was pretty sure it was just one—camped up in the canyon could at least tell her something about her other quarry, the man who had carried on into the night. And of course if the person up in the canyon did have the curse burning in him, she would have to extinguish it.

Solenne turned to her horse and took its head in her hands, bringing their foreheads together and feeling its breath on her neck. She pulled back slightly, smiling as she blew softly into its nostrils, whispering words the Witch-woman had taught her. After a moment, her voice drew a contented half snort from the Appaloosa, and she stepped away. The horse would not move until she came back unless driven by danger or an extremity of thirst.

Noiseless as a snake gliding cross the sand, Solenne approached the edge of the canyon entrance. She could see just enough of the rough plateau walls to map a way up. Pulling off her boots, she tied them to the back of her gun belt. Looking up at the stars, she wiggled her toes and flexed her feet, digging them into the gritty sand and letting them get a taste for purposeful movement again.

She began to climb.

\*\*\*

Turak and his fellow Apaches had made camp not more than a half mile from where they'd slaughtered the white man. His horse was now their horse, and his accoutrements, guns, and meagre food had been distributed among the group. Once stripped of anything useful, they had left his body twisted where it had fallen for desert scavengers to take.

The coin-filled saddlebags had been a pleasant surprise. The coins were dirty, but Turak could see they were made of gold. He had spent some time looking at the designs on them. One side showed a shield and crown, and the other the likeness of some man—some important man, he supposed. He believed the writing on the coins might be the same the Mexicans used. Grunting as he hefted the saddlebags, he glanced at the white man's scalp, drying on a stick by the fire. It had been foolish to come through this territory alone with such treasure.

Turak watched Burin lift the rabbit he was cooking away from the fire and begin to share it around. After they ate, they would tell stories and discuss the huge war the whites were making upon each other in the east until they grew tired enough to sleep.

Around them nocturnal desert creatures emerged and began their life under the moon. A thin and mangy desert fox scampered across the sand, pausing every few seconds to sniff the air. His acute sense of smell led him unerringly to the corpse. He feared the nearby fire, but the dead thing was a comfortable distance from it, and so the fox crept closer to the meaty smell until another scent intruded—something foreign and dangerous. The smell came from the dead thing . . .

And now the dead thing moved.

The fox watched the corpse vibrate and shudder for a moment, and when it did, the full power of the thing's stench reached its nostrils—like water poisoned by corruption and decay—and fear trickled into the fox's brain along with this new odour. Then the body lurched into a sitting position, and the fox skittered away.

The dead, empty hulk that had been Jake began to rise, intestinal gas exiting both mouth and anus in a groaning belch. Though most of its brain was now a mush of necrotic cells, a very particular hunger ruled what was left. More gas burped out through the arrow holes in its chest as it rolled to its feet. It became aware of the intoxicating smell of flesh nearby and began to lurch toward the camp and the only food it would ever crave again.

\*\*\*

Brennan had stumbled upon the canyon by accident as it was getting dark. It was a rare find in the desert—a relatively hidden and secure place to spend the night. There was even a small stream running down the middle of the canyon.

Brennan's horse had been exhausted even before the gunfight. Partly because of that, his horse was the only one he'd been able to catch afterward, and he had known if he drove it through the night without water, rest, or food, it was as likely to end up dead as not, and in the desert, a man without a horse was as good as dead himself.

A less circumspect person would perhaps have carried on despite entering Apache territory, despite the darkness, despite an uncertain horse under him. Brennan had known such overly "courageous" men mostly through cautionary tales. A man who called himself the Chicago Kid going up against three gunfighters at once and, to no one's surprise but his own, dying in a hail of bullets. A man selling bad moonshine to some Comanche, then scoffing at warnings to cut and run afterward; his scalp had eventually left town, though, as Brennan recalled, most of his body had remained. Then there was the Gregory gang, riding out of town after a bank robbery and deciding to shoot their way through the platoon of Union soldiers they encountered riding in; the only ones among the gang not dying that day were the wounded who were hanged a day later.

Anxious as he was to reacquire his gold, Brennan was also keen to live long enough to spend it. As he gathered scattered bits of mesquite for his evening fire, he reassured himself that Jake had looked sick as hell even before Brennan had sunk an arrow into his leg. The man would not be able to go long without resting, and once dismounted, it was doubtful he'd be able to get back on his horse. Brennan would set off just before dawn and pick up the trail, and he expected he would find the ailing thief still huddled in his bedroll—if Apaches had not found him first.

The Apaches would be a wrinkle if they found him first, of course, and Brennan swore at that thought, but nothing could be done about any of his worries until morning. He crouched closer to the fire and sniffed at the supper he was grilling—a rattlesnake he'd caught in the midst of crawling underneath its rock for the night. The snake looked about done and he plucked the skewer off the fire, cursing softly at the heat as he pulled out his knife. Slicing off a piece of meat, he held it up in the air over his mouth and blew on it before digging in. The meat was dry and had a metallic tang, but hungry as he was, he barely tasted it as he gulped it down. On his second swallow, he heard a soft crunch behind him that could have been his horse moving around. He almost didn't look, but—a cautious man—he turned and saw a woman appear as if from nowhere out of the dark dead end of the canyon.

She was tall with long black hair and was dressed like a man—no, more than that—like a gunslinger. He noticed this last thing in particular because the woman had a pistol in her hand, and it was pointed at him.

Brennan watched her for a moment, watching him, and then bit off another piece of the skewered rattlesnake and chewed at it. He noted scars on her neck and a nose that looked like it might have been broken once or twice—and the startling beauty that shone through just the same.

"You can start by putting the knife down."

Brennan was so distracted he almost forgot he was in trouble. Surprised by the woman, and doubly surprised by the deep, resonant tone of command in her voice, he laid his knife in the sand beside him and threw a slightly malign glance at his horse, standing serenely behind him. He'd previously been able to depend upon the animal whinnying if anyone unfamiliar approached it. The horse stared guilelessly back at him, and his gaze flitted to the woman again, and then inevitably to her gun.

In many of the gunfights Brennan had witnessed or—more rarely—participated in, he had noticed that people seldom fired a shot when they were in the midst of speaking. It was as if they could not do both at once. Without his own weapon near at hand, Brennan's instinct was to get the woman talking.

"Howdy. Remington, right?"

Her eyes narrowed.

"Your gun. A thirty-six?"

The woman ran her eyes up and down him and sniffed the air.

Brennan tilted his head. "No . . . a forty-four, I think. I've heard they're better'n the Colts."

"Are you bit?"

"What?" He looked puzzled. "Hit?"

"Bit. Bitten. Are you bit?"

Brennan was surprised again, this time by her question, and his face clearly showed it. *Drop your guns, Get your hands up,* and *This is a stickup* were all familiar forms of greeting by someone with a gun on you when your own was in your holster—or in his immediate case, lying by his bedroll a few yards away. He couldn't help thinking he'd heard her wrong.

"What?" he finally said, unable to keep the bafflement out of his voice.

The woman stepped forward—not *too* close, he noticed—and pulled the hammer back on her pistol. Clearly and articulately, loud but not quite shouting, she said, "Are. You. *Bitten?*"

Brennan considered this for a few moments.

"You one of those newspaper fellas?"

He watched the woman frown.

"Did you—"

And that was the moment. He threw the remains of the rattlesnake at her and dived for his guns.

\*\*\*

When the yelling intruded, Turak had been dreaming a tangle of pleasant things—his son grinning as he caught a trout, watching the sun rise on a cool spring morning, he and his wife naked under bearskins in their tent with a warm fire beside them. Things that, though he did not know it, he would never see again—at least not with eyes that understood their meaning anymore.

Another yell and he was torn from his wife's arms and awake suddenly in the desert cold by the dying fire, and madness was in their camp, roaring and tearing and raging with hunger. At first he thought a cougar or bear had come hunting among them. Old or diseased animals were sometimes driven by desperate hunger to attack groups of humans, but amid the chaos around him, he could detect only the cries of men.

Blinking slumber away, he rolled out of his furs toward a wet gurgling sound and saw his friend Burin crash to the ground beside him, his eyes bulging in panic. His hands clutched at his throat, and blood— dark in the moonlight—bubbled out in foamy rivers between his fingers as he tried to speak. Burin rolled to his side, choking, as he sought without success to staunch the flow of blood from the wound, and Turak flashed back to the memory of a long-ago battle, of burying his war axe in an enemy's throat and hearing those same desperate, bubbling gasps.

But where was the enemy now? Burin had been on watch when they all bedded down, and the fire was dying now, so it had been at least an hour since Turak had fallen asleep. With difficulty, he tore his gaze from the wide, frightened eyes of his dying friend and looked for the source of this mayhem.

A few yards away two figures were struggling on the ground. The one on top had his head down by that of the man underneath him, almost as if they were lovers engaged in a kiss. That momentary illusion was destroyed when the attacker on top jerked his head up and back as if stung. There was a sound like gristle being ripped from bone, accompanied by a geyser of dark, glistening blood jetting from the neck of the man below. The attacker used his fingers to shove a ragged bit of the victim's bloody flesh into his mouth as the man beneath writhed in panicked struggle, a short, gurgling scream erupting from him before he lapsed into the same choking sounds Burin was making.

In the dim light, it took Turak several moments to realize the attacker looked just like the white man they had killed and scalped not more than a few hours before. Then with a shock, he realized it *was* the man they had killed. Bare white bone gleamed on the head where Turak himself had peeled back the thin layer of flesh covering the man's skull, scalping him.

It was impossible. Unthinkable. For several seconds Turak was frozen into immobility as stories of evil spirits, told by old men around the campfire to frighten youngsters, flashed through his mind. Was this truly the *nunasish*, the demon that fed on men, come to life? Turak had seen many men die in his life, enough to be able to tell with some assurance when life had left a body. The white man had been dead, as sure as he was up and moving now.

This was only possible if he *had* become a *nunasish*.

The remaining men had been belatedly roused from their sleep by the liquid screams of their fellows, and they rushed forward to help as the *nunasish* plunged its teeth again into the neck of the unfortunate man on the ground. It was Tyee, Turak realized.

Turak cursed himself for his hesitation and moved toward the creature. Demon or not, he would fight the thing. He groped on the ground for his war axe as the first of his comrades, Taza, reached the fray and kicked the *nunasish* away from Tyee. When Turak reached his side, Tyee was looking up into the sky with frightened white eyes, making watery gasps and shivering like a man freshly pulled from a freezing river. Flesh was torn from his face and neck in long, ragged strips, and his hands trembled as they tried to stem the tide of blood that flowed from the wounds.

Taza's kick had thrown the *nunasish* off onto its side. It landed near Turak, and the warrior found himself staring at the gaping arrow wounds he and his comrades had left in the man's chest just a few hours ago. Bright yellow pus mixed with strands of dark fluid was leaking from the wounds now.

Turak had only a moment to stare. Growling and snapping at the men around it, the *nunasish* rolled onto its hands and knees and scrambled back on top of Tyee again. Taza kicked at the thing once more, and this time it grabbed at Taza's leg, snaring his ankle and pulling him off balance. Taza fell as the *nunasish* sank its teeth into his lower leg, shaking its head and tearing at the flesh like a starving dog.

Taza began yelling and beating at the thing with his hands, and that was when Baishan and Turak buried their axes almost simultaneously in the thing's chest and side. The *nunasish* reared back, ripping a piece of bloody flesh out of Taza's leg as it whirled its arms, clawing at Turak.

The fight had move closer to their guttering fire now, and Turak got his first good look at the demon that was trying to kill them all. It had the face and form of the white man they had killed, but it did not look the way Turak had imagined a demon might, with glowing eyes and sharp white fangs. This thing simply looked dead, its face dark grey and its eyes clouded over with a yellow film that resembled boiled animal fat. Its upper lip was ripped half-off, and the irregular brown teeth exposed by the injury were swimming in the blood of those it had attacked.

Turak had killed many times before—whites and men from other tribes, defending his people or on raids against enemies. From experience he knew even the strongest of men could not withstand the trauma of one—let alone two—war axes buried in their torso without collapsing, but this demon-thing merely ignored the wounds, instead hissing and scratching at them like some kind of wild cat, unhurt but simply frustrated at not being able to reach its prey.

"Again! Hit it again!" Turak yelled and pulled back on his axe only to find it was embedded so deeply between the thing's ribs that he could not draw it out again easily. Placing one foot on the struggling demon's torso for leverage, he heaved with all his might, straining so that when the axe came free, he flew backward and sprawled out on the ground.

Baishan now had his axe free too and hacked at the creature as it launched itself toward him. It spat black gore in growls of fury as Baishan, screaming a warrior challenge, danced out of its reach and swung the axe at it again and again, his weapon repeatedly finding its mark on the creature's body—the practised blows of the strongest warrior Turak had ever seen. It was obvious that Baishan's assault was breaking bones and carrying away chunks of flesh from the thing's arms and face, and yet while the *nunasish* faltered and stumbled, it never fell, and it never ceased its desperate attempts to sink its teeth into its assailant.

Turak jumped back to his feet, bringing his own axe up to come at the creature from behind as Baishan continued his assault from the front. What remained of the thing's right hand, half-severed by previous blows, was carried away by Baishan's next swing, and a wild yell erupted from the warrior's fiercely grinning mouth as he watched the appendage fly off into the night.

Berserker warrior alive in him, Baishan screamed in challenge again—straight into the thing's face—taunting it as he readied another swing. But he was too close now, and the demon-thing flung itself at him far more quickly than he had expected, diving into Baishan and driving him to the ground, its torn right wrist pinning him as its left hand raked across his face and neck and opened half-inch deep lacerations. The monster bent toward his throat, moaning with a hideous, desperate longing as Baishan sought to push it away.

The demon's teeth were nearing Baishan's neck when Turak planted his axe several inches deep into the back of its head. The creature made a single short choking sound and fell—limp and lifeless once again—atop Baishan, its mouth still gaping open and leaking oily blood onto the face of its intended prey.

Exhausted by the battle, half-blinded and in monstrous pain from the wounds in his face, Baishan tried to lever the corpse off his chest but could not find the strength. Turak joined him, grabbing at the demon's tattered clothing and pulling it away from his friend as he yanked his axe out of its head. Baishan crawled away from the dead creature, moaning.

Turak straddled the *nunasish* and, drawing his axe above his head and taking a moment to aim, buried it exactly between the thing's eyes and split the skull fully in half in an explosion of sludgy black brain tissue.

Again he raised the axe and brought it down, slamming it into what remained of the thing's face. Around him, he could hear the cries and gurgles of his injured and dying friends. The thing was obviously dead. But Turak had thought it dead before.

The axe came up again.

\*\*\*

The woman with the gun had flinched when the remains of Brennan's dinner came flying through the air toward her—just for a second, a bare moment—but that was enough. Brennan dived for his guns.

Out of the corner of his eye, as her bullet whistled like a banshee past his face, Brennan saw the woman's right foot lash out like a bullwhip. It caught him in the upper chest, and he felt the crack of something that might have been a rib.

She shot again, but he was still moving, rolling past his gun belts and grabbing at a pistol as her third bullet exploded in the sand beside him.

Brennan's gun was in his hand now, swivelling to come to bear on the woman, but she had danced in toward him and her left foot whipped out, striking his gun hand and flinging his pistol away. He kicked out and swept his legs under hers and her gun slipped from her grip as she crashed to the ground, half on top of him. Afterward, he would remember her scent in his nose, a lovely cinnamon smell.

She was like a snake now, writhing all over him, punching and kicking as he whipped onto his belly beneath her, straining to reach his weapon. The woman landed two more jabs on his sore rib, and he winced at the sharp, grinding pain in his chest. Ignoring the wound, he strained forward and felt his fingers slide over the hilt of his pistol, but she was on top of him, trying to pin his arm down. Brennan shot his free arm back into her face and was rewarded with a crunch as his elbow impacted her nose, drawing a satisfying curse from the woman. He swept her hands down with the same arm and pinned them against his torso as his other hand took hold of the pistol.

"Ha!" he said. "Now—"

Coiling against him, her arms trapped but her face suddenly against his gun hand, she did not hesitate. She bit hard, twisting her head until she tasted blood.

Brennan swore at the sudden agony in his wrist, and the pistol slipped again from his grip.

"Holy hellfire, you—"

And that was as far as he got. The woman's hand had found a fist-sized rock. Her fingers closed around it and she jerked it up and into the side of Brennan's head.

The explosion of pain rattled through his head, and he curled up on himself and rolled away as she hefted herself off him. In the seconds that followed, Brennan tried to force himself to move, but the pain in his skull was too great to argue with. Around him, he heard scuffling and muffled curses as—he supposed—the woman recovered both his guns and her own, but the mist in his head rendered him immobile in the moments when trying to renew the fight might still have made a difference in the outcome.

After a few minutes, the throbbing grudgingly began to subside, like an inebriate partygoer loath to leave the celebration. Hands clutched to his head, Brennan rolled onto his back in slow increments, as if worried an impetuous movement would spill his brains from his pounding skull. He was acutely aware that the woman had not finished him off. He was alive for the moment, and if she had not killed him in the first few seconds, there was no use in hurrying to his feet now.

He felt swelling already in his temple, along with a warm wetness that could only be blood running like a stream through his hair. Beyond this were foggy nausea and the awareness of his head and ribs warring with each other at every breath over which hurt the most. As the fog receded and he realized he would neither vomit nor pass out, he levered himself up into a sitting position against the canyon wall with, he felt, all the grace and speed of an elderly decrepit. He heard the click of a hammer being drawn back on a pistol, and he forced himself to crack open his eyes.

The woman was standing several yards away—far enough back that he would have had no chance of taking her down again even if he had found the strength to try. Dim gratification came from the sight of blood streaming from her nose and the grimace that crossed her face as she touched it.

In the firelight, her eyes looked red as a devil's. She appraised him for a moment with the same expression Brennan had seen on the face of miners trying to decide if the dusty rock they held was worth anything. Then—gun unwavering—she shrugged and righted clothing that had become disarrayed in the fight. A snort followed, and she spat gore at his feet, crooking her head to the side as if preparing herself to address a stubborn child.

"I *said* . . . " She turned the gun a fraction away from his face and squeezed the trigger, and a piece of the canyon wall just beside him exploded in a spray of dust. "*Are. You. Bit?*"

Brennan blinked twice, again trying to make sense of the question, and finally looked down at his bloody right wrist. His head was beginning to clear and, as it did, other injuries asserted themselves, clamouring for attention—his ribs, every time he took a breath, and his wrist, bloody and torn from where she'd sunk her teeth into him.

"Well, I am *now!*"

## Chapter Six

Turak did not halt the rhythmic smashing of his axe into the dead thing on the ground until the *nunasish* was utterly destroyed—its brain reduced to a bloody pulp scattered in and around the bowl of its shattered skull and its torso a ruined mass of shredded organs and fractured bone, all oozing the same stinking, brackish liquid that se emed to serve as the thing's blood. He would have kept going still, but he could not raise his weapon anymore; the muscles in his arms were on fire and would no longer obey his commands. His upper body and limbs splattered and stained with the creature's gore, he fell to his knees, blinking away the black blood as it began to dry and threatened to gum up his eyes.

The sound of ragged, wet, dying breaths surrounded Turak as he climbed to his feet again, shaking his head to be sure he was not in some horridly lucid dream. He thought again of the stories of evil forest creatures, faithfully passed down from elders to children among his people. As children grew into adults, they came to understand these as mere cautionary tales. Long gone were the childhood days when he had ever expected he might encounter such a creature.

Turak kicked at the fire and threw more wood on it, stirring it back to life so he had enough light to properly assess the situation. He saw immediately that he was the only one of his group not injured in some way. Burin and Tyee had been dead by the time the battle ended, drowned in their own blood. Taza and Baishan were still moving. Of the two, Taza appeared most grievously injured. A fist-sized chunk of flesh was gone from his lower left leg, and Turak could see that the injury would cripple him for life.

"Baishan, wrap yourself in a blanket and sit by the fire. I must see to Taza first."

Taza looked up at him as Turak pushed him onto his back. "What was that thing? It looked—"

"Quiet. Let me look at your leg."

Though the wound seemed to have bled little, there were strange dark lines shooting out from around it like roots from a tree. Turak had seen such decay before in a wound turned gangrenous, but this change had happened impossibly fast. In any case, the bite clearly caused the man much more pain than it should have. Turak knew Taza as a stoic. He'd seen the man shot through the leg in a battle with some whites and still kill three of his adversaries without flinching once from the pain his wound must have caused. Now he writhed and groaned as Turak bound his wound, trembling as if in a fever. His face was grey and slick with sweat, and there was a cloudy, unfocused look in his eyes. Turak bundled him in a robe and turned to his other friend.

Baishan was not as badly hurt. The creature had scratched at his arms and face and inflicted a superficial bite or two. But though his wounds were minor, Baishan sat on the ground as if exhausted, sharing the same blank stare—and apparently the same fever—as Taza, trembling uncontrollably despite his proximity to the newly stoked fire.

After tending to his friends, Turak checked the horses. The animals were nervous but otherwise fine. When he came to the fire just a few minutes later, Baishan and Taza looked truly ill. Turak dug some jerky out from among his belongings and offered it to them both.

Taza refused. "No, I cannot eat. I feel sick . . . My belly feels cold but the rest of me is burning, and I cannot stop my hands from shaking."

Baishan took some of the jerky and ate a tiny portion. Turak watched him for a moment as he chewed and fought to swallow it.

"I will keep watch the rest of the night," Turak said. "Try to rest."

"That man," Taza said, "the one who attacked us . . . was dead."

Baishan nodded. "The white man from yesterday. Perhaps we did not leave him dead and—"

"*He was dead,*" Taza said through chattering teeth. "Do not talk foolishness. We all saw he was dead."

Turak nodded. "Some kind of evil spirit. We pursued the other white man far from our usual places. Perhaps this place is cursed. We will leave in the morning."

Taza nodded toward the saddlebags they had taken from the dead white man. "The gold. Perhaps *it* is cursed."

Turak thought about this and nodded slowly. "Perhaps."

A number of the legends Turak's tribe shared with many of the plains peoples revolved around icons of power that drew evil toward them. Greed was often an integral part of stories of cursed items, and everyone knew that the white man's appetite for gold was insatiable. Was the gold meant to bring this curse of greed to Turak's tribe? He would have dismissed such thoughts as nonsense mere hours ago, but that was before he had seen a demon rise in a dead man's body.

Baishan nodded in agreement. "Yes, maybe we took the possessions of a cursed man and the curse came over us."

"You should rest now." Turak gestured at the remains of Jake's twisted and butchered body. "In the morning we will go and leave this man's things behind with him. The gold too."

Baishan and Taza lay down beside the fire Turak had continued to stoke while they talked. The fire was hot enough now that Turak was warm some distance away from it, but his companions still shuddered beside it as though naked in the midst of a winter's storm. Still, they fell into sleep within seconds, as if utterly exhausted.

Troubled, Turak peered into the night, his gaze moving over the rough landscape around them. He must miss nothing that could harm them further this night, but he found himself distracted by the scent of the creature's blood that had dried on his body. It had a foul stink of decay, like the blood of no other creature he had ever come across. The group had filled their water gourds at a stream a mile or so behind them, but there was never enough water in the desert, and certainly not enough for him to waste on washing himself clean. He tried instead to rub the blood off his arms.

It was slick and tarry, and he could not seem to get it off.

\*\*\*

"All right, then." The woman considered Brennan, who was still lying propped against the canyon wall. Her gun was at her side but no longer pointed directly at him. "What's your story?"

"My story? *My* story? My story is, I'm kinda cold, kinda pissed"—he lifted his bandaged arm and touched his head where she had smashed it with the rock—"and definitely fucking hurt."

She kicked at the fire, stirring it to life again, then glanced around at the canyon walls as if worried about what the brighter light might reveal.

Brennan sighed. "Look, I appreciate you're insane and all. Lone woman out here in the desert. Attacking armed men. Worrying 'bout if I'm bit and then biting me yourself, by the way—"

"What's your name, mister?"

"Brennan."

She nodded. "Well, Mister Brennan, let's just skip all the 'lone woman out here in the desert' shit."

Brennan nodded back and then regretted it, clasping his freshly pounding head in his hands for a moment. "All right, then."

"Good."

"And you are?"

"What?"

"You have a name? So I don't have to call you 'lone woman' and piss you off some more?"

Brennan saw the woman's lips flicker briefly in what might have been a smile.

"Solenne."

"Solenne. You can guess I'm pleased to meet you, I'm sure."

"I can guess, yes."

"Right. Well, then, maybe you can just tell me what you want? I don't have much. I ain't no desperado, or murderer"—Brennan mentally crossed his fingers—"or thief. Fact is, I was robbed myself just earlier today—"

"Is that when you killed those two men a few miles west of here?"

Brennan pursed his lips in obvious reluctance to speak and saw a flicker of impatience in Solenne's face as her gun hand rose slightly and waved in his direction as if she were shooing a fly away.

"Yeah, I expect so. Deadly as this country is, there ain't likely more than a couple of dead men a person'd come across on an average day. I hope they weren't friends of yours . . ." He watched her closely for any indication she was lying as she shook her head. "But the fact is they stole from me."

"Looks like one got away." Solenne flipped a gold coin at Brennan and he caught it easily in mid-air, even in the dim firelight. "This what they took from you?"

Brennan needed only a second to see the coin was one of his. He nodded. "Yeah. Look, now, I ain't no thief. I came by it rightly."

"Those coins're old. Where'd you get them?"

"Found 'em."

"Where?"

"Rather not say."

A flicker of a smile again. After a moment, she shook her head. "Doesn't matter. Fact is, I don't care where you got it. Don't care if you are a thief. Don't care if you steal food out of your grandma's mouth or kill preachers on Sundays. I'm only interested in the man who stole it from you—just one man, right?"

"That's correct . . . You're interested in the man?"

"Yes."

"Not the gold?"

"That's right."

"How come?"

"It's a long story."

Brennan looked unconvinced but nodded. "All right. I'm gonna pick up his trail as soon as it's light. That is to say"—he looked sourly at her—"if I survive the night, my plan is to catch up with him in the morning."

"Going to ask him for your gold back?"

"We'll see what happens. *Ask* might be understating it a bit."

"This man, was he hurt at all? Bitten? Even a small injury maybe . . . ?"

Brennan squinted at her. "Why on earth are you so interested in who is or isn't bit?"

"We'll get to that . . . maybe. I'm the one with the gun, remember? Answer my question—truthfully, if you please—and yes, I promise I'll know if you don't." In the silence that followed, she added, "No reason to lie. Told you I'm not interested in your gold."

"Just the bites?"

"I should remind you again, it's traditional for the unarmed person to answer questions so as not to make the person *holding* the gun angry."

"That's a point. Okay. All right. His hand was injured—no

question about that. He had some cloth wrapped around it and there was a smell about him . . . You ever smell gangrene?"

A flat, humourless smile. "I have."

"Yeah, well, smelled like that, a little. Fella looked pretty sick, actually. Didn't seem nearly as keen to rob me as his buddies were."

Solenne shuddered and winced abruptly. She closed her eyes, and her free hand moved to her chest. Brennan thought about going for her gun, but she recovered quickly, swearing softly. "*Chingame*. He's turned."

"What was that?"

"Never mind."

Brennan watched Solenne look to the east and thought she might be estimating how many hours until dawn.

"Come on—tell me. Why you so worried about bites and such?"

Solenne looked darkly at him and spun the cylinder of her gun. "Do you see any empty chambers in this thing? I'm sure I loaded them all."

"I realize I'm at a disadvantage here, but I am naturally curious." He raised his brows.

She thought for a moment. "I doubt you would believe me."

Brennan shivered. "If I say I will, can get a little closer to the fire? It's colder than a witch's tit out tonight."

This remark caused a burst of laughter from Solenne. Then she was looking to the east again, as if she could somehow will sunrise to come. Finally she holstered her gun. "All right. Let's talk."

\*\*\*

Just before dusk, the troop had come across a small stream. Hot on the heels of his prey, Johnston had been loath to stop—his men could have gone without for all he cared—but the horses were the life of his troop, and they desperately needed water after riding in the day's heat, and so he had ordered a halt for the night.

Five supply wagons and one prison wagon followed the troop, catching up with the men on horseback each night, and as they did every evening, Johnston's men had broken out supplies for supper, made cook fires, watered and fed their horses, and, most importantly, provided for the comfort of their colonel. The troopers would sleep on bedrolls of rough blankets, if they had them, but Johnston and his senior officers had tents and at least some of the comforts of home. For Johnston that meant a desk and chair. They were crude and rickety things, but they meant he could write in his journal each night in front of a fire. Sounds familiar to him from hundreds of nights in camp surrounded him, and he knew that all was as it should be. The men were restless—scared perhaps, still talking about Carter—but in Johnston's mind, that was as it should be too.

At his desk by the fire one of the privates had built, Johnston lifted his cup, sipped, and let the raw southern whiskey settle into his gut. He was now into the last of five bottles of the stuff he'd set out with. If he was lucky, this one might last until he saw civilization again. The whiskey warmed him at least as much as the fire, and he gazed into the flames and let the alcohol swim through his brain, dragging his thoughts back, as always, to the shrine in the jungle . . .

When Johnston's group had breeched the sealed inner door, Johnston himself was at the far rear, his hand on his gun. He intended to kill his comrades as soon as he was sure there was treasure to be had and take it for himself.

His plan of betrayal saved his life. The miasma of rotting flesh that wafted out of the darkness brought the men nearest the door to their knees. Behind it came the cries of hungry longing, and then the decaying yellow-eyed monsters themselves stumbled out into the sunshine, tottering like marionettes on strings. When the skeletal hands closed on the first of the men and began to rip and tear, Johnston had already backed far out of reach. He watched in horror as the things began to eat, tearing flesh from bones and ripping into the entrails of their still-living, still-struggling victims. One of the ravening monsters turned to him finally, moaning and reaching out for him, and Johnston emptied his pistol into the creature, each shot punching into the monster's torso with explosions of black flesh and bone that stalled its approach but could not stop it. Only by chance did Johnston's last bullet—fired with a trembling hand—enter the creature's mouth and blow the back of its head apart, leaving it a collapsed ruin of decay.

Johnston turned and ran, screams echoing in his ears for miles. When night fell, he reluctantly halted and built a fire, eventually falling into an exhausted, fitful sleep. He was awakened by something large thrashing through the bushes toward him. Then he heard moaning—the same moaning he had heard from the creatures in the temple. Ice ran down his spine and he shivered in the heat of the jungle night as he realized the creatures from the shrine had pursued him. But what burst through the undergrowth was one of his former companions—skin grey, eyes yellow, and abdomen gaping empty and open. He had been fed on by the things in the temple. And had changed. Dead . . . and yet living again.

Johnston had fled once more, smashing blindly through the jungle and eventually falling into a river. He had surrendered to the warm, cascading water, knowing it would probably kill him and yet preferring that death to being torn apart as a meal for a demon. But he had been washed ashore miles later as the first glint of daybreak shone through the trees. Somehow he had managed to follow the river to its tributary with the Amazon and to a tribe of heathens who had fed him and had led him back to civilization.

*Just one,* he found himself thinking again. One was all he needed to fulfill the destiny God had chosen for him. He knew he was very close to catching *her* and, therefore, close to one of the creatures she—for some godforsaken reason only she knew—chased and killed. But if she somehow killed them all before he caught her . . . well, then *she* would be the one to help him realize his plans. He *knew* it. Despite how disappointingly little Quinto had revealed about her, he could sense that she was tied to these creatures in some way. Only fools believed in witches or demons, but anyone who tracked these cannibal-things and killed them would know enough to help him realize his plans.

And of course, she *would* help him, whether she wanted to or not. Johnston smiled. He felt sure he could persuade her.

There was a low cough, and he realized Lewis had been standing beside him for some unknown period, quietly waiting for his colonel to notice his presence. Nothing urgent, then. Johnston grunted and swallowed the rye he'd been swirling around his mouth, savouring the gradual dissipation of the burn it left on the way down his gullet.

"Captain Lewis," he said finally.

Lewis saluted. "Sir. You asked to be called if . . . Private Carter is near death, I believe, sir."

"Very well." Johnston stood, feeling a bit dizzy. He had indulged in a trifle more whiskey than he supposed he ought to have. With an effort, he steadied himself. "Show me."

"Yes, sir." Lewis led Johnston among the tents and groups of men clustered around campfires, who were sipping what passed for coffee, if they had any left, and speaking in low tones. The talk ceased abruptly and the men averted their eyes as he passed, and he was pleased.

Away from the firelight and the view of most of the others, Carter had been chained to a tree on the camp's periphery. Barrett stood guard beside him, his rifle in his hands and pointed in what might have seemed a desultory fashion at the man on the ground, but Johnston suspected Barrett could have shot out both of Carter's eyes in less than five seconds had he felt the need to do so. Barrett watched the two men approach and lifted a hand in what Johnston would have characterized as an overly casual salute. Johnston would remember the infraction—he remembered everything—but for the moment more important things were afoot than chastising underlings.

Even in the moonlight, Johnston could see the magnitude of the savage change that had been wrought in Carter over the last few hours by whatever strange force now ran through the dying man's veins. A spiderweb of gangrenous darkness had woven its way from the dead man's bite on Carter's arm, spreading to invade most of the left side of his body. He stared up at the endless sky above him, his eyes glazed over with a mucky yellow film while his body shook with irregular, violent shivering.

"How long has he been like this?" Johnston asked.

"He was unconscious for the last couple of hours," Barrett said, checking the colonel's expression but never quite taking his eyes off Carter. "'Bout a half-hour ago, he woke up, a little. Eyes are going yellow"—Barrett paused and spat—"just like the others . . ."

Johnston nodded more in dismissal of the comment than in agreement. His eyes were searching the man on the ground for some difference in the progress of his deterioration compared with Johnston's previous experiments. Each of the earlier subjects had died a slow, torturous, and (in Johnston's eyes) unfortunately final death. It had come to seem that only an animate monster could pass on the curse.

But the corpses he'd used in his prior attempts had been dead far longer. This last one had been . . . fresh.

Perhaps this time the change would come.

He leaned in and examined Carter, who was riding waves of bone-shaking rigours that drew incoherent moans of agony from him. His panting, like that of a dog left too long in the midday sun, seemed to have accelerated even in the few moments Johnston had been watching, as if Carter's body could no longer draw in enough air to power the engine of self-destruction it had become. Johnston could almost swear he felt the fever heat coming off the man, who was paying no attention to any of those around him, focused entirely, it appeared, on his own inner suffering.

Johnston gave Carter a hard kick in the leg, drawing a fresh groan from the man, who slowly focused his gaze on this new source of torment.

"How you doing, son?"

Carter stared uncomprehendingly, his jaundiced eyes wandering back and forth with the desperation of a caged animal. "Wha—"

Johnston kicked Carter again, and this time the reaction was instantaneous.

Carter's eyes flared like struck flint and his convulsions vanished as he surged toward his former commander, cracked black lips drawing back over crooked yellow teeth. A low growl tore out of his black mouth as he was brought up short by the chains. His teeth snapped shut like a guillotine inches from Johnston's leg, neatly severing the tip of his own tongue. The piece of cyanotic flesh fell to the ground in a spray of inky blood.

"Jesus!" Barrett jumped back as he brought his rifle to bear on the demon suddenly among them. Lewis had drawn his pistol and aimed it toward the creature as well.

Startled, Johnston leapt back too, but he was shouting at the other two even as he did so. "Don't! Don't shoot him, by God."

Carter strained against his bonds to get at Johnston, spitting and snarling as the chain cut into his neck and shoulders. After a moment, he seemed to relax and began moaning in a low-pitched singsong. The sounds were different from those he had made before, and it took Johnston a moment to identify the distinction. This wasn't pain anymore.

The man—the *thing*—was *hungry*.

Excitement shot to life inside Johnston with the ferocity of the fever that had gripped the dying soldier. The others had not done this. They had died writhing in agony as their skin darkened, hemorrhaging black gore out of their every orifice, never really aware of anything or anyone around them once the infection took hold.

Johnston saw scowls of disgust on both Lewis's and Barrett's faces, but that was all right. Not all men could be visionaries. He could not help staring at the thing he had created as if it were a priceless work of art, quaking not with fear but with the possibility that he'd finally won. He stared into the yellow-eyed demon's face and saw the raw savagery he had been chasing all this time. Though they hungered for different things, the depth of his appetite easily matched that of the creature.

Barrett spat again, and the monster's eyes darted toward the noise. Moving like a wounded snake, Carter slithered back and forth, seeking a way out of his confinement so that he might reach the warm flesh so tantalizingly close to him. Groaning and snarling, black spittle spraying from his mouth, he began clawing and snapping at them.

Johnston chuckled—a cold sound that rattled like the tail of a viper in the thin desert air and drew a look of disbelief from Barrett. Unable to keep the self-satisfaction out of his voice, Johnston glanced first at one and then the other of his captains. "Well, gentlemen. Looks like we've finally got one."

Barrett stepped back from the soldier turned rabid beast and looked to Lewis and then Johnston.

Lewis looked bewildered and scared. Johnston appeared triumphant and almost gleeful.

"Do you know what this means?" Johnston waved his hands to indicate their surroundings. "No more chasing across this hellish desert." His smile widened. "Praise God, we can finally complete our mission and wipe the North from—"

The nightmarish demon—which had once been a poor boy, who'd grown up on a dying farm in south Arkansas and who had never ventured more than ten miles from it his whole life until he was pressed into service by Johnston's passing troop scarcely six months ago—heaved once more against his chains, roaring and raging at the meat so close to him . . .

And then it collapsed like a fallen tree, trembling briefly before lying immobile, unblinking yellow eyes on the starry sky above him.

Lewis, Barrett, and Johnston shared a shocked moment as they stared down at the suddenly quiescent thing on the ground.

After a few empty seconds, Barrett—rifle levelled directly at Carter's head—stepped forward and kicked the thing in the stomach, eliciting a burping gurgle of gas from the corpse's mouth but nothing more. Barrett looked unsatisfied and kicked at the thing again. It remained stubbornly mute and still.

Lewis knelt and leaned forward.

"Watch out, Lew." Barrett stepped sideways so his gun was still trained on Carter. "Don't get between us."

"Yeah, yeah." Lewis reached out slowly, eyes on Carter's still form every second, and held his hand over the man's mouth as he counted thirty slow beats to himself in silence before looking up at Johnston.

"Believe he's dead, sir."

Johnston—whose eyes had lost all evidence of their prior joviality—now began kicking at the corpse himself, his accompanying curses of frustration building in volume.

"Go on! Get up! Get up, you motherfucker!"

Barrett and Lewis stood back a pace as Johnston continued to assault the body, screaming and swearing all the while. The two captains darted worried looks from their commander back toward the camp before locking eyes. Each read the same in the other's expression—if the men heard their colonel shrieking like a man gone insane . . .

The troops were a generally loyal bunch, as much as any Southerner who'd rather be home by his own fire at night might be devoted to a cause that brought exhaustion and hunger as its chief immediate rewards. Most had a fierce hatred of the North and, loyal or not, the colonel's merciless leadership had bred more fear than respect among the ranks. Soldiers expected to see malcontents and thieves punished, but they were used to penalties such as short rationing, extra duty, or reduction in rank. They might expect a hanging for severe offences, such as murder or treason, but they were also used to any justice being meted out quickly— not the slow torture and agonizing death that it seemed had become Johnston's only form of punishment.

Weeks of hard riding, lack of food, and now seeing their fellows die in screaming anguish and misery had left them poised. Poised on the knife-edge of desertion, or worse. He had heard angry mutterings in the ranks after dark the last few nights, when the men felt they would not be heard by the officers or at least could not be identified. Barrett had heard the words *crazy* and *Johnston* together in the same sentence more than once.

This yelling, these insane screams . . . At best, Barrett and Lewis might hope the men took it for Carter's dying cries.

Johnston's rant abruptly played out. Taking control of himself, the colonel stood deliberately straight and upright and turned back toward his captains, pointing at the corpse.

"Leave this . . . thing . . . chained and appoint a guard. Someone you can trust not to kill it if it moves again. We can yet hope it may rise again, and if so, I don't want it loose, understand?" He said this without any real hope in his voice. It was obvious now that this curse or disease or whatever it was could only be passed to a human from one of the "living" demons.

Both men nodded as Johnston continued. "We'll break camp just as soon as the sky lightens, mind me?" More nods. "Make sure Quinto's up and ready to track." He looked to the east. "Guess we're gonna have to find that bitch after all."

\*\*\*

Dawn was a few scarce hours away by the time Solenne had finished telling Brennan—among other things—what the bandit he was chasing would have become by the time Brennan caught him.

Despite professing a deep, innate suspicion of supernatural tales, Solenne noticed Brennan had become absorbed as she spun stories of dead things risen hungry and eager to eat the living, her voice cold and her face curtained by flickering shadows from the firelight.

Solenne's horse had wandered up the canyon and come up behind Brennan halfway through her story. He abruptly jumped to his feet, startled and cursing, mind full of visions of monsters and his gun half out of his holster before he realized what benign thing had disturbed him. Unfazed by the man's antics, Solenne's horse had nuzzled Brennan's mount before dipping its nose in the stream for a long-awaited drink.

Brennan cursed a bit more for good measure and then settled back to the ground, eyes meeting Solenne's in embarrassment. She could see the gears turning in his mind. How much of her story he believed did not matter to her. All that mattered was that he'd told her the truth about there being a single wounded man. And she knew he had—she could sense it, just as she had sensed the thrum of the man ahead of them turning reaper as pain in her chest minutes earlier.

Might this be the last of them? Was there truly just *one* left? *One* more she had to kill? The curse always seemed to find a way to survive . . .

After this, she would spend weeks drifting back and forth through Mexican border towns and indigenous villages, as she had many times before, searching for stories of madmen or signs the curse had found others and then looking to pick up the trail if it had. One day, she supposed, she would have to find her way back to where the curse had originated. If she could find the source and destroy it . . .

But she couldn't do that until the last of the reapers was dead.

Her mind's eye held no clear image of a life beyond hunting the dead. Like a slave bound by chains, she dared not dream of a time beyond the captivity of the chase that was her own curse. She closed her eyes for a moment and let the night breeze wash over her face while Brennan built up the fire, complaining all the while about his throbbing head and bitten wrist.

"Might as well share the heat," he finally said after he'd quit complaining. "If you're on the other side of it, leastways you're not gonna be sneaking up on me again."

Her intuition had been legendary among her people even before she reached adolescence. In the wild country of even wilder people she had found since leaving her home, she had found her instinctual sense about people confirmed again and again. Often, a kind word and a sunny smile hid darker intentions, but this one—

"Watch out for the rattler under that rock."

She'd been looking for a place to sit, near the fire.

"Saw him crawling under there just as I rode in. Caught his brother for my supper." He had retrieved the half-eaten dinner he'd thrown at her earlier and made an unenthusiastic attempt to dust it off before tossing it aside with a grimace and a sharp glance her way. "Likely won't bother us, but I expect you wouldn't wanna sit on top of where he's sleeping."

This one, Solenne thought, was the survivor type. As best he could, he would studiously avoid both sides in this war the whites had going on. He wouldn't look for trouble, didn't seem violent or—like many of the wandering bandits out here—a sadist who viewed viciousness as a dearly relished form of entertainment. Obviously, he had no trouble killing when threatened, though. She could see that he would be a danger to her only if she put herself between him and his gold, and she had no intention of doing that.

Brennan poked at the fire, stirring it up. "So, the guy I'm chasing . . . He's gonna die and then turn into some kinda monster . . . and kill anything he sees?"

"Only humans. They're not interested in animals. Don't know why."

"And you've been tracking this thing—"

"Not always just one, of course. The sickness spreads easily. There have been times when there were many of these things. But this is the last one I know of." She paused. "Not many people out here"—she waved at the surrounding desert—"so with any luck, I can catch him before he infects anyone else."

Brennan scowled. "I suppose it seems sensible to ride out at first light and run this guy down together."

Solenne considered. "Yes. Sensible. I'll assure you again, I don't want any of your gold."

"That's good, 'cause that's *all* I want. Not sure I credit all you're saying about this curse or rabies or whatever—no offence meant."

"None taken."

Brennan rubbed at the bite on his wrist, bandaged haphazardly with a piece of his shirt.

"Sorry about the arm."

He shook his head and winced, holding a hand up to his temple. "Not to worry," he said finally. "Head hurts worse."

Solenne touched her own nose. It was slightly swollen but the throbbing had settled down, and she knew she would heal quickly. Bruises, wounds, and even broken bones had been no more than passing troubles for Solenne from the time she was a child. Early on, she had assumed it had something to do with being raised as a witch, but as a teen she had realized that even the Witch-woman seemed in awe of her ability to recover from injury.

Still, for now her nose hurt. She had washed the blood from her face in the stream as Brennan cleansed his own wound, but neither one of them looked particularly attractive.

"Gotta say, you're a pretty good fighter for a woman."

Solenne noted that in Brennan's mind, the notion of dead men rising to feed on the living fell somewhere on par with the possibility of a woman getting the better of him in a brawl. "Kind of you to say so." She made no attempt to keep the sarcasm out of her voice.

Brennan winked at her. "Not that it's the first time a woman's bit me. Just wasn't . . . ." He laughed and appeared to regret it instantly, holding his hand against his head again.

Solenne pointedly moved her hand closer to the knife on her belt. "Just so we understand each other, there'll be no more biting tonight . . . or anything else."

"Shit. Think I'd let you get near me again?" He shook his head. "Sooner bed down with that rattler over yonder."

"Me too."

"Yeah. All right. We'll ride out soon's it's light." He stirred the fire one more time before hunkering down and pulling his blanket over himself. "Oh, by the way, you were saying 'not many people around here'?"

Solenne had retrieved a buffalo robe from her horse and was drawing it around herself, ready to give in to the exhaustion she was feeling.

"Yes," she said, wary.

"Well, apart from you and those three guys yesterday, the reason I was headed this way in the first place was that I ran into some Apaches a few hours east of here."

"*Hijo de puta*," she whispered, her earlier thoughts—*What will I do after?*—mocking her now.

"Yeah, I know. They were none too friendly . . . Nearly put an arrow in my ass."

"You should have told me sooner."

Brennan pulled his blanket closer, paying no attention to the anger in her voice. "Well, now, must tell you I've had a bit of a busy day, what with gunfights and thievery and women smashing my head near open . . . Can't imagine how the Apaches slipped my mind."

Solenne threw off her robe and started to rise. "If that thing gets in among a tribe, within a day there'll be thirty of those things."

"Now, now"—Brennan held out a placating hand and pointed to the east, where the sky was still jet black—"I'm sorry I left that out. I can see it's important to you, but—" She glared at him and he repeated, "*But* . . . there's nothing to be done about it right at the moment."

An energetic venom danced in Solenne's eyes.

"We'll sleep for an hour."

"Still be dark then."

"Two hours, then. No more."

"Whatever you say." Brennan pulled his blanket up. He was snoring within a minute.

Exhausted and resigned, Solenne found a comfortable spot and lay down.

Just over a year ago, she had found a dog-eared copy of a book called *Smith's Illustrated Astronomy* among the discarded belongings of some pilgrim killed by Comanches. "Illustrated with Numerous Original Diagrams" the cover had proclaimed enticingly.

Solenne had kept the book, and over the coming weeks she had read it with some fascination. It was an exploration of the larger universe in which she inhabited one small dusty corner. Apparently the world she walked across was one of many that whirled around the sun, and every star she saw circled something greater than itself even as her own life seemed trapped by forces she could not control, in orbit around a ceaseless pursuit of death.

Above her, Jupiter chased the waxing moon across the sky. Orion was up—the constellation a people called the Greeks had long ago named after a legendary hunter, who was elevated by the gods, on his death, to stalk his prey forever among the stars.

Solenne could not imagine such a thing. She longed only for an end to the hunt.

## Chapter Seven

In her dreams, Solenne was never sure how much was memory, how much was imagination, and how much was . . . the rest, the spiritsense. She knew that some portion of her dreams, as well as some measure of her extraordinary awareness in the waking world, came from her special talents. While in the real world, she could usually tell those sources of knowledge apart. In dreams, this was not so easy . . .

This was the old dream, the first dream, the dream of her origins. She did not have it often, and it always preceded great challenge and great change. It was not a pleasant dream; from experience she knew she could not avoid it, could not wake herself from it, and she had long ago given up trying. So she swam into the vision now, focusing on the one thing it brought her that she had never had in the waking world—the face of her mother.

In the dream it was hot, as it always was in the canyon at the height of summer. The houses carved into the ravine walls faced south and were therefore touched by the sun year-round. Above the two-hundred-foot-high walls lay desert in all directions, but the canyon itself was a lush microenvironment with abundant vegetation and undergrowth that attracted a variety of animals and birds. Coupled with a river surging with fish, the canyon housed a rich source of food for the people who had come to live there.

Her ancestors had left the lands of their origins in the southern continent and made their home in this place after a migration lasting generations. The oral history of the tribe told that they had fled metal-clad invaders from the eastern sea, who poisoned the people's ancestral mountains with betrayal, sickness, and death.

Running a gauntlet of plagues, hostile peoples, and unfamiliar lands, the tribe had continued north, never able to rest for long. The natives of most lands they passed through viewed them as enemies and made war on the refugees from the south. Eventually, though, the tribe had found this canyon—an uninhabited, isolated oasis and a haven in which they sought to re-create the paradise of their faraway birth land.

The other peoples living near them here were mostly peaceful. Though the tribe avoided interaction with the natives, they were wise enough to realize it was worth copying their ways. They learned to catch and ride horses, along with which plants were good to eat or could be made into medicines.

They built homes into the raw cliff of the northern wall of the canyon, and their windows looked down onto the wealth of life the canyon offered in the shady river-carved valley. As their population slowly recovered from the losses suffered on their long run from the metal-clad men and their plagues, the number of houses grew, eventually climbing halfway up the cliff face in a honeycombed network of ladders and stairs carved into the soft red rock.

Now the dream moved Solenne abruptly into her parents' dwelling.

Her gravid mother lay supine on a bed of straw mats and animal hides, smiling at the husband who brought water from the stream far below, carried in carefully balanced gourds on a pole across his shoulders. The dream showed her father to be a tall, lean, bronzed warrior, with many scars on his body and a pleasing smile that she somehow knew her mother had fallen in love with at first sight. She could see them laughing as he stumbled and a few drops of water spilled before he lowered the gourds to the earthen floor.

Her mother was in active labour, and her smile became a grimace for a few moments as she closed her eyes and suffered through a contraction.

Her warrior father touched his love's face as she lay on the bed. The two old women at her side clucked disapprovingly at this interruption, but Solenne saw her mother smile again as the contraction eased. The old women—veteran mothers, wet nurses, and midwives to every child born within the last twenty years—had told her mother weeks ago that today would be the day of her child's birth, and of course they had been correct, as they always were about such things. The contractions had started just after her midday meal, and as this was her first child, her mother had simply thought her stomach was bothering her.

Her father made as if to squat on the floor beside his love, but the midwives shooed him away, telling him it was a woman's time. He went outside but did not go far. He was worried for her, of course, but he had an additional distraction. Some of his friends who had left on a mission many days earlier were long overdue in returning to the village.

Nearly two moons before this, the earth had trembled, as it often had in the southern continent, so the elders said, and sometimes did here as well. This time, though, the tribe had afterward noticed a change in the river. The water had turned dark, and many fish were found dead and washed up on the banks. Those who drank the water grew ill, vomiting blood and nearly dying.

A day later, bits of leathery cloth—rotted and torn but plainly the clothing of people—were pulled out of the river. The remnants stank of death, and when some of the people threw the cloth carelessly on plants by the river, the vegetation shrivelled and died within hours.

The Witch-woman had not slept nor taken food during this time. Instead she had knelt in front of her home in the full heat of the sun, sweat dripping from her haggard face, and spent every moment making spells and praying to the spirits of the land to protect them. More than the earth moving, more than the death in their drinking water, more than anything else, the sight of the Witch-woman in such a state had terrified the people.

Nevertheless, several days after the ground had trembled, the river had run clear again, and the Witch-woman had been first to taste it despite many protests and volunteers from among the men in the tribe. She had crawled to the edge of the flowing water and nearly collapsed when she bent over to drink. Two of the men supported her as she drew a shaky hand through the torrent and then up to her lips. When she cried out, the rest of those nearby rushed to her aid with horror plain on their faces—but it had been a cry of joy.

The water was pure and clean again.

The tribe had thought their troubles over and praised the Witch-woman's gift in allying the spirits to help them. But that night she looked up and read the moon and the stars and told the chief—standing trembling before him—that something evil remained far upriver, ripening itself like fruit in the summer sun to make death and disease among the people.

The men of the tribe—friends of her father—had been asked by the chief and elders to ride up the canyon and investigate.

She could see in her dreams that these were young men and that they respected their elders and even half feared the Witch-woman; but still, they had young men's minds . . .

Despite the fog of the dream, Solenne saw clearly that these were good, courageous, honourable men. But they had the lightheartedness of those who had led a nearly idyllic life. They had never seen the terrors their grandparents had known, and despite the stories they had all heard as children, they could not truly imagine such things. They were flush with the strength of youth and knew themselves only as agile, mighty, unconquerable warriors. They made plans to ride up the canyon, far beyond where anyone in the tribe had ever ventured. They would search out any threat to the people and destroy it.

These same men had exchanged knowing looks and chuckled with their typical gentle good nature when Solenne's father made ready to come with them, shaking their heads and teasing him—telling him they needed only focused warriors with them, not a distracted man who would be worrying about a first-born child. Her father had been the eldest of the young warriors in the tribe, and the only one married, and he had understood they were being kind to him, knowing his wife would soon give birth. In the bright sunshine, standing beside the singing surge of the stream, it was easy to forget how afraid they had all been days ago when the water had run dark as blood. So her father had remained in the village while the others set out.

Now came the moment when Solenne tried to resist the forward current of the dream. Always she tried to hold back, tried to see her father's eyes, blue as the sky, in the sun again.

But the inexorable flood of the vision drew her onward as it always did.

The party that had set out so full of banter and confidence was many days overdue. Everyone knew that, no matter what the men had encountered, they would have sent word back to the tribe by now if they could have. The Witch-woman had cast spell after spell without result, and the evening prior she had descended into a shivering trance from which the other women had been unable to rouse her.

So, on the afternoon of the fifteenth day after the party had left, her father sat outside the doorway of the house in the cliff and watched the canyon below for signs of his friends, feeling at odds with being idle but not knowing what else to do. Tonight he would see his child born, and tomorrow, once he knew his love and his child were healthy, he would set out with three or four others to see if they could find their friends.

Solenne was always somehow aware in this dream that her mother had had plans for her. She knew, for instance, that her mother sensed the child she carried would be female and that it would grow to attain both strength and intelligence. Others in the tribe had told her much later that her parents had looked forward to raising many children, and as she grew Solenne had often mourned the loss of these potential siblings and the bonds they might have shared as much as the loss of her parents.

Now—inevitably—the dream turned dark.

She heard the midwives telling her mother that the child would be born after sunset and that this meant it would be a wily hunter with excellent night vision and power over creatures that moved in the darkness. She saw her mother smile at this and at the many other assurances the women gave her—promises she suspected were given every birthing mother even while hoping they were true—that her child would be strong and tall and destined for greatness.

Her mother laboured through the afternoon, taking water so often that her father had to go fill two more gourds. By his last trip, darkness was descending and the tribe was lighting their cooking fires. Her mother could see he was concerned about his friends. She knew that some in the tribe now believed that they would never return.

They did come back, however, that very night.

But not all together, and no longer alive.

Solenne, sleeping by Brennan's fire, shifted and moaned. The inescapable events that came next were always a torture to see, yet each time she hoped she might learn something new among the pain of the vision.

All they knew—all they had to know—was that among the darkening narrows of the upriver canyon with its mazes of arroyos and contributing streams, where no human had walked for ages, the strong, lighthearted warriors who had set out days before had found a curse. A curse that took their spirits and their minds but left the empty husks of their bodies still walking . . . And hungry.

So very, very hungry.

In her mind's eye, Solenne saw people turn from their evening fires when they heard the moans. Out of the darkness, a half-dozen men slowly approached, shambling like those who had been injured or had lost their minds. As they got closer, everyone in the tribe recognized the men as the ones who had left days ago. There were even shouts of celebration—at first. The tribe had no warning that the men who had departed as lifelong friends and family were about to enter their lives again as relentless, ravenous monsters. Skin torn and flesh already decaying, but with teeth sharp and strong, what the people would eventually come to call reapers came among them.

Over the years, Solenne had come to understand that those newly risen retained both some of their former speed and a fine sense of smell. Reapers that had been dead a few weeks were easier to deal with as they were slower moving and less sensitive to nearby humans. These freshly dead things had been drawn downriver by the smell of the living. With the curse came the hunger, and the hunger was all-consuming. It became their only purpose, their only drive, their deepest need.

*Kill. Eat.*

And they did.

The reapers entered the village well after dark. Fires were dying and few people were outside their dwellings. Some were roused from sleep by the first few whoops of greeting, and when the screams began everyone in the village wakened to the pack of rabid demons suddenly in their midst.

For the hundredth time, Solenne saw the one that charged into her parent's house . . .

She whimpered in the real world, loudly enough that Brennan woke and rolled over to squint at his companion in the dying firelight.

The grey-skinned warrior was limping, his leg hacked halfway off, perhaps by one of his companion's weapons or maybe by one of the tribe who'd tried to stop him from reaching the houses. The same ochre-yellow pus that oozed from his mouth dripped from the wound that had half-severed his leg and from several other ragged black slashes on his face and neck, but the wounds were bloodless.

The thing stumbled into their house with her father hanging from its back.

Solenne always wondered why it did not attack her father first. Instead, it surged past him and through the doorway of their home. She had decided in years since that it must have been attracted to the coppery smell of the blood spilling out of her mother as she gave birth.

Her father latched onto the reaper as it tried to lurch past him toward her mother. She felt him thinking *Protect the child!* as his arms wrapped around it, muscles of iron holding the creature back from its chosen prey. She watched her father struggle to pull it away from his love as he drew his knife, but the reaper coiled within his grip and slashed at him with fingers worn down to bone. A typical specimen of the revivified dead, this one had likely worn the flesh off its fingers trying to forge its way up the cliff. Like all of them, it would have traded any wound or injury if the reward was the taste of living flesh.

This one's bony taloned fingers clawed into her father, drawing blood and tearing muscle. But her father hung on regardless, hammering at the thing with his knife, stabbing it in the torso again and again without any visible effect.

The struggle went on for some minutes, the creature and her father twisting back and forth in a macabre dance as he tried vainly to kill it. The demon seemed immune to harm, while her father grew steadily weaker, blood running all over him like snowmelt in spring from the many scratches and tears the creature had inflicted on him.

The women in the room screamed for help, but similar death struggles were being played out all around the camp, and no one came.

The blood from her father's wounds had now made him at least as appetizing to the creature as Solenne's mother. The monster began biting at him now, tearing chunks of flesh from his arms so that he lost his grip on the knife and it slipped from his fingers. The reaper heaved finally, and her father fell back onto the ground.

The old women shrieked and scattered to corners of the room as the bloody, snarling reaper twisted like a viper, leapt onto Solenne's mother, and bit deep into the taut flesh of her abdomen.

Sometimes at this point in the dream, her mother's screams were enough to wake Solenne and rescue her from the rest of what she might see. But she was exhausted from days of hard riding and the fight with Brennan, and salvation in the form of wakening would not come. She writhed and whimpered as she watched the monster attack her mother.

The monster tore a chunk of flesh out of her mother's upper abdomen, then reared back and threw its head up, wet smacking sounds echoing in the small chamber as it chewed like a starved animal on the bloody chunk of meat. Her mother struggled to free herself even as the force of another contraction shook her, but the reaper held her mother down effortlessly as it swallowed and then bent down in search of more.

Her father managed to gain his feet and took up his knife again, diving at the creature and knocking it off her mother as he rolled on top of it.

The reaper scrabbled desperately to get up, spitting and growling in a frenzy as her father held it down by its neck with one hand while bringing the knife up with the other. As the creature tore at the arm holding it with its bony claw-fingers, her father brought his knife slowly and deliberately down onto the thing's neck and put all his body weight over it, driving the blade deep into the reaper's flesh.

Her father was a warrior, and their trek to this place had not been without struggle. They had been attacked more than once by natives of the lands they passed through. Her father had killed many men, and he had killed prey animals without number. He knew what to expect from a neck wound—a wellspring of blood flooding over his hands, bubbling with the last desperate gasps and gurgles of the dying.

There was none of that here.

Her father's knife cut through dry flesh, empty of blood, exposing arteries filled only with sludgy black goo. Despite the grievous wound, the creature still struggled with demonic energy beneath him, though its moaning ceased as its windpipe was severed. Solenne had seen something white men called oil once, flowing out of the ground when they had drilled far into it. Now this black fluid oozed like oil out of the thing's lacerated neck—nothing like human blood.

Her father began a sawing motion as his knife finally hit the resistance of the cervical vertebrae, and still the thing below clawed at him, raking his arms and chest as the midwives and his wife shrieked in unintelligible pain and fear.

Her father's arms were in shreds, not one inch of flesh bare of the bloody crimson rivers running down them now, when he finally severed the reaper's head and it lay still at last. In agony, he rolled off the lifeless demon and lay clutching his torn arms.

The midwives saved her father's life. Briefly, at least. Once they saw the creature was dead, they tore strips from their clothes and bound his wounds. Her father could hear more cries of pain and anger coming from elsewhere in the camp and tore away from them before they could completely finish, running out into the night to battle the rest of the things. To protect the tribe, the family . . . the child.

Her mother was panting through another contraction, crying as the midwives pressed against the bleeding wound on her torso, trying to staunch the blood that stubbornly refused to clot even after several minutes of direct pressure.

Solenne gushed from her mother's womb a few minutes afterward. She arrived shrieking loudly, as if already demanding to take part in the battle. Solenne's mother shook with the usual relief the midwives saw in mothers once they had finally given birth. But minutes later, she still shook as if an illness was digging its way into her.

The midwives dried the baby and placed her on her mother's chest to suckle at her breast. Solenne felt the embrace of her mother for the first and last time as she took the nipple in her mouth and began to drink.

The Witch-woman and midwives of the tribe had known far more about pregnancy and birth than any white Solenne had ever met, and Solenne had learned all of it from them while growing up. She certainly knew enough to guess that sometime in between the bite and her first meal nursing at her mother's breast, some essence of the curse had passed into her, twisted into something quite different by the surge of nutrients and immune factors any newborn receives from their first sip of breast milk.

The fever spiked into her mother scarcely fifteen minutes later, not long after the baby had drunk its fill and been bundled up by the midwives. They piled robes on Solenne's mother and fed her as much water as she would take, peering out the doorway every few minutes and cringing as screams and cries continued to echo down the canyon.

All of the reapers were destroyed within an hour of entering the camp, but in that time, they had wounded many people. Scratches, bites—it took very little for the curse to take root. In the next few hours, the illness began growing in all of them.

If not for the Witch-woman, the whole tribe would have been wiped out. It was she who realized that all the wounded and even those who had died would inherit the contamination. Those who showed signs of illness were watched closely by the remainder of the tribe as they sickened and—again because of the Witch-woman—even after they died. The Witch-woman examined all those ailing cautiously—two stout and steely-eyed warriors armed with war axes beside her—since it was now obvious the curse could be easily spread, and all knew the tribe would not survive the death of the Witch-woman. They learned quickly that the disease was universally fatal and that the dead did not remain still for more than an hour or so—sometimes far less. When the yellow eyes snapped open and they rose—hungry as all the walking dead were—they were quickly dispatched.

And so killing and loss and mourning descended on the tribe like a burial shroud for the next three days. Death and unholy rebirth and final death, until it seemed it might never be over.

At the end of it, more than half of the tribe were dead, truly and finally dead, and the Witch-woman directed the construction of a huge funeral pyre far downriver. Once all the dead had been dragged there, it was set alight and stoked for two days, tended carefully by several warriors to ensure it burnt—as the Witch-woman instructed—continuously and with great heat.

Baby Solenne grew a fever like all of the others who'd encountered the reapers, but in her, and her alone, the fever died out several days later, like the ashes of the funeral pyre.

There were many adoptions, remarriages, and family realignments afterward. But the families who adopted were uniformly wary of Solenne, born on a night of demons and the sole survivor of the fever. Her destiny lay elsewhere.

A day after the attack, when the Witch-woman picked up Solenne—wary herself, at first, of this feverish, toothless babe—she experienced a warm surge in her bosom. Two days later, her breasts were swelling with milk, and she sought out the girl again. Solenne's temperature had normalized and she cried in hunger, an orphan who had survived what no one else in the tribe could. When she touched Solenne, the Witch-woman again felt the surge in her bosom. In a daze of wonder, she pulled her robe aside and drew the babe close, watching it find her breast and begin nursing.

The babe Solenne was adopted by the Witch-woman. She likely would have been tutored by her in any case. Early on as a child, along with the spiritsense, Solenne demonstrated that she had intelligence and powers that demanded she learn the witching ways so that she might protect the tribe when the Witch-woman died. But the events of that night, and Solenne's coincident birth during them, meant most others in the tribe would have found adopting her too disturbing to contemplate.

As Solenne grew, the Witch-woman taught her about medicine and spirits and about listening to the world around her in ways others could not. All her life, Solenne had seen sorrow etched in the face of the Witch-woman. Even when she laughed or smiled, there was a shadow just beneath it. When Solenne was sixteen, the Witch-woman told her a secret and the reason for the sorrow that she carried with her like a wound that would not heal.

One evening, when only the two of them remained around the dying fire, the Witch-woman began to cry softly. She made hardly a sound, and yet her body was racked with soul-wrenching shudders, as if unbearable grief was surfacing and finally being released.

Solenne was horrified. She had never in her life seen the Witch-woman cry, and she had unconsciously come to the conclusion that perhaps Witch-women could not cry, perhaps did not even possess tears. She found herself believing that when she matured and became the tribe's Witch-woman, all the tears would evaporate from her body as well. In fact, she secretly longed for the day when she would no longer be able to cry.

By the fire, in the waking world, Solenne moaned softly again as if in pain, and tears ran down her face.

"What is wrong?" she asked on that long-ago night after recovering from her disbelief.

The Witch-woman was a long time answering. She looked up at the stars and back into the fire as if somewhere between what the whites called heaven and hell she might find the words she so desperately sought.

"*Cielito* . . ." The Witch-woman had not called her *Cielito*—little flower—since she was five years old. "It was my fault, what happened to your parents . . . to the tribe. My fault."

Solenne frowned and shook her head. "No—how could that be? Many times people have told me the story of what happened and—"

The Witch-woman shook her head. "This is my secret shame, *Cielito* . . ." She sobbed—a gasp for air that seemed not nearly enough to fill her lungs. "I was very young when the Witch-woman who taught me died. She caught the lizard-skin disease. I remember, though, her telling me she could teach me everything except how to let go of the arrogance I felt at my power . . . and she was right, though I did not think I was arrogant at the time. No one does, of course.

"When we came upon this beautiful land, it was like the answer to all our dreams. But when we settled here, the spirits of this place talked to me at night. They showed me a time long ago, beyond remembering, when a fiery stone came down from the sky and made a hole in the earth many marches away from here."

Solenne swallowed a gasp.

"Yes," the Witch-woman said, "you can guess where." She waved upriver. "In my dreams the pit was covered over by the desert, but it remained a cold and evil place, and I knew somehow that all this time some evil thing from the sky lay beneath the earth . . . waiting."

"You couldn't know—"

"But I did, *Cielito* . . . Or I should have. But"—she sobbed again—"the people had come so far, and so very many had died on the way. They were so happy we had found a new home. In my conceit, I believed I was powerful enough to protect us. Every day I cast my spells and asked the spirits to keep the evil buried."

She sighed, and it was as if her very spirit was leaving with her breath.

"And for twenty years, they did. Forgive me child . . . I beg you."

Without a second's hesitation, Solenne leaned forward and placed her hand on the Witch-woman's arm. "I forgive you . . . Mother." She had never called the Witch-woman that before, and it set her to crying again. Solenne hugged her and looked up at the stars, blurred with the moisture welling in her own eyes.

Other than Solenne, no one in the tribe ever came to know with certainty what the men had found upriver. Afterward, the Witch-woman had pronounced that the canyon east of them was cursed and that none of the tribe's survivors ever venture there. The passage to the land upriver was forever after guarded by warriors.

The dream began to fade as Solenne saw the Witch-woman again, tears rolling down her face.

Solenne settled back into her sleep by the dead fire, but not for long.

What woke her now came in real time and shattered her slumber, a shock like lightning running through her. She bolted upright, emerging from sleep with the harsh cry of a wounded animal. Heart pounding, she shivered in the cold desert morning.

This was part of her connection to the curse. If she was near enough when a reaper first rose into its dark new life, she would feel the shock of its wakening, as if the curse called to whatever piece of it had been left inside her. Sometimes the jolt was slight, like the one she'd felt earlier when—she assumed—the man Brennan was chasing had turned. Other times, like this, the pain was like fire in her chest.

Somewhere nearby a newborn reaper was rising.

She turned to Brennan. Woken by her yell, he had torn his blanket off and was groping for his guns before realizing there was no visible threat. He glanced up at the lightening sky and then looked hard at Solenne.

"You okay? Nightmare?"

"No." Solenne cast her robe aside and stood to gather her belongings. "Something's happened. A reaper—a dead man—has come alive, not far away."

"How do you—"

"Never mind." She whistled, and when her horse cantered over, she saddled it, working with urgent efficiency.

Brennan watched her for a moment and then began readying his own horse for the ride.

She talked over her shoulder, cinching the saddle tight around the horse's belly. "Should warn you again, trying to get your gold back could kill you."

"That's not exactly news to me."

"Just saying—this might be ugly."

"Seen ugly before."

"Not like this."

"Are we gonna spend time arguing about 'ugly' now? Gonna get my gold back, one way or another."

"Come with me, then, if you can keep up."

"Believe I can," Brennan said. He touched his still-aching head thoughtfully, the shade of a smile on his lips. "Suppose it's worth mentioning again, just so we're clear—"

"*Hijo de puta, cabron.* Don't want any of your *chingada madre* gold. Said it near a dozen times now."

"Just so we're clear."

Solenne's answer faltered and died on her lips as another icy shock swept through her chest, a twin to the one that had woken her.

She was on her horse now and stared hard at him. "The gold's all yours. Just make sure *you* stay out of *my* way. No misunderstandings."

He held a hand up in submission. "I will, I will . . ." She looked at him grimly as he mounted his horse, and he said, "What?"

"It's worse than I thought. The man you're hunting has contaminated others."

Cold fire in her chest again. The curse, nearby, worming its way into new hosts.

## Chapter Eight

Nights in the desert were always cold, and when Barrett and Lewis ordered their sergeants to rouse the camp before dawn, the usual mutters of complaint could be heard among the just-woken men, aching from a night sleeping on hard ground and waking to bone-chilling cold.

Barrett watched for a moment to ensure the troops were quick in beginning their preparations to depart, then glanced over to where Quinto rode back and forth over the ground east of them, picking up the trail of those they chased. Johnston gave an inquiring shout at the Apache, and Quinto offered a confident nod back.

"Very plain trail. Three riders, but none travelling together. Each trailing the last. Only one is wounded."

Johnston turned to Barrett, grinning and clapping his hands together as if to warm them. The fury he had demonstrated the night before had vanished entirely. Barrett would never have expected any show of regret from his colonel on account of Carter's agonizing death, but he found himself swallowing his own ire at Johnston's near-festive attitude.

"I can feel it, Captain. Today's the day. Make sure the troops are reminded of my orders regarding the infected—and especially my orders about the girl." He clapped his hands again, anticipation lively in his eyes.

"Yessir." Barrett flicked his gaze away from Johnston's smile, a smile he had always found slightly disturbing and that was all the more so now that he knew the man better. He doubted any of Johnston's men required reminding about his orders, given the oft-demonstrated consequences of violating them.

"Quinto," Barrett shouted. "How far ahead, you figure?"

"If they made camp at dark, maybe we catch them by midday. Looks like they're riding fast though." He glanced at Johnston as he said this.

Johnston nodded and clapped Barrett on the shoulder. "Then we shall too."

Not for the first time, Barrett wondered what he was actually riding into; but as ever, there was only one answer to give to a superior in the army, and most assuredly only one a sane man would give Johnston.

"Yessir."

***

Turak was startled awake near dawn by something he could not immediately identify. Exhausted, he had fallen asleep when he was supposed to be on guard. Never in his life had he slept during watch, and his first conscious thoughts, as his eyes leapt around, directed intense anger at himself. Around him was the chaos of scattered belongings that had emerged from the battle with the demon. The fire had died and nothing appeared to be moving—nearby or on the horizon—but his hand wrapped around the hilt of his war axe as if of its own volition. Something felt wrong.

The morning was cold and he kept his buffalo hide wrapped around him as he got to his feet, eyes still seeking the source of his disquiet. In some ways, his wakening felt like an emergence from a terrible sickness, with the demon and their battle just a nightmare delusion. He ached from the fight, and his restless sleep had not refreshed him much. Running his hands through his hair, he again chastised himself for falling asleep and then silently expressed his thankfulness to the spirits for guiding him alive through the night.

Tied a few yards away, the horses whinnied and pulled against their ropes. They peered cautiously at him, as if wondering whether he was going to be the author of more noise and commotion. Perhaps the noise of the animals had woken him, but what was scaring them?

Turak caught movement out of the corner of his eye, but it was gone when he turned toward it. He saw that Taza and Baishan were still in their robes, slumbering around the dead fire. He and Baishan had wrapped Burin and Tyee in their robes last night and dragged the dead men slightly away from the camp. Before leaving today, they would burn the bodies. The motion he had glimpsed had come from near the corpses, and he wondered if some desert scavenger might already be making a meal for itself out of his dead friends. Coyotes could survive anywhere and had a keen sense of smell, so where death lay, they always followed close behind. When the heat of the day came, there would be vultures as well.

Movement again, at the edge of his vision, near the dead.

Turak walked toward the bodies. He could see no large scavengers near them, but he thought perhaps a snake had taken shelter under the fading warmth of the dead men. He glanced at those still sleeping and considered waking them, but for what? They were both hurt and exhausted, and he would likely be disturbing them only to help him investigate a mouse moving in the desert.

Then Tyee sat up.

Turak stumbled backward, gasping, and almost fell.

Burin was moving too now, writhing like the snake Turak had imagined moments ago. The dead men were both trying to claw their way out of their death wraps with spastic, awkward motions that reminded Turak very much of—

*The demon.*

A tremor ran through him and he cursed himself for it. Even after the strange, supernatural events of last night, it was difficult to believe what he was seeing. The white man had been a stranger. These were

friends whose deaths he had only barely begun to accept, and some evil
force was changing them into devils before his very eyes. In the growing
light, he watched Tyee thrust a pale grey arm out of the robes and begin
tearing the cloth away from his face. Burin continued to roll and twist
convulsively like a fish thrown on the riverbank, slowly working his way
out of the confining material wrapped around him.

Turak raised his war axe. Tyee had pulled free and was struggling
to his feet like a child trying to stand for the first time. Turak saw cloudy
yellow eyes staring out of the man's slack grey face. His torn-out throat
still gaped open, leaking a dark, viscous fluid. Now he sniffed the air and
turned his blind gaze toward Turak, drawing blackened lips over sharp
yellow teeth in a demon's snarl. After a moment, he began to stumble
toward Turak with an obviously malevolent purpose.

Burin was nearly on his feet too, ripping away his wrappings with
clumsy swipes. His eyes were on Turak now, his mouth working as if in
anticipation of the taste of Turak's warm flesh.

Turak found his voice. "Baishan! Taza! Wake up!"

The Tyee creature was too close suddenly, clutching at Turak as he
danced backward. The corrupt stink of the thing was almost beyond belief.
Tyee had died only hours before, but this monster smelled like something
disembowelled and left to rot in some damp, dark hole for weeks.

"Taza! Baishan!"

Turak yelled again and again for his companions as he scrambled
backward, just ahead of the Tyee-thing's spastically grasping hands.
Turak's surprise transformed into a reflexive will to survive, and as the
thing took another step forward, he swung his axe at it with all his power.
There was a dull, meaty sound as the weapon sank into the creature's neck,
and a geyser of brackish fluid sprayed from the wound as the Tyee-thing
fell sideways onto the ground, partially decapitated. Turak blinked away
the fresh gore on his face and yanked back, pulling his axe out of the
thing's neck, chunks of grey flesh flying out along with it. The creature lay
on its side for a moment, glaring at him with sharp hate in its cloudy eyes
while its mouth spasmed open and shut in irregular gasps. Then it pushed
itself up, head lolling to the side but eyes still fixed on its prey, irregular
streams of oily black fluid gushing out of its half-severed neck.

"Baishan! Taza!" By now, Turak realized that the lack of response
from his friends was not natural and likely foretold something about their
own fates. Both men still lay unmoving by the fire. He dashed over to
them, keeping his eyes on the demons as they moved slowly but
determinedly after him, a choking, rasping sound that might otherwise
have been a growl coming from Burin's torn throat.

Turak reached Taza first and pulled him out of his robes, yelling at
him to wake up even while he kicked at Baishan. It took a moment for
Turak to realize that the shoulder he clutched was cold as death. He

dragged his eyes from the two demons approaching him and looked at Taza closely. The man's eyes hung half-open in death, but they swam with the same milky yellow colour that he'd seen in those of the cursed white man and that he saw now in the eyes of the monsters coming toward him. The same spiderwebs of blackness crawled over Taza's face. Now he felt the thing that had been Taza shudder like some dark insect disturbed in its nest, and he dived backward, falling across Baishan. His body, too, was in the process of growing into a demon like his fellows.

The demons were only a few feet away from him now, huffing and gasping through their torn necks as they reached out to take him into their cold embrace.

Turak was a brave man. No one in his tribe would have believed that he feared battle with any living thing. He saw no reason to fear fighting dead things either—after all, he had defeated the demon of the previous night. But there were other considerations here. Last night they had made camp no more than a two- or three-hour ride away from the village. If Turak were defeated, the *nunasish* inhabiting his friends' dead bodies might well find the rest of his people . . .

He stepped back from Taza as the dead man shuddered again and made a choking moan. The Tyee-thing was near and reached out for Turak, his near decapitation hampering his movements only a little. Turak swung his axe underhanded and caught the thing in the chest. There was a sharp crack as his weapon cleaved through ribs and impaled itself several inches into the creature's chest in a well-aimed strike to the heart. The force of the blow caused the *nunasish* to stagger slightly, but otherwise it seemed to ignore what—again—should have been a killing blow.

The snarling monster grabbed Turak's shoulders, and Turak punched it in the face, mashing its nose into mush. This would have brought any man to his knees with pain but failed to faze the creature, which only drew Turak toward it with an impressive strength that Turak was hard-pressed to resist. He pushed away, only to find his axe stuck fast in the creature's chest. He yanked hard on the weapon, but this served only to tumble them both to the ground, with it atop him. Turak struggled to hold the thing away from his throat as the demon raged and lunged toward the warm flesh it desperately craved.

There were sounds of movement behind Turak, and in the growing light, he sensed shadows move over him. The Baishan-thing was close now, and Burin and Taza were getting to their feet, waking into their new demon lives.

Desperation ruled Turak now. He knew he had but moments left to break free before the demons all piled atop him and devoured him like a pack of wolves. He brought his knee up into the Tyee-thing's groin and heaved it off him, rolling away and groping for his knife. The Burin-thing was beside him as he rose, yellow eyes narrowed with savage intent, but

Turak had his blade now, and he plunged it with all his strength into the soft flesh under the creature's chin.

The long blade buried itself to the hilt in the underside of the *nunasish*'s jaw. Turak felt the brittle tremor as the blade smashed through the thin bone at the base of the skull and entered the brain. The thing shuddered, and Turak watched the animalistic awareness in the yellow eyes fade away to a blank stare of death. The creature slumped to the ground, Turak's blade sliding out of the bloodless wound as it collapsed in a heap beside him.

Turak turned to face the Tyee-thing again, fully expecting it to have regained its feet in the few seconds he'd been busy with the Burin-thing, and it was this expectation—that the *nunasish* would fight like men—that doomed him to become one of them.

The Tyee-thing was not on its feet. Its hunger, its drive, was not to defeat or overcome an adversary but simply to feed—to feast on the delicious, coppery flavour of warm flesh. The hunger was its sole purpose now, a driving vector of need that supplanted all higher impulses. So instead of standing, the thing had merely crawled toward the smell of the nearest warm meat.

As Turak turned, the demon grabbed his ankle, slapped his leggings aside, and drove its teeth into the living flesh it found beneath with cannibalistic ecstasy. Warm blood gushed into its mouth as it tore deep into the muscle, igniting necrotic nerves in the pleasure centre of its dying brain, and its head whipped back and forth as if in a seizure of ecstasy.

Turak cursed as he brought his other foot up, kicking it in the head until finally the thing loosed its grip enough so that he could yank his injured leg out of its mouth.

Despite the screaming pain flaring up his right leg, Turak managed to stumble away from the monsters grabbing for him. He looked down to see a sizable chunk of flesh missing from just above his ankle. Blood ran freely from the wound but did not pump, so he knew the injury would not kill him in the next few minutes, but that was little comfort. He knew he was doomed. He could guess now that the merest of wounds from one of the *nunasish* would turn those stricken into similar creatures, and this hardened his resolve. He *must* escape and survive long enough to warn his people. If even one of these things reached his tribe without them being aware of its nature, its curse would spread like a grass fire on a dry summer day.

He kicked out again as the Tyee-thing reached for him, using his wounded leg because he knew he would fall if he tried to stand on it. Pain flared from his wound as the kick connected and threw the creature back. The others were closing in, but Turak retained the agility that went hand in hand with his humanity, whereas the creatures were clumsy, walking as if the demon grown in their bones needed time to learn how to move within them. The monsters' yellow eyes flashed and they swiped at him as he limped by them, but none managed to touch him.

The horses shied away from Turak as he drew near. He could not know it, but the smell of the undead was clamouring alarm into their brains, and the ropes holding them went taut as the straining animals sought escape from the approaching creatures. Turak swiped his knife through the ropes, slicing them all free as he grabbed at the ropes holding the animal he'd always judged fastest and strongest. The beast was near panic, but Turak managed to struggle atop it, panting hard with the pain lancing up his leg. He could feel whatever evil substance the *nunasish* secreted working in him already, spreading like venom from a snakebite.

*Warn the tribe!* Turak glanced at the rising sun, knowing this would be the last dawn he would ever see. He was already trembling with fever as he rode hard toward home.

## Chapter Nine

The midmorning sun was warming the day quickly, and Johnston's troops rode below it at a pace they could not hope to keep up for long lest they run their mounts to death. But Johnston—so close to his goal—cared little about such things at this point; if a few beasts perished, his plans would not suffer for it now. He knew today would be the day. It *must* be the day. He had given orders that anyone or anything falling behind should be left behind to join the supply wagons that trailed them, if they could.

Quinto rode well in front of the rest on the fastest horse in the company to ensure he had the best look at the trail. Johnston watched as the man reined his horse back abruptly and rode slowly through a stream breaking out of a canyon in a mesa just south of them, reading the tracks in the dirt before circling back to ride alongside the colonel.

"Very close now. Two riders left here less than an hour ago. The third was ahead of them and passed by yesterday afternoon sometime." He gestured toward the canyon they were approaching. "Want to follow the trail up the canyon or the one they took out this morning?"

Johnston replied as if he'd been asked a pointless question. "Keep going."

Quinto nodded and spurred his horse forward.

\*\*\*

Solenne and Brennan followed the outlaw's trail until they came upon the large stain of blood upon the ground where he had met his first death at the hands of the Apaches. Eyeing the ground, the two circled their horses around the bloody scene, reading the hoofmarks and traces of gore on the ground.

After a few minutes of silence and contemplation, Brennan halted his horse and squinted at Solenne. "Seems to me someone met a bad end here."

Solenne nodded. "Prints from at least four horses, I'd say. Only one of them shod, though. You met the Apache near here?"

Brennan gazed around. "Near as I can tell. Wasn't taking in the scenery at the time, you understand."

Solenne smirked and pointed ahead. "Looks like when the Apaches left, they kept close to the river. Wind has hardly touched these tracks. They must be close."

"Ahhh, you happen to notice the—"

"Footprints?" Solenne was still staring down at them, and Brennan imagined she was arranging in her mind what had happened here. "Yes, I did."

"Right. So . . . how do you read this, then?"

"You tell me."

Brennan glanced off to the west. All his adult life he had been either causing trouble—on the whole just minor inconveniences that people got themselves overly worked up about, truth be told—or running *from* trouble. As a result he was wont to watch his back because those he'd inadvertently gotten worked up had a tendency to pursue him on occasion.

Over the last hour or so, each of Brennan's regular, reflexive glances behind him had shown him a growing dust cloud on the horizon. Too small and discrete to be a storm of any kind, there were few other things aside from a group of men on horseback that could disturb such appreciable amounts of dust.

He shook his head and turned back to Solenne.

"Okay, I'll give it a whirl. If I had to guess, I'd say the man I was after came across, or was more likely *come across by* the same Apaches I met." He gestured at a flat spot on the ground. "Lots of blood there . . . the man I was after, I expect. Wasn't like the guy I met would've done well against a bunch of Apache braves."

Solenne followed his thoughts and eyed the ground as he pointed. "Sounds about right."

"So, we've got one guy killed, and whoever left took all the horses." Brennan watched Solenne glance off to the west, just as he'd done moments ago.

"Seems likely."

"Except the dead guy is gone." Brennan paused, tipping his hat forward and scratching his head. "Now, it ain't impossible that coyotes or some such thing might drag a body off—"

"Don't see any coyote tracks. You?"

"Can't say I do."

"Just the footprints."

"Like he just got up and walked away."

"Suppose it's *possible* he was just wounded. Maybe faked being dead and then walked off later." Solenne sounded as if she might be entertaining the possibility on his behalf.

"Oh, like a possum, then." Brennan laughed. "From the tracks it looks like he was limping. I'll give you that."

"But you think not."

"You ever heard of Apaches *accidentally* leaving a man alive— and so uninjured he could still walk?"

"Hardly seems likely, does it?" Solenne's voice had the patient tone of a teacher waiting for a slow child to finish a simple math problem. "Maybe if there was some big battle. Then I suppose you could maybe imagine a person playing dead and getting missed. But this looks like one guy against"—she considered the tracks again—"five others."

Brennan's eyes rolled briefly skyward. "So, if I was to believe what you've been saying about this disease or curse or whatever . . ."

Solenne waited.

"Then, I'd expect the Apaches killed the guy I was chasing, took his horse—and my gold, by the way—and rode off. Then later . . ."

"He got up."

"It would appear so. Got up. Got up and walked . . . Walked *after them*, incidentally. Again not something you'd expect a mortal wounded man would do—chase after the people who near killed him."

"I tend to agree."

"Well, I suppose you would." Brennan looked at her from under the brim of his hat with an unreadable expression. "Being as that seems to support your story."

"Better explanation cross your mind?"

Brennan sighed. "Doesn't."

"So . . . ?"

"Well, I may just be one of those folks who has to see such things to believe 'em."

She nodded. "Fair enough."

"I guess under any circumstances, might be best to draw our guns and ride forward careful and quiet. What say?"

"Sounds about right."

Pistols in hand, they nudged their mounts to a canter and followed the trail of stumbling footprints.

"By the way."

"Yeah?" Solenne said.

"Interested in telling me who's chasing us?"

Solenne glanced at the dust cloud on the horizon behind them.

"Or should I say chasing *you*?"

Brennan heard irritation creep into her reply. "You carry stolen gold around in your saddlebags—"

"Ain't 'stolen'."

"'Liberated,' then?"

Brennan threw her a dark look.

"All right. Anyway, you want to tell me there's no likelihood that cloud could be a posse after *you*?"

"Not saying it's impossible. Still . . ."

"Okay." Solenne sighed. "You're right. That cloud's likely someone looking to find me. Could take a while to explain, but it's not good news."

"Can't say I'm shocked. A posse is *never* good news. I'm impressed, though. Takes a lot to make that many people angry enough to ride after you."

"Ain't a posse."

"Oh?"

"Listen, I do appreciate you riding with me seeing as how my story is hard to believe, but given what's behind us"—she nodded toward the approaching cloud—"I should likely ask you again just how bad you want that gold?"

Brennan considered. "'Bout as much as the next man would, I suppose."

"The *next man* you meet will likely be more interested in ripping you to shreds than anything else."

"So you've said . . . And what is that behind us, then?"

"Most likely a regiment of Confederate cavalry."

"Out here?" Brennan was genuinely startled. "You're shitting me."
Solenne smiled. "Wish I was."

"Shit."

"Oh, that's not nearly the worst of it. If I'm right, the man who's leading them is as much a monster as the things ahead of us."

"And he's chasing you because . . . ?"

"Let's just say there can't be any good reason."

Brennan looked baffled and she continued. "We have what you might say is a conflict of interests. He wants one of the creatures alive, and I want all of 'em dead."

Brennan cleared his throat and spat. "That does sound like a conflict of interests, sure enough. Still worth the chance, though, if we can be quick. They look at least a half-hour behind us."

"Understood. Just the same, thought you might want to know all the facts before it got too late for explanations."

"Obliged."

They continued following the irregular tracks the newly born creature had made as it reeled like a well-oiled drunk over the landscape. It was easy to see where the thing had fallen, but always it rose and carried on, following its desperate need.

"Anyone ever told you you're an unusual woman?"

"It has been said."

***

Turak could feel illness growing in him like decay in a rotting piece of meat. He tried to concentrate on guiding his horse, urging it at its best speed back toward the tribe, but he was finding it more and more challenging to ignore the throbbing pain in his leg—an agony that was slowly burrowing its way upward into his groin.

When he drew his clothing up, he could see tangled lines of darkness moving from the bite up into his torso. The bite itself was leaking a dark greenish pus that smelled of corruption, and he could no longer feel his leg around the wound.

He found his mind narrowing as the infection flowered in him. He knew he was dying. He could feel the alien thing embedded by the bite surging through his veins like floodwater gushing into a dry riverbed, washing away his humanity in favour of something eminently darker. But this realization and all others were increasingly difficult to concentrate on as the flood wore steadily at his thoughts, eroding them down to a single basic need.

*Hunger.*

He was now less than a mile from the verdant canyon that was his people's home. He had swum and fished in the river and had played endless games of war with his friends as a youth among the trees in the ravine. He had grown up with the woman who had become his wife and had first kissed her by that same river, but recalling these things with any clarity was rapidly becoming impossible. He fought the deluge of nothingness descending over his mind, knowing that he could not win but trying to postpone the inevitable because—

He was *so* hungry.

*Blood. Torn flesh. Taste of fear.*

Startled, Turak threw up his arms to thrust the visions away, and he nearly fell off his horse. In contrast to the fog enveloping his mind, the visions of blood and the *need* for it had been clear as the shock of plunging into an icy river on a hot day. The hunger was accompanied by a cacophony of sensations—screams, warm red liquid, and the sharp coppery tang of raw bloody flesh as he bit into it. He knew that the demon's mind was consuming his own and that when it was done, it would own him as surely as it had his friends.

Through cloudy eyes, Turak thought he could now see wisps of smoke from fires in the village. The wind was blowing toward him from the camp, and he caught the scent of meat roasting; the hunger returned immediately, slamming into him like a wild horse.

Visions of corpses grinned at him as they pulled themselves up from the ground . . . And now, the taste of bloody meat was in his mouth—deliciously sweet because it was torn from living flesh, and sweeter still because the taste was accompanied by screaming.

Turak's horse could sense its rider's confusion and fear and was near panic itself, driving itself forward at the edge of its strength, foam flying from its nostrils and mouth. The horse had known the man who was riding it for years, but now the man smelled *wrong*. The man smelled like a predator, like death itself.

This time when the visions descended, Turak's flailing as he tried to wave the phantasms away *did* overbalance him, and the horse slid out from under him. Hurtling to the ground, he tumbled several times, slamming into a boulder with force enough to snap ribs throughout his chest.

Its newfound terror of its rider driving it, the horse ran on without pause, legs pumping desperately in an attempt to put as much distance as possible between itself and the creature its rider was becoming.

The crash had winded Turak, but after a couple of useless efforts, he managed to draw a halting, shuddering breath and felt pain lance his chest. When he rolled onto his back, the movement caused one of his broken ribs to shift inward and puncture his right lung so that his coughing fit a few seconds later produced both agony and the taste of blood in his mouth. The demon part of his mind gibbered in joy at the metallic tang.

Turak moaned with frustration. He was close; a few minutes of riding, or even running, and he would be able to warn his people. But now simply breathing was nearly impossible. Every inhalation took tremendous focus and effort and brought renewed shocks of pain throughout his chest. When Turak tried to get to his feet, a new source of misery flared to life in his pelvis, and he collapsed back onto the sand, a tortured moan dying on his lips as he fought for consciousness. Lying still, he drew shuddering, shallow breaths in an effort to avoid further angering the injuries in his chest, and he looked around to see if, per chance, he might spot some member of his tribe nearby.

*Motion . . . there . . .* A tall cactus stood just a few feet away from him, and through the yellow mist dimming his eyesight, it seemed to him that the top of it was swaying. Then he realized that a vulture sat there, fluttering its wings with lazy patience—waiting for its soon-to-be next meal to die.

Home was less than a mile away, but it might as well have been on another continent. The horse might even have arrived there by now, perhaps sparking worry among his family and friends. They would raise a search, but likely not soon enough to find him alive. Turak's tribe had lived for a long time by fighting—fighting the elements, the harsh lands they inhabited, animals, other natives, and white men. They were a tribe of survivors, and they would not readily believe that five of their best warriors were dead. They would certainly not guess that one of those warriors—bred from birth to ride—had fallen off his horse just a short walk away.

The vulture folded and unfolded its wings, restless as it watched the human on the ground try to gain his feet again. The scavenger was long familiar with the smells of helplessness and desperation that preceded death, and it instinctively knew it did not have long to wait until it could feed.

Waves of pain radiated through Turak now, rolling through his chest and up from his bitten leg. As his breathing became more laboured, he felt the odd sensation of his heart pumping blood through some torn vessel into his chest, collapsing his lung. He tried again to get to his feet, but his legs had become unwilling lumps of clay, and he cursed as gravity dragged him back to the ground once more. Eventually he managed to roll onto his belly and tried to crawl toward the village, but he had only gained a few feet when—in his last moments alive—he had an awful flash of insight. Once dead, he would without doubt rise again as a flesh-eating demon, as his friends had before him. Inevitably, he would be drawn toward the tribe like a moth toward a flame.

Instead of being his people's saviour, he would be their ruin.

It now took supreme effort to move his arms to try to draw his dagger. If he could bring himself to cut his own throat . . . but his strength was fading and his hand would not obey him when he tried to bring the knife up. It slid from his grasp, and his trembling fingers could not pick it up again.

Shimmers of bloodlust ran through him, like ripples crossing the surface of a pond, as death slid like a maggot under his skin. His parched lips, desiccating as his life's blood drained into his chest, thirsted not for water, but for blood—fresh and warm and dark.

The vulture cocked its head as the dying human emitted a long moan and then lay still. It watched for several minutes, detected no movement, and then flapped once, dropping from the cactus to alight at the dead man's side. Habitually wary, it stepped around the carcass, head bobbing up and down. Finally, hunger overcame caution and it jumped onto the corpse. Satisfied that this produced no response and that the human was well and truly dead, it stretched down to rip its first bite from his arm. Then, just as beak touched skin, it stopped, blinking rapidly and then jerking its head back, wings flapping in confusion.

The corpse did not smell like food anymore. It smelled . . . bad . . . tainted.

The dead man began trembling beneath the vulture's feet, limbs jerking spastically.

Squawking alarm, the vulture took to the air again, circling the reaper as its movements became more purposeful. By the time the bird had become a distant flicker in the sky, Turak's corpse, after some faltering attempts to stand, had gained its feet.

Hunger drove it now. It caught the scent of fire and meat and turned toward the village, seeing nothing of what Turak would have seen—friends, family, memories of a life. The curse had washed it all away.

Ravenously hungry, the reaper moved forward.

*** 

Brennan saw the horses first, five of them milling around by the river ahead of them. He pointed and reined in his own mount, and after a moment Solenne followed suit. Together, they moved forward at a more cautious pace.

"Apache horses." Brennan's eyes narrowed. "I think I recognize them, same ones as chased me. No riders though. Where—"

"I see the riders."

"What? Where—"

But then Brennan saw them too, slightly behind the horses but plainly visible now as the two rode over the rise. One was standing almost motionless, looking away from them and weaving slightly like a tree swaying back and forth in the breeze. The second was bent down on his hands and knees as if in prayer, face pressed against the earth. He appeared to be eating or perhaps licking something off the ground.

"What the hell are they doing?" He turned toward Solenne and saw she had holstered her pistol and drawn her rifle out of its sling. "Hey, hold on."

Solenne kneed her horse in the ribs, and it cantered forward as she brought the rifle up.

"Wait."

The sound of their conversation had carried and caused the creatures to turn their way. Solenne paused but did not lower the gun. "Why?"

Brennan hesitated, at war with himself.

"They've turned." The creatures were moving toward them now. "They're not human any longer. They are walking dead."

"Ah, shit . . . ."

"Even if you don't believe me, didn't they try to kill you?"

"There is that." Brennan reflected. "But if they're sick . . . Just doesn't seem fair somehow."

The Apache nearest to them had begun an ungainly lope at what was obviously the best speed it could manage with its dead and misfiring nervous system. The one that had been kneeling on the ground was getting to its feet.

Solenne took her eye briefly from the rifle sight to glance over at Brennan. "Kinda looks like they want to meet us pretty bad, wouldn't you say?"

Brennan was squinting at the things lurching toward them. As they got closer, their lack of humanity became more and more apparent. What he had at first thought was ragged clothing was visible now as torn skin, hanging in shreds here and there on faces and arms, but no blood flowed from the wounds in the things approaching them, and now he could hear inhuman, toneless moans and growls.

Brennan raised his pistol as the creatures surged toward them at greater speed, mouths stretched open as if in terrible hunger. The nearest of them drooled brackish saliva, staining its lower face. It snarled at him and more of the black fluid sprayed from its mouth.

Brennan locked eyes with Solenne. "Guess you aren't crazy after all."

"This rifle's getting kinda heavy. Let me know if you need a closer look. You know, just to be sure . . . ."

"Reckon not." Brennan shot the closest man—*Reaper*, he thought, *reaper . . . not a man*—twice in the chest. The two black circles that bloomed just above the creature's left nipple spat dark yellow gore but no blood. The thing faltered briefly, thrown off balance by the force of the bullets, but after a moment carried on as before.

"Head," Solenne said. She looked down the barrel of the rifle again, training it on the second monster. "Gotta shoot 'em in the head."

She fired, and Brennan saw her shot smash through the forehead of her target and explode out of the back of its skull in a spray of reddish-grey matter tangled with tendrils of darker material. The creature dropped, rolling once in the sand before lying still.

"Right."

The creature he'd shot in the chest was only about twenty feet away now, and Brennan settled himself in the saddle and took careful aim. His shot struck precisely between the thing's eyes, and it pitched forward, tumbling before skidding to a halt so close to the feet of his horse that the animal danced back a step, whinnying in fright.

Brennan stared down at the thing he'd just shot. Its grey-yellow skin was ragged and torn, like the thing had been dragged over a washboard of sand and rocks. Black spiderweb lines criss-crossed all of its exposed hide, and its yellow-fogged eyes stared back up at him as if even in death the thing still hungered. With an effort, he restrained himself from shooting it again.

"Looks deader than most dead people I've seen." Brennan holstered his gun. "Guess I owe you an apology."

Solenne shook her head. "It's a tough story to credit."

"So, if that thing had got me, it really would've—"

"Would've cracked your bones open and sucked out the marrow if you'd given it half a chance."

"Hell."

"But just the same, I *am* glad you didn't have to see it *too* much closer before you shot it."

***

Quinto, still thundering ahead of the main group, slowed his horse and tilted his head as if listening for something, then turned back to join those behind him, again falling into place beside Johnston and yelling to him over the noise of the galloping horses.

"Gunshots ahead! Maybe a mile or two away!"

Johnston grimaced. "Hellfire and damnation! If she's killed the last of them, I'll whip the skin off her bones . . . Barrett! Lewis!"

The two men rode up and Johnson pointed forward and yelled. "We're almost upon them. Lewis, drop back through the ranks and get the first wave ready. Guns *holstered!* Anything that's upright and moving, throw nets over it. Just as we planned, got it?"

Lewis nodded, his *yessir* barely audible over the riotous background noise of hoofbeats, and waited for the threat that accompanied every command issued along these lines. He was not disappointed.

"And warn the men. This may be our last chance. Anyone who fails to follow orders will not live to see the sun set tonight."

Lewis nodded and dropped behind to ride down the ranks.

"Barrett!"

"Colonel."

"You'll ride close to me. If for some reason there is gun work needed, it will come from you. Understand?"

Barrett knew that "if there is gun work needed" meant if Johnston himself was in danger, but he did not hesitate to answer. "As you say, sir."

Johnston grinned at Barrett. "This is a great day, Captain. If we succeed, this will be the beginning of the end for the Union."

Barrett had heard this many times before during the troop's chase back and forth across this hellish desert, tracking the mysterious girl and the creatures Quinto claimed she pursued and killed. He had seen enough of the aftermath of the woman's passage to credit at least some of what Johnston said. Humans apparently torn apart by other humans. Corpses that seemed weeks dead with what looked like recent gunshot wounds. Wounds that were always in the head. And the locals always had the same stories of madmen who attacked others as if rabid dogs—violent, raving lunatics who were almost impossible to kill.

What Barrett had never been sure of was how tracking the source of any of these bizarre oddities could possibly help the South's fight against the Union. It was true that, from the rumours he had heard, there was no question the Confederacy *needed* help. It was always possible things had changed for the better—news travelled slowly to the frontier— but every scrap of information he'd heard before they'd set out suggested the Union was winning battle after battle, grinding the South under its heel, while Confederate forces were said to be stymied, battle-worn, and starved of supplies and food.

Barrett had tried a half-dozen times over the last month or so to tease Johnston's plan out of him, but the colonel had only smiled and assured him that their mission was crucial to the cause and that this—of course—was all any *loyal* man need know. When he'd heard *that*, Barrett had known enough to shut up.

He saw Johnston watching him now, as if reading his mind, and he gulped away his train of thought. After a second the colonel turned to Quinto, and Barrett found himself grateful the man's eyes were away from him.

"Lead us to them," Johnston barked.

\*\*\*

The Apache tribe lived in rough and dangerous country. It had always been so, but in the last decade, the dangers had mounted. There had always been other communities that might want their weapons, their women, or simply their territory. Now the whites were invading too, wanting all that and everything else they could lay their greedy hands on. Part of the reason the tribe had survived so long in such conditions was that there had always been sentinels on horseback wandering the perimeter of the camp day and night, watching for danger.

It was one of these watchers the Turak-creature first encountered as it staggered into the camp that morning.

Almost everyone in the village called the guard on horseback *Bruised-Head* because of a large purple birthmark covering the left side of his face. He accepted this nickname agreeably as that was his nature. So when Bruised-Head saw Turak limping toward him, his first impulse was to smile and tease the warrior about losing his horse. It would be a matter of great sport for months whenever Turak was around the evening fire. Then he realized his friend of many years looked distressed and wounded and that none of the men who had left with him were in sight.

"Turak!" Bruised-Head yelled at the thing coming toward him and then turned and shouted the name back toward the tribe too, unsure if anyone had heard him.

Bruised-Head got off his horse and waited for Turak. He looked . . . odd. Bruised-Head had seen many wounded warriors in his life. He had seen men with arms or legs crushed, broken and half-torn off; men impaled by arrows; and warriors lying like bathers in the middle of a red puddle of their own gore, panting the last of their lives away between lips turned blue, their skin pale as ghosts.

Turak looked worse than any wounded man Bruised-Head had ever seen.

There was a yellow cast to his skin, and he was covered in blood and some other kind of dark gore. His upper body was torn as if by the claws of a cougar, flesh hanging in ribbons from his face and torso. As the man got closer, Bruised-Head could see that his eyes were fogged and looked sightless and that there was more black fluid leaking like tears from them.

The Turak-thing opened its mouth, and Bruised-Head watched the lips pull impossibly far back over elongated teeth as the creature growled at him.

"Turak?"

Bruised-Head took a step back and reached for his axe. Despite a natural hesitation to hurt a lifelong friend, he might have successfully defended himself if he had not been suddenly distracted by whinnying and snorting from his horse as it caught wind of the dead thing. He himself caught the same scent seconds later, a stink of decay almost incomprehensible in its intensity.

And then the dead thing was unexpectedly close, running toward him with bony hands stretched out like the claws of a predator.

The creature slammed into him, and Bruised-Head fell below it, his axe and his right hand trapped behind his back as the monster pinned him to the ground. He felt the thing close its teeth around his throat as he wriggled beneath it like a deer struggling its last moments away under the jaws of a lion.

Cold teeth tore into his skin, and he felt the creature shake its head to drive them deeper into his flesh as he struggled beneath it. Bruised-Head was left wondering why there was no pain as his throat was torn apart. With already-dimming eyesight, he saw the creature on top of him slurping and choking as it swallowed the piece of flesh torn from his throat with obvious abandon. Arcing jets of blood that Bruised-Head was vaguely aware came from torn vessels in his neck obscured his fading vision. More sloppy chewing sounds, and he felt another ripping tug and some brief pain that signalled the second bite, but the sensation receded rapidly into the growing darkness.

***

Brennan and Solenne rode in to what had been the Apache braves' campsite and immediately saw two bodies lying on the ground. Brennan immediately recognized and pointed out one to Solenne as the remains of Jake, his body dragged away from the camp. He appeared to have been scalped, though whether in his first encounter with the Apaches or after his later resurrection, Brennan could not be sure.

The other was the man who had once been Burin. Brennan dismounted and examined both corpses while Solenne watched. To his experienced eyes, the bodies appeared weeks dead, but despite the amount of decay each superficially appeared to have undergone, he saw little dust or sediment on them. Their slaughter must have occurred only hours ago, and just like the two men Solenne and he had left dead less than a mile behind them, there was no evidence of blood leaking from the wounds—only a thin, oily gore that gave off an abattoir stink.

Brennan spat and got to his feet, waving his hand back and forth in front of his nose as he backed away from the body.

Solenne slid off her horse, briefly checking the corpse's for lethal head wounds before turning her attention to the mosaic of tracks and marks on the ground around them that told the tale of the life-and-death struggle that had occurred here.

"One got away." Her voice was barely audible to Brennan, as if she were musing to herself. Then, even more softly, she said, "One always gets away . . ."

Brennan absorbed this as he looked around the camp. His heart skipped a beat as his eyes lit on his saddlebags lying beside the remains of a fire. Beaten up and dusty though they were, they still bulged with the gold coins he had stuffed into them just a few days ago. He grabbed them up and shook the worn leather bags, obviously pleased by the weight and the sound of coins clinking together inside them.

"Gotta hand it to you, you were right about those men. It *was* like they were rabid. Maybe it *is* rabies, this thing?"

Solenne shook her head. "I've seen those things up close. They don't breathe." She shot a flat look at him. "They're dead things come back to life. It was my elders—not knowing what else to call them—that gave them the name *los segadors*—reapers." Her eyes were everywhere, searching. "And it's near enough true. They wipe out humans like death with a scythe."

"Hellish things, anyway." Brennan threw the saddlebags atop his horse, and the animal's resultant grunt suggested it was at best ambivalent at having the load back.

"Looks like it's all there, or most of it, anyhow. Hey, how 'bout we skip outta here and find some town that's got a decent saloon. I'll buy us some drinks and chow."

"There's one of those creatures missing. I have to find it."

"Then we'll get some grub and a good night's sleep, and you'll pick up his trail in a day or so."

Solenne shook her head with the dismissive, distracted look teachers reserve for the dullest of students, and Brennan noted with irritation that she wasn't even bothering to look at him and was still directing most of her attention to the ground.

"I just meant—"

"Brennan, you don't understand—" She stiffened. "*Mierda!*"

"What?" Brennan was distracted. He was attempting to climb onto his horse, but the beast was suddenly restless and shying from him.

"Two things."

Solenne pulled her pistols and raised them in opposite directions. She spun slowly, eyes darting like a hummingbird at everything around her.

Brennan's right hand moved down toward his own weapon. A glance to the west told him that the men following them were closing in. "I see the one thing, anyway . . . We'd best leave quick as possible."

"*You* should." Solenne strode with obvious urgency in widening circles around the campfire. "I can't. There's at least one more, maybe two. One left on horseback, going southeast."

Brennan had seen the departing hoofprints himself. "Okay . . ."

"How many horses did we see back there?"

Brennan's horse shook its head and whinnied, and Brennan reined it in absently. "Well, shit. Six. We killed two guys and there's two dead guys here. Maybe the last two went off together, or maybe—"

Out of the edge of his vision, Brennan caught the blur moving toward him from his right, too close and too late to do anything about it. The creature was on him as if out of nowhere, and he realized afterward that his horse had sensed the thing nearby and that he had ignored its unsettled state—partly because he was happily distracted at having retrieved his gold and partly because he was unhappily worried about the authors of the dust cloud approaching them. Much later, he would admit to himself that some portion of his distraction had likely been due to Solenne herself. For most of the morning, he'd found his eyes wandering toward her whenever he thought she wasn't looking.

When the creature rushed at him, Brennan's horse shied sideways and reared up, and he instinctively clutched at the reins to bring the animal under control. He heard rasping moans then, like wind rushing among dead leaves, and felt a sudden pressure as the reaper that had been Tyee closed its hands around his left leg.

"Shit!" Brennan's horse reared again, and he grabbed for his pistol as he struggled to stay on.

Solenne was running at him, guns up and firing. His horse came down hard, swinging its rear end around in an effort to get away from the predator clinging to Brennan's leg like a leech. He saw at least two of Solenne's bullets hit the reaper's legs, and he wondered at the fine marksmanship or simple dumb luck that caused her shots to miss both him and his pitching mount and to hit their attacker. Finally his own gun was out, and he swung it around so he could blow the creature's face off, but his horse's increasingly panicked gyrations made aiming almost impossible.

Solenne fired again, once more miraculously hitting nothing but the creature. Legs punctured by numerous bullets, it collapsed against Brennan, still clutching at him with the desperation of a drowning man. The creature had fastened a solid grip on his ankle now, and its weight and the pitching of his horse combined to drag Brennan out of his saddle. He fell to the ground on top of the reaper, his gun spinning out of his hand.

Savage with hunger and whirling like a dervish, the reaper clambered on top of Brennan as Solenne lost precious moments dodging around his panicked horse. Drool splattered out of the monster's yawning mouth and into Brennan's face, momentarily blinding him as the demon lunged for his throat. Brennan's hands shot up as he sensed the reaper move in close, and he managed to lodge an elbow under its jaw. Its skin felt cold and slimey, like that of an eel, and its stench of decay washed over him like a tidal wave. Even as he blinked the creature's secretions out of his eyes, he was keenly aware of its jaws snapping only inches away from his neck. He groped for his lost gun with his unoccupied hand.

And then there was a rapidly moving shadow above them. Solenne's gun was at the thing's head. She fired—

"Stop! No!" The voice came from far away.

Solenne's shot shattered the top of the monster's head, splattering grey matter and black-red gore over both of them. The creature slumped to the ground, a fist-sized chunk of its forehead gone, and—with some difficulty—Brennan pushed the limp monstrosity off him, trying to gain his feet as he wiped bloody black muck from his face.

More shouts erupted from westward, and Brennan struggled to clear his vision so he could see what new trouble was coming at them. He was rewarded for his efforts by the blurry vista of a group of Confederate cavalrymen racing down the hill directly at them.

Brennan saw Solenne frowning down at him, paying no attention at all to the shouting men behind her, as if the troop riding hell-bent toward them were a cloud of buzzing flies. Instead, gun held at the ready, she appeared to be looking him over with the same expression a cook might employ on finding that the dinner meat had gone rancid.

"You're bit."

"What?" Brennan said.

"Mistakes," Solenne mumbled, looking angry with herself, as if somehow she should have been able to prevent all this.

Solenne raised her pistol until it was pointed at Brennan's head. "I did tell you to leave, didn't I?"

Brennan looked into her blue eyes, icy chips of merciless computation. The shock of the attack was fading, and he could feel various aches and pains asserting themselves. But one singular sting was suddenly screaming for attention—on his left side just above his gun belt.

With some effort, he tore his gaze away from Solenne's eyes and looked down. His shirt was flecked with bloody black liquid and grey matter from the dead thing, but there was a larger patch of red blood—human blood—just above his waist.

"Halt what you are doing immediately or we will shoot!"

The voices were closer, but Brennan was ignoring them now just as Solenne had. His hands shook slightly as he pulled his shirt up, knowing what he would see before he saw it.

The reaper had bitten him. A shallow bite to be sure, but his blood was oozing from well-defined tooth marks on his lower belly. Perhaps the creature had got hold of him briefly as they tangled on the horse. Brennan supposed it didn't really matter. According to Solenne, bitten was *bitten*.

He turned his eyes to the pistol pointed at him, blinking rapidly. "Reckon you did mention leaving was a good idea."

"Halt immediately!"

Solenne sniffed and stared back at him, lips pursed, her eyes flickering back and forth as if her mind was racing, but the gun never wavered.

"Don't really wanna wind up like one of those things," Brennan said.

"Don't expect you do."

"Don't you do it, you bitch! Stop!"

"Friends of yours, I expect," Brennan said.

"Not exactly." The corners of Solenne's mouth twitched—what Brennan had decided counted as a smile. "I'm afraid this is going to hurt."

He tore his gaze from the blackness of the gun barrel, looked her in the eye, and said, "All right, then."

He closed his eyes and waited for nothingness . . . and waited . . . When the shot didn't come, he blinked and then opened his eyes again, astonished to see Solenne holstering her gun and turning away from him.

Then the troopers were all around them suddenly, racing to a stop in a flurry of sound and dust. He saw that some of the soldiers surrounding them had nets and—in what seemed to be a well-rehearsed manoeuvre— cast them over both him and Solenne and then quickly dismounted, grabbing up the tethers trailing from the netting.

"Not a shot, you hear? Not a shot, but I want her down! Put her down!"

Brennan fought against the netting and watched Solenne do the same. In his brief acquaintance with her, he had found that little seemed to surprise the woman, but even she seemed unprepared for this, and the soldiers were efficient and well drilled in their tactics. They hauled back on the tethers, drawing them tight as Brennan tried to get to his feet and Solenne fought to keep hers. He was almost upright when a tall, lean man pulled up—a colonel by his insignia—barely halting his horse before sliding off it. In the fine detail that Brennan imagined every condemned man saw, he noticed spittle covering the man's grey mustache and beard and realized that this was the person who had been doing all the shouting in the preceding minute or so.

A second later, a soldier ran forward and kicked Brennan in the side, and he fell. Another man reached through the netting and yanked his gun away, then kicked Brennan again for good measure. He watched the colonel rip his rifle out of its sheath and stride over to Solenne. She had been knocked down to her knees but was still fighting to free herself despite the many men heaving on the net, trying to bring her down. A rail- thin captain shadowed the colonel, holding what looked to Brennan to be a sniper's rifle as his gaze flicked everywhere at once.

\*

After the first two soldiers near her had earned punches in the face for venturing too close, others had grabbed Solenne's arms as they tightened the net. More hands reached for her guns. As she thrashed against them, in her peripheral vision Solenne saw movement, and with dawning horror she realized that the reaper she had shot in the head mere moments ago was—impossibly—rolling over and getting up on its hands and knees.

"Chingame!" she muttered, realizing with frustrated dismay that the wound she'd inflicted on the creature had only destroyed the front portion of its head. The dead thing was shambling up onto its feet again.

*Mistakes . . .*

Reapers were not driven by the higher, thinking part of the brain, which withered and died as the disease asserted itself. As long as the brainstem functioned to some extent, reapers could move and hunger . . . and kill.

Brennan had seen the creature rise too. "Watch out, you men!"

With difficulty, Solenne raised an arm, pointing behind the soldiers at the reaper wobbling on its feet like a drunkard. "Kill it!" she shouted.

All heads turned to follow her gesture. Soldiers who actually had experience fighting dead men might have taken the obvious precaution of casting nets even over men who appeared deceased. But these troopers had only training drills and cautionary tales to rely on, and in a flash Solenne realized many of them were like the long-dead warriors of her own tribe—young and overly convinced of their might and invulnerability.

"Kill it!" she shouted again.

The reaper seemed bewildered by the abundance of warm flesh that had sprung up around it while it had been incapacitated. The soldiers nearby watched the creature in growing shock as the realization sunk in that all the things their colonel had told them were actually true. This was a dead man come back to life—a rabid monster whose merest bite or scratch could doom them.

*

Barrett noticed that despite Johnston's warnings about the nature of what they were hunting, the thing's appearance was enough to render most of his soldiers immobile in disgust and horror. The Witch's shot had destroyed most of the monster's upper head so that remnants of torn brain matter dangled out of the impressive injury she had inflicted upon it. Dark liquid oozing from the lesion had stained its face and perhaps impaired what vision remained in its clouded eyes, but it seemed it could still smell warm blood in the moving shapes all around it.

The creature's fleeting confusion gave the cavalrymen near it a few precious extra seconds to get over their shock, draw their guns, and start to bring them to bear. Barrett was a heartbeat ahead of them, his rifle coming up to focus squarely on the thing's head.

"Halt! Halt, damn you!" Johnston screeched.

Barrett reflected afterward that Johnston's near-panicked scream would have made many men shoot simply out of reflex. He eased his finger back on his own trigger and waved at the other men to lower their guns. Those not on horses backed away from the creature, torn between the terror itself and the consequences they might face should they try to defend themselves from it.

It was a measure of the fear that Johnston commanded in his men when most of them felt compelled to turn away from the monster and toward the colonel's voice.

"Use the nets, men. Capture it!" Johnston yelled again, his voice a little less shrill now.

Several men were still on horseback, and Johnston's command seemed to force them out of their stunned reverie. Two of them unfurled a fresh net between them and moved forward. As they did, Johnston looked to Barrett, who stood like a statue with his rifle still aimed at the awakened dead thing like a machine waiting to be activated.

"Take its legs, Barrett."

Without hesitation, Barrett lowered his rifle and fired twice. The Witch's earlier shots had half destroyed the reaper's lower limbs, and now the creature's legs buckled as large chunks of bone and muscle were torn out of its knees, but it staggered forward nonetheless, its inhuman hunger driving it toward the men nearest it. Barrett could not help being startled, and he lifted his head away from his gunsight to stare in amazement at the monstrosity. He knew that his shots had hit—had seen the explosions of ochre gore and flesh as the bullets impacted the creature's legs. Any normal man would have collapsed to the ground in agony, disabled and thrown into shock, perhaps dying. This *thing* still shambled forward, an eager moan escaping its mouth as it moved toward its prey with a horrid determination.

The two mounted soldiers had stretched the net between them with an efficiency born of many weeks' practice, and they rode forward now, sweeping up the creature and bringing it to ground. The thing lay supine, pawing at the netting and growling but otherwise unable to move.

"Go on, men. Secure that thing."

At Barrett's command, the troopers on foot moved in toward the feral creature, glancing at each other with fearful eyes. Barrett could see they were weighing whatever threat the gibbering monster before them posed against Johnston's potential displeasure and determined there was no sane choice but to obey their orders. Still, all hesitated at first to draw too close. Then one man jumped atop the thing's legs, pinning them to the ground, and this seemed to embolden the rest, who similarly dived on to the clawing, snarling monster.

Johnston turned his attention away from the Witch and her accomplice toward the men engaged in capturing the creature. "That's it, men. Wrap it up good and tight. Hurry now!" He turned to Barrett. "Captain, make sure that thing's secured properly."

"Right away, sir."

Barrett dismounted and strode over to the wretched thing that roared and ripped at the netting encasing it, all the while snapping at any of the men who got too close to it. The monster's desperate spasms were quite obviously not intended to achieve escape. The demon longed only to taste the warm meat moving all around it, but after a few moments it was restrained so completely that it could barely move, though it continued to writhe uselessly in the twine, snarling in frustration.

"Good job, men. Excellent work." Johnston was grinning, turning as he spoke to take in all the men surrounding him. "You may not know it, but you have struck a blow for—"

His voice—and the grin—died as his eyes fell on the Witch once more.

*

Solenne had been captured a few times in the past—always briefly, mind you—by lawmen, bounty hunters, or outlaws. Given the life she had chosen, or perhaps more correctly the life that had chosen her, running afoul of such men was simply inevitable. Those who had caught her tended, once she was in their hands, to remember only that she was a woman and therefore, in their eyes, much weaker and less intelligent than they were.

They always tended to forget what she had done that made them want her in the first place.

The soldiers holding her had wrapped her tightly in the netting and taken both her guns, but once that had been accomplished, they had been distracted by the capture of the creature unfolding just a few feet away from them. Solenne observed that the smelly corporal holding her right shoulder was left-handed, his pistol holstered on his left side. Unwatched for a few precious seconds, she had wiggled her right arm free of the netting and found the gun within easy reach.

The colonel's eyes widened as he caught sight of her.

A pistol was in her hand, moving sideways to point at the monster, and her left eye closed—almost as if she were winking at it—as she aimed.

The colonel opened his mouth to yell at the men holding her, but his shout was drowned out by Solenne's first shot, which took off most of the monster's left ear.

"Stop her! Stop her, you idiots!"

He brought his own gun out and levelled it at Solenne but then hesitated as if unsure whether he could afford to kill her. He watched as Solenne's second shot sailed through the black hole of the creature's snarling mouth and blew out the back of its head.

Still enmeshed in the netting, the monster buckled and went limp, dead weight now against the hands of the men holding its bindings. Truly dead.

Too late, mere moments after the killing shot, the horseshit-smelling corporal whose gun she had taken punched her twice in the face. She briefly glimpsed the trembling, fearful rage on his visage before her vision blurred and the gun was yanked from her hand.

"Leave her be, you bastards!"

Brennan, yelling on her behalf. She took the smacks and grunts that followed to mean that the troopers had more than enough willing fists to go around for both their captives.

Her vision cleared and she saw a crowd of hostile, frightened faces looking down at her. They parted as the colonel came into her field of view, an animal fury having eclipsed the triumph writ upon his face scarce moments before.

Solenne attempted to rise and, with an effort, wrapped her lips around the words as she said, "G'morning . . . Colonel."

*

Brennan struggled to see what was happening, taking more punches and the odd kick from the soldiers around him as he twisted to watch the confrontation. He realized what the colonel was going to do a second before it happened, and he strained without result against the netting and soldiers beating him down. But he could only watch as Johnston lashed out with the butt of his rifle and caught Solenne square on the left side of the head.

Brennan was amazed to see that she remained conscious. Bleeding from her temple and lip, Solenne looked up at the colonel and spat at him, spraying a fusion of blood and saliva over his torso.

The colonel cursed and raised his rifle again.

"Hey, you yellow piece of shit."

The colonel froze and his head swivelled toward Brennan in the silence that followed his yell. Heart pounding and instincts for self-preservation having apparently deserted him in the wake of his bite wound, he continued, "Yeah, you, you piece-of-shit coward. How about you let me loose and you and me—"

"You, men!" the colonel fairly screamed. "I have to do every damned thing myself?" He wiped with one hand at the bloody spit staining the breast of his uniform and pointed at Brennan with the other. "Put. That. Man. Down!"

Brennan saw the colonel raise his rifle above Solenne again, and then he was among a hailstorm of kicks and punches. Head . . . gut . . . head . . . and blackness closed over him.

## Chapter Ten

Besides his old friend Bruised-Head, the Turak-thing managed to kill three others before the alarm was raised that morning.

The thing had burrowed into Bruised-Head's guts and begun to consume them when it heard giggling and laughter coming from the river north of the camp. Attracted to the noise, it abandoned Bruised-Head's corpse and pitched toward the stream. In moments, it found itself looking down the riverbank at four teenage boys playing in the river.

The quartet of friends had set out earlier in the morning, having told their elders they intended to fish. One of their fathers, a close friend of the Turak who was now gone forever, had rolled his eyes and promised the playful boys if they didn't catch at least one fish each, they would feel his bow across their backs.

The boys had slung lines into the deeper part of the stream and then waded into the shallows with spears. Fishing with a spear requires that the hunter stand still for long periods of time, scrutinizing the water below, ever alert for an unwary fish chancing by. Being teens, though, this activity quickly evolved into tricks, splashes, laughter, and screams as they began pushing one another into the water. They had done this before on many a summer morning. More often than not, they caught several fish, but on this day, their antics were a lure that attracted hungry death.

Drooling at the feast of warm flesh before him, the Turak-thing half fell down the riverbank and staggered into the nearest of the boys. Napi shrieked as the stinking creature dragged him down into the water.

At first the other boys thought this was simply more play and laughed in surprise and delight at this adult joining in to roughhouse with them. They recognized Turak—an admired and respected warrior—and it took several seconds for them to realize all was not well. He was covered in blood, his skin was a strange grey colour, and he was groaning and growling like a dying animal.

The other boys watched, stunned, as the Turak-thing darted a look at them—snarling—before plunging its head down into the water, mouth agape and lips drawn back. The boys saw Napi's struggles immediately intensify and bubbles erupt from the water around him. The water turned red, and the killer ripped its head up, spraying an explosive mix of water and blood into the air. The boys stared as the thing looked back at them through vacant, milky eyes, blood spilling over its lips as it gulped down flesh torn from their friend's throat. It still held Napi just under the water as it watched them, licking its bloodstained lips. Then quick as a snake, it darted down again, this time ripping a flap of bloody tissue off the dying boy's face. Surfacing again, it turned its dull eyes back on them as it chewed and swallowed, as if daring them to flee or attack.

Other boys, those raised in pampered surroundings, would simply have run. But these boys were Apache. The eldest of them—Kenoi—was the first to recover from the shock of what he was witnessing, and he rushed forward with his fishing spear, the war cry erupting from his lips an unconscious echo of his father's. He plunged his well-aimed spear directly into the creature's right chest with his full weight behind it, but the point of the weapon turned against one of the thing's ribs and tore only a shallow, bloodless rip across its side.

The boy immediately followed up with a kick to the creature's torso that knocked it sideways. Freed, Napi's lifeless body floated up just under the surface, blood leaking from the throat in a steady stream that stained the water around it as the river began to propel the corpse downstream.

The others followed the lead of their elder, jumping atop the creature and stabbing the thrashing thing repeatedly with their fishing spears, screaming all the while in fury at the attack on their friend.

Young though they were, the boys had all witnessed the effect of multiple spear wounds on both animals and humans and knew that the thing should be mortally wounded from the injuries they were inflicting upon it, and yet the creature under the water still struggled to rise.

Joze took a moment to aim, slipped his spear under the creature's lower ribcage, and jammed it upward, grunting with the effort of driving the weapon's point through the soft flesh up to where he knew the heart sat. This, he knew, would kill anything that lived, and indeed, the thrust threw the creature off balance and it slipped beneath the water.

At that moment, Joze's attention was drawn to the body of his little brother, Napi, as it floated downriver, so he did not note the lack of blood from the wound as his spear slipped out of it, nor did he notice that the creature was still moving.

A yell of churned rage and grief escaped him as he ran after Napi's body. Chachu and Kenoi spun to look, and Kenoi ran after Joze, stumbling through the knee-deep water to help him recover their companion.

Eyes riveted on his friends, Chachu hardly felt it when the creature—unfazed by what should have been deadly wounds—wrapped cold hands around his leg. It was only when he felt the thing's teeth pierce his flesh that he realized it was still a threat and attacking him now. Then a bony hand suddenly ascended in front of his face, and he screeched as the creature drew him down into its embrace.

Before Kenoi had even turned toward the cry of his friend, the monster had torn Chachu's belly open. It was yanking loops of bloody intestine from the ragged wound as the boy thrashed and screamed, trying to worm his way out of the creature's grasp.

Focused on his brother to the exclusion of all else, Joze splashed onward and plunged into the river, grabbing at Napi's body and flipping it over. Wails erupted from his mouth as he took in the empty eyes and the ravaged throat. He cradled his dead sibling and sought to wrench him from the river's grip and up onto the riverbank.

Kenoi heard Joze's yell but could not tear his gaze from the unfolding horror of the creature filling its mouth with the strings of bowel it had torn from Chachu, who now spasmed just under the water's surface in increasingly weak death throes.

"Kenoi—hurry! He is too heavy for me." Joze's voice held abject desperation, and Kenoi's darting glance could see both that Napi was dead and that in the time it would take them to drag the body to the bank, the creature would be done with Chachu and coming for them.

Kenoi opened his mouth to try to explain this, to plead with Joze to run with him back to the camp so they could warn their people, but no sound came out.

"Kenoi!" Joze was struggling with the dead weight of Napi's body, refusing to surrender it to the river.

Torn between running and helping his friend in what was obviously a hopeless cause, Kenoi could only whip his gaze back and forth in indecision. Then Kenoi saw the monster rise from the torrent on unsteady feet, releasing Chachu's corpse in favour of the still-live prey mere yards away, teasing at the thing's limitless hunger.

It fell and was almost swept off as it stumbled toward the other boys through the river's twisting currents, but it regained its feet and came on toward them, Chachu's blood staining its lower face and neck. When the thing turned its vacant stare on Joze, its moans singing of its boundless, desperate hunger, Kenoi could not help himself. He ran. Blindly at first, falling forward into the shallow water, and then with more purpose, scrambling on all fours to get out of the stream and up the riverbank. He was barely aware of the warm spill of liquid down his legs as his bladder let go. Knowing he was leaving his friend, knowing he had to warn the tribe, knowing he just had to get *away*.

Joze watched the thing approach as he pushed his dead brother toward the shore. His heart was pounding with rage and fear, but he felt the warrior tradition of his people strong within him. He stood up in the stream, let his brother's body go, and pulled his knife from its scabbard. Then, filling his lungs, he let loose a savage war cry as he charged forward to meet his death.

***

Only a few miles away, Private Edwin Sumner splashed water from the very same river onto his lower right arm with trembling hands.

*It's just a scratch.*

He could not be certain exactly when he'd acquired the wound, though he was fairly sure it had not been before he and his fellows had brought down the clawing, growling inhuman creature that the strange girl had then shot.

And it *was* only a scratch, surely nothing to be concerned about despite the stories the colonel had spun to them over innumerable nights in the desert. Sumner stared at the long thin break in the skin just below his elbow and tried to recall exactly how it had gotten there.

The monster had been spinning like a whirlwind in the net, growling and snapping like a rabid dog while he and the other men had worked to tighten the ropes around it. Before the girl had killed it, they had been pressing closer, trying to grab it and hold it still long enough to bind it securely.

Had it scratched him? He didn't think it was possible, but he could not be *sure*.

A cavalryman could easily sustain any number of minor injuries in the course of a day's ride. He and the men he served with were always covered with trivial bruises and cuts in various stages of healing. It was a routine part of army life.

He splashed more water over the cut, telling himself again that it was no different from many others he'd received in the course of his duties.

But . . . it *felt* different.

It felt *cold*, and it ached with a wrongness he could sense but whose nature he would never have been able to articulate. All cuts and scratches got red, but his whole lower arm seemed inflamed now, only hours after the encounter with the demon-thing. That seemed like more than coincidence.

Sumner heard the scrape of boots as someone descended the riverbank behind him, and he grabbed at his shirtsleeve, yanking it down over the wound. Then he plunged his hands into the river and splashed water over his face.

A fellow private, Rufus something-or-other, had apparently come to fill his canteen. Rufus smiled amicably at Edwin as he squatted down beside him and sank the battered copper container into the water.

"Hot as hell, ain't it?"

Edwin nodded and tried to smile. "Sure is."

But Edwin didn't feel hot. He felt cold.

\*\*\*

Brennan woke to pain and to the overbearing heat of what he estimated, after a glance at the sun, to be late afternoon. He was in a prisoner's wagon—essentially a wooden cage—and he regained consciousness slumped in the corner, his face resting against one of the corner supports. Opening his eyes (his left eye was swollen and would not open easily) presented him with a view of a prototypical army camp—

tents, horses, wagons, and men coming and going. He had seen such camps before, of course, but only through a telescope as he skirted around them.

Movement brought numerous specific signals of pain. His head throbbed a drumbeat in time with his pulse. His chest hurt where Solenne had kicked him the previous night. There were other aches and pains all over his body, the remnants of kicks and punches, but crying above them all was a hot arrow of agony in his belly where the creature had bitten him.

If Brennan had woken in such circumstances a scarce few days ago, he supposed he would have found himself lamenting his lost gold, along with the equally likely possibilities of being "drafted" into the Confederacy or hanged as a traitor to it. Given the way he'd sworn at the troop's colonel, hanging was far more likely, but perhaps only if they didn't dally much in arranging it. But after what Solenne had told him and, it had to be said, what he'd witnessed himself, he believed that whatever was in the bite of the reapers, as she'd called them, was working in him now. The midafternoon sun was certainly wont to be oppressive, but he could not help noticing that though he lay mostly in shade with a breeze was blowing over him, he still felt unbearably hot.

It was more than the sun. He was cooking up a fever.

He struggled to turn over and found that his wrists were shackled, with the chains running around one of the very stout pieces of wood that made up his cage.

"You up, motherfucker?"

Brennan looked over toward the source of the taunt and saw two men in dirty, tattered uniforms, who he imagined must've been appointed to guard him. One was a scared-looking rail-thin private with raggedy red hair and a mangy beard. The rifle he pointed at Brennan shook. Ratty redhead's companion was an older corporal who looked as if he had made it through the war without missing nearly as many meals as his fellows. He held his own rifle out in front of him as if he intended to use it as a club rather than a gun. He looked frightened, too, and was sweating almost as much as Brennan was. Brennan guessed from their nervous demeanour that the guards knew about the result of a bite from one of Solenne's reapers and had no desire to be contaminated by their prisoner.

"Got a tongue, motherfucker?" the corporal said, with a tremor in his voice that—by his eyes—he knew Brennan had heard, and Brennan immediately tagged the fat corporal as one of those men who respond to fear by abandoning thought and embracing aggression.

Brennan drew a long breath to speak, but this brought on a paroxysm of coughing. Each bark felt as if it were rattling his brain around his head, and it was a moment before he found he could say anything. "Afternoon, gentlemen." He attempted a smile.

This seemed to stymie the two soldiers, and Brennan took the opportunity to scan the camp in detail, trying to confirm his first impressions of his place in it while assembling his thoughts into some kind of order. His first judgment had been correct; he was on the camp's periphery. That was good. However, there were no signs of his guns, his gold, or an easily accessible horse. That was disappointing.

He supposed worrying about anything other than the bite on his belly was probably wasted effort, but habits were habits. He wanted to be free, on a horse, and away from these men, preferably with laden saddlebags.

With a flicker of guilt, he realized he had also seen no sign of Solenne, though for no reason he could name, he instinctively felt she must be in one of the large tents he could see in the centre of the camp.

His guards were still looking at him as if wondering what to say. He sighed. "Corporal, Private. I wonder if I could trouble you for a drink of water?"

When they did not reply, he added, "And maybe I could speak to an officer?"

The two men looked at each other for a long moment.

"Shut up," the fat man said finally. "Ain't no officer gonna come just 'cause you want to see 'em."

"Is he dead yet?" the skinny man asked the fat man. "Do . . . do they still talk after they turn bad?" He snatched his left hand from his gun to scratch his head, and Brennan saw one or two squirming lice fall from his greasy scalp and onto his shoulder.

"Don't know," Fatty said, not taking his eyes off Brennan.

"I ain't dead." Brennan did his best to hold on to the smile. "If I was, I'd be trying to bite you, wouldn't I? And I ain't. Right?"

Fatty said nothing, but Skinny gave a nervous nod.

"It appears we're agreed, then. Still alive. Really would appreciate some water, gentlemen."

Skinny squinted, apparently thinking this through as he scratched his head, and more lice fell wriggling from between his oily curls. Fatty looked irritated by the idea of the complexities that might be involved in giving a prisoner water—and all the more hostile for the inconvenience of having to think about it.

"Ain't got no orders in that regard," Fatty said after a moment, appearing proud at having remembered the sort of noncommittal reply he'd perhaps heard previously from a superior officer.

"But you ain't got any orders *against*. Am I right about that?" Brennan asked.

"That's true," Skinny said, eyes on Fatty.

"We ain't going near him, you hear?" Fatty shouted at Skinny before turning back to his prisoner. "You ain't tricking us. We ain't going near you."

Brennan darted a look around the camp once more. No one else was near enough to see what might transpire in the next minute or so. Given that, the appropriate reply came to him immediately. He spat on the ground in front of Fatty.

"Ah, now, I remember your mother wasn't quite so standoffish."

Silence followed as Fatty and Skinny chewed on these words. Skinny got it first and chuckled before he could stop himself. Fatty turned red after a moment or two and immediately swatted his companion in the face with the back of his hand, knocking the smaller man backward before turning his anger on Brennan.

"You fucking bastard."

Fatty stepped up to the cage and threw his rifle butt forward, aiming for Brennan's face. Brennan pulled aside as best he could, but the stock struck a glancing blow to his left cheek, sending a bolt of lightning through his head to join the steady storm already raging within it. Still, there was just enough length in his shackles to allow him to catch a firm grip on the rifle stock. He jerked backward as he kicked his left leg out between the slats of the cage, his boot catching Fatty just under the chin, slamming the man's jaws shut with a hard snap.

Fatty was caught off balance and off guard. Throughout his short service as a jailor with the Confederate Army, he had abused his share of prisoners without ever having had anyone fight back. He clawed for his rifle even as Brennan pulled it into the cage with him.

"Get him!" Fatty stumbled backward and slapped at Skinny's shoulder. The redheaded man shot desperate looks between Brennan and Fatty, then brought his gun up on Brennan as Brennan in turn brought his newly acquired rifle to bear on his captors.

"Calm down, fellas. Just want to get out of here. Now, Private, why don't you lay down that rifle and unlock these chains."

Brennan had no specific plan beyond getting out of his cage, but luck had brought him inept guards and experience had taught him that when fortune handed you a chance, you took it. Right now only two people in the camp knew he was awake. If he could get out of the cage and slip away . . . well, things became a bit unclear after that, but freedom could only be a step in the right direction. If he was dying, he would rather die a free man, even if it was by his own bullet.

There was one other thing he could do before that bullet, and that was try to free Solenne, or perhaps buy her some distraction so she could free herself. This thought was immediately followed by the realization that his impending death seemed to have imbued him with ridiculously gallant ambitions. Brennan smiled at the thought, never realizing the chill his grin sent through Skinny, who thought it meant Brennan was about to shoot him.

Shaking like a tree in a gale, Skinny had nevertheless managed to get his rifle aimed at Brennan, with Fatty shouting at him to shoot all the while.

"Now listen, there's no need for anyone to get hurt—"

Giving lie to any negotiation skills Brennan thought he possessed, Skinny chose that moment to pull the trigger, but all this action produced was a popping sound and a slight puff of smoke from the barrel. A misfire. Brennan was gratified but not particularly surprised. He had not known Skinny long but did not have the impression he was a man counted by his fellows as a capable soldier. Fatty grabbed Skinny's rifle out of his hands.

"Hey! Knock it off!" Brennan growled this in a whisper with what he hoped was great emphasis. Freedom demanded he pull off his escape without any gunfire that would alert the rest of the camp.

"*Listen to me*. I will blow both your fucking brains out unless you lay that gun down right this fucking instant. Hear me?"

Both guards paused, looking from the rifle pointed at them to the apparently malfunctioning one they now possessed.

"Okay," Brennan said. "That's good. Now drop the rifle." They hesitated, and he cocked the hammer on his own weapon. "Go on, now . . . You got to know I ain't the least bit interested in anything but getting free, so—"

Brennan choked as he felt the cold edge of a sabre at his throat. He debated trying to fight. It made some sense to get himself killed *before* his favourite food changed from steak to raw human. Being decapitated by a sabre might spare him the nightmare of rising again, but his natural instincts still found him ambivalent about imminent death.

The sabre slid, featherlight, across his neck as he cleared his throat and played the last card he had. "I swear to God, I'll shoot these two men before you cut my throat."

"Please do try, sir. I may have them shot myself, in any case. They are obvious incompetents."

Brennan's eyes flickered to Skinny and Fatty. They looked terrified, obviously not at all in doubt that this might in fact be their fate. The voice behind the sabre spoke again.

"I have no intention of killing *you*, sir. Not as yet. Although if I must, I will dismember you and wound you to a great degree—just so long as I can watch you become one of those creatures your woman friend killed this morning."

Brennan considered this, and then he lowered the rifle's hammer and, with slow, deliberate moves, pushed the gun back out of the cage. Fatty grabbed for it, but it fell to the ground and he scrambled after it, fumbling for a moment before it was in his hands again.

The sabre drew back from Brennan's neck, but not slowly. It slid away with a gradually increasing pressure that forced Brennan's head back against the wooden slats of his cage to avoid being cut.

When the blade was gone, Brennan turned to see the same

Confederate colonel who had ridden them down that morning looking him over with the detached eyes of a butcher judging a cut of meat. He was swinging the sabre back and forth as if undecided about whether he might yet make use of it.

"Barrett! Lewis!" The tall, thin man with the sniper rifle that Brennan had seen alongside the colonel that morning stepped up beside him and snapped off a salute, and a slightly shorter man with a uniform as near to immaculate as any he had ever seen in the field stepped up beside the first.

"Mr. Lewis. These two men"—Johnston indicated Brennan's guards—"are, in my judgment, inferior soldiers. If they cannot be trusted to guard a sick, unarmed man who is both caged and chained, I'm not sure what other use I might make of them."

Barrett saw the two men start at that. They had both seen "what other use" Johnston made of soldiers who displeased him.

Lewis waited with practised patience while Johnston appraised the two guards. Every officer in the army knew that conscripts, though generally loyal, received little if any training. But in theory, at least, Lewis was responsible for the performance of all the men below him in the camp. In the previous weeks, there had been many drills and much instruction from the sergeants and experienced officers, but in the end, it was the quality of the metal that made the sword.

Many of those who joined the Confederacy—draftees and volunteers alike—were simply not cut out to be soldiers, and no amount of training would make up for their lack of natural talent for it. Such men, if they could do no other job well, were typically placed on the front lines and used quite literally as cannon fodder. But even such valueless soldiers should have at least been able to guard a chained man. It was the responsibility of their superiors to see to such things. Therefore, it fell on Lewis's shoulders that they had failed in even this simple task.

"Well, sir? Do you agree?"

"Yes, sir." Lewis snapped.

Brennan cleared his throat. "Excuse me, Colonel."

"Be quiet, you imbecile!" Lewis was red-faced with outrage at the source of his embarrassment daring to speak so freely with his colonel, but Johnston waved at Lewis as if shooing away a gnat, and Lewis stiffened into silence.

"Go ahead, Mister . . . ?"

"Brennan."

"Go on, then, Mr. Brennan."

Almost any movement hurt Brennan now. His joints ached with what he decided rheumatism might feel like, but he turned as directly toward the colonel as he could, given the shackles digging into his wrists. Light-headed with even this small exertion, he was breezily aware that the fever had made him feel drunk, and just as when he'd had a few whiskeys, he was becoming more talkative than usual—and too glib for his own good.

"Colonel, as I suspect you've guessed, I'm no kind of good man. I expect these two fellows just—"

"Underestimated you."

"Colonel—"

Johnston darted forward, and the sabre was suddenly back at Brennan's throat, the point imbedded expertly just under the skin. Brennan flinched. He could feel a trickle of blood erupt around the point of the blade and run down his neck, ticklish and hot even over his feverish skin.

"Not another word, Mr. Brennan. As I have said, I will not kill you. Whatever disease makes those bitten turn into rabid creatures, I won't risk ending it before it has worked its way into you." Brennan saw the colonel's gaze dart down to the bloody spot on his shirt that marked the bite he wore beneath it. "But I can make you feel a great deal of pain before you die. I may have questions for you, and if I do, by God you'll have answers for *me*. But I do not desire any . . . *conversation*. Understand?"

Brennan took a long measuring look at the colonel. He recalled Solenne saying something about there being monsters behind them as well as in front, and he reflected that she should have been a tad less vague about what that meant. He nodded—barely a twitch lest the sabre bite deeper into his throat.

Johnston chuckled and withdrew the sword as quickly as he had employed it, drawing the cut he had inflicted under Brennan's chin into a thin laceration that opened an inch under his jawline, oozing blood that Brennan sought to arrest by tucking his neck against his shoulder.

Brennan's experience was that not many army officers wore sabres anymore. They were considered relics by most. Those who did employ them tended to use them as clubs for breaking bones, not as a traditional cutting and slicing weapon. Johnston, though, had kept his sword razor-sharp, like a warrior of another time.

The colonel continued watching him as if eagerly awaiting the moment when the curse would overtake him, but Johnston directed his voice to the men behind his back. "Mr. Lewis, as I was saying . . ."

"Yessir."

He waved his sabre at the guards, who Brennan guessed were disappointed to be back at the focus of the conversation.

"Can you think of a way we might stimulate these two gentlemen to be more attentive to their duties?"

Barrett stared stone-faced at Johnston and Lewis, but Brennan noticed that he swallowed hard and suspected these men were destined for some substantial punishment.

"I can, Colonel," Lewis said.

"So can I. A horsewhip. Two hundred lashes."

Lewis stood stunned. Brennan snuck a look at Barrett and saw the same muted astonishment on his face.

Flogging had been outlawed in the military years before the war. Cowardice, insubordination, brawling, theft, and desertion were common crimes in the Southern armies. Likely in the North too. Johnston had previously utilized the accepted practices of gagging, twenty-four-hour guard duty, demotion in rank, and thumb-tying to punish his men. Only recently had he begun the beastly experiments with corpse bites, which were in effect a death sentence, it now appeared. But flogging was unheard of. The bullwhip and cat-o'-nine-tails were now thought more likely to *cause* mutiny than effect discipline in the ranks.

"Sir—" Lewis began.

Johnston's look was ice. "Something to say, Lieutenant?"

"Sir, whipping . . ." Lewis's voice petered out like a clockwork toy running down. Brennan suspected arguing was useless.

"You're quite right, Mr. Lewis. Two hundred lashes are more of a mercy than anything, given the nature of the offence. We must preserve discipline. Four hundred lashes, then. See that the men are assembled to watch. Understand, Captain?"

"Yessir."

Brennan watched as Lewis caught Barrett's eyes as he turned. Both men's eyes possessed the same dark, defeated look.

Lewis shot a finger toward the two failed guards. "You two—come with me."

"While you're at it, Mr. Lewis, I have a job in mind for Lieutenant Chapman. He'll need five or six men to go with him."

"Right away, sir." Lewis looked puzzled. "May I ask, sir—"

"We have a train to catch, Mr. Lewis," Johnston said. "By my reckoning, the south Arizona line begins its run not more than a four-hour ride north of us. You will instruct Mr. Chapman to take his men up there ahead of us and see to it that we . . . have seats upon it."

Brennan was vaguely aware that the south Arizona line was part of the Arizona and New Mexico Railway, a fledgling narrow-gauge rail line that had been completed only a few years before. As far as he knew, it ran north into Phoenix and from there west to California, but this knowledge did nothing to further his understanding of his colonel's interest in it.

"Commandeer the train, sir?"

"Yes, Captain. By my recollection, a train passes through there once every day, and please tell Mr. Chapman if it isn't waiting for us and under his control when the rest of the troop arrives tomorrow, I will be very disappointed."

Lewis nodded. "Very well, Colonel."

Johnston turned to Barrett and gestured to Brennan. "Captain, watch this man for a moment, will you? I'm sure Mr. Lewis will send you some guards we can trust."

Lewis nodded at Barrett and left, shooing the two men he had been tasked with punishing in front of him.

"You understand of course, Mr. Barrett, that I want this man kept alive no matter what. If you see any signs he's changing into one of the monsters, have the guards send for me."

"Yessir."

Johnston turned back to Brennan and darted two stabs in his arm with the sabre. Brennan swore and rocked back as blood began flowing from the new wounds.

"Still bleeding red, I see. Not turned yet, then." He cackled. "Got your attention, do I boy? I'll be back shortly to talk to you. Likely you just got caught up in all this, but I never like to leave loose ends."

Johnston laughed outright this time and swept his arms up to the sky, sabre swinging. "That witch thought she had me beat, but *you*"—he pointed his sabre at Brennan's face—"are going be part of a most glorious deed. The defeat of the Union and the unification of a *rightful* and *lawful* Confederacy. You cannot realize it of course, but you are part of history. I have foreseen it and—"

Brennan had seen one or two megalomaniacs before, and the pain and fever loosened his tongue again. "Colonel, I think you've been out in the desert sun a bit too long."

Johnston feinted at Brennan and chuckled when he flinched back. "Don't forget I can cause you a bucketful of pain afore you die, boy." He smiled wider and walked away, laughing in a way that left no doubt in Brennan's mind that causing him pain was an entirely enjoyable prospect.

"Hey!" Brennan shouted.

Johnston turned, his expression flat.

"What happened to Solenne? The girl."

Johnston smiled. "She's the prize, isn't she? Despite her interference in all this." To Brennan, Johnston's eyes had the tinny glaze of the insane. "Chased her halfway across this godforsaken land, but she's the prize. I know it. May just take a little . . . persuading . . . to get her to enlighten me."

"What's that supposed to mean?"

Johnston was striding away and waved a hand dismissively as he shouted back over his shoulder. "Barrett, make him be still, will you?"

"What're you gonna do to her?" Brennan was startling himself even in the haze of his fever. Was he already delirious? Drunk and floating, he wondered where his instinct for self-preservation had gone. "You touch her and I'll cut your heart out and make you eat it."

Out of the corner of his eye, Brennan saw Barrett stepping forward with his gun butt raised, and that instinct for self-preservation suddenly reasserted itself. "Now wait—"

Barrett pulled back on his strike, but the wooden stock still hit hard, catching Brennan in the chest and angering the rib that Solenne had perhaps broken earlier. The coughing spell that followed left him helpless on the floor of the cage, and for a moment he thought he would pass out. After a while he found that he could take middling breaths with only small stabs of pain. He became aware that blood continued to seep from the cuts Johnston's blade had made, and he struggled to pull his shirt up and bunch the loose cloth against his wounds.

"Nothing personal, mister."

When he looked up, Barrett was staring at him, arms crossed and rifle between them. His eyes were cold but held none of the insanity that Johnston's had.

Brennan sat up slightly and wheezed. "Hard"—*cough*—"not to take it that way."

"Just the same."

"All right, then."

\*

Barrett considered the man in the cage. He was familiar with the type. No kind of desperado, but certainly a man who was always at least one step over the line on the wrong side of the law. He could probably choose a fast horse, play cards with a skill that others saw as cheating, and handle a gun well enough that anyone who called him a cheat didn't profit much from it.

Barrett had been much like this man before he'd joined the Confederacy—a drifter with some skill with a gun but few prospects as a law-abiding citizen. Then one day he'd encountered a bunch of Red Legs—criminal gangs who looted and murdered in the name of the North—marching into a town they regarded as filled with "Southern sympathizers," and he had seen the carnage they had left in their wake.

Barrett had had a good view of the massacre. He had been lying on a rise just a mile or so out of town, his life's blood leaking from him, courtesy of several pistol shots to his legs. He had been taken unawares and left for dead by the Red Legs on their way into town. Lying there, he heard the screams and gunfire and saw men, women, and children shot down in the street. The slaughter played out in front of him like some macabre play as he tried to save himself, binding his wounds with makeshift bandages. By nightfall, the town was afire.

The blaze and the cries of terror and pain waxed and waned through the night as he swam in and out of consciousness. With the horizon lightening, he came to and saw the fires dying. A terrible silence came with the dawn.

Dizzy and barely able to stand, but with no bones broken and his bleeding mostly halted, he staggered into town. Bodies lay scattered along the main street, mostly shot, some run through with swords. All dead, anyhow. Murder, rape, every building set afire. People—children, even—had been burnt alive inside their hiding places.

The blood loss he had suffered ignited a desperate thirst in Barrett, and he stumbled to a horse trough, falling to his knees and plunging his face into the stagnant, filthy water, slurping and gulping it down as if it were as tasty as fine wine.

Only when his belly was distended did he open his eyes and see something floating at the other end of the trough. When he lifted himself up, he saw that it was the corpse of a baby, eyes fogged and half-open, staring up at the indifferent sun as it bobbed around in the water with flies buzzing about its open mouth. A woman's body lay not far away, quite obviously dead as dirt as flies buzzed all about her as well. The babe's mother? She had been shot in the head. In all the years since, Barrett nurtured a hope that she had died before the Northerner scum had tossed her infant into the water to drown.

For most of his life prior to that moment, Barrett had lived much as he imagined the man in the cage had—shaving an illicit livelihood off the edges of productive society. But on that day by the water trough, he'd seen that even a man living on the wild side, if he really was a *man*, had to stand up for something. He had joined up with the next Confederate unit he'd met.

Barrett was good with a rifle and a natural, if reluctant, leader. He had wandered through several assignments and promotions, developing an unequalled reputation as sharpshooter and commander. Johnston had handpicked him, and at the time Barrett had seen in the colonel something he greatly admired—a man willing to do whatever it took to defeat the North.

But that had been many weeks ago. Barrett had since seen what "willing to do whatever it took" actually meant to Johnston, and he had caught himself wondering more than once if the unknown murderer of that baby in the trough had also been a man willing to do *whatever* it took.

Brennan coughed and spat, drawing Barrett away from his reverie. "What will he do to her?"

Barrett considered not responding at all, but he found it hard to begrudge a dying man—especially one in whom he saw something of himself—some simple conversation.

"I'll be honest, mister. He's been chasing after her for some time. She's been killing all these . . . monsters he wants to get his hands on. And he's not a man who handles frustration well."

"And what's he want some rabid monster for, anyway?"

"I'm not privy to all his plans. But I do know she has been a sore frustration to him." Barrett paused. "Guess what you really want to know is if he's gonna hurt her."

"Is he?"

Barrett gave the thought some consideration. "Seems like he thinks he needs her. The whole company was told their lives weren't worth a thousandth of hers, or one of those creatures. Don't think he'll damage her if he can help it."

Brennan seemed to consider that. "*Can* he help it?"

Barrett pursed his lips. "Truth is, he wants what he wants and he usually gets it. He doesn't mind how."

"Figured as much." Brennan spat again and Barrett saw that what landed on the ground was blood-flecked.

"The way Johnston tells it, those that get bit . . . ?" Barrett said, the question clear in his voice.

"Far as I know, from what she told me, every man jack who gets bit by one of those . . . reapers, she calls them. Everyone dies of it and turns into one of those things."

Barrett thought again of the creature they'd captured that morning. "Well, I'm sorry about that. Truly am. Wouldn't wish it on any man."

"Thanks." Brennan struggled to roll onto his back and then stared up at the wooden planks that made up his cell's ceiling. "Fair warning. Don't care much for your crazy colonel—"

"Don't be saying that, mister."

"You saying he's not crazy?"

"I'm saying . . . I'm saying, don't say it."

"Just the same. Fair warning. Might just have to break outta here and see if I can't mess up his plans a little, before I die and all."

Barrett watched as Brennan adjusted his position in the cage, then grimace as the movement seemed to awaken pain throughout his body.

"Appreciate the warning, mister," Barrett said. "But we both know that ain't gonna happen."

"Oh, you never can tell. I drew four aces once in a straight game of poker."

Barrett offered him a wane smile. "I see your new guards heading this way. They're capable men. Suggest you don't try anything with them."

"Aww, they ain't gonna kill me no matter what, anyhow." Brennan's laugh lurched into a racking cough.

Barrett watched the other man hack and spit up more blood. He thought Brennan's skin had a tinge of yellow to it now, and sweat dripped off him in a torrent despite the shade of the cage and the breeze. Barrett didn't feel especially hot, but Brennan looked like he was on fire with fever. He unslung his canteen and passed it into the cage.

"Want some water?"

This sparked laughter in Brennan again, and Barrett had to wait for another coughing fit to pass before the man could take his canteen. "You know, all I asked Fatty and Skinny for was a drink of water."

"Guess they should've given you one."

Brennan rolled to his side and unscrewed the top of the canteen, sipping with great care between the rigours that shook him so as not to spill a drop. He managed to swallow several gulps of the warm water before he tried to pass the canteen back.

"You keep it," Barrett said.

\*\*\*

Joze had run as fast as he ever had in his life on his way back to camp, panting so hard he could taste blood in his mouth, but he arrived crying and ashamed after leaving his friend to die. Instead of raising an alarm, he had crawled into his family's teepee and hidden. It was nearly half an hour before his parents came across the boy and began questioning him.

The Turak-thing entered the outskirts of the village at roughly the same time Joze's parents were beginning to realize that something beyond a childhood prank had occurred. Joze had gone from sobbing to telling of a monster that looked like an Apache but that could not die and ate human flesh.

Even as his father shook him, his voice growing louder as his questions grew more insistent and frantic, the boy's story did not change, and eventually Joze's father began yelling for other warriors to gather their weapons. If Joze and his father had had just a few minutes more to properly warn the tribe, things might have turned out very differently.

If she could have, Solenne would have told Joze's father that recognition always played a large part in the spread of the curse. Those afflicted are often friends or family of those next victimized. Frequently they were caregivers to those dying of the infection. Even if strangers, people in the wilds might be leery of a man wielding a gun, but far less so of the cursed, who often appeared to be harmless addled drunks or those gone insane.

And so it was when the Turak-creature staggered into camp. The reaper he had become was still barely recognizable as one of them, as a friend and fellow warrior. This doomed them all.

First they tried to talk to the snarling, ravening thing. It ignored them and leapt onto the first man who came near it, driving its teeth into his face as it drove him to the ground. The man began to shriek, slamming fists into the creature atop of him as blood began fountaining from his torn cheek. Several villagers moved in and pulled the monster off the wounded warrior. Amid screams of terror and confusion, the thing turned on the first man's rescuers and quickly brought down another, a woman this time. Clawing her abdomen open in seconds, it tore loops of bowel from the bloody open wound and drew them to its mouth in a frenzy of gluttony.

A warrior stepped forward and swung his war club against the creature's head, knocking it away from the doomed, shrieking woman. The reaper staggered to its feet, hissing and snapping at the people gathered around it. Those watching saw that the club had caved in the right side of the thing's head and that it had sustained many other horrific wounds, all leaking black ooze instead of blood. Yet none of its injuries seemed to impair either its ability to attack or its appetite for human flesh. The reaper surged forward again, seeking new prey and the taste of the irresistible red liquid that flowed inside them . . .

But now the rest of the tribe—all having armed themselves now—moved forward to meet the creature. Their astonishment at the transformation Turak had undergone was put aside, and they raised their weapons and began to smash at the thing.

The reaper fell under the first few blows of clubs and axes but did not die easily. Legs shattered, it still scratched and clawed at those near it, desperate for the merest taste of meat. Its arms were then bashed into useless things, but it still growled and snapped as it sought to somehow move within biting distance of its prey.

The crowd of warriors moved in closer and began hacking at the demon's head, and in a few minutes the Turak-thing finally lay still, skull crushed, bones shattered, and yellow-grey flesh torn asunder. Black gore strewn around it as if from an explosion.

Annihilated though it now was, the reaper had nonetheless managed to bite or scratch many of those who had come together to slaughter it. The Turak-thing was dead, but the obscenity within it lived—a parasite squirming into all of those injured, growing like a cancer inside its new hosts. That afternoon, while a party of warriors ventured downriver to recover the bodies of the murdered boys, a fever sprung up in the camp in all those who had been wounded.

## Chapter Eleven

As the rifle butt sent her plummeting into unconsciousness, her mind's eye recalled—with astounding clarity—the arc her spear had made against the cloudless sky on that long-ago day.

She felt a simple but overpowering joy in judging wind and distance, in loosing her muscles in the savage movement of the throw and then watching the spear fly like a bird of prey to drop mercilessly down out of the azure sky.

The sky that Acalan said was the same shade as her eyes.

She rolled those blue eyes and laughed when he said it, punching him in the arm hard enough that he winced. There was little doubt Acalan had a crush on her.

It was her nineteenth summer, and Acalan—two years her elder—had agreed to teach her to hunt. In fact, she knew he had been chosen by the other men to act as her bodyguard since she had—in her adolescence—shown herself repeatedly to be far too precocious and headstrong to obey orders not to go hunting or do anything else she decided she wanted to do. By the time she was fourteen, even the Witch-woman could not control her and, to the rest of the tribe's frustration, appeared to have given up trying.

Everyone knew that the old Witch-woman would die someday and that Solenne—her apprentice—would take over as spiritual protector of the tribe. She was therefore far too valuable to be allowed away from the village to explore or hunt in the wide wild world around them, and she had frequently been specifically cautioned against doing such things.

Regardless, she disappeared for three days during her seventeenth year, slipping away in the night and returning with stories of having climbed a nearby mountain and of seeing a village far to the east battling a group of white men wearing strange blue clothing.

To the chief's consternation, the Witch-woman merely smiled and said this one was too strong to contain, but the chief was not satisfied with that and took his bow and beat Solenne's backside until it was red, telling Solenne all the while that she must learn her place in the world.

The very next day Solenne stole his bow and quiver. She was gone for nearly a week this time. She returned dirty and bloody, carrying half a dozen rabbits and dragging a freshly killed deer behind her.

The chief stomped up to her and she dropped the dead animals at his feet, and before he could say anything, she notched an arrow to the bow and put it into the trunk of a tree fifty feet away. She turned slowly, and in the next ten seconds drew and let loose six more arrows. Each found its mark in a tree, except for the last missile, which swept through a water gourd hanging outside a hut.

Perhaps one or two men in the village could have accomplished such a feat of archery with such accuracy, and those would have been bowmen for years.

Solenne had held out the bow and empty quiver to the chief and—in a respectful voice—thanked him for letting her borrow it. The chief had looked at her for a moment, livid with anger, and Solenne had looked right back at him with her lightning-blue eyes, and it was as though the electricity in them lanced his anger as if it were a boil.

The chief had laughed, snatched his bow from her, and walked away.

And so, Acalan—a compromise. Solenne could act like a warrior if she wished as long as she had some protection while she engaged in such foolishness. Solenne thought this silly, but Acalan was pleasant enough company and too bashful to be troublesome enough to tell her he loved her, though he quite obviously did.

The spear arced through the sky and landed amidst a herd of deer a hundred feet away, lancing through the chest of one of them. With the rest of the herd scattering around it, the wounded animal took two hesitant steps, coughed a spray of blood from its mouth, and collapsed dead in a cloud of dust.

Solenne was pleased—proud, even. She had been feeling unwell all day, and several times during the hunt, what felt like bolts of lightning had ignited in her chest. She had gasped at these jolting sensations, drawing disapproving looks from Acalan for what he considered her inability to remain silent during the hunt.

But now she was vindicated.

Solenne had only begun practising with a spear two days ago, and she saw Acalan trying to hide his astonishment at her preternatural skill with it as they butchered the deer with their axes and divided the carcass for their homeward journey.

They were gone scarcely twelve hours, leaving at dawn and returning as the sun kissed the horizon, but in that short time the universe had tipped over.

The curse had come again, and the blue-clad men had brought it this time. *Los segadors*—the reapers—had returned.

Much later Solenne had learned about the blue-wearing marauders—Americans—that had begun to run like bugs from beneath a toppled stone across the lands later called Mexico. An errant group of them must have come across the source of the curse upriver from her tribe. After it blossomed in them, they had come downriver, following the scent of the living beings that were—or had been—her tribe.

And Solenne had been away . . . Solenne the protector had been indulging her adolescent wish to prove herself at everything instead of guarding what was most precious to her, as every Witch-woman before her had guarded their people.

Solenne and Acalan stood at the top of the cliff that looked over the valley of their tribe and saw nothing but death and the hell that was death risen and feasting. Lurching shadows, shambling demon shades, moved among dying fires. Groups of monsters clustered on their knees, tearing and ripping at the last few still-living things squirming beneath them. Even as Solenne and Acalan watched, a partially dismembered body lying on the ground shuddered and began to move, struggling to its knees and immediately joining its fellows as they gorged on a nearby corpse.

In the darting shadows of firelight, Solenne saw a familiar figure get to its feet, a pale and ravaged ghost of the human she had been. The old Witch-woman—her mother—was risen from the dead.

Grief and anger warred within her and grew a hurricane rage, and Solenne went mad.

She ripped the war axe from her belt and flew down the trail to the valley below. Acalan followed, but he stumbled and fell on the steep trail as Solenne—always sure-footed—sailed on.

When Acalan reached the valley floor, Solenne had already begun her war on the reapers, and the love he felt for her drained from him as he watched her chew into the inhuman monsters like a dark, implacable force of nature.

The woman he saw as a smart, beautiful, gentle being became a blood-splattered demon herself now, screeching and roaring as she attacked. The axe she held flew through the air like a hummingbird, flitting back and forth among the moaning reapers almost faster than the eye could follow. Acalan watched the weapon explode through the lower jaw of a moaning soldier—the gold finery draped on his shoulders a match for his dusky yellow eyes—and saw the creature fold like a collapsing tent as the weapon was yanked away along with the thing's lower jaw. The axe then buried itself inches deep into the skull of a thing he recognized from another life as his uncle—a creature that now crouched, snarling, over the body of a young girl and spooned chunks of liver from her gashed abdomen into its black mouth. Acalan's uncle-become-demon collapsed onto the carcass of the girl it had been eating even as her tiny body twitched with the first stirrings of her own dark resurrection. The axe fell now between the girl's eyes, and they snapped open for a moment, opaque and staring up at the cobalt sky. Her mouth worked, began a moan, and then her face relaxed into the oblivion of true death.

Solenne did not hesitate to place a foot on the girl's forehead and lever the weapon out, pulling a chunk of brain and pieces of her fragile skull along with it. She was a whirling dervish now, sudden death in all directions as she slammed her weapon into anything that moved—for she and Acalan were now the only two living humans in the valley.

The reapers closed around her, attracted to the scent of her warm blood in the valley of cooling death. They clawed and snapped at her, tearing at her with their nascent claws, ripping clothing and skin alike. In the dimming light, her gore-stained muscles flashed as her constantly moving weapon snapped limbs and crushed skulls. Death came quickly to any of the reapers that got close enough.

Acalan stood watching her, dumbstruck, and she paused to yell at him.

"Kill them!"

He looked at her as she spun back to her savage work. Her face and body were splattered with red-black sludge, her own blood mixed with the putrescent oily fluids that spilled from the reapers she massacred. She was bleeding from a dozen gashes where the flailing demons had clawed at her, trying to bring her down beneath their teeth.

Acalan moved in, emulating Solenne, and in the dying light of the campfires, they brought final death to the undead.

The battle went on for hours. There was never any guarantee that a body on the ground was truly dead unless its head was smashed, the brain destroyed. Some of the newly killed rose within minutes, and others she had initially thought dead were still staggering to their feet hours later. Solenne knew the population of her own tribe, but she had no idea how many soldiers-turned-monsters lurked in the area.

She did not see Acalan go down under the reapers' claws, but she did see him later that night when he came for her, lurching out of the darkness with most of his neck eaten away and his eyes—eyes that scarce hours ago had looked at her with love—turned oily yellow.

She had been crying all night, tears of rage beyond measure, as again and again she brought down people she had known all her life—all the people she knew in the whole world. Old women and men, children and infants . . . every member of her tribe . . .

And now the last fell under her axe.

Acalan groaned once as Solenne swiped her weapon at his head and cleft a grapefruit-sized chunk of skull and brain out of it in an explosion of bloody black tissue and pus. He collapsed and Solenne looked for the next one—and found herself alone among a pile of the dead.

It took many minutes before she believed it was truly over. She screamed and raged and called out for more of them to come at her. Exhausted, muscles trembling and barely able to lift her arms, she still wanted to go on killing.

Because if there was no more killing, then she must find a way to die herself.

She looked down at her body. Her clothes were bloody tatters, and her skin was a patchwork of claw marks where reapers had gotten too close. One had even managed a shallow bite on her leg.

She knew she would grow a fever and die—and rise—and that must not happen.

The cliff . . . If she climbed the cliff again and threw herself from its peak, she knew the impact would destroy her body beyond the curse's power to make it rise again. But exhaustion and blood loss betrayed her. As she began her climb, she grew dizzy and fell just a few scant yards above the valley floor. When her head hit the rocks, she was knocked unconscious and knew no more until morning.

She woke to the heat of a noonday sun, amid the stink of a hundred rotting corpses. When she tried to move, a dozen strained muscles protested, and so much blood had dried on her body and matted her hair that, in moving, she imagined herself as an insect breaking free of its pupae, emerging as a thing reborn.

And she was reborn . . . in many more ways than she could have guessed at that moment.

She could taste no fever growing in her, and she knew intuitively now that none would, as she sensed also that the circumstances of her birth had somehow given her this gift even as it had taken everything she might have loved from her.

It was at that moment that the jolt of electricity ignited in her chest again—that same energy she had felt the day before. Now she recognized it, without knowing exactly how, as the static thrum of something dead come back to life. And this time she was somehow aware of a direction associated with it.

Somewhere downriver, west of her, a reaper was rising into its new life, unholy hunger tugging at what was left of its brain.

It could not be allowed to escape.

Stripping off the remnants of her ragged clothes, Solenne waded into the river and let the water wash the gore and tatters of grey flesh from her body. When she emerged, she found clean clothes and weapons. The horse—the only horse that had not been frightened away—stepped up to her as if presenting itself as an ally, and Solenne readied for travel.

For moments only, she allowed herself to think back to the afternoon before and the clean, pure joy of that time. She knew she would never experience that feeling again.

*\*\*\**

Solenne woke to find herself seated in a chair, wrists tied behind her, in a hot and musty tent. The sounds of men walking and talking outside and the smell of many horses confirmed her assumption that she was in the middle of the Confederate troop's camp. She remembered the nets, and the fight, and the final sudden explosion of pain that must have been a boot or a gun butt hitting her head. Around her she saw a cot and writing table, and she also noticed her gun belt and coat piled in the corner on a stool. Brennan's guns and saddlebags lay on the floor beside them.

She guessed she was in the colonel's tent.

There was something significant she did *not* see among the heap of belongings, and it gave her cause for a brief smile. Then it was time to take stock of her situation.

She could feel dried blood caking her scalp and stickiness where it must have run down the back of her neck. She was sore all over, and likely more so for being tied to a chair, but when she moved her limbs, she couldn't detect any broken bones or real injury that would not heal in days or weeks, if she lived that long.

She squinted and blinked her eyes. Her vision was fine. Her memory seemed intact. She suspected her brain was relatively undamaged since she was acutely aware how much trouble she was in and how much of a mess she might have to clean up if she didn't get out of here soon. Only one of the infected had gotten away, but one was always enough, and the one who'd escaped had been on horseback. Who knew how far he might travel before the sickness took him down—perhaps far enough that she would have trouble sensing him and those he inevitably contaminated. By tomorrow that one might be four or five or more new reapers, all hungry and inevitably creating more of themselves in a geometric progression.

To her advantage was that this area was sparsely populated and that those who did live or travel through the desert—native, soldier, or gunman—were all by habit and necessity watchful, merciless, and likely to kill any of the creatures if they felt threatened. Nevertheless, reapers had a way of taking people unawares, and their ability to survive wounds that would kill the humans they had once been meant that they often managed to pass the curse along before they were destroyed.

She had to get free, soon, and track down the remaining creature.

She closed her eyes and forced herself to relax, to recall . . .

Years ago she had been travelling through the mountains in Northern California and had encountered a caravan of strange-looking men after a harsh winter storm halted them all in a highland valley. Their skin was a similar colour to Solenne's, but their eyes were strangely slanted. Only one of then spoke English. They called themselves monks and had come from a land across the Pacific. They obeyed strict tenets of a religion that was in some ways quite similar to the beliefs that Solenne's tribe had held.

They were peaceful and friendly people, but they were ill-prepared for their journey, carrying few supplies and being poor hunters. All were thin and some were sickly by the time Solenne met up with them. Yet they seemed to think that lack of food was only a test to bring them closer to their beliefs. Solenne was surprised they had survived as long as they had. In the days that followed, she hunted for them and taught them how to build proper shelters.

They repaid her by teaching her some of their fighting techniques. Solenne could sense that, though they would never think to violate a woman, they were privately horrified that she travelled alone and—to their way of thinking—unprotected. She knew they were also surprised by her strength and fighting ability, but they—in turn—had surprised her as well. Though all of the monks were considerably older than she was and were half-starved into the bargain, when she began to spar with them, she found to her chagrin that all of them could easily defeat her in hand-to-hand combat. Solenne had spent many years hunting and killing reapers by that time and felt confident in her capability to defeat most anyone alive or dead with fist, gun, or knife. But she was humbled numerous times in that first day by the oldest—a man of at least sixty, who stared down at her with kind eyes and a paternalistic smile each time he flipped or kicked her onto her butt.

She had been an apt pupil and learned quickly during their three weeks held captive by the winter storms, and when they parted she was—in their estimation—a considerable fighter.

In evenings around the fire, they had also introduced Solenne to their ways of looking at the world and to their methods of knowing themselves in a much deeper way than those in the West did by bending their minds and their bodies into new ways of thinking and being. Often the techniques they employed to fight crossed over into their philosophies, and vice versa.

*You could try to force yourself against an obstacle, or you could shift and use the obstacle's energy to turn it and twist its force away from you . . .*

Solenne took ten slow, deep breaths and began tensing and relaxing the muscles in her arms. She was already sweating in the oppressive heat of the tent, and the movement, slow but intense, made her perspire more freely. The ropes looped around her wrists first resisted, biting into her flesh, and then—after several minutes—began to move slowly over her now-abraded skin. Eventually her wrists began to bleed, and the blood combined with her sweat to lubricate the rope just enough that she was able to slide her hands up into the loops that had been binding her wrists. Now she began opening and closing her fingers against the rope.

Sweat was running down her face now, and without thinking, she sniffed and spat.

"Hear that?"

The voice came from outside the tent, and Solenne cursed herself. Of course there were guards outside. Of course they would be listening for signs their captive was awake. They whispered, but she could hear them easily.

"Ayuh. Reckon she's awake. Better one of us go tell the colonel."

"Right . . . but maybe we should check on her, like, just to be sure. I want another look at her anyhow."

"But—"

"But nothing, dipshit," the guard whispered with urgency. "You see that girl when they took off her coat and tied her up? She's pretty, and that shirt she's wearing hardly covered anything. I got a good look at her titties when they brought her in, and I want another one . . . At least a look. You?"

Solenne grimaced and looked down. Her shirt had been ripped halfway open at some point in her capture. She supposed she should be glad they hadn't raped her while she was unconscious.

Apparently the first guard had been able to convince the second not to notify anyone about her return to consciousness just yet. Solenne watched as a dirty hand parted the folds of the tent and a grimy bearded man in a stained and torn grey uniform peeked inside. He saw her looking at him and smiled a sparse-toothed grin.

"Well, hi there, missy. I'm Darrell. How you doing? See you're awake. You thirsty? I could likely get you some water."

Solenne said nothing and continued to work the muscles in her hands against the rope, looking flat-eyed at Darrell until he began to frown and wonder if this woman was a bit slow.

"You speak English, right? I *said* would you like some water? You must be a mite parched. Am I right? Answer now, darling."

Solenne stared right through him, and Darrell was obviously bothered by the lack of immediate response to his considerable charm. He was used to women smiling at him and thought of himself as a bit of a lady's man. The fact that the girls who typically responded so positively to his overtures were prostitutes that he encountered in bars or brothels was not something he had spent much time contemplating.

Darrell turned back to the tent's entrance. "You let me know if anyone's coming, Ollie."

Solenne heard Ollie cough a noncommittal reply as Darrell stepped fully inside, removing his hat and laying it on the small writing table. He leaned in close, and Solenne smelled the unwashed rank of the man competing against the sour odour of his breath. He didn't smell quite as bad as one of the walking dead, but she thought it was a near thing.

"Still got nothing to say?" Darrell leaned in even closer, and Solenne saw he was looking down her blouse. "You sure are a pretty thing, ain't you?"

"Darrell?" Solenne said.

"Yeah . . . ?" His eyes were still focused on her breasts.

"Stop looking at my chest, *tu pedazo de mierda*."

Most southerners had some acquaintance with the Spanish language. It appeared that Darrell could at least infer he had just been compared to a piece of excrement. He stepped back, anger clouding his face and hand coming back to slap her. Before he could follow through, she continued.

"*Listen to me.*"

Darrell paused, not quite knowing why—something in her voice.

Solenne smiled, and it seemed to her that Darrell was just bright enough to see the poison in her grin.

"If you let me go now—right now—I promise I won't kill you."

Some of the anger faded from Darrell's face. He looked surprised and even giggled—a laugh that grated on Solenne's backbone.

Then he did slap her.

The force of the blow flung her back as far as the chair would allow, and she was dizzy for a moment. She had a visualization of her brain rattling around inside her head like a die in a cup, and she felt the warm, wet trickle of fresh blood flowing from her nose and into her mouth.

"Hey," Ollie whispered from outside, an edge of nervousness in his voice. "Keep it down in there, fuckhead."

"Shut the fuck up, Ollie," Darrell whispered back, giggling again and holding his hand up to his mouth as if he were unable to contain the laughter that continued to spill out.

Solenne decided Darrell was a type of man she'd met a few times before, whose amusement was chiefly fuelled by the pain of others. He leaned down, grabbed a fistful of her hair, and twisted as he pulled her toward him. Her head wound roared at this fresh indignity.

"You listen to me, you little *whore*," he hissed in her ear. "I know the colonel wants to talk to you, but I suspect you can do other things with your mouth than just talk. Am I right?" He punctuated this question by grasping her shirt and ripping it apart, exposing her chest completely.

Solenne spat at him, and Darrell let go of her hair with a sharp push. He stepped back to take in his handiwork. She watched his cruel, ugly smile die as he looked her over, and she hated him all the more because of what he was seeing.

"What the hell happened to you?" he said, astonishment in his voice.

She felt her skin flush and was angry with herself for it. Just like any other woman would have, she had to deal with the shame of being stripped bare like this. But Darrell—about to rape her—was having the same reaction to seeing her in the daylight as the few men she'd willingly been intimate with in her life.

Her torso was strongly muscled from years of living on the run, hunting the dead, and fighting for her life. Her breasts—*she* thought, at least—were attractive even if they weren't especially large. But always in the daylight, a man's eyes were drawn to the scars; the scratches, the *bites*. Solenne had spent most of her adult life seeking out and killing the undead, and she was good at it now—a finely honed blade, tempered and sharpened by experience. But her early years had been a different thing. To anyone who could read it, the scars writ upon her body told the story of misadventures and near-death encounters.

White, raised scar tissue in the shape of human bites was clearly visible on both arms, her left shoulder, and just under her left breast. In addition, four twisted, pallid claw marks trailed across her chest below her left collarbone. She knew there was an accompanying set on her upper left back where the thing she'd fought that long-ago day had latched onto her with both hands. The reaper's fingers had been worn to jagged bone from trying to claw its way out of the ranch house in which she had found it, and it had taken her by surprise, battening onto her shoulder and ripping a four-inch strip of skin and muscle off her upper back in the first few seconds of their encounter. She could still recall the feeling of her flesh being torn away, a ragged, ripping sensation that she was forever after doomed to recall whenever she worked her left shoulder too hard.

She'd shot the reaper in the head, spraying black gore, drool, and bone fragments all over herself, and then she'd lain bleeding and sick for days in the deserted house before she'd found the strength to drag herself out to the well. It had taken her two hours to draw up the first bucket of water as the roaring pain drew whimpers of agony from her all the while.

These memories flooded back as Darrell stood fumbling with his belt and running his eyes over her like she was a steak dinner that had turned out to be a bit overdone, though—she could see from his expression—still, without a doubt, edible.

"You like the rough stuff, huh?" He giggled again as he pulled his belt apart and bent forward slightly so he could see over his potbelly to unbutton his fly.

"Yes . . . I do." Solenne watched as his head moved down into just the right position.

Her right leg shot up—lightning quick—as she leaned back, allowing her hip and knee to flex as powerfully as possible. The movement seemed to happen slowly inside her mind, and she found herself musing that she would never have tied a prisoner only by their hands, nor would she have left them shod. Again, it was to her advantage that men seemed to automatically consider her weaker and less able than they were.

The toe of Solenne's boot slammed into Darrell's face with a sharp crack, and his nose exploded in a mist of blood that became a geyser as his eyes rolled back into his head under fluttering eyelids. He dropped to the ground like a stone and lay still.

Solenne leaned forward, still working her hands within the rope. In a detached way, she was curious to see if Darrell was still breathing. The monks had taught her that such blows to the upper nose often shattered bone and pushed it into the brain, which meant certain death. Darrell lay on the ground motionless for a moment, then twitched a few times before curling slowly into a fetal position, moaning softly as his hands came up to cup his injured face. She decided she had not kicked him quite hard enough.

The noise that had accompanied Darrell's fall, along with the silence afterward, apparently prompted some concern in his fellow guard.

"Darrell . . . ? Everything okay in there?" Ollie, if not the sharpest knife in the drawer, did at least seem to realize that molestation and rape of a tied woman would not be occurring in such silence.

Solenne considered. Almost anything she said might lure Ollie inside; perhaps close enough that she might incapacitate him as well. In a few minutes she would be free of the rope and then—

"What the hell is this, Private?" a new, low-timbre voice said from outside the tent. A voice of ultimate authority. She knew it must be the colonel. Johnston.

"Sir!"

She heard a shuffle and imagined Ollie coming to attention outside.

"Where is the other guard, Private?"

"Uhh . . ."

Solenne doubted Ollie would be able to do much in the way of dissembling, so she saved him the need and raised her own voice.

"He's in here, Colonel."

Solenne heard a snort from outside and then the colonel lifted the flap of the tent and peered inside. She saw his face harden as he took in the scene before him. His head disappeared for a moment as he leaned back outside.

"Private! Fetch the sergeant and two more guards. And mark me, Private, if you are not back here in thirty seconds, I will have you hanged. Understand?"

"Yessir!"

Solenne heard the private running off and watched Johnston stepped into the tent as if wary, his eyes on her all the while. She saw him tense as he got a close look at her, sweat breaking out over his brow. His stare was so penetrating that she thought one rapist was merely replacing another. She steeled herself. She knew she would lose a fight against this man while still tied, and it seemed unlikely he would allow himself to make the same mistake Darrell had.

After a moment, though, she realized he was not gazing at her with lust. Instead, Johnston surveyed her as a man seeing a priceless treasure for the very first time. He seemed unable to look away.

He was looking at her scars . . . at the bite marks. He was not interested in her breasts at all, and for a moment, she was at odds with herself over whether to be offended.

"Colonel—"

Johnston shook himself as if emerging from a daydream and stood—just for a moment—almost at attention. "Ma'am!"

He turned away from her and darted toward the corner of the tent, where there were some blankets piled on the ground. He lashed out with his feet at the private who still lay twitching on the floor. Darrell rolled out of Johnston's way after several savage kicks, groaning and crying as blood continued to flow steadily between his fingers. Johnston came around behind Solenne and wrapped a blanket over her shoulders to cover her before stepping back, taking obvious care to stay out of range of her feet. He must have noticed the blood on the toe of her right boot.

"Miss, I am so very sorry for the way this soldier behaved."

Solenne frowned. Given that this was the same man who only hours ago had clubbed her into oblivion, the extremity of his embarrassment at her mistreatment seemed bizarre.

"You kidnap and beat me unconscious, but you're sorry about this?" She glanced down at the injured man.

Johnston bridled. "In war, ma'am, many things are necessary. Rape is not one of them."

"Just the kidnapping and the beating part, then." The monks she had known had talked often about something they called "the duality of man," and Solenne knew she was seeing it here. All manner of killing and brutality might come easily to this man, even while he found rape simply . . . impolite . . . an offensive to his gentleman's sensibilities.

The tent flapped open again, saving Solenne the illogic that surely would have formed some large portion of Johnston's reply. A sweaty, scared-looking man she supposed was Ollie entered, followed by another bug-eyed private and a balding, paunchy sergeant who looked less pleased by the second as he took in the scene.

"Sir?" The sergeant saluted belatedly.

"Welcome, Sergeant." Johnston returned the salute, but his eyes were on Ollie, who stood trembling with such force that Solenne thought he might lose control of his bladder.

"Private?"

"Yessir, Colonel."

"You and your partner"—he indicated the bloody moaning man on the floor—"were detailed to guard this woman. Is that correct?"

Ollie nodded, unable to bring himself to speak.

"It is obvious your partner was about to violate this woman." This was hardly arguable. Despite the blanket, everyone in the room could see that Solenne's shirt had been ripped apart, and Darrell's open pants had slid down over hips during the time he had spent writhing on the ground.

"Was violation of this prisoner part of your orders, Private?"

Ollie shook his head, blinking hard, a veritable waterfall of sweat cascading down his face now.

"Speak up, Private. I am asking you a question, and therefore please honour me with the courtesy of a reply."

"No, sir!" Ollie erupted like a boil poked with a hot skewer. "No! We was just told to watch and make sure she didn't . . . get away, like."

Johnston pursed his lips and nodded, winking at the private as if pleased with what he'd said.

"And you stayed at your post. Am I correct? You had nothing to do with this?"

Ollie nodded and Johnston frowned at him, pleasure gone from his eyes. Belatedly Ollie spat out, "That's right, sir. That's right. I stayed at my post, sir. Followed orders, sir."

Johnston turned to the sergeant and drew his pistol. "Sergeant Ross?"

"Yessir."

"I imagine you were engaged to assist in the punishment of two men who were earlier found to be inadequate in their duties as guards."

"That's right, sir. We're setting up now so as to give 'em"—Ross paused and a tremble came into his voice, as if he was hoping his commander was going to correct the order Lewis had, red-faced, delivered to him minutes ago—"four hundred lashes . . . with a whip, sir? Was that right?"

Johnston nodded and Ross released the breath he'd been holding in his chest, along with the hope he'd been holding with it. Even the meanest and dullest of the enlisted men, volunteers mostly, knew that flogging a man was beyond the pale. A few lashes with a whip might have been tolerated, but southerners knew the whip as a punishment for slaves. After Johnston's other "punishments," it was no mean feat to imagine that this would enrage the men to the point of mass desertion or mutiny, but Ross knew better than to give voice to such thoughts.

"Mr. Ross, I've decided those men will be additionally punished by forming part of the burial detail."

Ross blinked while he thought this over. Eventually his eyes crept over to Solenne as if wondering if the colonel, after going to so much trouble to capture the woman, was done with her already and intending to kill her.

Then Johnston shot Darrell in the head.

The man's body spasmed. Three or four gasping, rattling breaths gurgled out from between his lips, forming bubbles of bloody grey matter around his mouth and nose. Then he relaxed into death.

Everyone in the tent except Johnston and Solenne started at the shot. Solenne's eyes had never left the colonel. From the moment he had covered her with the blanket, she sensed that Darrell was going to die, though even she was surprised at the rapid and personal manner of his execution. Often a commander liked to make a public example out of men who had been egregiously disobedient, and Solenne realized this was all about obedience. Not what the man had tried to do, but the fact that—in attempting to rape her—he had disobeyed orders.

The soldiers staring down now at Darrell's still, bloody corpse would spread this story through camp. From what Solenne could deduce from the few words exchanged before the shot, two men would be whipped this afternoon for failing to perform their duty properly, and now the whole camp would be well acquainted with the price to be paid for violating the orders of their commander.

Every ugly thing Solenne had heard about the man who had been chasing her all this time was apparently true.

"Sergeant Ross. As you can see, we are now in need of a burial detail." Johnston smiled as if enjoying a good joke with comrades. "Have these two privates remove this . . . man until the burial can be attended to. I care not where."

Johnston holstered his pistol and waited until the sergeant had rushed his two subordinates into dragging Darrell's body out of the tent, a trail of blood and brain matter staining the ground behind them.

"Sergeant Ross. Guard the tent, will you? No one in till I'm done with this one."

"Yessir . . . Begging your pardon, sir, but Quinto's outside. Wants to talk to you."

Johnston shook his head. "No one till I'm done with this one."

"Yessir . . . Um, he did look right anxious, sir—just so's you know."

Ross had been a thief and a sometime gunfighter before the war. He was reasonably good with a firearm, but not especially fast. He had killed several people, but more often by craft than by skill, he knew. Typically Ross would wait until the man he was gunning for was drunk before challenging him. Sometimes Ross himself would buy the man liquor enough to ensure utter inebriation. Given the nature of his chosen profession, though, in his travels he'd inevitably come across men far more talented than himself and far too wary for such tricks. Men best to be avoided. True killers. Crazy killers, some of them. The look in the flat steely eyes boring into him was familiar.

"Not till I am done, Sergeant. Understand me?"

Ross saluted, looking from Johnston's composed face to Solenne's equally placid—if bruised and bloody—face, and he exited the tent.

Ross's face had betrayed nothing but dismay and puzzlement, and Solenne realized Ross had absolutely no idea what Johnston might want with a desert-hardened waif. Perhaps no one else in camp did either. If she could somehow kill Johnston and get free, the rest of these men would most likely go home and let her finish her work.

Johnston sighed and dragged the other chair nearer so he could sit. She again saw he took care to stand well out of range of her kick.

"Miss, I am truly sorry for what you have suffered at the hands of one of my troops. I hope you know it will not happen again."

Solenne turned her head and assessed the man before her in the same way Johnston had seen predators do when sizing up their prey.

"And what about what I suffered at your hands? Myself and my companion? Let us loose, if you're really so sorry." She could still see flecks of blood on Johnston's coat where she had spat on him.

Seated, Johnston faced Solenne and took off his hat, tipping it to her before throwing it on the table behind him. There was a lingering scent of cordite amidst the coppery stink of blood in the air, and the mixture of smells reminded Solenne of the preachings of the white man's Bible . . . of what it said about encounters with the Devil.

"I'm afraid I can't do that, miss. I do apologize for striking you, though." He smiled. "But you *had* just killed what I've been chasing over this hellish land for months." He held a finger up. "Not for the first time, either. It seems everywhere I've been the last little while, you've been there first . . . and left me nothing of what I've been searching for."

"I know."

Johnston frowned. "You do?"

Solenne almost had one hand free now. Just a few minutes more. "I've heard about you too."

Johnston nodded as if satisfied that his adversary knew him. He drew a wad of tobacco from his pocket and produced a knife from the sheath on his belt. Solenne's eyes lit on it. The hilt was made of ivory or bone, and carved into it were symbols she recognized—symbols of the past her people had left behind in the southern continent.

Johnston noticed her staring. "Like it?" He smirked. "I took it from a heathen on one of my travels, long before this war began."

He cut himself a piece of the tobacco and tossed it in his mouth, chewing on it as if he had all the time in the world as he watched her thoughtfully. "The heathen I took it from didn't want to give it up . . . But I always get what I want in the end."

He spat on the ground, and the ugly black-brown colour of the sputum reminded her of the oily gore the living dead secreted.

"Now then, miss. Where shall we start?"

Chapter Twelve

In the confusion and horror of the afternoon at the Apache camp, no one had thought to look for the sentries who ought to have been guarding the village perimeter. Bruised-Head's horse had returned to the camp, but in the midst of the attack, no one had noticed.

Bruised-Head lay where he had been killed, twitching like a dog in the midst of a dream. Dead pathways in his brain were activating again, but haphazardly at first and only in fits and starts. The hunger in those awakening to their fresh urges quickly drove newborn reapers to their feet and toward their prey. The pain of the curse—the undeniable *need* of it—living in the undead things it animated could only be eased by the taste of live flesh.

Bruised-Head rose to his second life in the early afternoon, getting to his feet only after several abortive attempts, like a child learning to walk for the first time. The wind was blowing from the west, and so though his own tribe was nearer, the smell of the Confederate camp entered his nostrils first. Human smells . . . and just a hint of blood in the air.

Bruised-Head stumbled forward like a blind man, like all the risen dead, seeking some antidote to quiet the *need* clawing through his brain.

\*\*\*

As Barrett approached Colonel Johnston's tent, he saw two privates dragging another soldier's body away from it and he cursed. Johnston's pitiless style of leadership was unmatched by any other commander Barrett had ever served with, and his newly developed penchant for experimenting on his own men had created the kind of abject fear among the men that could lead to rebellion. This was not what they had signed up for. Through reports from other Confederate forces they had encountered over the last months, he was aware, as he supposed all the men were, that the war was not going well for the South, and they were all itching to inflict real damage on their adversaries. He found himself hoping again that all the miles of this chase would produce something worthy of the cost of the pursuit.

Ross pushed the canvas flap of the tent's entrance aside. Seeing Barrett, he stepped toward him, waving a hand to forestall Barrett's entrance.

"Sir, the colonel has given orders to be left undisturbed till he finishes talking with that girl."

Barrett grimaced. "Shit. All right." His voice dropped to a whisper. "Now what the hell happened in there?"

Ross hesitated, looked around and saw they were alone for the moment, and plunged on.

"The colonel just killed one of the privates that was guarding the girl. Stupid fuck tried to have his way with her, and she broke his fucking nose and laid him out on the ground, near kilt him herself. Never seen anything like it. Anyway, the colonel shot him in the head and finished the job. He was . . . pretty intent on talking with her alone, sir. Just saying."

"Very well. Dismissed."

Ross nodded and flicked his hand at a private passing by, speaking to him in an intense, low tone for a few moments while pointing at the colonel's tent. A fearful look came over the private's face, and he nodded and stationed himself by the tent's entrance. Ross watched him for a moment, as if only half-satisfied with the likely ability of the man, then turned and walked off, following the trail of blood left by the two privates dragging their dead colleague.

Barrett looked at the sky and saw night would be falling soon. He felt uneasy. Under Johnston's command, uneasiness had not been unusual, but this feeling was something new. Despite all Johnston had said, stories of dead men resurrected by some curse or disease had always seemed to Barrett to be the imaginings from some hellish nightmare. The men he'd seen Johnston punish by forcing them to endure the bite of a corpse . . . well, it made sense that they had died. Every man knew human bites were dirty and festered easily. He had seen his share of men die from much smaller wounds that became infected and gangrenous. The fact that the last man punished had turned delirious and rabid with fever just before the end . . . well, that had made some sense too. He had been able to reconcile that with things he'd seen or heard before.

But the man—*the creature*—from this morning had been wild,

rabid, and still moving with half of its head gone when the woman finished it off. Its body had appeared days dead when Barrett had examined it afterward, though it had been moving only moments before.

It could have been nothing *but* a dead thing risen.

And that the man in the cage just a few yards away would also die and then rise again . . . It *was* true, then. All of it, everything Johnston had said.

And that prompted the questions once again—the awful questions. What possible use could such abominations be? What could Johnston want with such demonic things? Barrett was becoming more and more certain he would not like the answers.

Quinto approached, interrupting Barrett's thoughts. He was obviously intent on speaking with Johnston. Barrett held up a hand and caught his eye.

"He's busy talking to that girl. Doesn't want anyone disturbing him."

Quinto looked troubled. "Maybe you ask him to come out? Very important I speak to him."

"And why would that be?"

In all the time Barrett had known Quinto, during all the weeks of his enforced servitude, Barrett had never seen the seemingly unflappable man look so distinctly uncomfortable. His face was flushed as if he was either embarrassed or worried about the news he had to deliver.

"Might as well tell me. If it's shit news, it's hardly likely to turn sweeter in this heat."

After a moment of indecision, Quinto said, "Where we found the girl and man? The ground was very confusing—"

"What? Why?"

"The ground was stirred up by your men. There were many horse tracks. Some shod, some not."

Barrett nodded. During the confusion of the capture and its aftermath, dozens of men and horses had tromped through the area. Afterward, they had searched to ensure they had found everyone. But the ground had been too disturbed for any tracker to easily read.

"There is flat rock for a long way east of there. Almost impossible to see where a horse or a man passes on that kind of ground."

Barrett had tracked one or two men in his time and was conscious of the difficulties. He knew that those aware they were being pursued often waded down rivers or found hard rocky ground to cross in an effort to evade their pursuers.

"A man, an Apache, rode east before we got there. He was wounded . . . I found blood."

"We found bodies."

"Yes. But one other rode away. Wounded."

"You think he got . . . bit or something? By one of those things the colonel wants?"

"Maybe." Quinto paused. "I should tell the colonel right away, I think."

Barrett looked back at the tent. He could hear the low murmur of voices. He thought he heard the woman raise her voice to say something that sounded like *honourable men*, and hard on the heels of this was the sound of a slap. He could guess who had done the slapping and thought of his conversation with Brennan.

*He won't hurt her if he can help it.*

Can *he help it?*

"All right, then—let's go tell him." Barrett was almost grateful for an excuse to disobey orders and enter that tent, maybe distract the colonel from his newest victim.

Quinto shook his head. "Better if the colonel can come out, I think."

"You . . . don't want her to hear what you got to say?"

Quinto nodded, but Barrett could see it was much more than that. Whoever that woman was, Quinto wanted no part of her, not even to be near her.

"You know something about her. I want to know it too."

Quinto stiffened. "It is nothing I haven't told you before. She is a witch . . . It is not good to speak about her when she is so close by."

"And why is that?"

Quinto frowned. "All this time we were chasing her, I did not think we would catch her. She is too powerful." He sighed and looked Barrett in the eye. "I thought only to make sure the colonel travelled far from my village. By now maybe my people have gone where he can never find them again." Now he looked confused. "I thought the colonel would give up when he could not catch her . . . He should not have been able to catch such a powerful being."

The derisive answer that formed on Barrett's lips, given a lifetime of listening to similar superstitious stories from what he had been taught were primitive people, died as the image of the monster from this morning swept into his mind like a cold wind.

"But now?" he finally said.

"She is very dangerous."

"What? Why?"

"It is very bad to speak of this, even in the sunlight. She is a witch, as I have tried to tell you. Truly, she is. Wherever she goes, guardian demons circle above her like vultures. Even whispering about her could draw their attention to us."

Two soldiers were walking by them, and their eyes swivelled when they heard the word *witch*. Barrett cursed softly. For weeks they had been chasing an ephemeral fugitive their primitive Apache guide had called a witch, but Barrett knew that—to the men—the thought of some Mexican witch had been a joke. Now, though, they had *seen* one of Johnston's monsters. What would they think of a real witch in their midst? Barrett was as yet unconvinced of the woman's supernatural nature, but the weak-minded among the men would begin to spin stories of fear and remind their fellows of the horrible deaths Johnston had inflicted on their comrades. It could lead to no good.

"Tell me anyhow."

Quinto pursed his lips, wondering for the thousandth time how white men could so trust his talents without valuing his judgment. "Is it not obvious?"

Barrett glowered at Quinto, moments passing in silence until he let it spill out. "How else could a woman survive alone in this country without protection from spirits?"

They both looked toward the tent, hearing the unmistakable sound of a punch and the low grunt of pain that followed.

"The curse your colonel chases will not touch her."

"What?"

"It is true. He knows. It is part of why he pursues her. She can be hurt but not killed. And she is powerful. Too powerful to be captured . . . *unless she allows herself to be.*"

"That's all just bullshit stories. No woman—"

"No. It is true. The people say that she can speak to *Death itself* and that she has bound him with a charm. Death cannot touch her, but he follows her like a jealous lover, turning his gaze on any who comes close to her."

"Quinto—"

"We should let her go, or Death will find us all."

\*\*\*

Johnston thought of himself as a charismatic man. His smile had appealed to a number of young ladies he'd encountered in Southern society as a plantation owner. On more than one occasion, though, when charm had failed him, he had won the lady over—as he thought of it—with *sterner* measures. A staunch exercise of will was all he had ever needed to achieve his aims, whatever they were.

Johnston was also familiar with what some in learned circles were calling *psychology*. He knew that the woman before him had been taken prisoner in a brutal fashion and that this would no doubt have frightened her. Then she had been tied and nearly raped just a few minutes ago. While Johnston would never tolerate such unauthorized behaviour in a subordinate, he had to appreciate the effect. The private's near violation of the woman and subsequent brutal murder before her could only have traumatized her more. Finally, Johnston himself had established his authority over her. All these things could only serve to make her more malleable. Her full and complete capitulation could not be far off.

"Now then, miss, where shall we start?"

"Start?"

"I know you're scared, and I promise—if you assist me—to protect you from further harm. But I do have a mission to perform and I need your cooperation."

On his adventures into the jungles of the south, Johnston had encountered all manner of lizards, and it seemed to him now that Solenne stared back at him like one of those reptiles, her blue eyes flat and uninterested.

"You really should let me go."

Johnston laughed. "I've been chasing you a long time. Apart from that, things I've heard here and there make me think *you* might be useful to me. So"—he spread his hands and smiled—"why on earth would I let you go?"

Solenne snorted. Her nose had almost stopped bleeding from the now-departed Darrell's punch. "You want one of those things."

Johnston grinned. "Actually—no thanks to you, I might add—I don't *want* one. I *have* one. Your companion—Brennan, is it? He's bitten, fevered, and, by my reckoning, just about to change."

"You've seen these creatures before . . . "

He nodded with disconcerting enthusiasm. "Many years ago. True horrors, they were. I barely escaped with my life. It was not until recently that I realized their . . . potential."

"Their *potential*," Solenne spat out the words, "is to be the final plague of mankind. They spread like weeds in an untended field. They destroy everything and never stop hungering for more. Don't you realize—"

"Oh, but I *do* realize. I realize everything." Johnston rose and paced in front of her. He kept his distance, yet he had not had her legs tied. Too arrogant to believe she could do to him what she'd done to his underling.

"My mission, my duty—as it is every Southerner's—is to win this war."

"The war is going badly for you." Solenne flicked it out as a statement of fact, and Johnston did not disagree.

"It is."

"And what would you use these things for?"

"You know already, don't you?"

"In many places over the last year, I heard you were looking for me. I had time to wonder why."

"The Confederacy *can* win this war. All it needs is a . . . distraction in the North. Something to draw their resources away from the fight.

Something like a plague—"

"A plague that turns the afflicted into monsters."

"You follow my train of thought exactly."

"I thought you were an honourable man."

Johnston's face flushed. "How dare *you* accuse *me* of being less than honourable? What kind of a woman dresses like this, rides around like a man, killing and—"

"If you're going to use these things against the North, you won't just be killing soldiers. You'll be turning defenseless women and children into those *things*."

Johnston pursed his lips and shrugged after a moment. "Sacrifices must be made sometimes to achieve a greater goal."

"Not these kinds of sacrifices. Not by *honourable* men!"

Johnston leapt forward and slapped Solenne, much in the way Darrell had just a few minutes earlier, though a bit harder, and her nose began bleeding again.

"Don't you dare lecture me, harlot!"

*"Vete a la mierda, tu—"*

Another slap. Blood ran in a river down her face, and she snorted and spat more gory phlegm onto the ground.

"You'll never stop the spread of it. When everyone in the North is dead, where do you think they'll turn next, you idiot?"

Johnston slapped her again, putting all his strength behind it this time, and she felt the inside of her head echo with it like a shout reverberating down a canyon. His face was beet red now, and he pointed a finger—a bloody finger—at her.

"You keep a civil tongue in your head, missy! I protected your honour, assuming you *have* any, a few minutes ago." A dark smile creased his face. "I can just as easily let every man jack in the camp have his way with you."

Solenne stared into his eyes with a black expression.

Johnston could feel the woman's eagerness to kill him, as palpable as the electric feeling in the air during a thunderstorm. In all his military encounters, and even in his long-ago experience with the walking dead, he had never felt such an emanation of homicidal intent.

He licked his lips and took a deep, shuddering breath, gaining control of himself again. "I apologize for that. Of course I would never do such a thing."

"Is that right?"

He hesitated for a split second before answering. "Yes." He waved his bloodstained hand in Solenne's face and chuckled. "You said I can't control this thing, but I know I can."

Johnston drew his sword from its scabbard and eased the point of the blade under the blanket he'd placed around her shoulders just a few minutes earlier. He could not help noticing that the woman never so much as flinched. Tilting the sabre, he lifted the blanket so that it fell away from her left shoulder and chest.

Solenne flushed, but not from embarrassment or a sense of violation . . .

She felt fear. But not the fear most women would have felt. Again, Johnston's gaze betrayed no sexual desire at seeing her naked and exposed. His only interest appeared to be in the claw-like scars and bite marks that covered her torso. She felt fear of what he knew. And how he might use it.

"Tell me now, miss. How many times have you been bitten?"

***

Captain Lewis believed he had never seen a man look at once so intent in his work and yet so pained about its purpose as Sergeant Ross did, having accomplished overseeing and directing the preparation for the impending corporal punishment. Fatty and Skinny, known to their troop as Wallace and Smith, stood with remarkable calm as their fellows stripped their shirts from them and secured their upheld arms to the rear of one of the supply wagons. With the exception of those on guard, the whole camp had been assembled to witness the punishment, and their combined voices were tinged with what to Lewis's ears sounded like angry murmurs, like a pot about to boil over.

Johnston usually attended such events himself, but Lewis did not expect him today. He knew the colonel was far too interested in questioning the woman. The whipping would proceed without him. Lewis knew it would be best if this was over quickly, and he checked the bindings holding the men to be punished to be sure they were secure. If one of the men worked themselves loose halfway through the flogging and had to be re-tied, that might just push the men over the edge.

An educated man, Lewis clearly recalled the first time one of the enlisted men—in line for punishment because of some much more minor offence—had asked him with a trembling lip if it was true that only corporals could be whipped. It had been ten minutes after he'd dismissed the man before he realized with a burst of laughter that the poor soul had mixed up the concept of corporal as a rank in the army with the notion of corporal punishment.

The recollection brought no smile to his face on this occasion, though. He suspected that Ross, as well as the other sergeants—officers too—were conscious that the men were at a breaking point. Thinking this made him realize suddenly that Ross had asked him something several times and was waiting for an answer with all the patience a veteran sergeant could muster when dealing with a much-younger captain.

"You're all ready, then, Sergeant?"

"Yessir. Begging a question, though, sir?"

Lewis was new to his career. He had just been finishing military college when the war broke out. In his experience, Ross was a capable soldier. When he raised a question in this manner, he was politely asking to give an inexperienced officer advice. Even in the relatively brief time he'd been in combat, Lewis had seen other officers disdain such advice from combat-hardened men and come to regret it.

"Of course, Sergeant."

Ross removed his hat and wiped his face with it. It was not particularly hot, given the breeze, but Lewis saw that Ross was sweating and examined the expression on his face. Ross was far more privy to the men's thoughts than any officer might be. If Lewis was wondering about the mood of the men, then Ross would be sure of it, and his uneasiness was a certain validation of Lewis's worries.

"I believe, sir, that the colonel ordered four hundred lashes."

Lewis nodded, frowning. Of course he had. They had both heard it, and now this unheard of and entirely over-the-top-punishment would further disenfranchise the men.

"I'm sorry, Lieutenant, but I don't rightly recollect whether that was four hundred *each*, or four hundred altogether. Two hundred for each man, as it were."

Lewis considered, nodding slowly. Johnston had quite obviously ordered four hundred lashes for each man and Ross well knew it, but four hundred lashes from a bullwhip would kill most men. If the wounds and the pain didn't end their lives, infection feasting on flesh peeled down to the bone often would. Two hundred lashes was still far too much for this penalty. Most commanders would have ordered the men on short rations for a day or two, or some such thing. But at least two hundred lashes might be survivable, and it might also mean the difference between a mass desertion and a mass murder of all the officers after darkness fell.

"Thank you for inquiring, Mr. Ross." Ross stood tense until Lewis carried on. "As you say, I do believe the colonel meant two hundred lashes for each man."

"Yes, sir. Thank you, sir." Ross used his hat to wipe more of the sweat from his brow before saluting in acknowledgement of the order. "Permission to continue with the punishment, sir."

"Yes, yes." Lewis waved his hand, anxious to be done with this and get the men back to work before they had too much time to speak of it. "Let's get this over with, Sergeant."

As Ross strode off toward the men he was tasked with whipping, Lewis raised his voice and turned to the soldiers gathered around their two tied compatriots.

"Listen up, you men of the Confederate Army! We are far from home and must be engaged each and every minute in doing our duty to the utmost. These two men were not diligent and were disarmed by a *chained* prisoner." Lewis paused to let this sink in. "Let this be a lesson to *all of us.*

Fighting for Southern justice and honour requires rigorous attention to duty at all times."

Lewis nodded at Ross, who had been engaged in inspecting the whip. If Lewis knew Ross, the bullwhip had been washed in the river and carefully dried so as not to drive dirt into wounds that would then inevitably fester. A wet whip caused far more damage and pain than a dry one.

"Carry on, Sergeant Ross."

Ross was an expert with the whip. It lashed out and, as if by magic, a foot-long welt appeared on Wallace's upper back. Each man had been given a piece of rawhide to chew on, so Wallace made only a loud grunt at the first touch of the whip, but Lewis knew they would both be crying out before ten strokes had landed, probably cursing Ross with every breath, never knowing what he had spared them.

The whip flicked out again, and a wound appeared on Smith's trembling frame this time. Smith screamed at the first strike, and Lewis supposed he must have less protection over his bones than the fat man. As the whipping continued, each man's back became a ragged criss-cross of angry red wounds.

Lewis fancied he could smell an odour of copper in the air, and he chastised himself for his overactive imagination. But as surely as if shed in shark-infested waters, the scent of blood *was* in the air—to any predator that could smell it.

\*\*\*

What had once been Bruised-Head stumbled toward the glowing yellow orb in the sky. He was not attracted to the large ball of fire, but his senses, first excited by the smell of men and now by that of blood, drove him westward in a frenzy of hunger. The Bruised-Head of yesterday had enjoyed a reputation among his people for having amazing eyesight. It was one of the reasons he had often acted as a perimeter guard, something he had been proud of in that former life. But cursed ones rarely blinked, and while their sense of smell intensified, the disease dried and clouded their eyes. Its eyesight was a shadowy, soupy-yellow mist now.

In the distance, though, through the creamy mist, it could vaguely see things moving. And with every step in that direction, the intoxicating scent of blood grew stronger. Its lips peeled back over its teeth and drool ran over its chin as it moved forward.

Miles behind it, the children the Turak-thing had killed lay beside each other at the edge of the village, sewn into their sleeping robes by their families. They lay unwatched for the moment as the tribe's medicine man chanted blessings in the centre of the village. By custom, at nightfall, their families would carry the dead to the village's burial site up in the shadows of the canyon. But dead neurons were switching on again in the bases of the corpses' brains. The bodies began to stir with the first erratically firing signals of their new mutated nervous systems. Finally the newly born reapers began to wrench against the confinement of their burial robes.

In shelters throughout the camp, the warriors the Turak-thing had scratched or bitten that morning were falling into a feverish coma from which they would emerge as the hungry undead.

## Chapter Thirteen

The woman still stared at him with those infuriatingly fearless dead eyes.

Johnston imagined this was the way one of the creatures would look at you when it came for you. His sword was only inches from her fragile-looking neck, still holding the blanket away from her naked body to expose her scar-covered torso. She should have been trembling in shame and fear, and yet she looked back at him as if she were the one holding the weapon. As if she were the one who could kill him at any moment.

He shivered, and anger surged through him at the way he was responding to her and at the way she was failing to react to him. She was key to his plans, but she was still nothing more than a tool to be used as he saw fit in fulfilling his destiny. He needed to make her realize that, to bend her to his will.

He lifted his sword slightly and tapped her cheek.

Solenne winced. The razor-sharp weapon left a thin red line on the left side of her face.

"Got your attention, have I?"

Still, the darkness never left her eyes.

"I *said* how many times? How many times have you been bitten?"

"I will not speak about this with you."

"Doesn't really matter to you, does it? You're immune. You can't be infected."

The girl stared back at him like a basilisk.

Johnston felt his anger about to boil over. "How does it work? The primitives in these territories say you're a witch . . . You tell me how you do it. Now." He tapped her again on the cheek and another red line appeared. He noticed she hardly winced this time.

"Colonel, what you need to understand is this isn't something you can control any more than you can control the wind."

"Tell me what I want to know."

*"Shut up and listen to me,"* Solenne hissed at him, and Johnston was startled speechless. "This . . . disease has remained isolated because it has its origins in places where there are few people. If you let this loose in a populated area, it will blow over this country like a hurricane."

No man in his troop would survive for more than ten seconds if he exhibited a tenth of the presumption this woman had. But he could not kill her while she held from him the key to her magic.

"Are you listening to me? You are on the verge of killing—"

Johnston threw his sabre to the ground, leaned in, and flat out punched her this time.

*

The blow nearly threw Solenne to the ground, chair and all, and she fought for consciousness . . . fought hard because . . . for an instant, he was close enough . . .

She knew Johnston was the apex of this madness, the beginning and end of it. If he died, this troop of men would revert to just another pointless tool of mortal warfare. The threat of the curse being perverted into some weapon of mass destruction would be gone.

Solenne stood up.

She had managed to work her right hand mostly out of her bindings during their conversation, and she tore it free now as she came to her feet, experiencing the flash of joy she always felt in movement with purpose, which was enlivened by the abject surprise that erupted on Johnston's face as she rose before him.

Quick as a rattlesnake she darted forward, smashing her forehead into Johnston's face. There was the crunch of bone on bone and a satisfying yowl of pain as Johnston's nose flattened against his face.

Solenne felt her brain rattling around in her skull again as the colonel stumbled backward. She blinked and tried to focus. The first clear sight she had was of the river of blood from the man's nose as his hands came up instinctively to cup his injured face.

Still tied to the chair by her left hand, Solenne bent her upper body away from Johnston and brought her right leg up, snapping it forward at the knee, just as the monks had taught her. The heel of her boot slammed into Johnston's abdomen and he gasped and fell to his knees, the wind knocked out of him. She could hear him wheezing with the effort of trying to draw breath back into his lungs. As she danced forward to finish him, she wondered at the stupidity of the man, not having secured her feet after she'd disabled one of his men even with both hands tied.

"*Bitch*," Johnston wheezed as he heaved desperately to draw air back into his lungs. "I think you broke my rib." He sank to his knees and slumped away from her, then shot his legs out blindly toward her, connecting with his left foot. Encumbered by the chair, she tripped over Johnston's legs and fell on top of him, dragging the chair with her.

Johnston grabbed at her, and suddenly she was on her side, pressed up against him with her right hand trapped. The reek of his unwashed skin and cigar breath was in her nose. She writhed, trying to get her hands free even while she tried again to strike at his face with her forehead.

Abruptly she found her face pressed up against his neck. The stink of him was awful, but she could feel the pulse of his carotid against her cheek. She peeled her lips back to rip into his throat and . . . hesitated.

If she bit him and he somehow survived . . . She could not risk it.

And the moment was gone. She felt the barrel of a gun press

151

against the back of her head and heard the click of the hammer drawing back.

A gravelly voice came from above her. "Move a muscle and you're dead."

*

"Don't shoot!"

Barrett flicked his eyes briefly at Johnston, whose muffled protest was followed by a coughing spasm that went on and on as he thrashed out from under the woman as she rolled slowly onto her back, gathering the remains of her shirt together with her one free hand.

"Did I not just tell you *not* to move?" Barrett growled.

The woman stared back at him with the flat, fearless gaze of a lizard.

"Don't shoot her—whatever you do, Barrett." Johnston struggled to his feet and yanked a worn handkerchief from his pocket to staunch the blood running from his nose. His uniform was covered with gore and his nose had taken on a crooked shape, obviously broken.

In the first few seconds of the skirmish, Barrett, like the other two outside the tent, had assumed that the colonel was employing force in interrogating the prisoner. They did not enter until they had heard Johnston's first cry of pain. The private was attempting to stammer out just such an explanation for not immediately coming to his colonel's rescue, but Johnston cut him off. Gesturing to Solenne and the rope that still held one of her hands, he said, "Get her tied up again—*securely*—or I'll have your head. Hands *and* legs. Understand?"

"Right away, sir." The private laid his rifle aside and knelt down, rolling Solenne roughly over before hauling her up and back onto the chair. Barrett saw that his hands were shaking as he tied the woman, and that Quinto was taking care to avoid even looking at her.

The woman observed the goings on with a disquieting equanimity, as if she cared not a whit what these men were doing.

When it was clear that the woman was under control again, Barrett holstered his pistol and turned to Johnston. "Sir, are you all right?"

Barrett watched the shade of Johnston's complexion deepen as he absorbed the question.

"Do not trouble yourself about me, Captain." The threat was implicit in his tone. If anyone who had witnessed this spoke of their colonel being struck by a woman, they would regret it.

Barrett nodded. "Sir, I know you're . . . in the middle of interrogating this prisoner, but Quinto—"

"Colonel," Quinto broke in, "I need to tell you—" He hesitated when he saw Solenne looking at him, and Barrett was aware that Quinto was taking great pains to stay as far from her as he could in the confines of the tent. Despite his earlier conversation with the Apache, he was astonished at the thought of any man being more scared of a bound woman than of Colonel Simon Johnston.

"Well, go on, man." Johnston spat.

Quinto was trying to concentrate on Johnston, but his eyes flitted toward the girl every few seconds. "There is at least one more of the things you seek out there. I found tracks from an Apache horse—"

"Apache?"

"It was not shod."

Johnston nodded. "Of course. Go on."

"There was blood too . . . leading out of the camp where we caught them." His eyes darted back to Solenne again, looking as if he expected her to strike him dead at any moment.

Johnston smiled. His face was bloody, and Barrett could see a bruise rising around his nose. The smile looked familiar, but Barrett could not immediately recall from where.

"When did you know about this?"

Quinto paused, fear evident on his face.

Barrett interjected. "A few minutes ago, sir. I delayed Quinto outside as I knew you were interrogating the prisoner."

"Very well. Don't delay in notifying me about such things again. Captain, take twenty men and get to following those tracks. Make sure they have nets and make sure they understand—again—we aim to capture these creatures."

"Very well, Colonel." Barrett glanced at Quinto. "Could use him along, sir."

Johnston nodded and turned to the private, who had finished securing Solenne again. "She properly tied up?"

The private nodded.

"On your life?"

The private hesitated and then plunged ahead. "Sir, my daddy was a lawman. He told me anyone can get out of rope if you give 'em enough time, and not to depend on them overlong, sir. But she's tied up real good. Best I could do, sir."

"Good man, Private. Honesty is a valuable thing in a soldier. Barrett, I'm making this man a corporal. See to it when you get back."

"Yessir," Barrett said with a nod and turned to leave, but he found himself unable to exit the tent without casting a glance in Solenne's direction, and her cool blue eyes held him for a moment.

"Captain, your colonel is insane. The things he is sending you after are a plague—"

Johnston leaned in and punched Solenne, and this time the blow knocked her near unconscious and left her slumped in the chair.

"Corporal, you take up guard again outside the tent."

The newly appointed corporal snapped off a salute and a *yessir* and exited.

"Gentlemen." Johnston grinned again, and Barrett almost caught hold of the memory that the man's bloody smile evoked. "You have your orders. You may leave her with me."

Barrett nodded and turned to go. Quinto was a step ahead of him, obviously glad to be leaving Solenne's company even though she was now, to Barrett's mind, clearly helpless.

Barrett heard another punch land as the tent flapped closed behind him, along with a muttered oath and the word *bitch*. He quick-stepped away from the sounds of other blows and felt a coward for it, but he well knew that interfering would probably just get him shot and only delay the inevitable.

As he walked toward his horse, already shouting orders that would assemble the party of men he needed, the memory that Johnston's blood-smile had disturbed in him suddenly surfaced.

When he was barely sixteen years old, he'd wandered into a small California town and found employment there for a time as an assistant to the smithy. The sheriff had ridden into town one day, a man staggering behind him, hands tied and roped to the sheriff's horse. The prisoner was a cattle rancher who had gone mad and murdered his wife and three children. More than murdered, in fact. He had cut them to pieces—butchered them. Then, so the town shopkeeper told it later, he had carefully wrapped some of the cuts of meat he'd sliced from their bodies and brought them in to sell to the butcher. The butcher, even if he had been dim enough to mistake human flesh for that of a cow, had been disturbed in any case by the giggling of the gory figure who tried to present the meat for sale.

The crazy man had turned to look at Barrett as they passed, and despite being tied and destined for certain death at the end of a rope, his bright eyes had danced above a bloody-faced grin that mirrored the one Barrett had seen on Johnston's face just a few minutes ago.

*** 

Sumner had been assigned to water the horses in his platoon, and he had managed—barely—to accomplish this despite his growing malaise and the fog that seemed to be forming in front of his eyes to match the one already in his mind. Rigid concentration had been necessary to complete the simple chore of leading a few horses to the river and then back again to re-tether them.

During the course of this task, one of the horses had brushed against his right side, and the contact had flung agony up his entire arm, drawing first a moan and then a curse from him. He'd dropped the reins— thank God none of the animals had run—and staggered away from the horses. Collapsing on the ground, he'd drawn his shirtsleeve up his arm with shaking fingers, gasping at what he saw. His lower arm had taken on a dead-looking grey cast, and dark blue web-like marks had arced around the original wound. Worse, they had looked as if they were flowing up toward his shoulder, growing like an unchecked weed. The throbbing had been slowly receding, but he had realized with a flush of new fear that he felt no pain in his fingers on that side, and he had touched them with his good hand. No feeling in them at all.

"No, no . . ." He had been halfway down the riverbank and the horses had wandered to the stream themselves to drink their fill. One of them had lifted its head briefly when he spoke, but it went back to the water immediately when the man had begun rambling to himself.

"No way . . . No way, no how. It's just a *scratch*."

Sumner had seen wounds turn bad before, had even seen men have limbs amputated after they'd become gangrenous. The idea of such a thing happening to him was awful enough to contemplate, but at least he knew—given quick treatment by a surgeon—that gangrenous wounds were potentially survivable. But Johnston's troop carried no surgeon with it. The Confederacy had few physicians to spare and, in any case, the colonel had judged it unnecessary. This far from any garrison, a man who became sick enough to warrant the attentions of a medical officer could be left behind in the next town they passed through. Or simply left behind.

The troop did carry an amputation kit, and two of the corporals had been briefly trained on the use of chloroform and the tools within, but rumour had it the two had used all the chloroform up over the months, in place of alcohol, to get themselves drunk.

But Sumner knew this wound could not be gangrene. The black stink of tissue that characterized the death of an extremity took days to manifest itself, and this scratch—this mere scratch—was only a few hours old. Even if amputation could help, Sumner knew Johnston would not allow it. Everyone knew he would sacrifice anyone in the troop if it should bring him a step closer to obtaining the kind of creature Sumner feared he might now become.

Avoiding the use of his right arm, Sumner had managed to collect the reins of the horses and return them to camp, where he now sat staring at the small hatchet he carried in his pack. Many soldiers carried an axe to chop firewood and such. It could double as a weapon as well, if a man needed it. Sumner thought now of using it on himself.

Months ago Sumner had been wounded in battle—a trifling graze to his head that had bled in such an impressive fashion that two of his fellow soldiers had dragged him to the rear and then into the putrescent stink of the hospital tent. In his few hours there, he had seen twelve limbs amputated. He'd watched the surgeons bind the limbs with leather straps above where they intended to cut, then incise the flesh and saw through the bone.

Now he thought through how he might accomplish the same with his axe. He would have no chloroform—could he do it? Could he do it alone? He had no close friend he could ask for help. It was late afternoon now. Even if he could bring himself to try, would he have enough light to see so as not to butcher himself?

Sumner knew it would never work. Likely he would not be able to bring himself to do it at all, and even if he tried, he would almost certainly kill himself in the process. He began to cry softly, careful not to make too much noise. He wished he had never left the farm. His father had been—in most folks' eyes—a failure who could barely make his land pay and who was always in debt. Sumner saw his father now for the wise man he had been, or at least for what he had told his son the afternoon the horse soldiers rode in looking for food and water. Sumner had admired their uniforms and their toughness. They had talked of defending Southern honour and of how they needed brave men. Eyeing the two horses Edwin's father owned, they talked of how horsemen were especially valuable.

His father had seen the look in his son's eyes and told him not to even think of leaving with them, but Edwin had taken one of the horses and had rode out after them that very night. He had not even bothered to say goodbye to his family, thinking he would be coming home in a few months. He had thought that his family would forgive him for his rash behaviour when he returned a hero—that from then on, the neighbours who had sniggered about the Sumner family would tip their hats and treat his mother with respect whenever they rode into town. But he looked at his arm and knew that none of that would happen now. He would die out here and never see his family again.

Unless . . .

The girl they had been pursuing all these months . . . the Witch. In point of fact, it was her capture that had led to the wound that was killing him. She had, in effect, doomed him. It was *her* fault he was dying.

But if she were a witch . . . He had never believed in such things, but he had heard the men talking. One of them had seen her stripped naked. The prospect of seeing a woman nude was cause enough for talk among the men, but the rumour was that she was covered with scars. Bitten. Scratched. By the same kind of thing that had scratched Sumner. Yet she had healed. A witch, indeed.

She was Sumner's only chance.

## Chapter Fourteen

The Bruised-Head creature tumbled into one of the dry arroyos that criss-crossed the desert landscape in its stumbling drive toward the scent of men. It briefly caught the odour of fresh meat passing by, but that was gone before it could focus, and so it continued toward the Confederate camp and the tantalizing coppery fragrance of blood on the wind.

In fact, it had scented Barrett and the group of twenty men he'd gathered, who had ridden almost directly east following the trail Quinto had belatedly come across, and so they passed right by one of the creatures their commander so desperately wanted. The group followed the tracks into a wide canyon mouth, and it was not long before Quinto spied smoke from campfires ahead of them and pointed it out to Barrett. They reined in their horses, and Barrett squinted at the village, trying to discern details.

"Tracks lead right into that camp," Quinto said, peering at the collection of teepees and fires still a couple of miles ahead and then looking down to study the ground.

Barrett grunted. "If we are following one of those things, I guess that's about what you'd expect it to do—get after some fresh meat."

Quinto did not answer immediately. He was concentrating on a disturbed area in the sand just before them. Eventually he pointed at the ground a few feet ahead.

"Man fell off his horse here."

"Any chance he was shot?"

"Who knows?" Quinto pointed again. "There's blood here. And here, but . . ."

He rode slowly ahead, leaning down and examining the ground. Eventually he grunted as if in satisfaction and shook his head. "The horse ran off toward the village." He gestured at the camp ahead, and then back at the ground. "Here—tracks of the man. Looks like he was limping and fell a few times."

"Injured, likely."

"Not just injured."

"What? Why?"

Quinto looked toward the village. "Something's wrong in that camp. Can you see it?"

Barrett looked up at the village. "Not rightly." He tipped his hat forward and squinted again. "Looks pretty much like any Indian village I've ever seen. Can't say I'm anxious to ride into it with this many men, but—"

"The fires are all going out, and there are no sentries." Quinto shaded his eyes and twisted his head sideways. "I see movement but . . . fighting. They are—"

Quinto paused as the sound of a scream echoed off the canyon walls around them. He saw Barrett looking at him, frowning.

"What your colonel seeks is there."

"You figure, huh?" Barrett turned to the men behind him. "Garrison and Smith, Jones and Green—spread those nets out between you. You'll ride in to capture. The rest of you men, rifles up."

The men needed little incentive to draw their weapons. Barrett saw that several already had their carbines out, but they were all quick to comply with his orders and arrange themselves as they had been trained.

"Men, you know our mission is to capture one or more of those things. Whether we find Apaches or the creatures, this camp will no doubt be hostile. Stay close and watch yourselves . . . Advance."

Barrett waved his arm and nudged his horse forward into a sprint, his men in step with him, and they rapidly closed the distance between themselves and the camp. As they approached, it became plain that Quinto's assessment had been accurate. There were no lookouts of any kind and no sign that their approach had been noticed. Barrett's nose caught the stink of decay when they were still two hundred yards out.

Screams continued to rise from the camp, but at longer and more irregular intervals. As they got closer, Barrett saw that the village consisted of twenty or so teepees arranged in a rough circle on the high ground just back from the stream that wound down the middle of the canyon. Whisps of smoke drifted up from the remains of what had been cooking fires. Sounds of horses whinnying and snorting in agitation came from some distance away, perhaps from the other side of the camp.

By the time they were perhaps a hundred yards out, Barrett could smell blood on the wind, and the scent provoked a memory flash of the massacre he had once witnessed. He felt his heart begin to hammer as a vision of the long-dead baby, drowned in the trough, floated suddenly before his eyes. There must have been a lot of blood spilled for the scent to carry this distance.

Now he caught glimpses of shadows beneath the tall mesquite trees, moving between the teepees. Some were small, perhaps dogs—or wounded men crawling? It was hard to pick up details in the shade of the camp with the sun behind them.

Barrett led the four men with him toward a gap between the nearest of the teepees. He slowed and gestured for the pairs of men bearing nets to go to the left and right of his group. Tense, grim, and not speaking a word, they wound between the outermost circle of teepees in this way without seeing anyone.

Quinto waved and caught Barrett's attention. He pointed to the ground their horses trod across, and Barrett realized there was fresh blood splattered on the soil below. Just ahead he saw torn pieces of flesh and glistening fragments of human innards scattered about like the remains of a deer torn apart by a pack of wolves.

The wind had died and a miasma of decay surrounded them now, and Barrett choked back the bile that rose in his throat. His heart was now hammering so hard he felt it might burst from his chest. He knew himself to be a brave man, but a sudden desperate urge to flee was afire in his brain. Something truly evil was at work here, and he could feel it grinding at his nervous system like a bow drawn across the strings of a fiddle.

The horses seemed to feel the same growing panic. When Barrett tightened the reins and tried to force his mount forward, he felt its muscles tensing and twitching as it tried to turn away. He could not help wondering if he should let the beast have its way.

As they rounded the next tent, Barrett saw the first of the creatures about a hundred yards ahead of them. What had once been three Apache braves were kneeling on the ground surrounding a dead man, as if at a picnic. Each of them was covered in blood, and all were engaged in tearing morsels of flesh and organ meat from the abdomen of the corpse and heaving the pieces into their mouths.

The nearest creature turned as Barrett and his companions came into view, its attention attracted by the growing volume of their horses' panicked whinnying. Barrett saw that half of the dead thing's face had been ripped away, leaving a raw black-red wound seeping oily yellow pus. Its left eye dangled from its socket like a deflated balloon against the side of its exposed skull, swinging gently on the end of its optic nerve. The monster growled at Barrett as it continued to chew on the ragged piece of intestine that hung out of its mouth, dribbling a mix of gore and yellow-brown intestinal contents into its lap.

Another group of monsters came around one of the teepees ahead of them as if a dinner bell had been rung, stumbling with the nerveless gait that Barrett would quickly come to understand was typical of them. All of the creatures looked many days dead and bore the ghastly marks of having been fed on prior to their own reawakening.

While Barrett and his men were concentrating on this bloody parade of the dead, the teepee just beside them flapped open and another of the things crawled out. It had been a young boy, perhaps ten when it died. Now its lower body was mostly eaten away and its torn guts hung like multiple tails trailing behind it as it clawed slowly toward them.

The horror of the moment took Barrett back again to the horse trough and the dead baby. He shook his head to rid himself of the vision and bellowed at his men.

"Garrison and Smith! Jones and Green! Deploy your nets and move forward. Aim for those monsters on the right."

Barrett saw that the men were quaking and wild-eyed. Garrison seemed about to speak, but there was no time for discussion now.

"Go on, men!"

They had rehearsed this for months, and Barrett was gratified to see that despite their fears, the men were already spreading the nets out between them and moving forward.

"The rest of you! We only need three or four of these things alive. You will shoot down any that are out of the nets and a threat to our men. Clear?"

There were nods and a chorus of *yessirs* as he turned back to the hungry dead things pressing in toward them. The ones that had been clustered on the ground were getting up and moving in as well. He now counted seven of the things coming toward them, and the number was growing. Between the tents in the distance, Barrett could see other ragged, bloody creatures moving to converge on the scent of fresh meat.

"Forward men!" Barrett set his horse to a trot and the others followed.

If Barrett had not been so concentrated on his task, he might have found the behaviour of the things fascinating. They were aligned and focused on the men before them but seemed to avoid coming too close to their own kind if they could help it. Once or twice he saw one move within hand's reach of another, and there were quick snarls exchanged before a greater distance was assumed by one of the two. Like a pack of wolves. He wondered what level of intelligence actually remained in them.

The closest of them was no more than fifty yards away now. This was the time to surprise them. "Full speed now, men!" He set his horse surging forward and the others followed suit.

"Net men! Take the ones on the right! Riflemen, ready to shoot."

The monsters were close enough now that Barrett could easily pick out details. Their skin tone varied from grey to brown to yellow, and their eyes had all clouded over as if with cataracts. Each of the things had some significant portion of their flesh torn away and—he supposed—eaten by the creatures that had killed *them*. Skin and muscle hung in tattered rags from arms and faces. *Defensive wounds,* he found himself thinking. Many were missing body parts . . . fingers, eyes—even a nose—torn off or eaten. Bloodless gashes, perhaps from knives or axes, gaped open on most of them and arrows pierced the torsos of several—wounds that would certainly have been fatal to any living man. Bile-coloured pus leaked from some of the wounds, and a black, syrupy drool leaked from their lips.

Barrett's horse skittered around something crawling on the ground in front of it. He looked down and felt his heart skip a beat. It was a grey-skinned baby, one leg ripped mostly away and the gash of an empty cavity where its abdomen should have been. And yet it arms were moving, flailing uselessly at him as he passed the thing by. Barrett stared for a moment into its yellowed eyes, and then the dead baby floating in the water trough was in his brain again.

*The woman . . . The Witch. She was trying to kill the creature that did this, and we stopped her. All these people are dead—dead and risen as monsters—because of Johnston. And what I allowed to happen.*

But they were in the thick of it now, with no time for anything but thoughts of survival. Barrett and the riflemen began shooting at the creatures to their left. By happenstance, one bullet found its way into the skull of one of the monsters, and it collapsed in a heap. The rest came on despite a hail of bullets rained into their torsos.

Now the horsemen were nearly among the things, and several of the men around Barrett found their mounts shying away from the creatures, rearing up when their riders tried to bring them under control. One man had fallen and was struggling to get to his feet.

Too late Barrett felt the close quarters around him, tents that could hide the creatures or prevent easy manoeuvring of horses. He should have tried to lure some of them out instead of plunging in among the teepees, but he couldn't have imagined there would be so many of them.

"Sir?" Garrison called to Barrett in an uncertain voice.

"Capture them!" Barrett shouted, shoving his rifle into its scabbard and drawing both pistols, firing at the monsters nearest him.

Disaster began to unfold.

The walking dead were in among them now. The riflemen continued to shoot into the monsters not targeted for capture. Every bullet hit, and had they been firing at living men, their attack would have had deadly effect, but as it was, only two more creatures fell from accidental shots to the head. The rest merely stumbled briefly from the impact of whirling lead shot exploding through their flesh. Undeterred, they came on like golems, never wavering, their dead minds fixed on the food that was so close.

While Simon Johnston had learned something about the nature of these creatures in South America, and more yet from his pursuit over the last few months, he had never trusted the secret of the reapers' only weakness to his subordinates, whom he had tasked with bringing in *still-animate* specimens. Though he had cautioned them not to shoot *for* the head, he had reasoned correctly that this was not the same as disclosing that destruction of the brain was the only way to kill them once and for all.

This lack of crucial information alone might not have decided the battle, but Garrison's early actions did.

In a later age, Garrison might have been diagnosed as having one or more learning disabilities. In this age, he was simply thought of as slow. Despite this, he had been an able enough soldier—strong, with decent aim, and endowed with bravery and loyalty. In the weeks of drills using the nets, he had been quick enough to read the actions of others and let them direct his own. Because he had never been frightened during the many capture exercises, he had always performed adequately.

Now, though, he was terrified, and as he galloped forward, spreading the net between himself and the soldier beside him, his disability betrayed him. All his life, no matter how hard he had tried, Garrison had never been able to tell left from right. Barrett's order to net the creatures on the right had meant nothing to him. With no time to clarify, and in the cacophony of the yells of men and growls of the walking dead, he had guessed—and guessed wrong.

Garrison and Smith were in the lead, the net held between them, and when Smith angled his horse to the right just ahead of the creatures, Garrison rode to the left. He realized his mistake almost immediately and tried to correct his horse's path, but it was too late. The net spread quickly between the two riders, both of whom were clutching it with one hand as if their lives depended on it.

"No!" But Barrett knew the cry to be futile even as it spilled from his lips.

The net tautened between the two riders, and Smith's wild-eyed horse rode straight out from under him and then spun, hurtling away from the snarling monsters as fast as it could.

Smith hit the ground with a bone-snapping crunch and tumbled forward in a cloud of dust, coming to a stop very near the fallen rider, who had been unable to get back on his own panicked animal, which had turned into a wheeling, wide-eyed dervish.

Hand still clutched in the net, Garrison managed to stay on his horse only a few seconds longer than his partner. Smith's tumble wrenched Garrison from his own mount and his horse carried on, dashing through the ranks of the undead in a haphazard dance before it disappeared among the trees.

Garrison fell between the three creatures he had been attempting to net, screaming as he slammed into the ground. He rolled onto his back to find himself looking up into the tattered faces of hissing demons clustered around him. The undead dived onto him like a pack of starving animals—a tearing, biting whirlwind of hunger. The creature with the dangling eye latched onto his neck, and even in his last moments, Garrison was shocked at how cold the thing's mouth was in the midst of this hot desert. Icy lips parted and sharp teeth tore out his throat. His shrieks faded to desperate, bubbling gurgles that were lost among the other yells and screeches erupting around him.

Smith—his face a mask of fear and pain—had thrashed to his feet cradling a broken left arm to find he was surrounded. His eyes darted desperately at the nightmarish creatures closing in from all sides, their charnel-house stink filling his nostrils as their growls and roars shut out the noise of all the living men around him.

Barrett angled his horse to come alongside Jones and Green, then brought his rifle up to take aim at one of the closest monsters. His shot sent the thing crashing to the ground in a spray of black gore, the back of its head gone.

Jones and Green had been barely twenty yards behind Garrison and Smith, and they surged forward as they had been trained despite seeing their fellows go down. There was no confusion in *their* attack. In fact, Barrett thought they deployed their mesh perfectly. The netting was stretched between their two horses with a rigidly maintained distance of twenty feet. As if one, they reacted to Smith's presence in their path and jogged their horses to veer around him. The group of reapers clustered, uncertain, between Smith and the horsemen riding down on them, and Jones and Green rode in and cast their net, ensnaring all three.

"Draw them together!" Barrett yelled. "Close the net!"

Securing their ropes to the horns of their saddles, the riders whirled around and drew back. The netting slammed the creatures together in a twisting mass of hate, biting and raging at one another other in between desperate attempts to claw at the warm, ruddy humans surrounding them.

Barrett, like the other riflemen, was spinning on his horse and shooting—mostly uselessly—at the undead, aware that there were many more of the things around them now, as if risen from the very soil below them. Several of his men had been thrown by spooked horses that had then charged out of the field of battle, and they were retreating on foot from the monsters closing in on them. Those who still had their guns fired into the line of demons coming at them, but it was a rare shot that entirely crippled one of the things.

It was time to regroup and retreat. Beyond time, in fact. Out of the corner of his eye, Barrett saw a man dragged from his horse by two of the creatures that had been shot numerous times without effect.

"Regroup!" Barrett shouted. "Fall back!" But the men were on the edge of hysteria now, and amid the screams and gunfire, he was not heard. He watched as several troopers fired wildly into the mob of fiends tearing Garrison apart. Bullets tore through the creatures' bodies, and several struck Garrison so that he actually died from a shot through the heart only moments after his abdomen and neck had been torn open. Other soldiers had begun shooting wildly at the monsters around them, hardly bothering to aim at all.

None of the battles Barrett had fought in this war had prepared him for this. He had always been up against *men* like himself, who fought tactically and attacked in an organized fashion. Most importantly, the men he'd fought previously had been mortal and, at least to some extent, fearful of losing their lives. These dull abominations feared absolutely nothing.

Over the noise, and again unheard by most of the men, Barrett heard Quinto shouting. "The head! Shoot for the head!"

The Apache was aiming and shooting with much greater care than the troopers. Barrett observed that any undead thing that came near Quinto went down quickly, a bullet through its brain.

When Johnston had told his men never to shoot at the head of their quarry, everyone had seen that as simple common sense when trying to capture something alive. But Barrett realized now that Johnston had known that only a head shot would kill them . . .

This was bad. An accurate head shot, even for an experienced marksman, was a difficult thing beyond a hundred paces and was additionally problematic on horseback when both target and shooter were moving. He began to echo Quinto's cry, yelling at the top of his lungs for his men to take head shots only. He was unsure how many heard.

Barrett saw that most of the horsemen were scarcely even aware that Jones and Green had successfully caught some of the monsters, too occupied by terrified horses and the nightmare demons clawing and reaching for them as they closed in. But several turned away from their frantic firing when they heard Jones begin yelling for help.

In retreating after their capture, Jones and Green had ridden their horses through the netting dropped by Smith and Garrison, and Jones's horse had caught a foot up in the mesh. The animal ran on for a few steps, but eventually the two nets and the creatures caught in them tangled and the horse was brought up short, its back right leg breaking with a sharp snap, like ice cracking on a frozen pond.

When the horse collapsed, Jones was hurled to the ground, landing headfirst in the dirt beside his fallen mount and lying still. His horse struggled to get back on its feet, foam erupting from its nostrils and mouth as its head whipped from the netted monsters no more than twenty feet behind it to the lumbering free ones closing in on its fallen rider.

Jones was at best unconscious and more likely dead, Barrett thought. Two of the monsters limped toward the unmoving man, and Barrett saw that even the creatures entangled in the mesh reached out to him, arms flailing through holes in the webbing, heedless of their capture and longing only to feed.

Barrett saw all this over his rifle sight as he brought it to bear on the creature closest to Jones—what had once been a fat old grandmother. He fired and watched her right ear disappear in an explosion of black-red particles. The demon-thing turned toward him and roared its malice before falling on the prone cavalryman, pushing his head back to expose his neck.

Barrett fired twice more and finally hit his mark. The bullet burst through the top of the fat grey thing's head as it fastened on to the soldier's neck and then collapsed on top of him.

A nearby soldier, unhorsed by his own frenzied mount, tried to help Jones. He grabbed the lifeless man's arm and attempted to drag him out from under the weight of the dead monster. Distracted or brave, he paid little attention to two other creatures who had fixed their eyes upon him, firing only sporadically at them while he heaved on Jones's arm. He hit one of them in the torso, and then they were on him, pushing him to the ground and ripping his skin away in strips as they tore into him like sharks.

Barrett's horse lurched suddenly rightwards, and Barrett instinctively whipped his gaze toward what the horse shied from. Death in the form of a half-naked young female demon stared back at him from no more than six feet away, having come up unseen on his left flank. Its face was far more intact than most of its fellows, so that it was almost possible to imagine the happy, carefree girl it had once been. The dead girl with the misty yellow eyes limped toward him, most of the flesh stripped off its left leg. Arms lifted and fingers curled like talons, it reached for him and opened its mouth in a gurgling roar.

Barrett whipped his rifle around with his right hand even as he sought to draw his pistol with the left. But the thing was too close, and as the monster clawed toward him, the horse chose that moment to rear up and Barrett was in the air suddenly, then crashing to the ground. The wind sailed out of his lungs with the impact, and it was all he could do to hold on to his rifle as he gasped and heaved like a trout drawn out of the river.

The girl-thing loomed over him, dark blue lips drawn back over yellowed teeth, and pushed his rifle aside with unnatural strength. Barrett went with the motion, pulling the rifle around and lowering it. When he pulled the trigger, it blew out the thing's left knee, finishing the job its killers had begun by severing the leg. The creature collapsed half on top of him, its mouth wide open in anticipation, and he knew he was done for.

Then the rabid thing's head exploded, showering Barrett with bone chips and sludgy black gore. One of the riflemen—Roberts—was suddenly beside him, his gun still smoking as he pulled Barrett out from under the lifeless monster and back to his feet.

"Sir. 'Bout to get our asses kicked here," Roberts said. And he was right.

Barrett's gaze darted around. Three of the creatures remained ensnared in the net. A half-dozen of them lay dead or at least incapacitated. Two or three were crawling, legs or lower bodies destroyed by gunfire, toward the soldiers nearest them as the rest of the men—only a few left on horseback—continued to fire into the demons.

More creatures were closing in. The troopers had not yet been overwhelmed only because several men had been lost to the creatures, and wherever a soldier had been taken down, it had attracted a crowd of reapers. There were at least five writhing mounds of creatures on top of their helpless prey, ripping them apart with savage determination. Even as Barrett watched, one of the things ripped a leg bone, covered in mere tatters of flesh, from the corpse of a victim. The thing snapped the bone in two and began sucking marrow from one of the ends.

Quinto rode back and forth among the remaining soldiers, yelling repeatedly, "The head! Shoot them in the head!" He followed his own advice, firing with great care at a reaper near him. The thing dropped lifeless, a ragged black hole in its forehead.

Some of the men seemed to have heard and understood Quinto and had shifted their aim toward the creature's heads, but they were scared and desperate now, shooting in haste and missing what they were aiming at most of the time.

Barrett guessed this village must have boasted a population of about seventy. He had set out knowing he was taking twenty well-armed fighting men into a camp that held perhaps twenty or thirty warriors, with the rest being elders, women, and children. But all were warriors in this village of the dead, and the troop was severely outnumbered and outmatched.

"Regroup!" Barrett shouted again, and this time the men seemed to hear him. They had been on the verge of breaking and running anyway, and they took heed immediately. Those few still mounted wheeled their horses and circled back toward Barrett. Men on foot backed toward him firing pistols or rifles wildly at the creatures approaching them.

Barrett caught sight of his horse and ran toward it, motioning to Roberts to remount as well. "Regroup! Fall back!" he repeated, conscious of the splinter of fear in his voice.

"Green . . . Roberts . . . Evans . . ." The three men tore their gazes from the dead things shambling toward them and focused on Barrett. When he saw he had their attention, he pointed at the monsters still writhing in the net. "Don't wait for us! Get those things back to camp! Go! Go!"

"Right away, sir!" Green said. He motioned to the others, and the three turned as if one and rode forward, their horses straining at first against the load strung behind them. Barrett watched the frenzied men kick brutally at the animals beneath them, shouting curses as each man took turns firing at the monsters closing in on them.

Green allowed one of the things to draw too near him. He fired his last shot at its head, and though the monster's lower jaw was blown away, it was still able to drag him from his horse. Barrett lost sight of the doomed man as several other creatures fell upon him, but he saw the other horsemen carry on. Their horses had established a momentum now and soon outdistanced the other lumbering demons pursuing them.

Barrett turned back to the massacre their encounter had become and began picking targets and firing, trying to cover his men's retreat, but he feared it was far too little, far too late.

The monsters had taken down at least ten men, and the screams of the dying surrounded Barrett, mingled with the awful sounds of tearing flesh and the guttural growls and moans of the monsters as they feasted. Blood was everywhere, staining the ground and misting the air as the monsters shredded any live human they got their hands upon.

He saw the dead baby again, crawling across the ground toward him as if it had chosen to punish him, specifically, for letting this happen.

*She was trying to stop this.* Again, the thought bobbed to the surface of his mind.

Any loose horse had long ago bolted away from the undead, and now any soldiers remaining followed suit, sprinting as fast as they could to be away from this hell. At least two of them seemed to make it between the teepees, running out into the desert, but he saw most of the others taken down in screaming terror by the demons.

Quinto fired repeatedly at one of the creatures as it latched onto him and sunk its teeth into his arm. Even as he fell, gun lost, he groped for the tomahawk in his belt and brought it up in an arc to bury it several inches deep into the monster's head. The creature collapsed below him, and Quinto pushed it away and got to his hands and knees, retrieving his pistol.

Barrett watched him look down at the wound the creature had made on his arm. It was bleeding freely and there was a large chunk of flesh missing. Quinto looked up and found Barrett's eyes in a stare devoid of hope.

Barrett heard the Witch's voice. *Your colonel is insane.*

Quinto shoved the barrel of his gun under his chin and fired. Barrett saw the back of his head explode and the man fall limp beside his attacker. His suicide seemed to Barrett like a well-planned action, as if the man had spent some time thinking about the afterlife and decided he wanted no part of wandering the earth as a hungry revenant.

Distracted by Quinto's death, Barrett started when he felt a sudden pressure around his left ankle. He looked down to see a reaper that would have once been an eight-year-old boy looking up at him, milky yellow eyes staring out of an empty grey face that sported a crooked, wide-mouthed smile. He tried again to sink his teeth into Barrett's leather boot.

Barrett kicked the undead boy in the face and watched him fall. Two more of the demons—what looked to be a former grandfather and a teenage girl—had come up on his other side, and his horse reared again, skittering away from them. Barrett managed to shoot the grandfather in the head, but by then the teenager had hold of him. Other hands joined hers, and he was dragged again to the ground as his horse skittered away.

"Dammit!" He had waited too long.

The girl-reaper was above him, and it took three shots from his pistol to bring it down. It fell beside him, empty eyes staring accusingly at him as oily red fluid drooled out of the bullet hole in its forehead.

*Just a girl. She would be alive now, perhaps tending to a cooking fire or gathering agave for the evening meal—if not for Johnston.*

The sudden sharp sting in his left leg was shocking, sending a bolt of fear up his spine. He tore his gaze from the girl's corpse as he tried to wrench his leg away from the pain. It was the boy reaper, battened on to his lower limb like a leech. It had ripped aside his chaps, and he could feel its teeth digging into his flesh. He kicked at it, struggling to free himself, but the demon-child just raised its head and growled at him, spitting Barrett's own blood from between its teeth before turning its poisonous mouth back to his leg. His next kick dislodged the demon-boy, sending it rolling over and up onto its hands and knees, the demon rictus still affixed on its face. The thing was still chewing on a piece of Barrett's flesh as it began to crawl back toward him.

Barrett groped to get onto his knees, kicking at other dead grey hands reaching for him as pain flared in his leg. His hand found his remaining pistol, and as the demon-boy launched itself at him again, he fired point blank into its face. The small, fragile skull disintegrated into bone fragments and foul-smelling black liquid as the thing buckled and fell still on the ground. Barrett stood, punching and kicking at the others pressing in on him, and limped away from the remaining monsters as quickly as he could.

He could see no other living man left standing. All around him, packs of snapping, growling demons fought over their victims, some of whom still gurgled hopeless, frothy cries for help as their killers ripped them asunder.

But not all of the demons were thus occupied. Several of the living dead continued to pursue him as he limped away—women and children mostly—perhaps driven away from the kills around them by stronger creatures. The baby had almost reached him, a few shreds of intestine still dangling like grey worms from the gash in its belly.

He heard the Witch's voice again.

*Insane.*

The baby's toothless maw yawned open, and it hissed at him.

Somehow, Barrett found the strength to run.

***

"Stop, Evans. Hold up a moment."

Evans stared straight ahead as if he hadn't heard a thing. There had been no reaction the other two times Roberts had yelled at him either, so Roberts sidled his horse up and took the man's reins, pulling slowly back and halting both horses.

This finally provoked a reaction from Evans. He flinched as his horse stopped and turned to Roberts, wide-eyed and horrified.

"What're you doing? We've gotta keep going."

He pulled at the reins in Roberts's hand, but Roberts held on firmly and leaned in close to Evans, near enough to know that sometime in the last half-hour's orgy of horror, Evans had shit himself.

"No. We've got to stop. Some of the others will have gotten away. We have to wait for them."

Behind them, the creatures massed in the netting sensed something had changed and reached arms out through the mesh and began dragging themselves, net and all, toward the men atop the horses. Evans noticed this immediately and jerked the reins out of Roberts's hands. This provoked Roberts to slap Evans, nearly knocking him off his horse.

"Shit!" Roberts cradled the hand he'd hit Evans with, cursing in pain.

Evans shot him a dark look. "Take a look behind us, dickhead. We stop and those things'll crawl right up our ass. Can't you see that?" He paused, puzzled. "What in hell's wrong with your hand?"

Roberts dismounted, not answering. "You stay on the horse. I'll go back behind the net. They'll fight each other to get at us both at the same time and go nowhere."

Wary, and with eyes always on the netted demons, Roberts walked wide around the mass of inhuman monsters so that the creatures were between him and Evans, and the demons fought against each other to reach the man closest to them and went nowhere. The horses seem nervous and less than happy about having stopped, but as long as the creatures remained a few yards behind them, the animals seemed controllable.

Roberts had long since lost his hat, and so he shaded his eyes with his hands as he looked back across the desert. He estimated they'd run several miles from the village.

"See anything?" Everyone knew that Evans's eyesight was poor at any great distance.

Roberts did—quite literally—see several *things*. Creatures had followed them out of the village and were on their trail, albeit a long way behind. He saw three soldiers running as well. It was easy to distinguish the coordinated running of a live man from the crippled, limping gait of most of the walking dead, though some of the demons were overtaking the living men, two of whom were wounded and limping.

Roberts watched an injured trooper tumble to the ground under the grip of what had once been a fat old man. He saw the creature windmill its arms, clawing into the man's face and neck, and then dip its head downward. The soldier struggled briefly and then lay still as the creature began ripping into him in earnest. Roberts cursed and skirted the net once again to return to his horse, barely able to draw his eyes away from the captured creatures that snarled and raved like cold merciless death behind him.

"Reckon you're right." He put his foot in the stirrup to climb back on his horse. "Ain't nothing for it but to head back to camp."

"Maybe not," Evans said, and when Roberts looked up, he saw the other man had his pistol out and was pointing it at him. "I asked you before . . . What's wrong with your hand?"

Roberts stepped back from his horse. "What the fuck you doing?"

Evans glanced back at the trapped creatures. They had begun crawling toward the warm meat amassed in front of them again. Evan's horse had noticed it too, and it shifted nervously under him.

"Your hand—what's wrong with it?"

Roberts licked his lips and glanced down at the hand he'd hit Evans with. There was an open gash across the palm that looked oddly black at the edges.

"Must've fucked up my hand tying those sons a bitches up," he said, nodding at the creatures. "Now what the fuck are you doing pointing a gun at me, asshole?"

But Roberts thought he knew all too well why Evans had his gun out. Now that he thought about it, Roberts could feel an unusual heat coming from the laceration, like a branding iron was warming slowly against it. And now he remembered, during the capture, that he'd snatched his hand away as one of the creatures had clawed at him.

"One of them things gotcha, didn't it?" Evans said.

"No. No!"

"Oh yeah, it did." Evans gathered the reins of the other man's horse and nudged his own forward. "You're staying here. You got my sympathy, but I ain't riding with someone who's gonna turn into a monster."

"Evans, you bastard, you are not fucking leaving me out here."

Roberts stepped forward and Evans raised his gun. At that moment, one of the monsters lunged toward them, growling, and Evans's wary eyes flicked to the creatures, busily engaged in dragging themselves closer to him.

When he looked back, Roberts had his own pistol out. The man stepped toward his horse again, his gun unwavering, the black hole of the barrel staring Evans in the face.

"I ain't got no quarrel with you. I ain't *bit!*" Roberts reflected that this statement was not entirely a lie, since he had been *slashed*, not bitten. But he desperately wanted to believe the gist of it, himself—that he was not contaminated, despite the unnatural warmth and the itchy feeling in the wound, as if maggots were scuttling around under the skin.

Evans cocked his pistol and pointed it deliberately at Roberts's head. "Only way you're coming back to camp with me is if you climb inside that net with those others." The sudden eruption of hate on Roberts's face gave him pause, but he carried on after a moment. "I'm sorry for you, but I ain't finishing my life as one of them things."

For emphasis, he motioned with his gun toward the demons they dragged behind them, and in the second his gun was off target, Roberts fired. Once, twice, and then the click of an empty chamber. He had used up most of his bullets in the fight at the camp.

Evans looked down at the two smoking red holes that had bloomed like spring flowers in his upper chest. He felt numbness spreading through his body but still managed to pull the trigger of his own weapon twice as he fell from his horse and struck the ground unconscious.

Evans's first shot tore Roberts's lower jaw away in an explosion of blood and teeth. The second entered what was left of his mouth and erupted out of the back of his neck, severing his spine and collapsing him like a house of cards.

Brain left undamaged but unable to breathe, Roberts found himself staring up at the darkening evening sky. His lower face was an orchestra of agony, but as his brain ran through the last of the oxygen in his blood, the pain slowly left him and the sky faded to black.

Evans woke a few minutes later with pain grating like shattered glass in his chest every time he took a breath. He coughed and was rewarded with a spray of blood from his mouth, black in the dimming light. He knew that the coppery taste meant death was coming for him. Even as it came up, he could feel more pouring into his throat. After a moment, he threw himself onto his left side. The agony from the wounds in his chest turned his next coughing spell into a paroxysm of excruciating pain. After it was over, he drew a cautious, shuddering breath and spat the last of the blood—for now, at least—onto the sand.

There were scuffling sounds around him. Evans looked up at his horse and saw it straining against the rope and pawing the ground as it twisted its head back and forth, looking from the man to the monsters behind it in the netting. Muzzle flecked with foam, Evans knew it would have bolted if it were not tied to the netted monstrosities. He tried to get to his feet and found himself dizzy and weak. He struggled to one knee and then fell back onto his side, hacking again and spewing yet more blood out onto the sand.

The smell of fresh blood seemed to excite the trapped creatures. Evans saw that they fought less among themselves now and exerted more of their efforts toward dragging themselves closer to Roberts and himself. Fear bloomed anew in his chest as he saw that each time the creatures inched forward toward the men on the ground, the horses took up the slack in the rope and began straining anew against it. In this way, the horses were now assisting the mindless demons in crawling toward their prey. The creatures would reach him within a few minutes if he could not get away from them.

He rolled toward the horses and, in doing so, provoked new bolts of agony in his chest. He was panting for every breath now and gurgling like a boiling pot as his punctured lungs filled, and he was forced to lie back prone. Unable to move without pain and every ounce of energy spent trying to breathe, the next time the hungry dead things crept closer he had no strength left to move away.

In the next few minutes, death shuffled over Evans in clumsy fumbles. Taloned hands scraped at his boots until eventually one of the monsters found purchase on his legs. Then came the weight of the massed bodies dragging themselves on top of him, the stink of decay and rotting meat a miasma around them. Blood and vomit filled his mouth as the first of the reapers bit into his legs.

*\*\*\**

Barrett came upon the bodies about an hour later. Against the twilight of the horizon, he had seen the two men's horses standing some distance from the heaped mass of netted monsters. The horses tried to trot away as he came near, but the weight of the net held them back.

A high fever was drilling into him now, and he suspected the horses could smell the stench of something unclean within him already. Sure enough, when he stepped closer to them, they began rearing up against the ropes, desperate to be away from him.

Barrett drew his knife and stepped back from the horses. He had no strength to fight for a ride and no desire to see the horses come to a bad end. Grasping the two ropes holding the netting, he hacked through them, cursing against the sweat that constantly swam into his eyes with the effort. First one, then the other of the ropes parted, and the horses took to their heels.

Barrett turned to the netted monsters, whose attention he had of course attracted. They looked like sated ticks, bellies bulging with their recent repast. Nonetheless, they reached for him as he came close, as frantic and greedy for the taste of human flesh as if starved for weeks. What remained of the bodies of Evans and Roberts lay beneath them, unidentifiable scraps of flesh and shattered bone.

Barrett stumbled around the netted mass of hungry death. His lips were cracked and his tongue felt as dry as a piece of leather. Grit was in his eyes, and it seemed every time he blinked, he must surely be sanding down his eyeballs. Feverish and half-baked in the heat, he had hoped he might find a canteen, but the only one he managed to locate was nearly empty.

What he wouldn't give for a single gulp of *blood . . . warm bloody flesh.*

He shook his head and shuddered, then slapped himself across the face until the visions of blood and the abrupt shocking *need* for it passed. Wiping the sweat from his brow with a trembling hand, he checked his gun belt. He had about a half-dozen bullets left, and he would not use any of them on the creatures unless forced to. He had other plans for these few shells.

A glance behind him revealed that the dead things that had streamed out of the Apache camp behind the retreating cavalrymen were gaining on him. They were perhaps a half mile behind now. The crippling injuries that many of the reapers had suffered slowed their progress somewhat, but Barrett was slowing as well. He had started at a good pace, even if limping, but the pain in his bite had grown from embers into a roaring fire, with the flames licking up his leg and into his hip. His body temperature had rocketed up in a valiant but useless attempt to fight the infection growing inside him, and both his balance and his vision were compromised, even as darkness was falling. He would have to hurry despite these handicaps if he wished to reach the camp ahead of the monsters behind him.

Though there was no water, he did find a rifle. It had a few shells in it, but for now it was more use as a makeshift crutch. He set out again, but he still could not move faster than a rocking limp. It would have to be enough so that he could warn them. Warn them and put an end to this madness. He had few bullets, but if he could keep ahead of the creatures, two were all he would need.

One for himself, of course.

But first, one for Johnston.

## Chapter Fifteen

Solenne woke to silence—but with the feeling that some noise had roused her. There had been dreams before waking, hazy now and impossible to recall clearly, filled with blood and screams. But had the screams been part of the nightmare, or were they real? She held her breath and listened. Her ears told her that she was alone for the moment. When she opened her eyes, the dried blood caking her eyelids cracked away. Her cheek was pressed against the sandy floor of Johnston's tent, the coppery smell of blood in her nose. Pain flared like a freshly lit lantern in her head and chest when she took a deep breath.

The tent was empty. Having obtained some self-satisfaction—if no new information—while beating her unconscious, Johnston had apparently left to attend to other things. She knew he would be back soon, though, and that no doubt at least one guard still stood outside; but she thought perhaps the fate of the last sentry who'd ventured in here would keep this one where he was if she made no sound and gave him no good reason to enter.

With any luck, Solenne would have at least a few minutes to herself. She closed her eyes and cautiously explored her injuries. Every motion hurt—she suspected even smiling would cause her pain. Her nose was clogged with blood and was definitely broken. Her left eye felt puffy and would not open fully. A slow, cautious breath evoked some pain in her chest but no point tenderness. Ribs might be cracked, but not broken. Her belly was sore—perhaps she'd taken a couple of kicks there—but she sensed that nothing was leaking blood inside her and that her body's impressive healing processes were already kicking in.

After consideration, she decided she was, all in all, still reasonably functional.

Someone had thrown the blanket over her again, and she twisted underneath it, testing her muscles. Her blouse was in shreds, but her pants were still on and she felt no pain where she might have if Johnston or anyone else had raped her while she was unconscious.

The private who tied her up *had* done his best. Despite his caveat that eventually anyone could get out of tied ropes, she was bound far more securely this second time. Her hands were still strung behind her back, but not her shoulders or elbows, which would have made things far more difficult. Her ankles were tightly tied as well, but not her knees.

And the private had left her boots on.

That had been really quite stupid.

Solenne arched her back and curled her feet up toward her hands. This brought fresh throbbing in her abdomen and lower back, but she embraced the pain as a friend. The raw ache in her midsection helped her focus.

It was difficult, but she managed to get her fingers into her right boot. The knife she kept there was still in its sheath.

And then the blade was in her hands and she was sawing through her bonds. In a few minutes, the twine around her wrists parted and she sat up. Conscious of the guard who was no doubt just outside, she silently swivelled and drew her feet up in front of her. A few more seconds, and she had worked through the ropes that bound her feet and she was free.

She rolled onto her knees first, trying herself out. Sitting up caused no dizziness. Well, not much, anyway. She got to her feet, wavering a bit until she got her balance, and stood still, breathing deeply as her equilibrium returned. There was a shirt draped over the cot that occupied one corner of the tent. It was stained with the blood, and she noted with what she supposed was perverse satisfaction that it was her own, which she had spit at Johnston when he captured her and spilled on it when he beat her. She discarded her own torn shirt and buttoned Johnston's around her. It stank of cigars and stale sweat, but that could not be helped.

Solenne looked around and saw her gun belt had been flung in a corner of the tent. She shook her head. Her captors had left a killer's guns within easy reach of the killer.

And that was not all. Her eyes lit upon Johnston's sabre. He'd left it on his cot.

She grinned. Smiling *did* hurt.

She could not know how long she had been unconscious, but she could see that it was just past dusk now.

*Precious time gone . . . and none left to lose.*

Now fully conscious, Solenne's dark senses rippled outward around her as if from a pebble thrown in a pond, and she felt a surge in her chest. *They* were out there, all around her, and not far away. Many more of the cursed had sprung to life as she lay unconscious. *So many more . . . and coming this way.*

At least they were approaching her and not pursuing some distant wagon train. The thought made her want to laugh. Few people on the planet would wish for reapers coming *toward* them.

There was a muffled grunt outside and Solenne whipped her head around. A scuffle followed, and she saw the tent wall bulge in momentarily as a body fell against it before—by the sound of it—tumbling to the ground.

Her time was up and she knew it. She snatched at her gun belt and was pulling out her pistol when the tent flaps parted and Edwin Sumner stepped in. He was holding a rifle with bayonet attached, and he had it aimed at her midsection.

"Don't."

His urgent whisper was laced with desperation, and Solenne could see why. The curse was ripening in him—even in the dying light, the yellow-grey cast of his skin and the tangled web of bluish veins growing up his left arm were readily apparent. The desert air was already cooling as evening set in, and yet the man was drenched with sweat. He was trembling too. So violently that Solenne nearly tried to beat him to a shot anyway. The way he was quaking, she half believed he might shoot her by accident.

Sumner stepped forward, and she saw that the bayonet was wet with fresh blood. Some of it was still dripping onto the ground.

"I'll let you go." The same desperate whisper. "But you have to fix me first."

It was not in Solenne's nature to lie to a dying man. "I'm sorry, but no one can help you now."

Sumner jerked his rifle forward in an angry gesture, and the timbre of his voice went up. "Yes, you can! I *know* you can. I heard about what you can do. You're a *witch*. You can *cure* this." Oily tears ran down his cheeks.

"No." Solenne shook her head. "I can't."

His voice hardened. "Fucking Witch. You *can* and you *will*." He stepped forward, and this time when he jerked the gun toward her, it came within inches of her belly.

"Soldier, I would help you if I could, but there is no cure for what you have."

"Are you *listening* to me? I will fucking run you through right now if you don't fix me!" He lifted the gun and shook it front of her face.

Like Brennan, in Solenne's many experiences with armed men, she had noted that people holding weapons rarely shot while in the middle of a sentence. It seemed the human brain was reluctant for some reason to converse and destroy at the same time. Solenne had pondered the philosophical implications of this while tending many an evening campfire, and she had employed the knowledge to her advantage more than once.

"How did it happen?"

"It . . . it was just a scratch." He snorted suddenly as a stream of black almost-blood began leaking out of his nose. He took his right hand—the one that had been wrapped around the trigger—and absently wiped the dark fluid away, and that was the moment.

Solenne moved—a blur to the feverish man holding the rifle. Except that he wasn't holding the rifle anymore. Solenne was. And now it was swinging toward him.

Sumner's vision exploded into a dazzle of white light as the rifle stock struck hard against his temple. He collapsed to the ground, apparently unconscious, but Solenne was thorough about such things, and so she methodically raised the rifle and struck him twice more. Dark blood poured from the wounds she had inflicted. She recognized the colour as well as the stink of it as a sign of the curse reaching its apex in the man.

She dropped the makeshift club and strapped on her own gun belt. Then she knelt beside Sumner. His eyes fluttered open, and she drew her hand back to hit him.

"No! Please." He drew his hands up in front of his face. "Please don't. I ain't gonna fight you no more."

"If I could help you, I promise you I would."

"I'm gonna die, ain't I?"

"Yes. I'm sorry, but yes."

He began to weep more sludgy, oily tears. Solenne could smell death flowing into him like a rising flood, mere minutes away.

"I . . . don't wanna be like that thing you was fighting with."

"What's your name, boy?"

"Edwin."

She smiled down at the man, whispering indecipherable words, and the look of pain on his face receded.

Solenne knew she should not spare precious seconds simply to offer this man a quiet death, and yet in her experience, she had found that whatever gods or spirits might be watching her, they never counted kindness against her. Not so far, at any rate.

She placed a hand on the man's neck and felt both the curse working in him and his body relaxing into the death that would precede it. This one had such an open mind. Solenne had seen a zoetrope once, a device that made still pictures dance as if moving, and her spiritsense could catch glimpses of this man's past stirring in his brain as though they were moving drawings.

"Imagine yourself at home, Edwin . . . at supper with your family."

"Yes . . ."

He closed his eyes, and Solenne moved her fingers over the pulsing arteries on both sides of his neck, pressing down until her fingers were occluding them. The man stirred slightly at the pressure, and Solenne murmured more indecipherable words until he was still again. She kept the pressure on his neck for nearly two minutes, until he was unconscious.

Sumner was still breathing, but what she might have done about that was interrupted by the sound of steps outside the tent. To Solenne's ears, it was someone trying to move in silence without being especially good at it.

Quickly, silently, her pistol was in her hand.

Brennan stepped into the tent and winced, though Solenne was unsure if his reaction was provoked by the gun in his face or by the evidence of the beating she had taken.

\*

With dried blood still covering Solenne's lower face and streaking her neck, Brennan thought she looked almost as if she were one of the creatures herself, just finished feeding on a victim. The gore barely covered the bruises and cuts Johnston's punches had ploughed into her face, and he observed that her nose had acquired a swollen and bent shape since he'd last seen her.

Brennan had killed about a dozen men in his life, including those in the last day or two. Bad men, not an innocent one among them, by his reckoning. There were also two or three assholes on a list in his head that he'd shoot on sight if they ever chanced across his path again, and Johnston had now added himself to this list.

Brennan saw Solenne seeing all this in him.

"Jeez, you're like to scare a guy, ain't ya?" he said eventually.

Solenne took a long breath, holstered her gun, and just barely smiled at him. "Come to rescue me?"

Without waiting for an answer, she bent and grasped Sumner's head and then twisted, the muscles in her shoulders tensing until the muted crack of vertebrae snapping broke the silence in the tent.

"Ah, jeez . . ." Brennan winced again. "Maybe, I guess."

Solenne looked up at him. "Help me roll him."

They pulled the man onto his side, his head lolling like that of a rag doll. Solenne placed her knife at the base of the brain, where the spinal cord enters the skull, and shoved it sharply upward. There was a cracking sound as the blade broke through the thin bone. She wiggled the knife around in Sumner's brain and then withdrew it and wiped it clean on the man's shirt.

Brennan took in the sickly grey appearance of the thoroughly dead man on the ground as Solenne stood. "He was gonna turn into one of those things?"

Solenne nodded.

"Just like me."

She stared back at him for a moment, looking him up and down. "Not exactly."

\*\*\*

An hour or so before, Brennan—imprisoned and doomed—had unaccountably begun feeling slightly better. The fever seemed to be waning, his wound felt less painful, and, though he was a bit light-headed, overall he didn't feel that bad. Still, he was loath to take this as any kind of good sign. He knew nothing about this curse or sickness or whatever it was. Maybe victims felt better just before they changed into monsters. His mild euphoria might be due to delirium—or even the whiskey.

The idiots who had imprisoned him had taken his gun belt, jacket, horse, and saddlebags, but they had left him his boots.

Normally a prisoner in his circumstances would have had any kind of decent footwear confiscated by one of their captors. In the army, a good pair of boots was beyond price. Brennan had heard of Confederate units where a third of the men went barefoot. He supposed he should be offended that not one of his guards had fancied his boots as worth taking, but in fact, Brennan credited his status as contaminated and doomed as the true source of his luck.

And it was lucky. Brennan had long had the habit of secreting valuables in a ragged cloth in those boots. It was very hard to steal a man's boots without him knowing. Out of habit, Brennan had hidden several gold coins there, and he had felt them, still pressing against his ankle, when he woke in the cage.

His new guards had been far more wary than Skinny and Fatty. For instance (and to Brennan's disappointment), they would not allow their captive within reach of their guns. Skinny and Fatty's fate after their short shift guarding him had apparently reinforced this elementary policy in his new guards' minds. But they had also possessed less soldierly aptitudes. Within minutes of Barrett's leaving, Brennan had seen one of his guards draw a small flask from under his shirt, take a sip, and pass it to his partner. Brennan imagined that in a troop on the march for months, only seeing a town every few weeks, obtaining whiskey was an estimable talent.

A complex negotiation had ensued. Brennan was sure that in a normal course of events his guards would simply have beat the hell out of him and taken by force anything he offered them. But again, Brennan's status of both a *protected* and *infected* man had left his guards unnaturally cautious and prone to keep their distance. This had allowed a trade to unfold on a more or less fair-market basis. Each guard gained a piece of gold, and Brennan wound up with half a flask of rotgut whiskey of uncertain parentage but undeniable potency.

He had reasoned that if he was going to die in a makeshift prison in a dusty old desert, he might as well buy himself one last drink. It had been a very expensive drink, as it turned out, but it seemed unlikely he was going to be spending the gold on anything else.

Feeling somewhat better with moonshine running through his veins—along with whatever else was cooking in there—had provoked thoughts of escape despite what were clearly very poor near-future prospects. Even while dying, his instinct was to frustrate his captors, to get out and take the girl with him. It would be a happier death knowing that more of these men, and Johnston in particular, would be left cursing his name afterward.

The shackles he had beat. During the brief moments he'd held Fatty's rifle, Brennan had managed to remove the firing pin, and it would serve nicely as a lock pick. After the shackles came the challenge of the cage itself. A problem, but not an unfamiliar or insurmountable one. Brennan had, on occasion, departed jails before without formal permission to do so. His experience was that jailors designed cells so that people could walk in or walk out only when the key holders desired it. No one seemed to think a prisoner would ever try to leave another way. Lying supine and sipping the dwindling firewater he'd paid a fortune for, Brennan could see that the roof of his cage was the weakest point of the enclosure—just a few planks nailed in what appeared to be a half-hearted manner to the top of the wagon. A few kicks would break one of those wood slats free.

All the possibilities for escape were there. Perhaps most importantly, he was now lubricated with enough alcohol to believe he might actually pull it off.

He had been thinking he needed something to distract the guards for a few moments when the screams began.

*\*\*\**

There was, of course, no calculated intent in the Bruised-Head reaper's approach to the army camp. The thinking part of its brain had devolved to necrotized sludge. Lizard hindbrain and insatiable hunger directed its actions now. Anyone not aware of this, though, might have seen tactical intent in the way it entered into the camp.

In the midst of open desert with little cover, any approaching enemy could be spotted miles away if there was any light at all left in the day, but the reaper was missed by the perimeter guards because it came up the channel cut by the passing river. Its quest for the source of the blood-scent on the wind had led him down a series of gullies to the riverbank and west toward the camp from there.

It was just past dusk when the Bruised-Head creature found a shallow part of the bank and managed to climb the ridge where its nose told it food was. It emerged no more than fifty yards from the camp, and the first man it encountered was a private named James Matheson, who was kneeling with his horse's left rear leg pulled up between his own, digging a pebble out of its shoe.

Matheson did not look up until his horse scented the undead thing and kicked its foot loose of his hands, whinnying in fear. Matheson fell to the ground cursing as his horse skittered away from the approaching creature. A group of soldiers preparing an evening fire among the tents looked up at the animal coming toward them, and one of them snatched up its reins, chuckling and pointing at Matheson, who was just getting to his feet.

"Hey, caught your horse for you, Jimmy."

"Yeah, we'll sell 'er back to you for—whatcha think, fellas? A dollar?"

More laughter followed, and Matheson was struggling to think of an appropriate retort when he caught a sudden overpowering smell of decay in the air and heard the grunting moan from behind him.

When he turned, a yellow-eyed nightmare stood before him, skin hanging in strips from its face and torso and black goo dripping from multiple wounds. The hands stretched toward him ended in bony claws, the flesh worn from its fingers. When the monster opened its jaws, a hole torn in its grey-skinned cheek also gaped open like a second mouth, exposing sharp, yellowed teeth in blackened gums.

"Shit!" Matheson skipped back a step and fell. "Help!"

His fellows behind him were still laughing. Matheson scrambled to his feet, holding the jackknife he had been using to clean out his horse's shoes in front of him as the creature came on toward him.

"*Help!*"

But the chuckling men around the campfire were too distracted by Matheson's horse, which was refusing to calm down. The animal struggled against the man holding its reins, snorting and wide-eyed in terror. When Matheson called for help a third time, only one of the men turned toward him. The rest remained occupied with the crazed animal that danced in desperate fear among them.

Matheson had been under Johnston's command for as long as any of his fellows, but that morning he had been driving one of the supply wagons and was far to the rear of the troop when the company had finally met one of Johnston's creatures for the first time. He had seen the dead body of the thing with its head destroyed, but he had never seen one of the creatures walking.

Taken by surprise, Matheson reacted the way he would have against any mortal attacker. As the creature with two mouths groped for him and dug its talon-fingers into his shoulders, Matheson buried his knife to the hilt just under its ribcage. His unintentionally well-aimed upward thrust pierced Bruised-Head's heart, but that heart no longer beat, and the reaper drew the dumbfounded Matheson toward him and sank its teeth into his face.

Matheson began shrieking.

The men around the fire all turned toward the cries and, seeing Matheson fall to the ground with what looked like an Apache on top of him, dashed toward the struggle. The first troopers to reach Matheson found the creature bent as if in prayer over the man's body, shoving tattered bits of its communion—torn flesh still weeping blood—into its mouth. Even in the dim light, it was plain that most of the left side of Matheson's face and neck had been shredded in the space of the few seconds it had taken the men to reach his side and that an artery in his neck had been opened, a shower of blood gushing from his carotid. The first of those arriving to help saw the creature scrabble on the ground after Matheson's left eye, which bobbed across the ground like an errant cherry until the creature captured it between its fists and popped it into its black mouth.

One of the troopers kicked at the creature as another stepped forward and speared the thing's belly with his rifle bayonet. After a dozen or more swipes he stepped back, panting with exertion, and to his astonishment, the creature simply rolled away from the source of its torment, utterly unaffected by what the trooper knew should have been a fatal assault. On its feet, the growling reaper lurched toward its attacker, oily fluid gushing from the fresh wounds in its lower torso.

From the direction of the main camp came a shout, a corporal well acquainted with Johnston's orders and the consequences of disobeying them straining to achieve a voice of authority.

"Don't kill it! Don't kill it!"

Despite this, as the reaper moved to attack them, several men blazed away and shots rained into the thing from rifles and pistols at point-blank range. The force of the shots staggered the creature, and fresh black wounds appeared in its chest and abdomen. More gunfire knocked it back onto the ground, but the men could see the thing still moving purposefully, snarling as it struggled to gain its feet once again. They began reloading.

One of Matheson's friends knelt beside him to offer aid, realizing belatedly that he knelt in a pool of gore, his friend's lifeblood emptying from him. The geysers of pulsing blood from Matheson's neck had slowed to the waning trickles of a river running dry, the last of it dribbling out of the savage wounds he'd sustained. Matheson's friend saw that the man's eyes were wide and unmoving, staring up at a darkening sky he could no longer see.

A new voice rose above the pandemonium.

"Don't kill it! Capture it! Stand back, you men, and capture it!" Johnston himself was running toward them now, men with nets keeping pace beside him.

The corporal turned toward Johnston, and his gaze lingered just a moment too long. The creature surged to its feet, unbalanced by bullets that had shattered its left arm and shoulder but still mobile and deadly. It drew the corporal into a clumsy embrace, mouth open to receive the gift of his warm, ruddy flesh, and dragged him to the ground, a growl of wild joy muffled in blood as its teeth found his shoulder and burrowed into the flesh.

"Stay back!" Johnston roared, waving his hands at the uncertain, panicked men witnessing murder in front of them. "Nets! Get the nets on it!"

"Please! Get it fucking off—" The corporal's screams dissolved into gurgling shrieks as the reaper's claws tore into his neck.

"Get back, you men. Get back for your lives!"

Johnston fired his pistol into the air. When he had the men's attention, he motioned to those at his side to move in for the capture.

"Over both of them. Now! Move!"

As the other troopers watched in confused horror, the netting was cast over both the monster and the corporal who still struggled in vain to free himself from its unholy embrace, incomprehensible wet sounds bubbling now from the man's torn mouth and trachea.

The two soldiers who had deployed the nets now drew back on the ropes attached to them, tightening the webbing around predator and prey and knocking them to the ground in a writhing, bloody mass.

One of the corporal's comrades, tears of rage streaming down his face and perhaps still hoping to save his friend, raised his pistol at the creature, but Johnston was watching for just such a failure of character and, without hesitation, he shot the corporal's would-be rescuer in the heart. The man looked down at the hole in his chest, his eyes widening with surprise. Dying senses sent final desperate signals flittering through the man's brain—taste of blood in his mouth, smell of burnt flesh and cordite, and an arrhythmic stuttering in his chest as his heart trembled to a halt. Then he collapsed dead onto the ground.

"No more shooting at that demon or, by God, you'll *all* die!"

"Colonel—"

"Shut up. Not a word!" Johnston shouted, waving his gun with deadly emphasis at the men left standing beside the trapped creature and the dying man entangled with it. The demon-thing seemed to be settling down now that the corporal had stopped moving, and in the relative silence ensuing, all those nearby could hear the wet smacking sounds of the monster beginning its feast in earnest.

"Now, you men! Aid these two." He gestured at the soldiers who had cast the net over the creature and its prey. As they had been trained to do, the men were leaning back and keeping a constant tension on the riggings. Both looked pale, and sometime in the last minute or two, one had vomited. There was bile all over his chin and shirt, but he had never stopped pulling on the net. He would not have dared.

Johnston gestured toward Matheson's body. "Drag it up there, too, men. Throw them all in the prison wagon with the gunslinger."

After a moment, the bystanders moved to obey, their faces slack and pale as they began to assist the two men at the ropes.

From all over the camp, more men came running toward the source of the yells and screams, guns out and ready for battle. Brennan's cage was close to the riverbank, and so his guards were among those who were attracted by the hue and cry.

\*\*\*

"No?"

"No."

"Just *no*?"

"That's right." Solenne wiped bloody hands on her thighs and then cupped them around her nose, twisting. Brennan grimaced at the popping sound—like knuckles cracking—as she straightened her nose into something resembling its previous shape.

"We should go now."

"No kidding."

"We should go *now*."

"I *know*. But, just to be clear, I'm not gonna die like . . . " He waved a hand at the body on the ground between them.

"Dying is still possible if you want to stay here and talk for a few more minutes."

"But—"

Solenne rolled her eyes. "I'm leaving. Coming?"

"I'm with you . . . I am. Might take a moment to find that gold before we go, though."

Brennan noticed Solenne watched him with undisguised exasperation as he looked around and quickly spotted his saddlebags.

"Aha!"

"We don't have time for this."

"Oh, hell, we got a couple more minutes." He waved a hand back toward the river. "Everyone and his dog was running down thataways last I saw. Some sorta commotion."

Solenne's eyes flickered. "Yes. There's a cursed one nearby."

Brennan threw the bags over his shoulder, grunting with the effort even as he smiled with evident pleasure at the weight. His gun belt was beside the bags, and in seconds it was buckled around his waist again.

"I'm ready now."

He watched Solenne hesitate and that flicker of a smile touch her lips again. She leaned forward, grabbed Johnston's sabre, and tied it to her belt. Then she grabbed Brennan by the shoulder and dragged him out of the tent.

"There're a lot more reapers out there now, among all the others who wouldn't want to see us leave." She kept her voice low, but the intensity in it was unmistakable. "Quiet as you can."

It was almost completely dark now, and though some cook fires and torches had been lit, the dying light had created a maze of tents and shadows. Brennan could plainly hear shouts way off to their right toward the river, but Solenne pulled him in the opposite direction.

"Okay, okay." He shook her hand off and fell into step beside her, trotting among the tents and bedrolls scattered around the campfires. "You see any horses?"

"I can smell them up ahead."

They jogged on in silence. Brennan could smell horses too. They were in the middle of a cavalry camp, after all. But he had no idea how she was able to determine from what direction the odour originated.

The shouts behind them were dying down. There had been a flurry of gunshots not long after his guards had left him, and now two isolated shots echoed in the cooling desert air.

A ragged bearded soldier stepped out of the shadows in front of them. Without pause, Solenne threw all of her weight behind her right hand and smashed the pistol she held into his face. The soldier's eyes rolled back and he dropped to the ground like a felled tree with a long, sighing groan. Behind him, they found a group of horses tethered to a mesquite tree. Beside that was a supply wagon, along with saddles, gear, and cases of what Brennan imagined must be weaponry, food, and other supplies.

He rooted through several saddlebags and grunted with satisfaction. A knife and some pemmican went into his pockets. He then came across a case full of fist-sized packages of what his nose told him must be black powder. He had used explosives once before to open up a bank that would have been otherwise unwilling to extend him a loan, and he took the powder out of simple practicality. You never knew when something like that might come in handy. Fuses of various lengths lay at the bottom of the case, and he pocketed several of those as well.

"There's no time for that," Solenne whispered. "*Hurry.*" She had found her own horse among the rest and had begun getting it ready to ride. She frowned at Brennan as he picked through a stack of rifles looking for the best one, and he felt her eyes on him.

"I *know,*" he whispered at her. He snatched up a rifle and then quickly picked out a horse that looked speedy and fit. He began applying reins and bridles and securing his saddle, his hands flying in practised haste to ready the animal.

Once Solenne's horse was ready, she stepped toward the others and drew Johnston's sabre. With what looked to Brennan like expert strokes, she whipped the blade back and forth through the ropes holding the remaining horses. The freed animals stumbled back from her, snorting uncertainly.

"That's smart."

"Quiet."

Something in her voice made Brennan obey.

Solenne closed her eyes and grew still as a rock, as if gathering her strength.

Brennan watched as she drew a sudden, deep breath and threw her head back. Her hands danced in small circles and *something* leapt out of her, rippling like a cracking whip.

Brennan stumbled back as it hit him. The *thing* that radiated outward from her was like a physical blow. Every horse except the two they had chosen took flight, turning and running as if from a banshee's shriek.

Solenne shook herself, saw Brennan eyeing her, and arched an eyebrow. "Every horse within a mile of us is turned wild. They'll fight any man that tries to ride them . . . save ours."

"How'd you—"

Brennan stopped because Solenne's nose had begun to gush blood again, as if whatever she'd just done had cost her something, had taken something from her. There was pain in her eyes as she drew her hand gingerly across her face, looked at the gore staining it, and then wiped it against her already-bloodstained shirt.

Brennan's gaze flickering again over her damaged face, a flash of compassion in his eyes.

Solenne turned a baleful look on him.

"How bad'd he hurt you?" Brennan asked after a moment.

"Shut up."

\*\*\*

Three soldiers armed with hammers were punching nails back into the roof of the prison wagon that Brennan had vacated when his guards were drawn to screams by the river. Sergeant Ross was on the roof of the wagon with them, directing their work with occasional muttered oaths and constant exhortations to greater speed.

Ross could hear barely controlled rage in the muttered replies of the men and knew they were on the verge of murder and mutiny. Johnston's very ruthlessness had forestalled his own assassination or the mass desertion that had followed when many Confederate units had deemed their commander unworthy, but the murders and the flogging had pushed his men over the edge. The only thing that held the troops back from murder now, Ross judged, was the unholy nature of the creature that had come among them and their uncertainty as to the fate of the raiding party that had gone out that afternoon.

Had the party encountered creatures such as this one they'd captured? Had they prevailed against them? Who knew how many more of these demon cannibals lurked out there in the night . . . ?

In the darkness, at least, Ross thought the men would rather the relative comfort and protection of their ruthless, maniac leader than the unknown atrocities that might be just beyond the flickering of their campfires, but Ross was all too aware their collective fear would wither in the light of the coming day. What might they do then, after Johnston's latest insanity, the spoils of which lay moaning in agony in the cage below?

All these men had seen it—seen Johnston take in the report of the lost prisoner, Brennan. He had nodded as if deep in thought and then had drawn his pistol with the carefree air of a man taking pen to paper. His two carefully aimed shots had pierced the bellies of the errant guards and driven them to their knees, clutching at their ruptured innards.

Johnston had watched them for a moment as they tried to staunch the flow of blood coming from their wounds with shaking hands, and then he stepped forward and spit on them, one after the other. Some of the witnesses, who had been working on the cage their comrades now resided within, had heard what Johnston whispered to his victims as he leaned over them, and Ross heard it repeated in low tones of anger and disgust as the men reassembled the roof.

*You too shall serve.*

He had seen Lewis walk into the torchlight and salute Johnston with a shaking hand as he stammered under the icy gaze. "There is no sign of the gunslinger, sir. I have tasked every man not on guard duty with finding him."

"And the girl?" Johnston spat.

"She remains under guard in your tent, sir."

"Very well, Captain. I—"

"Sir."

Ross had watched Lewis's eyes dart for a second to the two men who writhed within the cage before continuing. "The gunslinger escaped under my watch, sir. I take full responsibility for it."

"I agree that you should, Captain." Johnston spun the cylinder of his pistol slowly, taking bullets from his belt to replace the ones he'd not long ago fired into Brennan's two luckless guards.

Ross's eyes were drawn to the monster the troops had captured. Only yards away, four men still shook and grunted with the effort of holding the raving monster secure. It had been almost quiescent, for a time, in its roped confinement as it stripped the meat away from the neck and face of the dead corporal who had been ensnared with it and then burrowed into the man's belly, gorging itself on his entrails. The men holding the ropes were hardly grateful for the respite in its urgent efforts to escape, for they then had to endure the wet, sloppy noises of its feeding.

And yet now it appeared to Ross that the creature was tiring of its most recent meal. Perhaps the corporal's body had grown too cool for its tastes, for it had begun clawing again at the ropes that held it, eagerly searching for a way out of its prison so that it might focus its appetite on warmer flesh. Ross hoped that, if Lewis was to die, it would be a quick death, by a bullet to the head.

"You *were* responsible, sir," Johnston continued. "But you are *not* culpable. You did your duty." He looked into the cage at the wounded men, their eyes turning a dull tarnished-silver hue as torn arteries gushed blood into their abdominal cavities. "As will these men do theirs. They shall through their own punishment yet serve our cause."

Behind Johnston, the netted creature growled as if in agreement, perhaps catching the scent of fresh blood in the air. Johnston spared it a glance before turning back to the two dying soldiers. "Time to get that creature in the cage. The corporal too, if there's anything left of him, and the man he killed first."

There was a stunned silence—not at the order, but at the callousness of it—that drew out until Johnston added, "Mr. Lewis, I did not mean at your leisure, sir."

Lewis saluted, making an effort to still his trembling hand. "Yes, sir. Right away."

He turned to the soldiers around him. "Men, drag that devil-thing over here. We'll throw it in the cage. Matheson too. Quickly now!"

The three men pounding the wood and nails back into place had never halted their banging, but they all felt Johnston's eyes fall upon them. Ross was the only one who dared look back.

"You fellows repairing this cage, you mark me. Anything gets outta there this time, and you'll spend your last moments inside a cage with one of those demons." Johnston pointed at the creature as the others dragged it toward the cage.

"Bastard," one of the men muttered a little too loudly, and the colonel came alive, leaping toward the wagon as if hit by a bolt of electricity.

"What did you say? Repeat it! Which one of you spoke?" Johnston half climbed up the cage. "I'll have you down in there with your fellow miscreants—"

"Colonel." Ross spoke up, sweat welling up on his brow. "Colonel, I will make sure the cage is secure, sir."

Ross knew he had just placed himself in the crosshairs of a possible death sentence, or worse. But he would have said anything at that moment to prevent more killing.

"Sergeant Ross—" The colonel's tone was near a growl, but he had no time to finish his sentence.

"Colonel, sir. Best step back from the cage, sir." Lewis's desperate eyes flicked up and met Ross's for an instant as he continued. "Don't want that creature getting too close." Lewis gestured to the men dragging the monster toward the cage.

By providence—in Ross's eyes, at least—the two gut-shot soldiers in the cage began at that moment to plead for mercy. They knew they were dead. Every soldier was well acquainted with the fact that deep belly wounds inevitably led to corruption of the inner organs and a slow, painful death. But now they realized they were to be imprisoned with the cannibal-thing. Even death was preferable to that, and they began to plead with Johnston for a quick end to their suffering.

The colonel—now twice distracted—merely threw Ross and the other men on top of the wagon a black look before climbing down. He glanced at the weeping, gibbering soldiers in the cage.

"I wouldn't waste another bullet on you. You were poor soldiers in life—let's see how you do in death."

Ross saw one of the men beside him raise his hammer and take aim at Johnston, and he elbowed him in the ribs, snatching the instrument away. An urgent whisper came from him as he glared at the man. "You want to end up in there too? Do ya? You got family at home. You want to see 'em again?" Then louder, to the others, he said, "Get back to work. Let's finish this, boys."

When he saw them obey, Ross jumped down and stole a look at the two pleading, shivering soldiers. They were already trying feebly to tear their way out, scraping their fingers bloody on the cage walls as the netted creature was dragged closer. The creature seemed to have lost interest in the corporal entirely now, snarling and biting at the net as it focused on the smell of the fresh blood and meat it sensed nearby.

Lewis looked at Ross again, and each immediately recognized the look of disgust on the other's face as two men slung Matheson's limp body into the cage.

"As you said, let's get it finished, Sergeant."

Ross's jaw hardened and he nodded. "All right, men. Listen up. We're gonna do this fast—hear? Need four of you on the netting and one of you on the cage door! Mind you don't get bit, now!" The men moved to obey, wariness evident in their every move.

"Heave!"

In one smooth, rapid motion, the demon-thing was raised up to the cage entrance and the netting was loosened. The men behind it poked at it with rifle butts to push both the dead corporal and the rabid creature all the way in, but the demon needed little urging with the coppery stink of warm blood tugging at its hunger. It yanked itself free of the netting and lunged toward the men cowering at the back of the cage with the eagerness of a slave loosed from chains. The men directed feeble kicks at the roaring yellow-eyed nightmare, and the demon raked its claws into the flesh of their legs. When the creature finally caught hold of one of them, the man, too weak to be anything but resigned to his fate, only groaned as the undead thing tore a long strip of flesh from his leg and began to eat.

Ross slammed the cage door shut, swallowing against the bile rising in his gorge. He yanked several times on the lock, satisfying himself it was secure.

Johnston held out a hand. "I think I'll hold on to that key, if you don't mind, Sergeant."

"Of course, sir." Ross placed the key in his colonel's hand and felt as if he'd rid himself of something dark and unclean.

Lewis pointed at the men who had rebuilt the cage roof. "You men! You will guard that cage and keep it tight and secure. Any piece of wood that breaks off, you will nail two back in its place. And don't let that thing near you or you're—"

One of the men inside the cage had found the strength to scream— a stuttering wail of utter hopelessness.

Lewis paused only a second before raising his voice to shout over the noise. "Or you're dead as those men in that cage! That thing'll rip a chunk outta anything comes near it."

Ross saw Johnston twitched slightly and rub his neck, a pained look on his face, but there was no time to ponder the cause of this. Two privates, one of them carrying a fizzling torch, ran into the firelight by the cage and came to a stumbling halt, brought up short by what they saw in the prison wagon.

"Captain! Colonel!"

The demon-thing was now ripping in earnest into the two former guards, who screeched and wailed and waved their arms through the bars of their cage as though succor would come if only they could catch the attention of one of their fellows. The corporal's corpse, slung in alongside its slayer, was a ragged near-skeleton from the neck up. Bloody black sockets were all that remained of the eyes, and the nose and ears were gone, as was most of the neck, ripped down to the off-white gristle of tendons and cartilage.

The newly arrived men stood gaping until Johnston reached out and pushed one of them in the shoulder. They both fell back as if joined together, but still neither spoke.

Johnston slapped the nearest one across the cheek. "If you have something to report, man, spit it out!"

"The W-W-Witch . . ." It was the other private who stuttered this out, his gaze never leaving the hellish theatre in front of him. "The Witch . . . she . . ."

"What?!" Johnston roared, beating at them both now with his fists and knocking the torch to the ground.

"She, she's gone, sir . . . Killed her guards . . . She's gone."

Ross backed away as Johnston screamed in an inchoate rage, as unintelligible as the growls of the demon creature just yards away. Then he leapt forward and punched the private across the face, knocking him to the ground before racing off toward his tent.

The creature in the cage lay across the two dying soldiers, its head haloed by irregular bursts of blood as its talon-hands and teeth raked through the men's bellies, sliced through arteries, and spilled ragged lengths of gut and flecks of unidentifiable organs all around it. Every so often, it dipped its head into the gashes and chewed like a pig brought to the trough.

The men outside the cage stepped back and watched the demon feast.

"Sure as Jesus wept, we're going to hell for this," one of them muttered.

This was greeted with silence, but the only ones among them who might have disagreed thought that perhaps they had already arrived.

## Chapter Sixteen

It was fully dark now, a thin crescent moon rising east of them. Brennan guessed they were nearly three miles south of the camp.

"Slow down . . . Hey! Pull up a second."

Solenne slowed her horse and both she and Brennan looked around. In the weak moonlight, Brennan could see no signs of immediate pursuit, and he heard nothing apart from the heavy breathing of their horses.

"There are a mass of them west of us. Dozens, I think."

"The creatures? Reapers?" He squinted. "Where?"

"Too far to see. But not for long. I can sense many—"

"*Sense* them?"

"Yes, just like yesterday." He caught the flash of her teeth as she grinned at him. "There's a reason they call me a witch." She pointed toward the rising moon. "One of the reapers must have made it to a local tribe or a wagon train, or the like, and infected them all."

"That quickly?"

"They spread like rats. Johnston sent a group of men to follow the reaper that escaped us. If any of that party survived, the dead may be following their scent back to the camp."

"Why? Why does he . . . ?" Brennan trailed off as Solenne explained Johnston's plans for the undead. He was left blinking for a moment. Finally he offered, "Knew that man was crazy the first minute I met him . . . Ahh, shit!"

"*Shh . . . Quietly* . . ." Brennan looked daggers at Solenne and she added, "What is it?"

"I heard him. While I was in the cage. He sent some soldiers up to commandeer a train on the south Arizona line, about four hours' ride from here."

"I know that train."

"Yeah, me too. Runs straight west all the way to California."

"And California is held by the Union."

"Mostly, yeah. He's likely planning on putting a few of those things aboard and running 'em out there."

"I think you're right. We have to stop him."

Brennan grimaced. "Ahh, *we*?"

Solenne looked away for a few seconds. When she turned back to him, he swore her sapphire eyes were just barely glowing. *Tears?*

"I've been lucky all these years, Brennan. Chasing these things. There's never been more than a dozen alive at one time that I had to deal with, and generally they're stupid and easy to kill if you know what you're doing. In large numbers . . . I need your help."

"You need the law. Or the Union Army. I ain't a good guy."

"You tried to rescue me."

"Well—"

"Even if I didn't need it."

"Like stink."

"Johnston only needs to get one or two of them aboard that train. He'll probably sacrifice the passengers or his own men to grow their numbers, but even one would do. In a big city, they'll spread like a prairie wildfire. No army could stop them. In six months there'll be nowhere for you to spend your gold."

Brennan poked a thumb at himself. "How you think I came across that gold, anyhow? Think I mined it and smelted it and pressed it into coins? Think someone gave it to me? I told you, I *ain't no good man*."

"Don't need a good man. Need a man who's good with a gun."

Brennan was silent.

"There are enough reapers heading toward camp that it will be a bloodbath there tonight. The soldiers will never be able to kill them all before the dead are among them. Reapers'll eat some of the bodies to the point they can't rise, but most of those men will die and wake hungry. By tomorrow, there'll be well over fifty of them. They won't move much because they won't smell humans this far out in the desert."

"If you're lucky."

Solenne's voice hardened. "I have to be lucky. I can get them all. Just me—no problem. I can kill them all in a day or so just with all the guns and ammo they'll leave lying around."

"So? Johnston'll be one of them too. He won't make it to any train. Look, I'll stay behind and help you kill 'em if that's what you want."

"It's not enough. Johnston knows about them, knows enough not to get caught. He'll abandon his troops and run for that train with as many of the demons—"

Solenne shuddered suddenly, eyes closed, pain flaring in her chest. "*Chingame!*" She looked toward the east. "More rising, and they are much closer than I thought. The dead move fast when they smell blood."

"We can still make it to—"

"Nowhere!" She hissed. "Nowhere *in time*. I need your help to stop him making that train."

"So we're gonna let all those troopers get ripped up and eaten."

"If you recall, I never said I was any kinda good guy, either."

"True enough."

"Thirty of them"—she nodded at the camp—"or tens of thousands on the coast."

Brennan thought about that.

Solenne drew her gun.

Brennan's gaze flicked from the woman's stony cobalt eyes to her pistol. She was staring right at him when she raised the weapon and fired. He flinched, his own gun hand flickering too late toward his pistol. But her bullet sailed over his shoulder, and there was a meaty crunch behind him.

Brennan tore his eyes away from Solenne and turned to see one of the reapers lying on the desert floor, perhaps thirty feet away. Even in the faint light he could see black liquid leaking out of the hole Solenne's bullet had punched through its left eye. It had been an Apache, an old man.

"That was a wanderer. Most of them are coming up on the camp. Those soldiers are dead men. I'm going to circle west of the troop and try to cut off Johnston."

Solenne lowered her gun and smiled at him, but the smile was just muscle movement around her mouth and never touched her eyes. "I need your help, and you *owe* me."

"For that?" Brennan nodded over his right shoulder.

Solenne shook her head. "No. For the gift I gave you."

Brennan's eyes narrowed and were drawn down to his stomach. He could feel the wound on his belly was healing and his fever was long gone. "That dead thing bit a chunk outta me. How come . . . ?"

"Because I bit you first."

Brennan held up his arm and squinted at the mark Solenne's bite had left. It was, in comparison to his other injuries, a relatively minor wound, forgotten in the midst of the many other insults his body had suffered over the last day. Her bite had been deep, but he could hardly feel it now. The bandage he had wrapped around it had fallen off, and he could see that the individual tooth marks were scabbed over and healing.

"Your bite . . . ?"

Solenne frowned and nodded absently, turning her gaze leftwards. Her gun rose again suddenly and she shot another creature that had drifted in toward them. It collapsed to the ground not far from the first one she had shot.

"The curse cannot touch me. And it will not touch you now, either."

\*\*\*

"Did you hear something?" Taylor whispered this to his partner, Moore, who was dozing as best he could as he sat on a boulder a few feet away and leaned on his rifle.

Moore snorted mid-snore and looked around. "Huh?"

"Thought I heard something. That-a-way."

Moore squinted into the night and listened carefully.

A shuffling sound.

Moore stood up and both men aimed their rifles toward the noise, which grew steadily in volume and seemed to be increasing in frequency, as if whatever was scuffling toward them was accelerating.

"Who is that? Who . . . Who goes there?" The phrase felt awkward in Taylor's mouth, but he had heard somewhere that this was the proper way to challenge an unknown person in such situations.

A reaper stumbled out of the darkness, and at first Taylor took the demon for just what it *had* been up until a few hours ago—an Apache warrior.

*"Injuns!"* he hollered as he raised his rifle and fired. His shot caught the thing in the chest, throwing its spastic gait off balance and causing it to fall to the ground—preserving for a moment in the minds of the two guards the idea that this was the beginning of an organized attack.

"Injuns coming! Attack! Attack!" Both men screamed this toward the camp as they peered into the moonlight, looking for more attackers.

The reaper rolled over and groped its way onto its knees. Moore saw this and turned his rifle on it again. This time the shot struck the thing in the back but did not stop it from regaining its feet and turning toward them.

As answering shouts from the camp echoed in their ears, both men turned back to what they thought was a man; a murderous, heathen Indian, but a man, nonetheless. It was only when the thing lurched closer, black fluid drooling in a stream from its mouth, that the thing's true nature dawned as a possibility in their minds. Even in the indistinct moonlight, they could see that irregular chunks were missing from the man's face and arms, as if ripped away by some scavenger, and that the teeth in its wide black maw looked unnaturally sharp and elongated.

It moved toward them, arms wide as if to embrace old friends.

Taylor shot it again, and both men watched a chunk of grey tissue explode out of the reaper's right arm in a spray of inky gore.

"No!" Moore said, the creature's true nature and his colonel's views on disobedience meeting like two careening trains in his mind. "Johnston wants them things alive." He turned to shout back at the camp. "We got one of them creatures here. Send out men with nets!"

"Get back, then." Taylor said, his voice shaky. "Get away from it."

Moore and Taylor both moved back from the monster, and it, in turn, moved after them. After a moment of observing its uncoordinated attempts to latch on to them, they chuckled and began to dance around it, poking at it with their rifles. The creature lurched first one way, then the other, trying in vain to catch either of the men who moved just out of reach around it.

"Clumsy thing." Taylor tripped the dead thing with his rifle and it nearly fell.

The sounds of running men came now and Moore, feeling suddenly emboldened, laughed. "That ole Johnston, he's probably gonna promote us for this. Huh? Whatcha think, *Corporal Taylor?*"

Taylor giggled back, the fear draining from him. And that was when a squaw—barely into her teens, with her face half-gone and her left arm missing from the elbow down came out of the darkness and clamped onto Moore's neck. Tearing. Ripping.

Moore screamed and dropped his rifle, batting at the girl-thing with both hands, but it had wrapped both legs around his torso now, and blood spurted up around its mouth from his neck.

Dumbfounded, Taylor watched Moore fall to the ground, his attacker keening with what sounded like pure joy as it dug into his flesh. Then he felt a cold hand close upon his shoulder and heard a moan behind him. He tried to move away, but more hands were upon him. A graveyard stink filled his nostrils as soulless eyes and a craggy mouth came into view before him.

The moaning stopped as frigid teeth sank into his face.

\*\*\*

Someone had lit a lantern in Johnston's tent, and the guttering light painted dancing shadows across the face of the dead man on the ground, giving it an illusion of animation and expression it would never have again.

Not for the first time tonight, Johnston felt a sudden urge to scratch a non-existent itch on his neck.

*It'll rip a chunk outta anything comes near it.*

Something about Lewis's words nagged at him. He rubbed at the prickle just below his jaw as if soothing the itch would pull together the disjointed connection his mind was trying to make.

Johnston, along with a private, and a sergeant—Smith, he thought the man's name was—stared down at the corpse, it's neck twisted and a wound at the back of the head leaking black fluid that might have been blood but shimmered like oil in the lamplight. There was a stink of corruption in the air that spoke of something long dead and left to rot in the sun.

Smith was a tired-looking man with sparse grey hair and a ragged sword scar that ran down the left side of his face, but Johnston knew him to have a reasonably sharp mind and watched as the man toed the rifle lying on the floor and pointed at the bayonet.

"Ain't no detective, sir, but those two outside appear to've been stabbed, and you can see the blood on this pigsticker's fresh. Almost seems like Sumner—that's the private's name, sir—"

"The private stabbed the guards? Is that what you were going to say?"

"Yes, sir." Smith nodded.

Johnston knelt over the dead soldier. He recognized the progression of the disease in the man and guessed at what might have occurred. He pulled up the man's sleeves and found the dark blue network of veins coursing up his right arm. There was no bite, but the black necrotic scratch that must have begun the infection was prominent.

*No bite.* Johnston rubbed at the itch that was suddenly on his neck again.

"Reckon he let her loose, sir?" Smith inquired. "She was a witch after all, right?"

Johnston nodded, but he wasn't looking at Smith. He was looking at Sumner, and the word *bite* was going round and round in his mind.

"Maybe she did something to him. Cast a spell, like?"

*Bite,* Johnston thought again, getting to his feet. *And the gunslinger escaped. But he did not turn. Or die. He was bitten but he did not turn. Bitten . . .*

Johnston tore his gaze from the dead man and looked around his tent. She—his prize—had been here and then escaped. He had trusted cannon fodder to guard a being of unknowable ability. The two had taken their weapons and—

Now his eyes darted to his cot, where he had left his sabre.

*Gone.*

His sabre was gone. She'd taken it. Taken *his* sword.

Rage boiled in him now, almost uncontrollable, and he felt his teeth grind together with such force that he wondered that they did not crack apart. His neck was itchy again, and he finally knew why.

The Witch.

During their fight, there had been a moment—just a brief moment—when she had been on top of him, pinning him down, and he had felt her teeth against his throat. She could have torn his neck open, but she had hesitated.

In his experience, women—especially women of low birth—commonly bit a man in the midst of a fight. He'd seen enlisted men return often enough from town carrying bites and scratches from some harlot they had offended. Sometimes the wounds festered, but usually they were not truly serious.

But the Witch was no simple barmaid scorned. He had seen her handiwork a dozen times over while on her trail. She was a savage, ruthless killer. She might easily have torn out his throat at that moment, had she tried.

*Why had she not tried?*

*Her bite . . .*

When the gunslinger had been captured, it had been obvious that he had sustained several injuries, mostly from the assault by Johnston's own men—but he'd already had a bandage on his wrist.

The gunslinger had not turned. Had the Witch bitten *him*?

"Smith. There are men chasing the escapees?"

"Yes, sir. Got 'em going right away. But truth be told, sir, with this moon, they'll be picking their way. They're not likely to find a trail proper now till morning. Maybe that injun Quinto could've, but . . ."

Johnston's dark expression was not softened by his nod of agreement. "Understood. Any sign of Barrett's group?"

Smith shook his head. "No, sir. They was supposed to send a rider back with news, but no one's come back, sir."

"Very well. Go tell Mr. Lewis I wish to double the perimeter guard tonight—"

"Expecting trouble, sir?"

Johnston turned a savage look on Smith, and the sergeant felt as he had when he woke in his bedroll one morning to find a snake squirming round his legs. It had turned out the snake was not deadly, but of course the same could not be said about Johnston.

"I expect, Sergeant, not to be interrupted when I'm giving orders."

"Yessir. Sorry, sir."

"Good. Tell Lewis to double the guard and that we'll decamp at first light. We'll be headed north toward the railway at double pace."

Smith waited a moment to be sure Johnston had finished, then saluted and turned to go.

"One more thing, Sergeant."

"Sir?"

Johnston pointed to the corpse at his feet. "Get this thing out of my tent."

Smith nodded and motioned for help from the private, and they dragged the body away.

Johnston stared into the flickering light of the lantern and tried to smother his rage. He had caught the Witch once; he could catch her again. What mattered was that he had the *weapon* in his hands now. *That* was the crucial part—the part the Witch had been able to deny him up until now.

The crack and echo of a distant gunshot focused his mind. He became aware that there were cries in the distance and that they had been going on for some minutes. His initial instinct as a commander was to race toward the commotion to assess the situation, but he could tell from the panicked tone of the yells reaching his ears that this was no attack by natives or by a force of Union soldiers. The noise was coming from the same direction he had sent Barrett's expeditionary force. If they had come to a bad end and some sizable number of the risen dead came now among the troops, things might easily spin out of his control.

He knew he must act quickly and decisively in the next few minutes for his plans to come to fruition. Some might see his next steps as less than honourable, but victory *would* bring honour, even to those he must now sacrifice, for what he would do next, he would do for the greater good of the Confederacy.

*Honourable.* He would never be able to think of that word again without remembering the Witch spitting it in his face with disdain.

Almost without willing it, Johnston's hand came up and he smashed the lantern to pieces, throwing the tent into darkness. He walked out of his tent for the last time, stepped around a sergeant trying to get his attention, and headed for the caged monsters. The sergeant—Clark, Johnston thought his name was—chased after him.

"Sir! Begging your pardon, sir. There's Injuns coming in from the east, sir."

Johnston kept walking but turned to the man sidling along beside him. "Attacking?"

"I think it might be some of those things. Those things you're after, sir."

Johnston halted and placed a hand on the sergeant's shoulder. "Excellent, Sergeant. I assume you've sent men out to capture them?"

The sergeant nodded, his mouth working as if searching for words he did not have.

"Yessir, but . . ."

"But what?"

"There's . . ." His mouth opened and closed several times before he managed to stutter out, "There's an awful lot of 'em, Colonel."

Johnston's gaze hardened. "Capture those you can, then, and kill the rest. Bring the captured ones down to the river, understand?"

"Yessir, but . . ."

"But what?"

Johnston could tell by the look in Clark's eyes that some of the men had been bitten. Just as obviously Clark couldn't bring himself to give voice to the thought.

"Nothing. Nothing, sir."

"Get on with it, then, man!"

Clark saluted and scurried away as more shots rang out, and Johnson resumed his trek to the river. He could feel time pressing down upon him and looked up at the sky.

The thin blue arc of moon might offer just enough light to travel.

It was time to go.

Johnston could see the guards milling restlessly about the prison wagon, keeping a respectful distance from the dimly lit and now indistinguishable mass of creatures and dying men inside the cage. As he approached, he could hear moans and growls mixed with the wet sounds of flesh being ripped apart, and in the torchlight he could see that blood dripped from between the bars and onto the ground below as if from an overflowing fountain. A horrid stink of intestinal fluid permeated the air.

"Guards! Listen up. I want—" Johnston halted abruptly, attention turned to a figure staggering out of the shadows and toward him. One of the creatures? It was a moment before he recognized the man.

Barrett. Barrett limping like a cripple into the firelight.

"Colonel," Barrett said through gritted teeth, his face a mask of pain.

The man stumbling toward the colonel looked nothing like the one who had left hours earlier. Even in the weak light, Johnston could see that Barrett was dying and soon to be as one of the ghouls in the cage behind him. His skin had turned a mottled bluish grey; his eyes and nose leaked a jellied, inky fluid; and the odour of corruption coming off him rivalled that of the prison wagon. In the torchlight, Barrett's jaundiced eyes looked like those of a devil.

Johnston took a startled step back from the apparition, and then old habits reasserted themselves. "Report, Barrett."

"Did you say *report*?"

Barrett spat the words back—without the customary *sir*, Johnston noted. He also noticed that Barrett held a pistol. Johnston's right hand wandered down toward his sabre and twitched when it found empty space where the blade's hilt should have been.

*The Witch.* She pricked at him as if hoping to kill him with a thousand small cuts instead of one fell blow.

The thought brought a fury so pure it was liberating.

"Yes, Captain," Johnston roared. "As in *report the results of your expedition.* And by the way, Captain, you will call me *sir* or I will see you shot for your impertinence."

The men around the prison wagon heard the tone of the conversation and moved nearer. To the east, Johnston was aware of escalating screams and the sound of more and more bullets flying.

Barrett wove back and forth, dizzy with fever. His throat felt increasingly clogged, and he gurgled and spat pus-yellow saliva on the ground at Johnston's feet. "My report . . . sir . . . is that all of the men are *dead*—dead for now, at least—and that they all died in a hellish, fashion, *sir.*" He slurred the second *sir* with thick and unmistakable sarcasm.

Then Barrett raised his pistol. He moved slowly, as if in pain, but Johnston could not help thinking of the many circumstances in which he had depended on the man's accuracy with a gun.

"I will not let you put anyone else on this road to hell, you bastard."

"You will not *let*? *Me*? I am your *commander*, you pissant little shit." Spittle sprayed from Johnston's mouth, showering Barrett, who took no notice.

Barrett cocked his pistol and Johnston stepped back again, one hand still clawing automatically for his missing sword while he went for his own sidearm with the other. Barrett closed his left eye and steadied his aim on Johnston's head . . . and fiery agony was suddenly washing up into him as if someone *had* plunged a sword into him, raking it up his leg and into his back.

It was the infection, growing exponentially in Barrett now—surging up into his brain. His leg spasmed, muscles locking in excruciating, fiery pain as if the infection *knew* it needed Johnston to propagate itself, as if it *knew* Barrett killing Johnston would hinder its growth. As if the curse was more than the component of its individual parts.

Barrett fired then, but rolling bolts of shocking pain shook his aim. Instead of plowing through Johnston's head, Barrett's shot skimmed across his left cheek, digging a rough furrow through the flesh and tearing away a small chunk of his ear. Struggling to move closer, Barrett fired again, but his leg gave out as he did so and he collapsed to the ground, the shot gone wild. He levered himself onto his back as more ripples of tearing, black pain tore through him.

There were other men around Barrett now, staring down at him, guns out, with puzzled looks on their faces.

Johnston, too, stood over him, face grim. A cataract of blood was coursing down his cheek, and his shirt was wet and slick with it. He pressed his hand against the side of his face to try to stem the flow of blood, but it was no significant injury.

Drops of gore from Johnston's wound fell onto Barrett's upturned face, and the coppery smell caused Barrett to lick his lips in hunger. Then a look of disgust crossed his face and he rolled and vomited up a stream of bloody black bile. When he could breathe again, he wiped his mouth, turned his gaze back up to the colonel.

Johnston's pointed the gun between Barrett's eyes, and Barrett slumped back, as if eager for the the bullet's release.

But Johnston grinned, a cold, wintry rictus, and his aim lowered.

"You, too, will serve," Johnston said, then shot him in the belly.

Barrett's gun fell from his hand as the bullet exploded in his abdomen. He tried to crawl toward the weapon, but a cold weakness was stealing through him, sapping his strength. He flopped again onto his back, staring up at the pitch-black sky.

"We've caught more, sir."

"Bring 'em in."

"Get 'em in the cage!"

"Dump the captain in, too."

The infection purred in Barrett like a contented animal.

\*\*\*

The newly risen reapers from the Apache village had naturally followed the scent trail of blood that Barrett and his fellow soldiers left behind them as they fled west. Apart from Barrett, the few troopers who had initially escaped the rout at the village had been felled by the creatures chasing them and would be rising themselves in a few hours to join the ranks of the new army into which they had been drafted. Each of the reapers could now smell the humans in the camp west of them and was drawn toward it like a moth to a flame.

Among the shuffling mob of hungry dead, those that had risen with their limbs mostly undamaged by the predation of their sires were the first to reach the Confederate camp. A second and larger wave of the worst injured lagged behind, shuffling with the crippled gait common to the undead or dragging what remained of their half-consumed bodies across the rough desert soil.

Despite the paucity of their numbers, the first wave all managed— before being captured or killed—to bite or scratch some of their living adversaries and so distribute the plague they carried.

Though Taylor and Moore, stationed a hundred yards north of him, had been the first to meet the nightmare things, Travis Wilkerson was the first of the perimeter guards to survive the initial encounter. He had stumbled back toward camp after a desperate struggle with a dead Apache woman, who had lunged silently out of the darkness and raked her claw-like hands down his arms as she drew him into her cold embrace.

She would have bitten Wilkerson too except that her lower jaw was mostly gone, half-ripped off by the reaper who had chewed into her face during her own agonizing death. Nevertheless, she had tried to latch onto Wilkerson's neck, and while she could not bite, exactly, he had felt her upper teeth abrading his skin as her dry, leathery tongue whipped back and forth across it, desperately seeking the taste of the blood running in the arteries just below. Wilkerson had fallen, dragging his attacker down on top of him as she raged and clawed at him. Then he had kicked her away and was on his feet and running as the toneless keening of disappointment fell behind him.

Heading for the nearest source of light, he had run into a group of soldiers loading rifles by a hastily stoked fire and stumbled to a halt with horror on his face and streams of blood running from the gouges his assailant had inflicted on him. In whimpering, gasping breaths, he had told of the demon-things, but after a few seconds he realized none of them were listening to him, though they were all staring at him with the stony-eyed glare of men readying themselves for battle . . . for killing.

Then one of the soldiers—one of his friends, someone he'd marched and ridden and eaten with—spoke.

"You bit, Travis?"

The man's eyes were not on Travis's face but on the rips and tears that marked his arms and on the blood running from them and dripping into a growing pool on the desert sand below him.

"N-n-n-no . . ." Wilkerson had grown out of his childhood stutter as he entered his teens, but it returned in times of stress. He clutched at his bloody arms as if he might somehow hide his wounds and looked back and forth between the men around the fire, searching the faces of his former friends for any indication of kindness or mercy.

Out of the night behind them, the tuneless moans of the risen dead became audible, growing louder even as the soldiers shifted their gaze, like nervous prey animals, from one another to the hollow sounds coming out of the darkness. It seemed to Wilkerson that there was a desperate hunger in the unnatural howls, and he tried but failed to suppress the sudden sob of fear that burst from his lips. Suddenly, all eyes were on him again.

"You *are* bit, ain't ya?" Sloan said. Sloan, whom he'd shared his canteen with when Sloan's had leaked and gone dry.

Wilkerson gulped, staring at Sloan and attempting to wrap his lips around another denial when one of the other men shot him in the head.

\*\*\*

When the second wave of the undead arrived, the soldiers had, for the most part, continued to attempt—as they had been trained—to capture them. But the troop had been drilled in capturing single specimens in daytime. They were unprepared to deal with packs of rabid, hungry marauders approaching at night. Some of the undead were captured and dragged off toward the prison wagon, but—unguided by Lewis, Barrett, or Johnston—confusion quickly took hold. Panic spread, and soon the troops began trying to kill the things coming toward them.

But reapers were not like men.

Every trooper in the regiment had been in battles before, had shot at human enemies without caring much where the bullet hit since adversaries were often brought down by any substantial wound, no matter where it struck home. Head, torso, arm, or leg—the pain and trauma of any direct hit was likely to at least disable a man in battle. Even once word began to spread that only a head shot could kill the monsters, men were often struck dumb as one of the demon-things—a former friend, sometimes—continued to stumble forward like a broken puppet even after being shot in the chest or belly—wounds that would quickly kill any mortal man.

Likewise, the soldiers were used to enemies that *feared* death or dismemberment, that *retreated* from superior numbers or weaponry. The reapers had no fear of injury or death. They felt no pain and were disabled by only the worst of wounds, and they came at the soldiers like a river rising to a torrent, a flood that would wash over the camp and leave nothing living behind.

\*\*\*

Johnston felt the change in the air—the tide of battle turning. It came to him as a subtle transformation in the yells he could hear in the distance. Though at first startled by the attack, once alerted, the men's yells had quickly become the hearty, blustery cries of warriors engaged in battle. Now the yells had turned into shrieks of fear and desperation. The volley of gunshots had risen in number and was now on the decline as—Johnston imagined—more and more of the undying nightmares with pus-coloured eyes dragged his men down. He knew they would reach his position soon.

Several more of the netted creatures, snapping and clawing at the living men around them, had been packed into the prison wagon to join their fellows. Barrett had been slung in with them, and his struggles had quickly waned to feeble twitching as the creatures had moved in and begun to tear at him. Lewis was using the flat of his sword to batter against the last of the captured creatures as they slashed and bit at the men lifting them into the cage.

"Shut that door now!" Lewis shouted. "Lock it up!"

Lewis turned to Johnston, a tremor in his voice. "Total of eleven of the creatures secured, Colonel. There is another prison wagon—shall I have it brought up, sir? For the rest?"

Lewis pointed at another group of the foul things that writhed like a ball of snakes in frustration under nets staked to the ground some feet away. Several soldiers prodded the reapers with rifle butts while others pounded with rocks at the stakes holding the netting, frantically seeking to drive them further into the unyielding ground lest the creatures should tear themselves free.

Johnston glanced around at the ravening creatures in the cage and at the netted ones desperately groping toward their captors. Blood—slick and wet—and bits of flesh were scattered all over the ground as if they stood on the floor of an abattoir. He grinned, and out of the corner of his eye, he saw Lewis back away from him.

It didn't matter. None of it mattered now. He had what he needed.

"Sir?" Lewis repeated after a moment. "Shall I—"

"No, Captain. The other wagon will not be necessary."

There had been a sharp increase in the number of screams coming from the eastern front of the camp in the last few minutes, and Johnston knew it was past time to depart.

"Instead, Mr. Lewis, I'll have you hitch up this wagon with your best horses. And while you're about it, bring up my horse and get him ready to ride."

"Yes, sir."

"I'll need four good men to ride with me. We'll be departing directly."

"In the night, sir? It will be treacherous, even—"

"Yes, man, I know that. Listen to me and obey my orders, do you hear?"

Lewis nodded and belatedly added another *yessir*.

"Will you be one of those good men who come with me, Captain? Are you up to it?"

Lewis looked at him. Johnston's grin was undiminished. "And the rest of the men, sir?"

"They will hold station here till we return."

Lewis paused and licked his lips. "Will they, sir?"

Johnston's grin disappeared and he looked at Lewis as if he were looking through him. "Make ready, Captain. If we're not travelling in five minutes, there'll be at least one more person in yonder cage." He nodded at the wagon, crammed full now with stinking, disembowelled corpses and the ravenous living dead that continued to feast on them. As they both watched, one of the corpses twitched and twisted into its new life, roaring with a newborn demon's hunger.

"Understand, Mr. Lewis?"

Lewis saw the newly born monster pluck an eyeball off the floor of the cage and pop it into its mouth as if it were a grape. He swallowed hard and nodded. "Yessir."

## Chapter Seventeen

"There he goes. Looks like he managed to corral a few horses after all."

Brennan pointed just toward the south, maybe a mile or two away, where several men carrying torches and riding atop a laden wagon were moving away from the camp. Brennan saw them splash through a wide, shallow part of the river and climb up the opposite bank. The two horses hitched to the wagon reared every few seconds, and Brennan could hear repeated whipcracks as the wagon's driver sought to control the animals. There appeared to be two men on horseback suffering similar difficulties with their own mounts.

"Uh huh," Solenne answered absently as she sighted through her rifle's scope and fired, the sound lost in the multitude of shots erupting in and around the camp now.

Away from the torchlight of the camp and with his eyes acclimated at least somewhat to the darkness, Brennan found the sliver of moon lit the desert night just well enough that riding at a moderate pace need not be a deadly undertaking. But he still could not imagine how Solenne could see anything clearly beyond a few yards away.

Despite this, as they had picked their way around the Confederate camp toward the river over the last hour, Solenne had found and fired on a number of targets that Brennan had never seen, always sounding satisfied with the results. That her night vision was better than his was a small surprise compared with her other abilities, but it was still strange to see her firing off into what appeared to be blackness and vague shadows and to know that with each bullet she was taking down one of the creatures.

"Didn't you want to be chasing after him, then?"

Solenne lowered the rifle, continuing to stare into the darkness for a moment before she turned back to him.

"I do."

"Looks like about half a dozen men altogether. Only two on horseback, and they're having a devil of a time staying that way." He arched an eyebrow at her.

Solenne grunted in reply. "Anyone who managed to saddle a horse in that camp tonight would've had to beat it half to death."

"What'd you do back there? To the horses." He nodded back toward the camp. "Some sort of spell?"

Solenne smiled at him, eyes flashing, and ignored the question. "Probably he's got his best marksmen riding with him."

"Not what I'd call great odds."

"If we can catch up with them before first light, I can shoot one of the wagon horses. Once they're stopped, I can pick off the things in the cage . . . after I kill Johnston."

"Might try a shot at him myself," Brennan whispered.

Brennan eyed the injuries to Solenne's face again. She flashed him an irritated glance before a particularly loud scream drew their attention toward the Confederate camp.

In the flickering light of the cook fires, shadowy figures moved back and forth against a riot of background shouts and gunshots. Some of the dark shapes were running, moving like live men, but many others shuffled with the singular, lurching gait of the risen dead. As they watched, one of the running shadows was cornered, darting back and forth among a group of reapers until he was immersed and taken down like a deer falling to a pack of wolves.

There was a low keening to Brennan's right. An undead child with flaming yellow eyes loomed out of the darkness, dragging itself forward on hands and knees as its lower right leg trailed behind it in the dirt, held to the rest of its body only by a thin string of tendon. Brennan's horse shied back from the reaper, and the demon-child turned its empty eyes up to the man atop the animal and hissed, mouth yawning open and moving in spastic chewing motions as if already anticipating the rush of blood that would follow teeth penetrating flesh.

Brennan raised his pistol and hesitated. The girl could not have been more than eight years old. She wore a crude beaded necklace that looked as if it might have been made with her own hands.

Solenne's gunshot took him by surprise. He saw the back of the girl-thing's head burst open and watched it collapse to the ground, scrambled grey brain matter oozing out from the shattered skull like yolk from a carelessly dropped egg.

"They're all dead." Solenne's voice was sharp. "They're past being children, past being human, past—"

"I *know*." Brennan's face was dark. He was still thinking of the handwoven necklace and the innocent girl who might have considered it her most prized possession a mere day ago. "Let's go."

They followed Johnston at a fast trot toward the lightening eastern horizon.

\*\*\*

Lewis wiped his eyes and tried in vain to forget for a few seconds the sight of the creatures in the wagon bumping along only yards away from him. They had been travelling for about an hour, and the sound of gunshots from the camp had faded behind them. Lewis hoped that this was a good sign, that the men they'd left behind were winning their battle against the undead, but there seemed no credible reason to actually believe that. Lewis had never credited the idea of witches or the supernatural or any of that rot, but he could see now that he had been wrong.

Even their journey away from camp had been cursed. Nearly half of the troop's horses had been cut free and were nowhere to be found. The remaining ones had been nearly impossible to catch or mount. He had worn the muscles in his arm to a tremble in beating Johnston's and his own horse into submission, leaving both animals bleeding profusely, cowed into a shivering mass as saddles and reins were laid upon them.

Hitching two others to the wagon had been only slightly less problematic, and steady use of a whip had been required to keep each of the horses from bolting. The animals had quieted as they moved away from the camp, but they were still on edge and prone to rearing up, trying in vain to escape the hellish accompaniment of savage growls, rending noises, and the stench of blood, shit, and decay they towed behind them.

The reapers had long grown tired of the dead human prey beneath them and had turned their hungry gaze on the men riding alongside their cage. They snatched at those riding atop their wooden prison whenever they could, and one of the men—a dullard private named Scott—had made sport of this briefly, hanging his hand down close to the bars and then snatching it away, giggling, when one of the demons reached for him. The third time he had done this, Lewis had put a hand on the hilt of his sword and told Scott he would be joining those in the cage if it happened again. Now Scott sat wordless atop the wagon as if for all the world in a sulk at having his game halted.

Lewis imagined that Scott's near imbecility (the man could barely load a gun) allowed him to overlook what Lewis could not—that these ravening monsters had only hours ago been men like himself and, save for the Apache, men he had ridden with and fought alongside.

His eyes turned almost against his will to look at Barrett. Barrett, the colonel's favourite and second-in-command. Barrett, who had returned from his mission contaminated and doomed and tried to kill his own colonel. One of the monsters had ripped at the hole Johnston's bullet had torn in Barrett's abdomen until his belly had spilled open, and then it had picked through and gorged on the intestines with mincing, darting bites that had reminded Lewis of crows feasting on carrion. But Lewis had noticed that the demons had tired of Barrett's flesh quickly. Perhaps— already infected—he was not as . . . palatable . . . to the creatures as living men. Obviously, they did not feast on each other, so—

Barrett was looking at him.

Lewis felt a shudder run down his spine. Barrett sat half propped up against a corner of the cage, his intestines lying across his lap and dangling down through the bars of the cage like a carelessly spilled plate of sausages. Lewis had thought his fellow captain long dead, but Barrett was looking at him again—with intelligence. His eyes were the jaundiced yellow of the demon undead, but it seemed Barrett still struggled to assert himself behind them.

"Lew." It was barely a whisper. If Lewis hadn't been looking at him, he might not have heard it.

Lewis's eyes flicked toward Johnston, who was just in front of the wagon. He had not heard.

Lewis edged closer to the cage.

Barrett tried to wet his lips with a tongue dried to sandpaper by blood loss. "The . . . the Witch was right . . . He's insane. Johnston's . . . insane."

"Hey, Colonel! One of these things is still talking!"

Scott, of course. Lewis could have run the man through with his sword happily at that moment.

Johnston started and pulled back on his horse's reins until he was riding level with Lewis, his eyes flickering briefly to Barrett.

"Lew . . ."

The creatures that Barrett shared his cage with seemed disturbed by the conversation. Though they no longer seemed interested in feeding on him, they moaned and snapped at Barrett and renewed their clawing attempts to reach the men riding just a few feet above them.

Johnston stared at Barrett and drew his sidearm. "Silence, sir. I am still your commander till the second you die. Now—"

"He's insane, Lew . . . Just like the Witch said. He's—"

There was a moment when Lewis could have intervened, could have stopped or altered events; he could have listened to Barrett, perhaps even put the dying man out of his misery—even shot Johnston. But as always, Lewis found himself unable to act against authority. He was scared of death. But he was even more terrified of winding up in the cage like Barrett, with the inhuman things feeding on him and with only the promise of rising as one of them—soulless, cold, and hungry—beyond that.

And then the moment was over and Johnston had fired, a black rose erupting in the centre of Barrett's chest as the bullet tore through his heart. Barrett coughed twice, dark black blood spraying from his mouth, and then he was still.

Johnston holstered his pistol and turned back to Lewis. "I have a mission in mind for you, Mr. Lewis. It will require stealth, though . . . Perhaps you would permit me to carry your sabre for you?"

Without a word, Lewis unbuckled his sword. He knew it was true enough that such weapons tended to rattle against other belongings when a man was riding. He also knew it would have been easy enough for him re-rig it so that it made no sound. But Johnston had lost his own sabre somehow, and Lewis suspected no good could come from asking where it might have gone.

"Is your marksmanship as good as the late Mr. Barrett told me?"

Lewis swallowed. "Not quite as good as his, sir, but—"

"Much better than average."

Lewis knew he should be looking his commander in the eye, but he could not tear his gaze away from Barrett's dead yellow eyes. It seemed like they were staring into his very soul.

"I'm a very able shot, sir."

"Let's find you a worthy target, then."

\*\*\*

Brennan and Solenne had gradually closed up the distance between themselves and Johnston's wagon until they trailed them by just a few hundred yards. Though the sky was lightening, it was still too dark for Brennan to see much detail among the shadowy torchlight of the party travelling ahead, just a hint of figures silhouetted against the barely brighter horizon. But Solenne could see well enough that she brought her rifle up and sighted experimentally on the mass ahead of them.

"Johnston first," Brennan whispered, and Solenne murmured agreement before lowering the gun. The first shot had to count because after that the whole party would be shooting back.

Later Brennan decided that it was Solenne's fixation on Johnston that allowed him to sense the subtle change in the noises of the desert just off to their left before she did. He heard the faintest sound of something wrong—something shifting in the sand and the soft click of metal striking against rock. He knew, without knowing how he knew, that the noise was not from one of the reapers.

"*Solenne.*"

Brennan urged his horse toward the source of the sound and raised his gun. There was the crack of a rifle shot and then a half-second for him to wonder who had fired. The impact punched like a hammer into him and he fell off his horse, pain flaring just above his heart as he slammed into the ground. The shock blew the air from his lungs and left him panting in shallow gasps, wondering when he would begin to taste his own blood, and blinking at the stars fading into the brightening cobalt sky.

Then he heard the sound of Solenne's horse as she galloped away, and after that, things became quiet.

\*\*\*

Lewis lowered his rifle and allowed himself a barely audible grunt of satisfaction. His shot had hit centre mass on one of the two figures on horseback.

With practised stealth and speed, he worked the bolt of his gun, chambered another round, and brought his right eye up over the rifle scope, and saw . . . one riderless horse.

The other was nowhere to be seen.

He swivelled and swept his aim back and forth across the area where he had last seen the two. His targets had closed together just before he'd fired, but the chance of a single bullet taking both of them off their horses was astronomical, and no decent gunman would credit the possibility.

He heard a loud groan then, and he could tell by the tone it was the gunslinger who had escaped with the Witch. In the dim light, he had been unable to distinguish the shadowy figures against the subtly brighter horizon, but it seemed by chance his first shot had felled the Witch's companion. The thought disturbed him for no reason he could identify since obviously the gunman was the greater threat.

He searched again for the shadow of the woman and her horse against the dim blue background of the sky. Where was she? Down in a gulley, perhaps? Surely crawling away, trying to make her escape. Surely . . .

Again it came, the restless moan of a man in pain. It reminded him of the sounds the demon creatures made, and the thought sent a shiver through him as he lay on the cold desert ground searching for his second quarry. He could imagine the nightmare things out there in the darkness hearing the man's cries and turning toward them. Coming for him.

A series of laboured gasps now. Lewis paused and drew several slow breaths, listening to the man he'd just shot panting and wheezing away not more than fifty yards distant. The woman was still nowhere to be seen, but that was all right. He could walk in and finish off the gunslinger and then track down the Witch at his leisure.

He stood up—almost soundlessly, he thought with pride—and stepped forward with cautious deliberation, sweeping his gaze from side to side. He could see the man on the ground now, both hands clutched over the left side of his chest.

"If you tell me where she is, I'll let you live."

The gunslinger laughed and then choked, coughing for a moment. Finally he said, "Don't think so."

Lewis raised the rifle and—

A black shape surged past him and was gone again as suddenly. As it passed, there was a feeling—something like a feather stroke—just below his jawline. Lewis blinked, sensing a sudden wet warmth on his neck, and felt a thrum of fear vibrate through him.

Again the black shape flew past him—almost too quickly to see— and this time Lewis felt a veritable gush of hot liquid ripple down his neck.

His rifle slipped from fingers gone numb and he fell to his knees, hands coming up to staunch the flow of what he knew now must be his own blood, cascading like a waterfall from severed arteries just below his jaw. He could feel his heart labouring already, the organ an unknowing accomplice in his death as it dutifully pump his lifeblood out onto the desert floor around him. A figure came up beside him, and he looked up to see Solenne staring him with the passionless gaze of a reptile. There was a knife in her hand, and he knew the oily black sheen on it gleaming dimly in the twilight was his blood. The woman stepped forward and kicked him in the chest, and he fell over sideways, still clutching at the warm liquid that oozed between his fingers as if he might somehow stem the tide of death rising over him. He could no longer feel his legs, and he felt blanketed suddenly with cold, as if a rain shower was washing over him.

The woman stood over him for a moment, and he knew she was satisfying herself that he was finished. Her long black hair was restless in the wind, as if a living thing itself, and when his eyes found hers again, they found a depthless arctic blue—a cold wasteland without mercy. In his last moments, he was reminded of the Greek myth of Medusa, who could kill men with her stare.

She turned away, and his last vision was of the Witch striding over to the gunslinger and frowning as she bent over him.

## Chapter Eighteen

"Shit . . . shit, shit! That hurts!"

"Be still." Solenne had torn Brennan's shirt apart and was running her hands over his chest.

"Ow! Shit! Stop that!"

"Quit shouting. Where are you hit?"

"Chest!" He coughed. "Goddammit!"

Brennan watched her frown in puzzlement. "No. You're not. There's no blood . . ."

She gently probed the bruise rising on his chest—a large welt about the size of a fist. Her eyes narrowed and she pawed through his jacket and shirt, sure of what she'd find even before she drew it out and held it in front of Brennan's eyes.

"You're not shot, you asshole." She laughed as she said it, dangling a whiskey flask, dented and buckled, before him.

"What?"

But Brennan recognized the flask, the one he'd bought from his two guards with the gold coins tucked in his boot.

"Damn, that—" He coughed again. "That was a good investment."

Solenne was probing at his chest again, drawing gasps of pain as her fingers touched two snapped ribs that ground together under her fingers.

"Cracked a couple of ribs though. Gonna have to bind them."

Ignoring Brennan's protests, she rolled him half out of his jacket, tore the rest of his shirt off, and began folding it into a wide bandage.

"You gotta go after him. Just leave me here."

"It's too late. Won't catch him unawares, now. 'Sides, I need you. One extra gun might make all the difference."

Pulling him to a sitting position, she wound the makeshift dressing around his upper chest and yanked it tight, drawing another curse from her patient. Then she helped him back on with his coat.

"That'll keep 'em still enough that you don't puncture a lung." Solenne grabbed the lapels of Brennan's jacket and leaned back, hauling him roughly to his feet. "Mind if we get going now?"

Brennan hacked again and ran his hands over his chest as if still unwilling to believe his good luck.

"Yeah . . . Just give me a minute."

Solenne looked up at the sky.

"Don't have a minute. Dawn's coming and they're almost out of sight. Can you ride?"

Brennan pushed on his sternum, wincing.

"*Can you ride?*"

"Yeah." He looked around and saw his horse just a few yards away, eyeing the two humans who were the source of so much noise with some suspicion.

"By the way." Solenne slapped him in the face, stunning him for a moment. "That's for being stupid."

"What?"

"You heard him, didn't you?" She gestured at Lewis's cooling body. "You rode between me and that bullet."

"It was an accident. I'm clumsy."

"Well, there *is* that."

"Yeah, yeah . . . What now, then?"

Solenne frowned. "He's too far ahead, and he'll have heard the gunshot—just *one* gunshot, mind—and know that his man is dead."

"But the train—"

Solenne sighed. "There's another way. A harder way, but . . ."

Brennan had gathered the reins of his horse. He watched as Solenne flicked a hand at her own mount, and it whinnied and trotted over.

"What way?"

"You don't know this country too well, do you?"

Brennan's eyes narrowed. "No. Was just trying to run through it, truth be told."

Solenne pointed after Johnston. "He's headed to Copper River— small town where the train stops to pick up ore from the mines, but"—she shifted her finger toward the west—"it swings back south to cross the Gila River."

Brennan considered. "Those trains ain't especially fast."

"Right. We can cut across and make the Gila River bridge in four hours. It'll take him at least that long to get there."

"Getting on a moving train ain't easy, you know." Brennan was climbing on his horse with the caution of an injured man, but the pain in his ribs had already faded a little. It seemed the knowledge that he wasn't going to die—in the next few minutes, anyhow—was something of an analgesic.

"Didn't say it'd be easy. Said it'd be harder."

Solenne urged her horse forward and Brennan fell in beside her.

"Just so you know."

Solenne arched an eyebrow at him. "You've gotten on trains from horseback before."

"Had occasion."

"Figured you might've."

The sun was just breaching the horizon as they set their horses to a canter.

"Hey! Did you check the man you killed? For bites and the like?"

"You're learning. But he's not gonna turn. He's dead for good."

A pause as Brennan took this in. "How d'you know?"

"I'd have smelled it on him."

***

"No, sir, you will not! You will absolutely not do any such thing." The Copper River sheriff stamped his foot like a five-year-old in the midst of a tantrum.

Johnston and his group had reached the Copper River railroad junction an hour after sunrise, two hours after they had heard just a single shot behind them in the direction Johnston had sent Lewis. Since his captain had not returned, Johnston could only assume that Lewis had been killed either by the undead or by the Witch.

*The Witch* . . . If he ever got his hands on her again, he would take his knife and peel her skin from her body as if it were a ripe apple.

Even after escaping, she continued to haunt him. The horse below him had bucked and tried to throw him at irregular intervals throughout their journey. Furious beatings had been necessary to bring the fine beast under control, and now it was a stunned revenant, dull-eyed and looking hopelessly into oblivion as blood from a dozen or more blows from Johnston's crop dried on its torn face and neck.

The horses drawing the wagon had exhibited similar unpredictable bursts of erratic behaviour, bucking and wheeling without warning every twenty minutes or so, each time having to be coerced into moving forward again with whips. Each of these episodes had delayed their journey somewhat, and Johnston sensed that the Witch was responsible . . . somehow. He was sure of it. But perhaps Lewis had delayed her in turn, because now he had arrived and all that remained was to load his precious cargo on that train. Once that was done, nothing could stop him.

Standing in his way was this idiot sheriff.

*

Lieutenant Chapman had at first been exceedingly glad to see his commander ride up a few minutes ago, then surprised that the whole troop was not behind him, and finally horrified by the cargo his commander carried with him in the prison wagon.

"Report, Lieutenant," Johnston had said, halting his dead-eyed horse with a sharp tug on the reins.

Chapman had not answered right away, absorbed as he was by the sight of the twisted grey arms reaching for him and the yellow-eyed faces yawning at him from between the bars of the cage.

"Lieutenant! Report!"

"Sir." Chapman licked his lips, gone suddenly dry. "The train arrived approximately eight hours ago, and we secured it as you ordered, sir. We allowed some mail and other cargo to be unloaded this morning since there seemed no harm in that, sir. But the train was scheduled to leave"—he squinted at the sun, now sitting about a third of the way toward its zenith—"about two hours ago. There're thirty passengers already aboard, and they're starting to complain." Chapman pointed at a tall, pear-shaped, grey-haired man. He was surrounded by several people who were obviously berating him for not being able to begin their journey. "That's the sheriff over there, sir."

"Thank you, Lieutenant." Johnston drew his pistol and leaned toward Chapman, who sat, heart hammering, on his horse as the gun's muzzle came to rest on his right shoulder. "And mind me, sir. The next time you fail to answer me immediately, I shall shoot those lieutenant's bars from your shoulder. Understand?"

"Yessir." The words shot out of Chapman's mouth as if from a slingshot.

The sheriff had initially been cooperative when Chapman had ridden into town with his party. Copper River was far from both Confederate and Union forces, and troops from both armies had passed through the town at one time or another. The copper mines surrounding the town were the reason it existed, and most of the mined copper was shipped west to California on the very railroad Johnston was now intent on using. But the town was not important enough strategically for either army to occupy.

Nevertheless, everyone in town was well aware that this kind of situation could easily change, and they did their best to remain on friendly terms with any Union *or* Confederate force that happened through their peaceful little burg.

But the soldiers had been unable to explain exactly why they were holding the train, and the passengers had begun complaining. Some of them were Copper River residents, who had begun wondering aloud in front of the crowd that had gathered why they should vote for a sheriff who couldn't even get them on a train.

"Colonel!" The sheriff had stepped forward as Johnston got off his horse.

Johnston had looked at the men and women peering out of the train's windows for a few moments before turning and smiling at the sheriff. "Sir, my apologies. I can assure you these people will all be on their way very soon indeed. Is that the engineer I spy up yonder?" He pointed at a tubby man who sat leaning up against a supporting strut of the water tower beside the train.

The sheriff thought for a moment and nodded. "Jess! Jester!"

The sleeping man blinked and then lurched to his feet, shading his eyes and peering at the group near the rear of the train.

The sheriff motioned for him to get aboard. "These folks are ready to go! Get the engine fired up!"

The engineer drew a flask from his pocket and took a drink, grimacing at the taste before climbing up into the engine. Johnston watched until he heard the machine begin to chug to life and then turned back to his men and the waiting sheriff.

"Sheriff . . . ?"

"Parsons."

"Ah, Sheriff Parsons. Thank you for your patience, and for assisting my men. We'll be on our way just as soon as I've loaded my cargo."

That was when the wagon moved into view of the sheriff as well as the passengers leaning out of the train windows, and Chapman saw that things were about to go wrong.

In the rising heat of the day, the smell of the things in the cage was almost unbearable, like decaying meat fried up in hog grease. The stink wafted ahead of the wagon, and Chapman could see the sheriff turn away and the gawking passengers begin to gag and retreat into the railroad car.

"What in hell . . ." Parsons had taken his first good look at what the wagon held. One of the drooling, yellow-skinned reapers was looking him right in the eye as it reached for him, clawing at the air as it tried to force its head—ragged with torn skin and dripping black slime—through the bars of the cage.

Parsons turned back to Johnston. "Don't you tell me you're thinking of loading those things on this train?"

"Not thinking of it, sir. Doing it." Johnston turned to Chapman. "Mr. Chapman, you and your men will lock and enclose the passenger compartments and—"

"Sir?" Chapman could not keep the puzzled look off his face.

"Attend me, sir," said Johnston, steely anger in his voice. He continued in a low, deliberate tone. "You will see to it that the passenger compartments are secured. You will then load my cargo"—he gestured at the flailing undead in the cage behind him—"into those same compartments—"

"But, sir—"

Johnston pointed his pistol at Chapman. "One more *but*! One more interruption, and I shall shoot you and throw you in with them." Johnston flicked his eyes toward the cage. "Do. You. Understand?"

Chapman nodded and gulped out a belated *yessir*.

"Good. Secure the compartment. Load those things inside, and mind neither you nor any of your men get bit or scratched. If they do, they'll join the others. Understand?"

"Yessir." Chapman turned to one of his sergeants. "Begin getting the passengers off that train and—"

"No!" Johnston shot his pistol into the air, and all eyes were upon him. "Mr. Chapman, I gave no orders to unload those carriages. Secure them. Load those things in, and then batten the doors behind them. Am I clear?"

There was the slightest hesitation as Chapman took this in. "You . . . are, sir."

"Good. Do it."

Parsons had listened to this exchange while whipping his head back and forth from the train to the wagon full of rabid-looking savages.

"Hold on there, Colonel." Parsons said, holding up his hands. "You wanna take this train? I ain't gonna interfere—"

"Glad we agree on that, Sheriff."

"But you ain't putting those . . . *things*"—he pointed at the wagon—"in with those people."

And that was when Johnston shot Parsons, about as casually— Chapman thought—as one would swat a fly. His hand flicked up and his pistol fired, and the sheriff went down, clutching at the bloom of red growing over his abdomen.

Two of the sheriff's deputies stepped forward at that moment, their hands moving toward their guns. But stone-faced Confederate troops had filled their own hands with weapons all around them, and after a moment of watching the sheriff writhe on the ground, shrieking and cursing, the deputies lowered their eyes and their hands and stepped back.

"Mr. Chapman. Carry out your orders."

"Yessir." Chapman turned and nodded at the group of soldiers closest to him and pointed at the train. "You heard the colonel."

Several people within the two passenger carriages realized what was about to happen and began trying to disembark, but Chapman's men— eager not to fall afoul of Johnston's temper—ran to station themselves at each door, rifles out and barring anyone from leaving.

One of the men inside the train drew a pistol as he pushed others aside to get down the carriage stairway. Without hesitation, one of the soldiers raised his rifle and shot him in the chest. The man fell back inside, bubbling sounds coming from his throat as blood frothed up into his mouth.

A woman began screaming and tried to push her child out of a half-open window, and more soldiers moved to stop her.

Johnston smiled and looked down at the sheriff, who continued to slither around on the ground like a snake with a broken back, but with steadily decreasing energy, his skin losing more and more of its ruddy hue as death began to write its signature on him.

"Seems like you'll be riding with us, Sheriff."

Chapter Nineteen

In the last hour, electric shocks had been jittering back and forth in Solenne's chest like bolts of lightning among clouds in a gathering storm—the shade of the curse that ran through her calling out, as if taunting her as it took root in new victims. And they all came from the direction they rode toward. Her best guess was that Johnston had thrown the living dead in with the train passengers to swell the ranks of his reaper army.

In the last few minutes, though, the shocks had slowed and then halted, leaving an empty, sick feeling in Solenne's stomach. She knew that all the passengers on the train were dead; dead and being reborn now as empty-eyed reapers.

*Mistakes . . . Would those people be alive, if I had left Brennan? Or would I be lying dead along the trail, with nothing left between Johnston and his own personal Armageddon?*

Solenne had seen the wispy trail from the train's smokestack a few minutes before, and as they now rode over the last rise to meet it, she realized there was still a modicum of luck on their side. They had come across the train as it began to ascend a low hill, and their galloping horses would be more than a match for its reduced speed as it laboured up the rise. She pointed at the trailing carriage as they rode in steadily closer, aiming for the rear of the train as it rattled roughly along the tracks. Solenne saw that Johnston had detached all of the railcars save the passenger carriers.

No train passed through this country carrying only people. All carried cargo as well, usually on the cars set furthest back so the smell of cattle and other such freight would not offend the paying passengers. The cargo cars were gone now though. In the remaining passenger cars, Solenne could see figures stumbling against each other, rocking with the movement of the train like boats bobbing in rough seas. As she and Brennan moved closer, Solenne could make out grey-skinned faces pressed up against the windows, empty yellow eyes staring out at them, dead mouths open and tongues weaving tangled oily patterns over the windows, thirsty for the warm flesh they could sense moving nearer. Infected and deadly, they waited only to be loosed among a large populace to complete the arc of Johnston's insane plan.

Solenne's keen eyesight was occasionally a curse. She could see that one of the vacant faces at the windows belonged to what had once been a little girl, perhaps ten years old. She was still wearing the blue bonnet that Solenne imagined her mother had helped her put on that morning. Now it was askew and bloodstained, and the left side of the girl's cheek was torn away, giving her a permanent ghastly, lopsided smile.

The girl returned Solenne's stare with soulless, dandelion-yellow eyes and chewed at the glass that held her inside, which only stoked Solenne's anger. In her many years chasing and running down reapers, she had met rapists, sadists, and murderers. But her long experience had also acquainted her with a special kind of evil—men who deluded themselves and others into believing that any dark holocaust they might author was entirely justified for a greater good.

She had chided Brennan only hours ago for just such contemplations. She knew there was nothing of a little girl left in that face staring at her now. There was only a demon reaper that would tear her apart if it could. But she had been hunting the dead for so very long, and for just a moment, she could not help imagining the little girl looking in a mirror and admiring that pale blue bonnet, smiling at her reflection and looking forward to the adventures of the coming day.

All gone now, and just the mindless hunger left.

The dead girl had distracted Solenne, but three gunshots in a staggered staccato dragged her back into the moment. Another bullet zinged by her left ear as she spotted two men with rifles on the rear platform of the last carriage. Another man was stationed on the roof, and up ahead she could see at least two more leaning out from atop the locomotive tender and on the forward carriage.

The soldiers had all noticed Solenne and Brennan by now and were firing and reloading as fast as they could, barely taking time to aim. The reason for their haste was plainly apparent. The grinding noise of the train drowned out his shouts, but Solenne could see several soldiers leaning out of the engine cab bringing guns to bear, and Johnston was among them, face flushed with rage. His mouth was open and he was no doubt cursing at his men to take down the two approaching riders on pain of death, or worse.

*

"Here we go," Brennan yelled, beginning to direct his horse back and forth in an irregular rhythm. Solenne followed suit as they both drew pistols and began to return fire, concentrating on the men at the rear of the train, who were most likely to hit them. Brennan chose his targets carefully but knew only a lucky shot would tell from a moving horse. He would need to get closer to score a hit, which would of course mean that the men with rifles would have a much better chance at him.

"Get in behind the train!" he shouted at Solenne.

Solenne nodded and they both veered their mounts closer to the tracks. Now they would at least be out of sight of the men further up on the train and gunfire could reach them only from those stationed on the rear carriage.

Brennan was congratulating himself on this idea when his hat was blown off by a near miss. He swore and looked at Solenne. "This ain't gonna work! They'll get us long before we get close enough."

"I know!" she yelled back and holstered her pistol to draw her rifle out of its scabbard. "I have an idea!"

Brennan thought he saw a flash of insanity in the grin that accompanied this statement, but that was little surprise. "Best try it soon, then!"

They were less than a hundred yards behind the train now and gaining on it easily as it lumbered up the incline. At this rate, they would catch it before it crested the hill—if some stray bullet did not kill them in the meantime.

"Do your best to distract them." Solenne's lunatic smile vanished as she levelled her rifle at the back of the train.

Brennan bit back the indelicate response that first came to mind and occupied himself with the nearly impossible feat of hitting one of the gunmen. He might have tried his own rifle, but pain still leaked across his chest from his injured ribs, exacerbated by every hoofbeat. He was not entirely sure he would be able to hold a rifle and quite sure he would not be able to fire it with any accuracy.

Nevertheless, he snapped off two quick shots at the man atop the train and was gratified to see him flinch—struck in the arm. Brennan's following bullet took him in the chest and pitched him off the roof to land in a tumbling, bone-shattering heap beside the tracks.

Brennan shifted his fire to two men perched on the deck of the rear carriage. Both were crouched behind the meagre cover the railing offered and continued to fire at the approaching riders as Solenne opened up on them with her rifle.

Given everything he had seen over the last few days, Brennan expected Solenne to be a crack shot with a rifle, but her bullets went wild, striking far above the crouching men and shattering the windows behind them. Gunfire from the train ceased as both riflemen cringed and raised their hands to shelter themselves against the resultant shower of glass that rained down upon them. It was in that moment Brennan realized Solenne's shots had struck exactly where she had intended.

Graveyard-grey arms suddenly appeared through the shattered carriage windows, and—heedless of the dagger-like shards edging the window frames—the pack of undead surged toward the two gunmen crouching just below them.

The gunmen did not immediately notice the reapers reaching for them as they rose up to take aim again at Brennan and Solenne. And then one of the dead—a former soldier and comrade, by his ragged uniform—managed to force his upper torso halfway through one of the fragmented windows, falling forward with clutching hands that dug into the neck of the nearest man.

Dripping oily black goo from a dozen cuts in its shredded arms, the tattered nightmare tightened its hands about the soldier's neck as the man shrieked and whipped around in desperation, dropping his rifle as he was yanked toward the thing's yellow-toothed maw. Brennan could see the very moment when the man *knew* what had hold of him, and for a moment the soldier's eyes met Brennan's in a silent plea for help as he began to batter his fists against his attacker. Then the demon-thing bit deep into the soldier's face, and Brennan heard his scream even above the rattle of the train.

A second monster joined the first. Too portly to fit through the window, it nonetheless forced its arms through the opening and flailed to get a grip on its share of the warm feast set before it.

The doomed soldier's partner had been equally ignorant of the danger behind them until his partner began screaming. When he saw what was going on, he swivelled and surged to his feet, raising his rifle and clubbing at the demon that had hold of his friend, but the reaper ignored the blows. Moving its head back and forth in frenzied jerks, it ripped free most of the man's cheek and swallowed the bloody piece of flesh even as it opened its mouth for another bite. But the reaper's victim had managed to brace a leg against the carriage door, and now he pushed back with all his strength, breaking free of the monster's grip.

The soldier fell backward, clutching at his torn and bleeding face as he collided with the railing. He rebounded, crashing into his comrade, and the other man careened off the platform, mouth open in a soundless scream. He toppled to the ground in an explosion of blood among a group of boulders, limbs askew and skull smashed open like a ripe melon. Solenne spared him not a glance as her horse galloped right over him,

Brennan close behind.

*

Rifle fire still cracked around them sporadically as the men aft of the locomotive continued to try to take them down, but for the most part, the train shielded them. Still, Solenne could feel their moment vanishing. Their horses had been at a full gallop for nearly two miles and were beginning to tire, and the locomotive was nearing the apex of the hill. Once over the rise, momentum would quickly carry it out of reach. She could see that if they did not board it in the next minute, they never would.

She directed her horse in toward the carriage platform. The bitten soldier lay on the deck, kicking at the inhuman things reaching down for him, his hands plastered to the gaping wound on his face. As Solenne drew parallel to the deck, the muzzle of her rising pistol aimed directly at him, he whipped his head up and met her eyes.

"Please . . . No—"

Solenne shot him in the left eye, and his head snapped back, bloody grey matter exploding out of the socket as he sank lifeless onto the platform, moving now only with the shaking of the train.

Manoeuvring her horse directly beside the carriage deck, Solenne grabbed one of the rails with her left hand as she brought the pistol in her right to bear on the two reapers that had assisted her in eliminating the riflemen.

The dead men turned their attention to this new source of food as soon as she came within range, groping for her like clumsy, drunken lovers. One—a stocky former businessman by the look of him, now missing most of the right side of his face—was still mostly inside, unable to manoeuvre much of his bulk through the window, while the dead soldier who had managed a bite or two from the now-deceased trooper had tumbled headfirst onto the platform, his feet still caught in the shattered window above.

Solenne swung off her horse onto the platform and shot first one and then the other in the head, twin explosions of rotting brain and oily liquid. Other creatures in the carriage moved forward to take their places, but she saw she had some moments before they would reach her and took time to reload her guns, watching as Brennan rode up on the opposite side of the platform.

"Throw me your saddlebags!"

"What!?"

"Don't wanna leave your gold behind, do you?"

Brennan hesitated, frowning, and then finally nodded. Grimacing at the tightness in his chest, he reached around and yanked at the straps holding the bags to his saddle, slinging them at Solenne, who caught them expertly.

"You're next! Come on!"

A devout Quaker woman caught on the train when Johnston commandeered it—formerly reverent of the blood of Christ and now far less discriminating about the origins of the blood she worshipped—reached through the window for Solenne. Her yellow dress was stained a rusty red where the things that had fed on her had eaten into the soft flesh of her belly. She smacked her lips continuously, as if she had a thirst beyond measure and beyond quenching.

Solenne slapped the woman's hands away and put a bullet through her forehead. An apple-sized chunk exploded from the back of her skull and showered the monsters behind her in a viscous, pus-coloured fluid laced with bone chips. The woman fell backward, mouth open wide as if in surprise.

"Come on!" Solenne yelled again.

Brennan moved within a foot or two of the train and reached toward Solenne, who yanked him from his horse and swung him onto the platform. His feet slid on the greasy slop of blood and brain matter that covered the flooring, and for a moment he thought he might slip over the edge. Then Solenne steadied him as he watched their horses fall away behind.

Brennan eyed the remaining monsters in the carriage. Twenty, at least. More than half of those had been attracted to the noise and movement on the rear platform and were shuffling toward them, jockeying to be the first at the food trough that awaited them if Brennan and Solenne remained where they were. They might just be able to kill them all, but the forward carriage was likely full of as many or more of the monsters, and Johnston's remaining men would be upon them long before they could finish such a task.

"What now?"

Solenne pointed toward the carriage roof. "We go up top."

Brennan looked up at the roof and then back at Solenne as if she had just offered him a plate of shit for breakfast.

"Trust me. I have a plan. Now climb!"

Even as she said it, a reaper stumbled across the corpse in the yellow dress and reached out the window for her. Solenne slithered away from it and scrambled up onto the railing, grabbing the edge of the carriage roof and hauling herself up. There was an immediate resurgence of gunfire as the men further up the train saw her come in to view.

The train crested the ridge and moved downhill now. The view showed they were headed down into the Gila River valley. Brennan followed Solenne, climbing unsteadily up onto the railing, paying no attention to the protests the exertion caused his ribs.

Solenne reached down for him and pulled him up beside her, rolling him on top of her. A bullet whistle by just above them and Brennan reflexively whipped his head down, bringing him face to face with

Solenne, closer than he'd ever been to her except during their fight. Solenne notice him breathe in her scent. He looked almost intoxicated.

"You enjoying this?" She wore that half-insane grin again, her nose almost touching his.

He looked at his saddlebags, still slung over her shoulder, and frowned. "What's the plan?"

The shooting had stopped, and Solenne frowned, pushing Brennan off her and then rolling to her feet in a crouch, throwing his saddlebags up toward the apex of the train car. Johnston and two other soldiers had climbed out onto the roof of the car ahead of them and were advancing on them as quickly as the irregularly wavering train would allow. Johnston was ahead of the other two, and though they each held a pistol, they were obviously too scared to shoot. The train was rocking with ever-increasing enthusiasm as it picked up speed, and any shot from either was as likely to hit their commander as their enemies.

Solenne skipped on hands and knees, light as a lizard, toward the centre of the carriage, motioning for Brennan to follow.

Brennan struggled to a crouch and then slipped as the train rocked ferociously to the left. He fell prone, pain flaring in his chest, and skittered toward the side of the roof, hands out and fingers clawing at the wood as he skidded to a stop at the edge.

There was nothing below them for at least a hundred feet. The train had reached a bridge, and far below them the torrent of the Gila River ran, as eager as any of the creatures to swallow Brennan whole if he fell. With great care, he planted his hands beside his shoulders to push himself back, but before he could, a carriage window shattering just below him. A dull grey arm spidered with blue veins snaked through the window below, sinuous as an octopus as it groped upwards toward his face. All along the carriage, other windows were being smashed out as the reapers inside, perhaps disturbed by the gunfire, sought to escape. The soldiers stationed forward on the other carriage might soon have something to occupy their minds other than Brennan and Solenne

"Quit fooling around!" Solenne yelled at him. "We don't have much time—come here!"

Brennan took a deep breath and edged back toward the centre of the train, shooting Solenne a dark look. She was not paying attention, though. There were three vents spaced equally across the apex of the carriage roof, each about two feet across and topped with slatted tin caps to keep the rain out while allowing hot air to escape from the compartments below. Solenne was sitting on her butt, kicking at the cap of one of the vents. But she had not forgotten Johnston. Her pistol was back in her hand and she paused a moment to aim, squeezing a shot off at the three men approaching them as Brennan sidled up beside her.

Johnston saw the shot coming and fell to his hands and knees, nearly dropping his own pistol in the process. He had seen Solenne use a gun only once, when she had fired a nearly impossible shot that had struck its target—the head of the creature he had been so desperately trying to capture—even while she was being restrained and beaten two dozen feet distant. If nothing else, he had respect for her aim.

Solenne's shot flew mere inches over Johnston's head as he ducked, and the soldier directly behind him took the bullet in his belly. He tottered as he clutched at his punctured abdomen, and the train shuddered just at that moment, flicking him off the side like a flea off a shaking dog's back. His shriek died quickly under the rattling cacophony, though Solenne imagined it carried on for some time as he fell toward the river many feet below.

Solenne managed to kick the top off the vent, and it clattered in a chaotic tumble across the roof of the car, missing Brennan by inches as the wind whipped it away. He cursed as Solenne rolled toward him. Then her hands were in his jacket, groping through his pockets. "The black powder! Where is it? Aha!"

She tore out one of the sacks of powder he'd picked up at the camp from of his jacket and hefted it, testing its weight.

"What the hell are you doing?"

The mad grin was back on Solenne's face. Brennan watched her eyes flash from him to Johnston and to their final focus—forward on the locomotive.

"Unscheduled stop."

Solenne's right arm shot back and then flew forward like a catapult as she launched the packet of powder toward its target. In the moment of release, she experienced a powerful and unexpected jolt of elation in a flash of muscle memory. It took her a moment to recognize the origin of the feeling. Arm moving forward and the missile arcing upward—the joy of throwing a spear with the movement and power of that long-ago girl hunting on the plain . . .

Brennan and Johnston were both transfixed momentarily as they watched the packet fly through the air . . . over Johnston . . . over the forward carriage . . . and toward the cab of the locomotive.

At the start of the train's journey, Johnston had quickly impressed upon the engineer the necessity for speed, leaving the imprint of a pistol barrel on the man's forehead from the intensity of his lecture. Because of this, since leaving Copper Creek, the train crew had kept the firebox door open and the locomotive constantly stoked with a heavy fire.

With accuracy that had not diminished since she felled her first deer, the sack of powder sailed straight and true to its target—into the open firebox.

The explosion was immediate, an eruption of sound and light and overwhelming force that tore the cab of the locomotive apart. Fire shot thirty feet into the air, along with screaming comets of red-hot metal and wood that careened in all directions, like flares shot from a dying sun. Several errant pieces of shrapnel blasted into the soldier who had remained back atop the forward carriage, tearing him into a bloody mass of unrecognizable flesh that flopped back and forth like a dying fish for a few seconds before lying still.

The shockwave that reverberated throughout the train knocked all three left alive on its roof from their feet.

Solenne was first to make it back upright. Brennan was still climbing to his knees when she reached him. Swaying from the concussion and blinking as if to clear her head, she smirked like a drunkard as she plucked another of the packs of black powder from his pockets.

Secondary explosions rocked the locomotive in front of them, shooting geysers of flame and steam into the air as the engine began to slow and die like some mortally wounded primordial beast.

Solenne saw Johnston regain his own feet. His pistol was gone from his hand, and she watched him find it with his eyes—it had danced to the edge of the train's roof and was rocking there like a man contemplating suicide, uncertain about whether to jump. Johnston apparently decided against retrieving it and instead drew a sabre from his belt. Solenne had a moment to wonder where he'd acquired it as she still had the one she'd taken from his tent lashed to her side. Then Johnston was leaping across the gap, a bellow of inarticulate challenge escaping his lips as he did so, lost in the wind and the death rattles of the slowing train. Once safe on the rear carriage, he advanced on Solenne and Brennan as quickly as the shaking and lurching of the dying train would allow, the sabre in his hand trembling and his face red and twisted with murderous rage.

"Get the hell off my train, you scum! You shall not stop me! Do you hear?"

Solenne bent over, as if too preoccupied to pay attention to the ravings of the man approaching.

"Solenne!"

Brennan had somehow managed to maintain a grip on his own weapon, and he fired several quick shots at Johnston before his gun went dry, but the irregular swaying of the train skewed his aim and none hit.

He glanced at Solenne, who had his saddlebags and was packing the black powder into them with one hand as she patted the pockets of her pants with the other.

"Solenne!"

Johnston was nearly within reach of Solenne, and Brennan leapt forward and aimed for Johnston's legs, but Johnston saw the move coming and skipped sideways, lashing out with his foot and striking Brennan in the face. Brennan was thrown onto his back and Johnston turned to bring his sword down. Rolling instinctively away, Brennan scrambled over the dry wood to arrest his trajectory, but this time he could not stop and suddenly he was shooting over the carriage edge, twisting and—in a miracle—managing to grab the lip of the roof with both hands, feet dangling over the abyss of the Gila River.

"Brennan!" Solenne shouted. There was irritation in her tone, as if his predicament was somehow an inconsiderate distraction.

Johnston moved forward to finish off Brennan, but Solenne moved in front of him.

"See you found another sword, Colonel." She had drawn Johnston's own sabre in her left hand and was spinning it experimentally while her pistol came up to point at his face.

"Took this from an incompetent captain." Johnston spat. "But I'll have my own back from you, you bitch!"

"I don't think so, Colonel. I like this one—believe I'll keep it." She waved the gun in his face. "Need to borrow something from you, now. I recall you smoke—"

A shot rang out, and a look of surprise come over Solenne's face as a bright red stain blossomed on her upper right leg. She crashed down to her knees and then fell over on one side like a discarded rag doll, a puzzled look on her face as her gun slipped from her hand.

*

Brennan followed Solenne's gaze to a soldier crawling across the forward car. It was hard to believe anyone who had been in the cab of the locomotive when it exploded had survived, and Brennan had seen so many new forms of monstrosity over the last two days that it was strange to recognize a familiar one. The soldier who had shot Solenne had been seared alive by the steam explosion. His uniform and hair were burnt mostly off, and his skin had acquired the rich red hue of roasted pork, crimson blisters warring with blackened patches for control of his skin.

Dying, he had nonetheless tried to do his duty and had crawled close enough to use his rifle in defense of his commander. The man was attempting to reload, but his hands were fumbling ineffectually at the ammo pouch still clinging to his tattered belt. And now Brennan saw that his desperate, darting eyes weren't looking at him or Solenne but at the roofline . . .

Grey-blue hands, white-tipped with bony claws, had appeared above the roof of both carriages and were groping in greedy, spastic surges in an effort to climb atop the coaches.

Johnston was grinning again, moving toward Solenne with his sabre raised. She spun onto her back and tried to raise her own sword, but Johnston stepped in and kicked her in the gut. She rolled with the kick toward her fallen pistol, only to have Johnston drop down on top of her and drive his knee into her abdomen. Brennan was sure she would have screamed if the assault had not forced the air from her lungs.

Brennan had one forearm back on top of the roof. The pain in his chest made climbing difficult, but that was not his only hindrance.

A reaper had broken out the window below Brennan and wrapped its cold hands around his right ankle. It was leaning through the casement and trying to pull Brennan's leg toward its drooling mouth. From the look of him, the monster had been a businessman scarce hours ago, before his fellow passengers had eaten away most of his abdomen, and his subsequent unholy resurrection. Brennan saw that loops of intestine hung from its belly and had been shredded where they had fallen afoul of the wheels and rails below, creating a tangled apron of putrescent and bloody gut hanging from the creature's waist.

Brennan kicked at the monster, but the movement only loosened his own tenuous grip on the top of the carriage. Nevertheless, a cry drew his attention back to Solenne. He saw Johnston shift his weight and bring his knee down on Solenne's thigh, pressing it into her bullet wound and laughing as he did it, practically giggling as she screamed.

"Now, you little bitch! Before you die"—he shoved his hand down over her mouth—"you're going to give me your magic! Bite my hand! Bite it!"

Solenne reached a hand out toward her pistol, fingers groping at it only inches away. Johnston saw what she was doing, lifted his own hand, slapped her, and then immediately forced his fist back over her bloody mouth. She tried to bring her sabre up and he knocked it away with his own.

The weapon tumbled toward Brennan, slashing his cheek as it went over the edge. As it fell past him, it sliced into the arm of the reaper that had hold of him, and Brennan felt its grip weaken. He kicked again until whatever structures the blade had pierced in the creature's arm gave way and he found himself free. He jerked himself upward, doing his best to ignore the sharp, searing pain the movement loosed in his chest. He coughed and saw spots of blood splatter across the roof underneath him.

The locomotive was slowing appreciably now. Irregular blasts still shot from the firebox like desperate signals from a dying heart, and steam hissed a mad banshee cry from the failing engine, but the train was as good as dead. Other problems awaited them though. Even if Brennan could reach Johnston in time to aid Solenne, he saw that—among the many making the attempt—one of the reapers had won out and managed to climb atop their railcar. It was on its feet, swaying with the last convulsive tremors of the train.

Brennan recognized Barrett, turned reaper now.

*

"Bite me, you bitch!" Johnston moved to slap Solenne again and she twisted under him, bringing her legs up as she lurched and writhed within a finger's reach of the gun dancing on the wooden roof beside her.

Johnston was nearly thrown off, but he rebounded and slammed back down on her, driving his knee into her abdomen again. He looked down into the face of the woman he had pursued for so long, who had tried so hard to prevent this moment—his triumph.

She was *nothing*. A troublesome bug for him to squash. Her face was bloody. Her lips had split and her nose was broken. *She* should have been broken too. Shot. Beaten. Half suffocated. But those diamond-blue eyes . . . They stared back at him as if *he* were the insect.

Then—icy cold and hard—there was a short, sharp blow to his belly.

An involuntary gasp escaped him as he looked down at Solenne, down into those defiant cobalt eyes shining like gunmetal out of the face he'd bloodied.

She smiled at him through the blood.

"No bite for you . . . But I do have a sting."

Her smile widened as she jerked her hand upward; and the piece of ice in his belly moved with her. He saw the knife in her hand then, buried to the hilt at an upward angle just under his ribcage.

His blood began to ooze out around the knife. This woman, this *witch*. It was as if she had torn at a ragged thread and unravelled his life.

Where had she found the blade? Her boot? Her belt . . . ?

Then she let go of the hilt, as abruptly as if her hand were unlocking from a spasm, and he saw the intricate carvings on the bone hilt. It was *his* knife. He could feel his heart fluttering against the metal blade and knew it was pierced.

Solenne gave an inarticulate cry—mix of rage and triumph—and shoved hard against his chest with both hands, launching him off her so that he shot back onto his knees as she rolled away from him. She had the gun back in her hand now.

Johnston clutched at the knife in his chest and felt grey fog descending over his vision. He tried to get to his feet, and almost made it. He had dropped his sword . . . if he could find it . . .

A shadow fell over him and Johnston turned.

Barrett—dead and grey and leaking a black drool that looked something like molasses from the corner of his mouth—looked down at Johnston, snarling. He had ripped off his nose and most of his left cheek in whatever battle he had waged with the obstacles that had stood between him and this moment.

Johnston half rose. If he could get to his sword . . .

Barrett embraced him then, a nightmare apparition with half his face gone and his yawning mouth ready to bite, stinking like an open grave. Johnston struggled against Barrett, but the grey fog swirling past his eyes brought with it an accompanying heavy feeling in his arms. The dead nightmare pulled him in and plunged icy teeth into his neck. Johnston

229

uttered a stuttering shriek as the Barrett-revenant bit deep and began chewing into his flesh, even as his dying heart spasmed one last time around the knife penetrating it. When he fell, he dragged the Barrett-thing with him, and they stumbled together toward—

"Brennan!" Solenne yelled at the top of her lungs. Her gun came up, and she shot the Barrett-thing through the head, but it was too late to arrest the thing's trajectory.

Johnston and the Barrett-thing fell against Brennan, who had just regained the roof and climbed to his feet, and the impact sent all of them over the side.

## Chapter Twenty

*"Chingame!"*

In her long war against the curse, Solenne had only rarely had allies, and never for long. She had encountered few people who could stomach the slaughter her life involved, and one or two who came to enjoy it far too much. She regretted Brennan's loss. More than regretted it, if she were honest. But then, losing people had been part of her whole life. And now—as ever—she had no time for sadness.

She rolled onto her stomach, grimacing at the agony the movement produced in her leg and muttering more curses as she assessed her situation.

The train had lurched to a near halt perhaps three-quarters of the way across the bridge.

Her right upper leg was a lightning storm of pain, but it didn't seem to be bleeding too badly. No major blood vessels struck, then; and while she could feel the bullet had penetrated deep into the muscle, as far as she could tell it had not struck bone. She was fairly sure she would be able to stand and maybe even walk, and that would no doubt be very important in the next few minutes since several more reapers were in the process of dragging themselves up onto the car she occupied. That would become a bit of a problem if she could not complete her work quickly. Immunity to a bite was not immunity to being torn apart.

A glance ahead revealed that the burnt soldier on the roof of the forward carriage was still alive and still bravely struggling to reload his rifle despite what must have been horrific pain from his burns. He had company now, though. A reaper was crawling toward him, no doubt attracted by the aroma of his roasted flesh and the smell of blood from the soldier blasted apart not far from him. If the soldier managed to get the rifle loaded in time, would he aim it at the drooling reaper, or at her?

*Time slipping away again . . .*

Johnston's pistol was still jiggling on the gutter edge of the roof. She knew she might need every bullet, and so she scrambled toward it, pain flaring from her wound. Shoving the weapon into her belt, she turned back toward the vent she'd kicked open. The saddlebags still lay across the apex of the carriage roof, and she started to crawl toward them.

And then, barely audible over the wheezing and clattering of the dying train, came a shout from the side of the carriage.

Ignoring the protests from her leg, Solenne dove again to the edge of the roof. Brennan, like some proverbial many-lived cat, twisted over the abyss, looking up at her with grim desperation. He was hanging on to the arm of a reaper that had smashed its way out of one of the windows, his feet dancing over the gulf below him and desperately seeking some purchase so that he might climb back up. The undead creature seemed frustrated by the man clinging to it—food just beyond its reach—and it snarled and snapped at Brennan as she watched, but it was pinned on broken glass at the window's base by Brennan's weight, and Brennan remained beyond the reach of its teeth.

Solenne grinned. "Hey!"

"Hey!" Brennan grunted back. "Little help?"

The bridge was little wider than the train. If Brennan dropped, there was no chance he would not fall to his death.

Solenne unbuckled her belt and pulled it free, lowering it down toward Brennan and glancing again at the forward carriage as she did so. Two reapers were now bent as if in prayer, feasting on the seared soldier that lay atop its roof. As she watched, a child's face appeared at the edge of her carriage—the same girl she had seen earlier at the train window. There was a fresh oily black tear on the right side of her neck, and somewhere in the few minutes since Solenne had first glimpsed her, perhaps on her scrabble to the roof, she had poked one of her eyes out and the deflated eyeball dangled like hellish jewellry from the right side of her face.

Solenne's belt swayed a few inches above Brennan's hands. She looked into his eyes and shouted, "That's far as I can go or we'll both go over! Reach up!"

Brennan swore and lurched upward, letting loose his grip on the reaper and fumbling desperately at Solenne's belt before securing his grip.

Brennan's lunge nearly yanked Solenne off the roof, and she immediately noticed that his weight seemed to be causing things to move within her shoulder that should not be moving.

"Hurry." The pain in her voice was unmistakable.

"Doing my best."

"Do better."

Clad in the remains of a torn bloody dress that might have once matched her bonnet, the girl-demon had finished clambering up onto the roof, and Solenne shuddered at the look the girl-thing threw her. In nearly twenty years of killing them, she had never seen one of them do this before—the sightless adolescent devil-thing actually grinned as it set her sights on the only human left within reach.

Brennan had his hands around Solenne's wrist now. He had managed to get his feet up against the outer wall of the carriage in an attempt to brace himself and aid in his climb up. The reaper—free of his grip—had managed to lift itself up was groping for him, jaws working in anticipation and a river of brackish drool fountaining over its snarling lips.

"Pull!" Brennan and Solenne both yelled at each other at precisely the same time, and then they each grimaced at the other in irritation.

The reaper-girl with the ravaged face was lurching like a drunk across the roof of the train toward them. Something in Solenne's shoulder was slowing beginning to tear now, and every move on Brennan's part threatened anew to drag her from the roof.

"Hurry up, *pendejo!*"

Brennan was familiar with the Mexican term for *jackass* but was in no position to protest its use.

"Just—"

"Shut up!" Solenne screamed at him. She sensed the revenant devil-girl settle to its knees behind her as she lay prone before it, an easy meal, but there was no time to worry about her. Not when she had seen—

"Matches!"

"What?" Brennan twisted below her, utterly perplexed.

"Matches! That thing in front of you! It has matches in its pocket. Get—"

Brennan looked at the reaper he had so recently relinquished his grip on, still flailing away at him. The thing's shirt and jacket were bloody and shredded, but the grey hands reaching for him did have vaguely perceptible tobacco stains on the tips of the fingers, and sure enough, an indistinct outline that might have been a pack of matches was visible beneath the blood in the man's torn shirt.

"Are you kidding?"

"No! Get the matches!"

Solenne tensed as she felt the dead girl fall forward onto her injured leg, her nose no doubt following the irresistible scent of fresh blood seeping from Solenne's wound. She felt the thing's tiny, frost-cold fingers rip at the fabric around the bullet hole to make an opening large enough to feed from.

"Hurry!" She hissed at Brennan through gritted teeth.

Brennan shook his head but stretched to move closer to the creature reaching, in turn, for him. It now had competition at the window from others who had noticed food dangling within reach, and Brennan had to jockey his hand between numerous arms clutching at him.

He stretched—once . . . twice—and then he was ripping the packet of matches out of the thing's pocket. Placing the matchbox in his mouth, he grabbed back onto Solenne's arm with both hands.

Solenne's eyes were closed and her teeth were clenched in agony. The reaper-child was chewing into her upper leg. Little teeth ripped determinedly into her flesh, and now that the noise from the train had quieted to irregular, gasping burps of steam, Solenne could hear the slurping noises the monster made as it sucked at the blood flowing from her wound.

Brennan's hands slipped down on her arm.

*The moment is vanishing.*

With an effort, Solenne concentrated, seeking memories many years old. The words were still there, words she had been taught as a child—and likewise taught never to use. Never, unless there was no other way. The phrase was an ancient one, brought from the southern land, and was an appeal to the most powerful of forces, some of them dark ones. Such requests had a cost whose price could not be predicted, and so they must be used only in the greatest extremity.

The words flowed, and she bent her mind around a corner of reality, shifting into the spiritworld, disengaging the portion of her soul that felt fatigue, worry, and pain. No human could free themselves from the assaults of the outside world, but a *witch* could accomplish things otherwise impossible if she slid out from reality for a few precious moments.

It would have to be enough.

Marshalling strength no human was entitled to in the real world, Solenne twisted her body like a writhing snake, wrenching Brennan upward even as her shoulder threatened to tear itself from its socket, and Brennan—astonishment on his face—levered himself up and onto the roof.

Solenne released Brennan and kicked the leech-like reaper off her. It fell into a crouch, hissing, its dangling right eye still bobbling against its cheek and Solenne's blood staining the lower half of its face.

Solenne's hand found the sword Johnston had dropped, and as the demon-child leapt at her, she swiped the sabre sideways in a vicious cut that bisected its neck. Rusty black fluid flew from its decapitated body as its head—bonnet and all—went bouncing off the roof.

Solenne stared down at the frail-looking body, breathing hard. She could see a small homemade doll tucked into a pocket of its bloodstained dress.

Shaking herself, Solenne snatched the matches away from Brennan. She pulled him along as she moved to the peak of the roof, and she yanked him down beside her as she collapsed beside the saddlebags, digging through his jacket pockets again and plucking two more sacks of black powder out of them.

"Is this all you've got?"

"You mind telling me what the hell you think you're doing?"

Her eyes flashed like lightning. She waved a sack of the pungent stuff in front of his face. "Is. This. All?"

Brennan nodded.

"Okay." She began to shove the packs of explosive in among the gold coins. Among his treasure.

"Just what the hell are you—"

"Explosive isn't enough—there's gotta be shrapnel."

Brennan looked horrified.

"No—"

"Yes."

Solenne pointed toward two hissing reapers that had managed to get up onto the roof of their carriage and were climbing to their feet behind them.

"We're going to have to jump," Solenne said.

She watched him gulp as he noticed that one of the fuses he'd stolen had appeared in her hand and that there was a match in the other.

"Off the end of the *train*, you mean?"

"It's the only way. Stand upwind of me. It'll keep the match lit."

Brennan moved to stand forward of Solenne as she struck the match, and looked with sorrow down at his bulging saddlebags, the coins now mixed with enough explosive to destroy an entire town.

"Don't suppose there's any other—"

"Ain't no other way. It's a short fuse. Get ready."

A former soldier shuffled toward them with the fixated gaze typical of the hungry dead. His right arm was peeled down to the bone like a turkey drumstick after the feast, and his lower jaw swung haphazardly from his skull. It had as its companion the former sheriff of Copper River, its head canted to the left owing to the fact that most of the flesh had been stripped away from its right neck. Despite himself, Brennan was impressed that either man had been able to make the climb to the roof, given the nature of their injuries.

Solenne lit the fuse—a thirty second one, if she'd cut it right—and threw the saddlebags down into the vent hole, then rose to her feet, grunting against gritted teeth at the shocking hammer of pain in her leg when she moved it. Brennan grabbed her and they ran, as best they could, toward the back of the train.

*Twenty-five seconds . . .*

Two more reapers stood in their way—hungry, bloody, reaching for them—and the sword in Solenne's hands flew back and forth almost too fast for Brennan to follow. She decapitated one and split the other nearly in two with a strike that sliced downward through its neck and deep into its chest.

They shouldered past the two collapsing dead things, Solenne skipping over the rolling head of the one she had decapitated, and jumped.

*Twenty seconds . . .*

Solenne pulled Brennan to her as their feet left the carriage roof, and she twisted as they flew so that she would land below him and cushion his own fall.

In their brief seconds in the air, Solenne looked up at the blue sky, the sun shining down into her eyes—elemental primordial energy—and she whispered *the words* again and pulled the sun into her, warping its energy over her and the man she embraced.

They struck the rails and rolled, and she tried as best she could to continue the motion, knowing that every moment their movement continued meant energy dissipated. Still, she felt several of her ribs snap like twigs in a child's hand as they plummeted onto the railway bridge. They would heal quickly, as all her wounds seemed to, *if* she could survive the next few minutes.

*Fifteen seconds . . .*

Solenne was dragging Brennan to his feet the moment their tumble halted as if he were a reluctant partner at a dance.

"Move!"

Arms about each other, they hobbled like contestants in a three-legged race across the bridge and away from the railcar. Twenty yards . . . thirty . . .

*Ten seconds . . .*

They glanced back and saw reapers on the roof of the train's rear carriage reaching out for them like disciples calling to a failed saviour.

*Five seconds . . .*

"Down!" Solenne dragged him to the bridge deck, falling on top of him.

"Solenne—"

"Shut up."

She ducked her head down into the nape of Brennan's neck as a wave of fire and thunder rolled over them like an avalanche.

The concussion of sound and light shattered their senses as the bridge swelled and rolled, cresting with the abrupt force of a tidal wave shattering on the shore. The waves ebbed and died, leaving silence behind, broken only by the clattering rain of debris—chunks of wood, metal, bloody flesh, and shattered bone—cascading like hail on the bridge around them.

Solenne rolled off Brennan, a dozen wounds groaning at the movement, and Brennan sat up with the slow caution of an invalid. After a moment he managed to stand, vertigo warring with his middle ear, not helped in the least by the deep abyss still on either side of them. He reached down and helped Solenne get to her feet.

Solenne bent to one side as if her back hurt, and she realized her jacket was burnt and that fresh blood leaked from a half-dozen gashes where debris from the exploding train had struck her.

When they turned and looked behind them, they saw the remnants of the metal platforms and the wheels of the two twisted railroads carriages, with smoking splintered wood remaining at their bases and little other evidence of what they had once been. The back coach had been derailed entirely, and its rear portion hung listing off the east side of the bridge, held only by the hitch connecting it to the front carriage, gravity worrying at it like a vulture tearing at carrion. The fuel tender and locomotive in front looked deceptively intact, though scarred and burnt by the explosive atrocities Solenne had visited upon them.

No living thing moved among the wreckage. No dead thing either.

Solenne grabbed Brennan by the shoulders and looked into his eyes. Her face was a mass of rising bruises and a mix of fresh and dried blood. When she spoke to him he looked at her blankly, then stared at her lips, and she realized the force of the blast had near deafened him. She leaned forward to shout in his ear.

"I have bad news!"

"I can't hear—"

"Bad. News!" she shouted at the top of her lungs.

"Bad news?"

"Yes!" She yelled and pointed. "We're not done running!"

*

Brennan followed Solenne's gesture.

Sixty feet behind them, at the centre of the explosion, the bridge was beginning to sag like a papier-mâché construct left out in the rain. Though partially shielded by the metal in the carriage platforms, Brennan saw that the explosion had nevertheless ripped through portions of the bridge's supporting structure below.

In the warm summer wind, the bridge began to sway again.

Solenne swore—something Spanish and indecipherable—and grabbed Brennan's shoulder.

"Run!"

They clutched at each other and began limping away again as fast as they could. Irregular sharp cracks came from behind them and there was the sensation of the bridge shuddering beneath their feet as supporting timbers snapped, one after another. Brennan glanced back and saw the bridge begin to fail just underneath the train, lurching and buckling downward like a penitent man falling to his knees. With a scream of agonized metal, the rear coach platform let go and rocketed into the river below, destroying any remaining support that the bridge below it had offered. Rifle fire pops of splintering wood multiplied and rose into a discordant orchestra of destruction as the remainder of the train cleaved into the bridge and then tumbled with it toward the rocks below.

Solenne and Brennan ran and ran, the remaining bridge shaking beneath them as if in a seizure, threatening at any moment to throw them off or sink beneath them.

*We're not going to make it,* Brennan thought, and then he could see the southern bank and the shaking began to diminish. He and Solenne collapsed against each other and fell to the ground, near a half mile away from where they had started and only a few yards from the southernmost beginnings of the span.

As if in tune with the creaking and labouring construct below, they lay exhausted, gasping like consumptive old men until finally, minutes later, the tremors ceased. Solenne levered herself up on her elbows and saw that the entire north end of the bridge was gone, dragged down into the Gila.

Brennan had been tearing cloth from the inside of his jacket, and now he was beside her, binding the makeshift bandage around the wound in her leg. She gritted her teeth and swore under her breath as he tightened it, and Brennan found his hearing was beginning to return.

"All right, now. No need for that."

"You're not much of a nurse."

"That's too bad, 'cause I'll have to find *some* sort of job seeing as you *blasted my fortune to pieces.*" He finished tying the bandage and lay back on the ground again.

"Wait a minute." Solenne rolled onto her side, cursing some more as she dug at her lower back. She yanked something out with a gasp of relief and dropped a scorched and bloody gold coin—shot into her by the blast—into his lap.

"This'll get you started again."

Brennan sat up and picked up the coin, laughed, and then immediately began coughing. When he could speak, he said, "Think I might rest here for a bit."

Solenne took a few seconds to answer. "Can't."

"Just for a minute."

"All right . . . A minute."

"Ten minutes?"

"All right. Ten. No more than that, though."

"All right, then."

"Just shut up will you?"

"Think you got 'em all?"

"All that were on the train."

Brennan lay back and let the various insults his body had received make themselves known to him. His mouth was dry and he longed for a taste of whiskey. Much more than ten minutes later, they were both quiet, breathing easier, and still lying there looking up at the sky.

"I guess we should—" Brennan started.

Solenne rolled on top of him—careful, he noticed, not to lean against his broken ribs—and took his face in her hands.

She was still a mess, her face a mass of dirt and blood, and he supposed he looked much the same. There were those sky-blue eyes, though, and that overwhelming smell of cinnamon again.

She kissed him, hard, for a long time. When she broke the kiss, she said, "Thank you."

Before he could reply, she began kissing him again.

## Chapter Twenty-One

They caught their horses not far from where they had abandoned them. Both were chewing at some soft grass at the edge of a stream, and again Solenne thought her mount, though perhaps pleased to see her, looked a bit disappointed that they were to be on their way again so soon.

They mounted and rode in silence for a while, letting the sun bake the worst of the hurt out of their wounds.

Eventually Brennan said, "We're heading back toward that camp, I see."

"All that kissing and such make you forget all that? Gotta go back. Gotta kill them all . . . Doesn't mean you have to come."

"Suppose you could use some help, though?"

"It wouldn't be unwelcome."

"Guess I could come."

"Appreciated."

"More of those kisses . . . and such . . . in my future, you suppose?"

"Life is hard to predict."

"Can't argue that."

"Still . . ."

"Still?"

Her blue eyes flashed at him like stolen pieces of the sky. "Been my experience that almost nothing on this earth is entirely impossible."

#

## Afterword

I owe a great deal to my mother and father. I think I was a reasonably "good" child (my sister might disagree), but it was not until I began working as a Paramedic and got to peek into the lives of the rest of society that I realized how truly idyllic my own childhood had been. Among the many other things I am grateful to my parents for are the love of reading they instilled in me and, with it, the desire to write. Some of my earliest memories include trips to the library, and our house was always full of books.

My thanks to the many friends who expressed interest, support, and encouragement during this adventure.

## About the Author

Blair Lindsay grew up in Montreal with a ferocious appetite for reading, particularly within the genres of science fiction and the supernatural. He spent twenty years working as a Firefighter and Paramedic in rural Alberta. Since 1999, Blair has taught in the Paramedic and Respiratory Therapy programs at the Southern Alberta Institute of Technology, where he also runs the Centre for Advanced Patient Care Simulation. His other interests include astronomy, paleontology, digital art, and human factors science. He is an avid runner.

Sequels

*Solenne will return . . .*

**Hunting the Dead** is Part I of the *Solenne Trilogy*. Look for the sequels, coming soon . . .

### Reaper
For decades, in a hidden complex deep underground, a top-secret US bioweapons team has raced against counterparts in Russia, Iran, and North Korea to resurrect a legendary rabies-like virus known only from American Civil War reports and artifacts—a disease that could turn the tide in war by mutating the enemy into rabid cannibals that would annihilate themselves.

But their efforts have attracted the attention of a mysterious woman . . . Solenne is a merciless, icy-eyed killer with a blood-bond to the origins of the disease. She will stop at nothing to prevent the team's success . . .

But she may already be too late. Unknown to all of them, the project's head researcher has concealed both his homicidal insanity and his own plans for the disease.

Solenne must destroy them all before the infection breaks containment.

### Armageddon Machine

A disease of unimaginable virulence threatens the world—a highly contagious virus that turns its victims into rabid creatures with a singular and voracious appetite for human flesh. Killer, hunter, thief, and assassin, Solenne has seen such plagues before: reapers, zombies, the undead—call them what you will—all that matters is that the risen dead die only when their brain is destroyed.

But Solenne has learned that the infection is much more than it appears. Experiments by the military have altered it into something far more powerful and deadly than it once was.

Solenne believes she can halt Armageddon, but she must wander through the holocaust of the disease to find its source, all the while pursued by the walking dead, as well as something far more lethal: a mutant monster intent on ruling a world made into hell.

Only Solenne is standing in its way.

### Connect with Blair Lindsay Online
Author's website: blairlindsay.com
Facebook: https://www.facebook.com/pages/Blair-Lindsay/171931306175251

www.ingramcontent.com/pod-product-compliance
Lightning Source LLC
Chambersburg PA
CBHW071146260626
47162CB00003B/932